Starting with non...
hundreds of articl...
JJ Despain. In 20...
career with *The L*...
Medical Romanc...
and with more tha...
enjoyed writing ever since.

**Deanne Anders** was reading romance while her friends were still reading Nancy Drew, and she knew she'd hit the jackpot when she found a shelf of Harlequin Presents in her local library. Years later she discovered the fun of writing her own. Deanne lives in Florida, with her husband and their spoiled Pomeranian. During the day she works as a nursing supervisor. With her love of everything medical and romance, writing for Mills & Boon Medical Romance is a dream come true.

**Also by Dianne Drake**

*The Nurse and the Single Dad*
*Saved by Doctor Dreamy*
*Bachelor Doc, Unexpected Dad*
*Second Chance with Her Army Doc*

**Sinclair Hospital Surgeons miniseries**

*Reunited with Her Army Doc*
*Healing Her Boss's Heart*


*From Midwife to Mummy*

is **Deanne Anders**'s debut title

Look out for more books from Deanne Anders
Coming soon

Discover more at millsandboon.co.uk.

# HER SECRET MIRACLE

### DIANNE DRAKE

# FROM MIDWIFE TO MUMMY

### DEANNE ANDERS

# MILLS & BOON

First Published in Great Britain 2019
by Mills & Boon, an imprint of HarperCollins*Publishers*
1 London Bridge Street, London, SE1 9GF

Her Secret Miracle © 2019 by Dianne Despain

From Midwife to Mummy © 2019 by Denise Chavers

ISBN: 978-0-263-26980-2

**MIX**
Paper from
responsible sources
**FSC C007454**

This book is produced from independently certified FSC™ paper
to ensure responsible forest management.
For more information visit www.harpercollins.co.uk/green.

Printed and bound in Spain
by CPI, Barcelona

# HER SECRET MIRACLE

## DIANNE DRAKE

**MILLS & BOON**

To all my open-heart patients.
You were my inspiration to be the best nurse I could be.

# PROLOGUE

AS NIGHTS WENT, this was a beautiful one: still warm enough to enjoy being outside, with only a faint wind and the nip of a chill settling in. In the distance, Sapporo's snowcapped mountains stood tall and inviting, giving Eric that feeling that he could stay here, someplace different, someplace else. Someplace where there was time for this…for daydreaming, thinking about a future, having fun in his life. But it was up to him to let it in. Unfortunately, he'd never quite discovered how. But someday…

"Are you enjoying the seminar, Dr. Hart?" asked Dr. Michiko Sato, stepping up to the balcony rail next to him. Her seductiveness nearly blended into the night. Dark skin, black dress. All woman. He'd spent two days listening to her lectures, the dulcet tones that made the field of physiatry sound almost as sexy as she was. There were other lecturers, of course. But he only had ears for Michi. And eyes. *Especially* eyes. And he, as well as other experts in attendance, couldn't get enough of her smile, the way she turned her gaze downward as if she was shy…and her body to die for. But, most of all, her dedication and intelligence.

Dear lord, perfection in his view for only a few short

days. Michiko Sato was a woman who interested him in so many ways, and for a man who couldn't let himself be interested it was damned frustrating. Especially since he'd caught her staring at him a time or two, and it had not been a professional stare. Well, damn it. He'd done this to himself, hadn't he? Drawn his boundaries and stayed behind them. Lived a life without the interruption of real pleasure. And now here was real pleasure standing next to him and it was all he could do to keep his hands from shaking.

"It's a very good seminar. And call me Eric, please." He twisted to see the full length of her, and the sight of Dr. Sato in something more than her professional garb— white lab coat—caught him off guard, even though he'd been watching her for nearly an hour now. Tonight, she was stunning in her black sleeveless dress with its low-cut neckline and a side slit nearly up to her hip. The dress was not too tight to be indecent, but tight enough to show her curves. And what fine curves they were. Curves that would fit him so well if ever he got the chance.

"Eric. And I'm Michi." She moved closer to him, brushed against his arm, and stayed there rather than stepping away. "You've been sitting in the front row, I've noticed. Every lecture, every day. Should I be flattered?"

"I have." He chuckled. "All the better to see you." That was a bold statement, but a coziness was settling in around them, and it seemed to be calling for a bold move. Especially since after tomorrow he'd be gone, and she'd be on to her next lecture group or back to her medical practice.

"Did you like what you saw, Eric? And what you see right now?" She stepped away ever so slightly, to give him a better look.

"If I didn't, I'd have been sitting in the back row. The front row was never my style." She stepped into him a little more, and seemed so innocent doing it. But this wasn't innocent. They both knew where it was heading. He'd known it the instant he'd walked into her lecture hall and made eye contact with the most beautiful woman he'd ever encountered. There was destiny here. Maybe not one that would go beyond tonight, but it was inevitable. She knew it as well as he did.

"I'm glad you weren't. I think I was enjoying my view as much as you were enjoying yours."

Sliding his arm around Michi's waist, he pulled her as tightly to him as she could possibly get. "You don't mind, do you?" he asked.

"Not at all." She nudged her foot against his. "Not at all."

Then he pointed to the evening shadows of the mountains. "There's a little cabin up there. A very isolated cabin. My father owns it, and when I was a kid, he'd have a personal ski instructor bring me here to teach me how to ski. It was the only time I ever got to do something fun, just for the sake of doing it."

"So, you're a good skier."

"Depends on your definition of good, I suppose. In my day I was."

Michi laughed. "In your day? From what I've been seeing, you're still in your day, and it's looking quite good." She sat her glass of champagne down on the wall surrounding the third-story veranda and turned to Eric. "So, tell me, Eric, what else were you good at, in your day?" She wrinkled her nose and her eyes sparkled with flirtation. *"Or night?"*

He was good at being a surgeon, day and night, but

that wasn't the way he wanted this conversation to go. Not after listening to her and watching her so intently for what seemed like forever. Memorizing her movements, anticipating her words, trying not to be distracted by her beauty yet being distracted by every little thing about her—the raising of an eyebrow, the slightest hint of a smile meant only for him. "I'm good at picking up your signals."

"And what are these signals telling you?"

"That tonight's our last chance. Tomorrow we'll both be back in our normal lives." Why was his attraction to her so strong? There'd been other women in his life, other opportunities, but tonight, with Michi...

"And just what would that last chance include?" she asked him.

"We have options," he said. "Dancing, although I'm not very good at it. We could go for a walk. Or, stay here and talk."

"Talking's overrated," she said. "And these shoes are definitely not made for walking or dancing."

He glanced down, noticed that her shoes were strappy and spiky, and while he was no expert, he couldn't imagine that what she was wearing was going to make a walk much fun. Yet while he thought they were probably uncomfortable as hell, they also looked sexy as hell, making her incredibly long legs seem even longer. "Then maybe you'd like to go sit someplace where you can take off those shoes. They've got to be killing your feet."

Michi laughed. "So, you're a practical man."

"That's what my colleagues tell me."

"That's what my aunt told me when she recommended you to this seminar. That you're good at your job, not always as sociable as you could be, and that you're governed by practicality. But the best in your field."

"Your aunt?"

"Agnes Blaine."

He knew Agnes. She worked on the medical end of cardiology while he worked on the surgical end of it. Specifically, pediatric cardiac surgery. "Small world," he said.

"Not really. I'm trying to grow my practice in different ways, incorporate more physiatry into medical and surgical areas where it's not yet used. I asked her to send someone who might be able to make use of my specialty. And while I wasn't specific in terms of what kind of specialty I wanted to approach, she thought cardiac surgery and rehab would be good. Hence…you. So, let's get back to these shoes. Are you offering a foot massage?"

"For starters."

"Then what?"

He bent over and whispered something in Michi's ear that caused her to laugh. "That sounds very naughty," she said.

"Well, if you think that's naughty…" He whispered something else in her ear, but this time he grazed her earlobe with his tongue, causing Michi to gasp, then stand on tiptoe and whisper something back to him.

"Will that get me a passing mark in your class?" he asked.

"That, Doctor, will send you straight to the head of the class."

"My favorite place," he said, picking up her glass of champagne. "And I'm ready to start doing the homework that will get me there, if you don't mind being my tutor."

"I would love to tutor you, Doctor."

He was already regretting that it could last for only a night but come tomorrow the fantasy of the evening would have worn off, Michi would be back in her white medical coat ready to present the last lecture of the series, and his mind would be back on the list of patients he would be seeing once he was back in New York. But for now, Sapporo, Japan, or New York City were simply places on a map while here, before him, was a place in time he wanted to exploit. "So, can you walk out of this banquet room, or would you like me to carry you?"

"How about you go first and I'll follow in ten minutes?"

"So, this is to be a clandestine affair?"

"Clandestine and cautious," she said. "Because we have only tonight. This is just the fantasy. Do you understand? Tonight, the fantasy. Tomorrow, the reality."

"Yes," he said, because he wasn't a greedy man. One night was all he had in him. That was the way he structured his life. "Very good rules to live by. No relationship, no tangles. That's been my motto for years." Even though he imagined one night with Michi was more than anything he'd ever hoped for. But even in the fantasy there had to be practicality. That was the story of his life. He didn't want a real involvement. It was too complicated. Hearts got broken. Someone survived while someone else did not. No, what he did, what he had, worked. A life without those involvements suited him just fine.

"Ten minutes," he said, brushing a slow, lush kiss to her lips before turning and walking away. Yes, ten minutes before his world would change, even if only for one night. But, for the first time in his life, he felt oddly uncomfortable with that arrangement. To think about why or put thought into it would only ruin the moment, and he wanted this moment like he'd wanted no other before. So, he put it out of his mind as he pushed the elevator button and went to his room on the sixth floor.

Michi stood in the hall outside his door for several minutes, simply staring. Was she totally out of her head, seducing him the way she'd just done? She paced back and forth for a little while, downed the rest of her champagne, wished she had another glassful. Then finally she drew in a deep breath, bent down and took off her ungodly uncomfortable shoes, stepped up to his door and knocked.

When he opened to her, she simply handed him her shoes on the way in, and it took a full twenty seconds before she realized he'd already rid himself of his shirt. And there he was, the perfect image of the man of her dreams. Interesting, smart, a little intense. The typical tall, dark, handsome hunk. Smoldering. Sexy. Virile. Provocative. Seductive. All those descriptions from her fantasies come to life. All hers for a little while.

"You're thinking too much," he said, as he shut the door and tossed the shoes aside.

"Good thoughts," she said.

"About me, I hope." He started to walk toward her, but Michi held out her hand to stop him.

"Playing games?" he asked.

"Making memories."

He chuckled. "We haven't done anything to make memories of, Michi, and if you've changed your mind, it's not too late for you to turn around and go back downstairs to the reception you're hosting. That would be the practical thing to do."

"Maybe I don't want practical," she said, moving

closer to him, then raising her hand to slide it around his neck. "Maybe I'm always practical and tonight I want something else." Even though her mind was still a little wobbly, it was made up. One night, one time with one perfect man. The handsome stranger who would come and go in her life and leave her with a memory of the time she'd stepped outside herself to do something daring. No strings, no attachments. Throw caution to the wind this once, because the wind had never thrown anything back that wasn't painful.

So, no, it wasn't her style, but she didn't want it to be. Just once she wanted to know what being bold and reckless would feel like, as being anything else hadn't gotten her what she wanted. But one night of excitement with Eric and maybe that would be enough before she stepped back into her life and its harsh realities.

And Eric was… He was pure, raw sex and total excitement. And she wanted it all.

# CHAPTER ONE

MICHI SATO LOOKED UP at the massive building, wondering how many stories high it was. She guessed somewhere between twenty-five and thirty, all belonging to Eric and, maybe someday, Riku?

She really hadn't given Eric's status much of a thought up until now, and simply seeing his name in gold looming over the massive bank of revolving glass doors caused her stomach to churn. Even as outgoing as she was, she wasn't up to this. Finding herself so close to Eric now, after all this time, caused too many unanswered questions to come to mind.

Her motivation for that night, his motivation as well. Certainly nothing long term had been meant. They'd both made that clear during pillow talk and foreplay. Then look what had happened. Especially after her doctor had told her only weeks before it was an impossibility. That her condition had gone from bad to abandon all hope.

"I'm so glad he was wrong," she said, kissing Riku on the cheek. "Mommy hasn't done everything the best way she could have, but that's all going to change now." After Eric knew he had a son. After Riku's surgery. There were so many things weighing her down now, so much guilt she had to come to terms with, she didn't know where to begin. But she was here to start a new course. At least, that was what she kept telling herself. New course, new direction, new leaf turned over. It sounded good, but in practice…well, that was the part she wasn't sure about. But the first step was behind her now, and that was good.

Of course, she'd told herself other things, too, that she'd backed away from, hadn't she? Namely, not telling Eric he was daddy to her two-year-old. She'd tried, had made futile attempts at calling, texting and using any other means of electronic communication available. Then she'd given up. But that didn't make things better. In fact, in the long run it would make things worse than she could probably even imagine.

"Mommy's going to make it all better," she said. How? She didn't know. But she'd figure it out.

And now, on the second step of her journey—trying to figure out how to tell him—here she was, looking in Eric's window, holding his son, and so confused her head was spinning. In just a few days Riku's long-awaited surgery would take place—a surgery Eric should know about as it had been his specialty when he'd been a practicing surgeon.

Of course, that would have meant telling Eric somewhere along the way that he had a son, then also telling him his son had a heart defect. Neither of which she'd done. Yet. Except the *yet* part was looming like a black raincloud over her. All the good intentions in the world wouldn't stop it from bursting and pouring down on her. It was up to her to make the plan that would avoid it—step into a doorway or, in this case, Eric's office.

But, no. Instead, here she was, like a little girl with

her nose to the toy-store window, hoping for the prettiest doll inside. Expecting to get it but fearing she wouldn't. Expecting Eric to overlook that she'd kept his son from him all this time but fearing he would not forgive her. And in some fragmented way, hoping the three of them could become a family on some level. All while the black cloud was getting closer and closer to bursting.

"Be glad you're too young to know about responsibilities," she said to Riku, turning so her body would shield his from the slight gust of warm wind whipping up the streets and down the alleys. "Or how to make something right you've already made such a mess of."

Realistically, she wasn't counting on things turning out well as far as Eric was concerned. Sure, he could walk away from the entire situation, which didn't seem at all like the man she'd known for little more than a night. Or he might recognize Riku as his son, then want more of Riku in his life than she was prepared to give him. And that seemed the greater possibility. But would he go so far as try for full custody since she'd hidden his sick child from him for two years? Or argue that she was negligent given how he was an expert in the procedure his son needed to have done?

This was what scared her. And why Eric scared her. He might want more of Riku than she could bear to give up. Now, she feared, she was about to find out just how much, and she wasn't sure what she'd do once she knew. Wasn't ready for that, wasn't ready to face the consequences she'd set into motion, whatever they might be.

Still, she had always to remember this was about Riku, not her. Not even Eric. Right now, her son was the only one who counted, and when she did tell Eric about him, she hoped he would be able to see that was the case. At least until after Riku's surgery.

"Your daddy's inside that building, Riku," she said, turning again so the boy bundled in her arms could look through the window. "He's a very nice man. And kind. A perfect man to be your father. I know you don't understand what I'm telling you, but you will someday."

And she prayed he didn't hate her when he did understand, even when she'd finally gathered the courage to correct her mistakes long before Riku would be old enough to hate her for what she'd done.

That was another fear she had to live with: the possibility that Riku could turn away from her once he was old enough to know what his mother had done. If that day ever came, well…she wouldn't think about it. The way she hadn't thought about other consequences.

So, true to form, she wasn't going to deal with that now, when she was so confused, so angry at herself, and so afraid for her son's life. Especially not when every ounce of everything inside her was devoted to Riku and what was ahead for him.

"I wish you could tell me what to do," she told Riku, snuggling him in even closer to her. "Your mommy didn't make some wise choices and now she's very discouraged that what she's done might touch you in ways I never intended to happen."

Riku's response was to reach up and grab Michi's hair, then giggle.

"Do you know how cute you are?" she asked, trying to extricate herself from his playful grip. This child was her world, nothing else mattered. And it still surprised her how much she'd changed in such a short time. "OK, so you're not going to answer me. But take my word for it, you're the cutest little boy ever."

It was a mild November day, the sun was bright, the slight gusts of wind warm enough that people had taken off their jackets to enjoy the unexpected rise in temperature. But Michi tucked Riku's little fist into the blanket in which he was wrapped. So maybe she was overprotective. What of it? She'd had so much difficulty bringing him into this world.

She'd lost count of how many times she'd almost lost him before his birth; didn't know how long she'd been hospitalized to prevent a miscarriage early on and a stillbirth later. It had been such a struggle, then afterwards a beautiful baby boy…with a heart defect. All of it had been so much to deal with, the hysterectomy after Riku's birth being the least of her concerns. That mess with the social worker calling her unfit had been traumatic. So, if she wanted to be overprotective, she had good cause.

In her defense, she'd tried contacting Eric early on, but the information on him from the seminar had been old, and she'd refused to ask her aunt to forward information on to him as that would have revealed her pregnancy long before she'd wanted to. So, she'd put it off. Had promised herself she'd do it later. But later had brought her pregnancy difficulties, then a sick baby, outside complications…too many "laters" had added up until she'd known she'd passed the point of reasonability. All that, plus she simply hadn't been coping. One step at a time. That was all she had been able to manage. One difficult, often heartbreaking step at a time.

Still, she had always intended to find Eric at some point, maybe when Riku was through the worst of it. Or maybe when she wasn't so consumed by guilt and confusion and strange emotions she couldn't even identify.

Even with all the mistakes she'd made, though, look what she had. The world. Riku was the whole world to her. And now, as she hugged him and stood looking into the Hart building, the urgency to make this right was pounding at her. "He's in there somewhere," she said, hoping yet not hoping to catch a glimpse of Eric. "Anyway, it's silly standing out here, not sure what I'd do if I did see him," she said to her son. "Besides, look who's here."

She twisted so Riku could see his great-aunt walking with outstretched arms to greet them. Riku stretched his arms out to her as well.

"Just what we need," Agnes Blaine said. "A whole afternoon to spoil my nephew."

Michi laughed. "Not too much spoiling, I hope."

Takumi, Agnes's partner of twenty-five years and Michi's uncle, stepped to Agnes's side. "That would be between Riku and us." He bent over and kissed his nephew. "And maybe the clerk in the toy store."

Michi loved these people. They'd been there for her at the end of her pregnancy, then through some of Riku's early tests. And they were part of the small circle of family she'd trusted enough to let them care for Riku for a few hours, or even a full day.

"The amount of spoiling we bestow upon our nephew is a personal matter," Agnes teased, looking up at the gold embossing over the building: *Eric Hart Property Management.* "You haven't…?"

Michi shook her head, then stepped back. Agnes and Takumi knew to leave it alone. Her whole family did. Yes, everybody knew Eric Hart was Riku's father, but it was not a topic anyone ever discussed. At least, not in front of Michi. "He's just up from his nap, so he should be good for a while. And I shouldn't be gone long." Just long enough to spend some time alone, to think.

"We'll be back home when you get there," Takumi said, pulling Michi into his arms. "Be patient with yourself," he said. "Everything will be as it's meant to be."

And, in the blink of an eye, she was alone on the sidewalk in front of Eric's building. It was the first step. And her second step would take her inside.

"No, I'm not going to my afternoon meeting. We couldn't come to terms over the phone, so I cancelled it. No point in wasting everybody's time. But Bucky Henderson is still coming in this morning since he flew all the way from Texas before I could stop him, and I'm hoping we can come to some kind of terms. I like the land he's proposing I buy, but I'm not really into what he wants to do with it. Which means I need this meeting to see if he's open to compromise."

So maybe he wasn't the best businessman in the world. Lord knew, he wasn't his old man when it came to property management and land deals, but this was his lot now. People depended on him, and he tried his best not to let them down.

"Will you need the lawyers here for the meeting?" his secretary Natalie asked.

"No. And I don't need anybody from the real estate acquisition division here either." He'd settle for it to go all his way, or even for a compromise. But if Bucky didn't buy into that… "They know what the deal is, and what I'd like to see it become, so we're set." Besides, having too many people around the business table was intimidating and while that might have been his old man's way of conducting business, it wasn't his.

"Then you've made up your mind?" Natalie asked. She was an older woman. Nearing seventy, he thought. Efficient, smart, and his dad's mistress for more than a quarter of a century. One of the many. Only Natalie was the one who'd kept him on the business track and for that devotion, no matter how misguided, Eric had let her stay, despite the badly kept secret that she'd played some part in his parents' divorce. But Natalie wasn't alone—there was the part his mother had played in the story, a part he knew nothing about.

"Not entirely. But I'm getting closer."

"Your father would have had this deal wrapped up weeks ago," Natalie reminded him. Her gray hair pulled back into a knot at the base of her neck, her glasses riding low on her nose, her perpetual frown and critical tone…there were days he wished she'd retired. Pretty much most days. But, like everything else, he felt an obligation to right his dad's wrongs. And there were so many of them. As for Natalie, she was just a drop in his father's unfortunate ocean.

"Of course he would have. But I'm not my father. I'm a surgeon, and as a surgeon I don't just hop into a procedure without knowing every angle of it." He forced a friendly smile, even though he knew Natalie would take one more shot. She always did.

"You *were* a surgeon," she reminded him. "Past tense, Eric. Remember that."

"You're right, of course. I *was* a surgeon." At heart, he still was. But circumstances had changed when his dad had died, leaving him not only an international property management corporation but a billion dollars, windmills, camels and God only knew what else.

Oh, his dad hadn't expected he'd be able to run the company and had even gone so far as to make provisions to put the governance under the control of a hand-picked board. Hand-picked by his father, of course. In other words, ten daddy clones trying to rule his life instead of one daddy. He'd fired them and put into place various people who made sense to him. An environmentalist, a construction engineer, a social worker, even a teacher. All people he respected and admired and not a designer suit amongst them.

"Look, I'm going across the street for coffee."

"But we have that expensive coffee system your father had put in."

"We have a coffee system that makes espresso, latte macchiato, cappuccino and even milk foam. It makes café mocha, *frappé* and *yungyang*, whatever the hell that is. But what it doesn't make is a decent cup of black coffee. So, I'll run out and grab one, then I'll be back in time to meet with Bucky. Oh, and if the coffee machine doesn't make anything he prefers, text me and I'll bring him a cup of black coffee, too."

"He's a busy man, Eric," she warned. "Don't keep him waiting."

He never did. A habit from his doctor days, he supposed. But Natalie always said it, and he always responded with, "I won't." While gritting his teeth. "Anyway, would you like something?" he asked. "Regular coffee, tea, a scone?"

Every time he asked she always looked surprised. Probably because his dad had never made a simple, kind gesture toward her. Which, in a way, was the same boat he was in. Always trying to find a way to get noticed by his dad, and never succeeding. So, while she may have had the occasional romp in his father's bed and a paycheck, at the end of her day she'd always gone home alone. Just like he had, until he'd been sent off to boarding school.

Was there a term that meant more than alone? Because that was what he'd always felt growing up…more than alone. The one left out. Left behind. Forgotten. An obstacle in his dad's path.

"I'm perfectly fine with what your father's coffee system makes," she said.

Poor Natalie. Always the trouper. And always let down. Yep, he knew the feeling. "OK, then I'll be back in a few." Even though he would have preferred a nice walk, or maybe some people-watching in Central Park, he didn't have a choice. That wasn't his life now. Getting back to Bucky Henderson to discuss the purchase of a large chunk of Texas for a casino with all the frills was.

Sighing, Eric stood after Natalie left, then went to the window. His dad's office had always been at the top—the twenty-fifth floor. In a massive corner suite, with plate-glass views of the city in all directions. His own office, however, was on the second floor, one window, limited view, and small in comparison to what awaited him on the top floor. Occupying it was an egregious act, he supposed. One that signaled ambivalence. And being at the top signified power. So, his defiant little office on the second floor would probably speak volumes to a shrink, if he cared to go that route. Which he didn't. But none of it really mattered, did it? He did his job, his employees had their lives secured, and the world kept spinning.

For a moment, Eric scrutinized the people walking on the sidewalk below. Where were they going? Why were they in such a hurry? Were they happily married or cheating on an unsuspecting spouse? He liked speculating about other people's lives since he barely had one of his own. Speculating made him feel like he was still in touch, even though he knew damn well he wasn't.

One last glance before he headed out for coffee and someone down there caught his eye. From his vantage he couldn't see much of her, so he adjusted for a better look and what he saw was well worth the effort. *She* was walking with a purpose. Long strides that outdistanced all the people around her. Shouldering her way through all the congestion like a woman with a purpose. He could almost hear the click of her heels on the cement, she was moving so fast. Like a whirlwind whooshing in and out of the crowd. And beautiful. Black hair pulled back away from her face. A stunning figure that men could only dream about.

She was Japanese, he thought. Reminded him of Michi…her height, her stature. Michi…so often on his mind. The one he shouldn't have let get away. But in the nearly three years since he'd spent that incredible night with her, too much had happened. Too many responsibilities had pulled him away from what he wanted to do and dumped him into the pile of all the things he *had* to do.

There had been a time Michi had been what he'd wanted. Maybe in some ways, she still was. But it was too late for that. He'd made his choice the morning he'd left without a goodbye. After that, there was no turning back.

Michi was the one he regretted walking away from, though. The only one. Even now, she floated through his mind in the unguarded moments, taunting him for what he'd missed out on. One night only. It was what he'd told her because it was what he'd meant. Something had happened that night. Something that had unhinged him and compelled him to do what he'd never done before—given himself over to a casual fling that had turned out to be so much more. At least, in his thoughts. Still, one night with Michi…

Eric closed his eyes, conjuring up her image. Funny how what he remembered of her seemed to meld with the woman he'd just seen on the walkway outside. Maybe it was because he'd never truly gotten over her. Granted, they'd only known each other a few hours when the text that had changed his life had come. But in those few hours…it had been like he'd known her for days, or weeks, or months. Maybe his whole life. Could she have been the one? He didn't know as he'd never found himself in that mindset before. The possibilities hadn't escaped him, however. And as she'd lain there next to him, her breath sounds so tiny and precise, he'd simply listened, and wondered what would happen if they had one more night.

Unfortunately, the opportunity to go beyond that night had never happened. Still, in the very few—as in could be counted on one hand—dates he'd had with other women since then, nothing had ever seemed right. To himself, he'd nitpicked every woman to pieces before their date, then always cut the evening short because she hadn't what he'd wanted. And for sure, he'd never dated any of those hopefuls twice. Because of his job, he always told himself. Yes, because of his job.

But somewhere in all that mess, thoughts of Michi pushed everything away. Even now, when he should be concentrating on Bucky's proposal, his mind was wandering back to Sapporo, to that one perfect night.

Which meant it was time to go get that coffee, refocus, and figure out his next step in the Texas land acquisition deal. So, Eric put on his suit coat—he really hated wearing suits every day, but that was the dress code, so he observed it—took a quick look in the mirror in his private bathroom, straightened his tie, then traced, with his left index finger, all the new lines and creases that were beginning to show. So many changes to his body in the past couple of years. *What did it matter?*

There had been a time when he'd appreciated the sideways glances of the nurses who hadn't known he knew they were watching. And that obvious flirtation from Michi in Japan…something that had twisted and turned him in ways he hadn't expected then, and even now. So maybe the looks weren't going down too badly, but what he saw staring back at him from the mirror was a man who was…resigned to something that didn't make him happy. Didn't satisfy him either. Didn't give him the good, hard feeling of being tired but satisfied that made him sleep well at night. As long as he spent his days behind this desk, doing mediocre work at best, it would always be that way.

"But we keep promising to fix things, don't we?" he always said to his mirror, ever hopeful that saying it out loud to an inanimate object that wouldn't criticize him might actually inspire him to go out and find some of that old mojo again. And did he ever need that inspiration. Where and how, though? He didn't have a clue. But at least all hope hadn't died. That was something to hang onto. Although sometimes hanging only by a thread.

Once Eric decided he was "Hart-ready," as his dad

had called it, he headed for his office door. And his thoughts—on the woman he'd seen outside. The fairy-tale would have them bump into each other in the coffee shop, then spend hours talking, laughing, getting to know each other. They would make plans for dinner that night—someplace slow and dim, where they could talk quietly and tell secrets. Then they'd go back to his place...and that was where it stopped.

Those days were behind him even though he was only thirty-six, and now he was all about the corporate life where everything ran on fear and promises, and most of those promises were empty, like his social life.

"Sure you don't want something?" he asked Natalie again, as he headed out the door. The fact that she didn't even take her eyes off her computer screen didn't surprise him. Now, as she did so often, she was looking through her gallery of pictures of the only man she'd ever loved. Lost in his world. Reliving the life she'd never had. Sad. But sometimes the choices people made weren't easily shed. For Natalie, that was his father. For him...trying to please a man who would never be pleased. And now it was too late.

Would that be him someday? Sitting at a computer, looking through reminders of a life he had never had, and an undertaking in which he'd failed so miserably. He sincerely hoped not.

# CHAPTER TWO

IT WAS A cozy little café. Pastries, teas, coffee, flowers, and all sorts of gifty things that were cute, but not practical. And the café was full to overflowing with people. Loud, but nice. Michi had managed to snag the last table available, the one in the corner, the one with the worst view in the shop. But that didn't matter. She wasn't in the mood for being social or enjoying views. All she wanted was a tea, and some time by herself to think.

She was worried, naturally. Riku would be in great hands with Dr. Kapoor. She was sure of that. But right now, that wasn't her biggest concern. It was Eric, and what to do about that whole situation. He had a right to know he had a son. He also had a right to know his son had a heart defect. But hadn't she tried to contact him early on her pregnancy? Then later, after Riku was born, hadn't she tried again?

Well, that was the way she pacified herself when she got in the mood. Telling herself she'd tried. That she'd been so overwhelmed that her thinking hadn't been sharp. Sometimes it worked, sometimes it did not. Today it wasn't even coming close because her motivations were not even clear to herself anymore. Except for one. But that had nothing to do with Eric, and it was something she surely didn't want him to know: being accused of being an unfit mother.

So, there was that weight she always carried, as well as not telling Eric the truth from the start. And, of course, her default excuse...yeah, right, she'd tried. What of it?

Yet he was right across the street now. Easy, convenient. All she had to do was walk over there—and then what? Would she produce papers proving Riku was Eric's? Wait, she didn't have papers. Hadn't even put Eric's name on the birth certificate. So, would he simply believe her? *Hello, Eric. I had your baby two years ago.* Probably not. Then there was always the question of whether he'd want to be an involved father. She knew he'd be a good father, just from the little she knew of him. But would he want that?

There were so many questions with answers awaiting her. Answers she feared. So, for now, she'd sip her tea and hope for an angel or something to drop down from the sky and give her the solution she needed because she sure wasn't in any state to figure it out on her own.

"Would you care for a refill on your tea?" a young man asked, startling Michi out of her thoughts. "Another tea bag, more hot water?"

She looked up at him and smiled. "That would be lovely," she said, gazing beyond the server to the table where four women sat chattering away as they ate their pastries. "With a little more lemon," she added. "And maybe one of those scones I saw earlier when I was at the counter."

"Happy to oblige, ma'am," the young man said, then scooted through the tangle of people who weren't lucky enough to have a place to sit but who obviously weren't ready to go back outside and face the rest of the day.

Michi leaned back in her chair, trying to relax, but she was too wound up for that, so she simply sipped her tea, ate her scone when the server brought it, and stared out the window at Eric's building, like that was going to give her some kind of resolution. Intermittently, she flipped through her phone to various photos of Riku and only then did that feeling of despair go away. One perfect little face with such a calming effect. Who would have ever guessed that she could have fallen in love so deeply. But she had, and she would literally give her life for that little boy.

"I hope you like blueberry, because I've bagged up one to take with you. You look like you're in a blueberry kind of mood," the server said, handing over a bag. "On the house."

"Thank you," she said, as she repositioned herself in the seat. "So, tell me—what, exactly, identifies a blueberry mood?"

"Someone who's worrying or being contemplative. You've been in here quite a while and it's obvious something's on your mind. Something heavy, judging from all the frowning."

Was she so transparent that the young man with the scones could identify her mood? He was right—it was definitely blueberry. "Maybe if I come back, I'll be in a strawberry mood. Would that be better?"

"Yes, because our strawberry scones are one of the most popular and strawberry is a very happy state of mind."

"Then make sure you save me a strawberry and I'll work hard on my strawberry mood before I get here."

She took a bite of her blueberry scone, then a sip of her tea, and started to pop back into her photo gallery, but a voice at a nearby table startled her out of her plan.

"Help! Somebody, please, help. She's choking."

Instantly alert, Michi jumped up and ran to the table where the ladies she'd observed were sitting. Sure enough, one of them was choking. Sitting up straight, confused, trying to breathe, the woman rolled her eyes up at Michi, and her expression was beyond frightened. She was dying, and she knew it.

"Please, stand back," Michi yelled to the crowd, as she leaned the choking woman forward and slapped her back five times. She'd hoped that whatever was lodged in the woman's windpipe would come loose, but unfortunately that didn't happen.

So, from behind again, she wrapped her arms around the woman's ribcage, forming a fist with both hands. Then she pulled the woman toward her, giving an upward thrust each of the five times she tried. Still, nothing happened. And now the woman was turning blue. Her lips, her fingernails. Oxygen deprivation, Michi knew as she started the whole procedure over again. "Has somebody called for an ambulance?" she shouted to the crowd.

One deep, smooth voice stood out over the noise of the crowd. "ETA less than five," he said, pushing himself through the crowd, then kneeling next to Michi. "And she doesn't have five minutes left in her," he continued.

Michi looked over to see who was working with her, and gasped. "Eric?"

"Michi?" he said, as he took over the upward thrusts Michi was doing. One, two—on the third thrust it worked and the woman sucked in a deep breath.

"Stay still," Michi cautioned her, trying not to think what would happen next, when the ambulance took her to the hospital. "The paramedics will be here shortly, and they'll take you to the emergency room so the doctors there can run some tests to make sure you're good."

Gasping for breath, the woman nodded her understanding as Eric took her pulse again. "Much better," he said, giving her a reassuring pat on the arm. "You've come through the hard part like a champ, and this next part in the hospital will be much easier. And it won't be happening on a cold cement floor."

She smiled up at him, drew in a deep breath, then closed her eyes, not from fear but from trusting Eric, who'd taken off his jacket and placed it under her head.

The way Eric was with the poor woman…it nearly brought a lump to Michi's throat. This was a man who was born to be a doctor. A man who shouldn't have given it up. And he was Riku's father, she thought as a swell of pride overtook her. "Paramedics are on their way in," she said, glancing out the window, not so much to watch for the paramedics as to pull herself together.

Immediately, the onlookers in the café began to move tables and chairs back and push the display shelf of coffees and mugs for sale to the wall to make room for the two paramedics, their equipment and their stretcher. "Her vitals are stabilizing," Eric said. "So now it's more about her being frightened than anything else."

The woman looked up at him again and nodded, and Michi was still amazed by the way not only the woman but everyone in the room responded to him. Even in the middle of a medical crisis his voice was so calm, so reassuring she was impressed by how much she remembered the detail of it. It was the same deep, convincing undertone that had seduced her. The same richness that had enticed her into his bed. Yet now she could hear the edge, the command. And she could see the way people were responding.

"I was actually thinking about you earlier," Eric said.

There hadn't been a day gone by since he'd left her that she hadn't thought about him. She'd sculpted the perfect words to say when she did finally catch up to him. Practiced them. Edited. Practiced. Edited. And now that the moment had arrived, all she could think to say was, "How have you been?" Stupid. Stupid. And she didn't hear his answer between the noise of people still moving tables back and the mad flurry of the pounding feet of people trying to get out of the way.

"She's doing better," Michi said, as Eric bent down again, but this time not as keen to watch the patient as he was to look at her. "Respirations still shallow and fast, but nothing dangerous."

Ruth, the choking victim, smiled at Eric like he was the only one in the room as the paramedics took quick vital signs, then lifted her onto the stretcher. At that point, Eric took her hand and went with them to the ambulance, and it was only when they had arranged her in the back and were getting ready to shut the door that he let go. Once he did, he slapped the door to indicate everything was good, and the ambulance siren came on, then the vehicle nosed its way into bumper-to-bumper New York traffic.

"She really trusted you," Michi said, standing behind him.

"I think if you're in a life or death situation and there's somebody there to help you, you naturally trust them. Haven't been in one myself, but it makes sense."

"How have you been, Eric?" she asked again as they walked back over to the sidewalk.

"Busy. New responsibilities, a new job, a new life."

"Medicine's loss," she said, clearly uneasy. This wasn't the right place to tell him about Riku, neither was it the right time. But it was circling around her now, the reality of what she was about to face. "My, um... aunt mentioned you'd left surgery to take over your family business."

"Duty called," he said. "But that's life, right? Things happening when you least expect it. Like you. I thought I saw you outside my building a while ago," he said, following her back through the congestion of people and displaced tables and chairs in the café. "Standing on the sidewalk."

"I was taking a walk earlier, so you might have." Since he wasn't mentioning the baby she'd been carrying, she assumed he hadn't seen Riku. "I was on my way to order coffee and a scone," she answered, then laughed. "Which is pretty obvious since we met in a shop where they sell coffee and scones."

"Good coffee, great scones. So, can I get you something? The blueberry scones are the best, in my opinion."

Blueberry. That caused her to laugh. Today she must have simply reminded everybody of a blueberry, and that one little scone held so many ramifications, her stomach turned over and all she wanted was to turn around and get out of there, blueberry scone or not. "After what just happened, I'm out of the mood," she said.

"Well, I've got a secretary back in the office who's expecting delivery service, even though she'll deny it, so..." He stepped on ahead to the counter, placed his order, then turned back to Michi, who'd taken several steps toward the door. "Not that it's any of my business but are you in New York for any reason in particular?"

To find him? No. To find herself, perhaps. Mostly, though, for Riku. "Family," she said. "My uncle and his partner are here, and…" She shrugged as she took another couple of steps backward toward the door. Opened it, then hesitated for a moment. "Look, I need to get going. They're expecting me."

"I wish I'd known you were coming. Maybe we could have set aside an evening…"

"Maybe," she said on a wistful sigh as she stepped out onto the sidewalk.

"Is it too late for that? Since I'm the boss I can juggle my schedule. Maybe something tonight? Dinner?"

That could be the perfect time and place to tell him everything. Which was why she was hesitating. Her fear of what she had to do was finally turning into her reality. "It's not like we started anything real that night. Then the way you left me… I mean, I didn't have expectations. But when you do what we did, I should think there'd be a civil goodbye at the end of it." Except failed contraception had turned that into an impossibility because she had Riku now. And no regrets, except her actions.

But if she did decide to tell Eric, would he have regrets? Well, now wasn't the time to tell him, and now wasn't the time to discover the answer to her question. Maybe that angel had dropped down when she wasn't looking and left her with enough of a solution to get her by for a little while. But only for a little while as she still felt unsettled. "Seven," she finally said. "At my uncle's restaurant." A comfort zone she desperately needed now.

"Which is?"

"Tanoshī Shō, if you don't mind eating Japanese food.

It's small, quiet, and the chef…they don't come any better than Takumi. But if you'd prefer a steak, or something Italian…"

"What I'd prefer is an hour or two of your time, Michi. That morning when I left…it never felt resolved. You know, lacking the whole closure thing people talk about today."

"Waking up alone in bed is closure enough," she said, even though she felt the same way he did.

"Then bear with me. There are some things I need to tell you, for my sake."

"You left me," she said, slinging her purse over her shoulder. "We weren't…aren't…anything, and we knew what we were about, so what happened happened."

"I had a good reason."

"And the author Jean Renoir once said, *'The truly terrible thing is that everybody has their reasons.'*" She didn't want to be obstinate, didn't want to sound so harsh or rejecting since she too had her reasons. But this was fear bubbling up in her. Pure, raw fear. Everything that had scared her these past nearly three years was finally confronting her, and she had to get it right or too many people would be hurt.

"Look, I don't want to get into this here. I've got a meeting in a few minutes so tonight…"

Michi swallowed hard, then nodded. "Tonight," she repeated, then managed a smile. "But only if you try my uncle's peanut *amanattō*."

"I don't believe I know that one," Eric replied.

"He doesn't make it for the general public. Mostly for his family." And in a way Eric was family. "Here, in America, his desserts are a little more Western, but back home this was always a real treat. In fact, there's a version without the peanuts that Riku loves…" She caught herself before she said anything else. This wasn't the way to tell him. Not here. Not now. Not a casual mention in a going-nowhere conversation.

"Riku?" Eric questioned. "Who's Riku?"

"I'll meet you there at seven," she said, then scooted around him and headed down the sidewalk, not sure where she was going. But any place away from Eric was good. He'd had such a profound effect on her the first time they'd met that within the first hours she had wondered if their meeting could be the start of something more. Not expecting Riku to be the something more, of course. But everything about Eric was potent and powerful, which was everything she'd needed that night. Someone to push out the reality and offer the fantasy.

And look at her now. All about the reality, and nothing else. But as she thought every time she looked at her son, *No regrets*. Her medical practice was nearly a thing of the past now, she spent more time in doctors' offices and doing online research than she'd ever imagined could happen in her life. Every waking minute was fixed on Riku and the next thing she needed to do for him, whether it was bathing him or feeding him, adjusting his oxygen when he required it, or simply cuddle time.

Definitely no regrets, though. Only love for Riku, and maybe a little bit left over for the man who had given her Riku. Because, after all, without knowing it, Eric had redefined her life, given her a purpose far greater than anything she'd ever known. For that, her soft spot for him was large. Larger than she could have ever imagined.

## CHAPTER THREE

MICHI WALKED WITH a purpose. He'd noticed that when he'd seen her on the sidewalk below and hadn't known who she was. It was that walk that had captured him. Maybe because it had been familiar? Maybe because he'd remembered it so keenly from the first time they'd met, then tucked it away as part of a memory of a night he'd wanted to go so right yet had gone so wrong.

So, she was here to visit family. Agnes and her husband, he presumed. But she'd also mentioned someone called Riku and for a moment he fixed on that. Maybe a little jealously, even though he didn't have that right. So, who was this Riku? Was he a friend or lover? Maybe a husband? He'd asked, but she'd avoided answering. Did she wear a wedding ring now? Or even an engagement ring? Why hadn't he looked?

Michi married? That was an idea he didn't want to consider, maybe because somewhere in the middle of their one night, he'd caught himself wondering if that had the potential to turn into something more. She'd simply seemed to…fit, and he'd even caught himself planning some quick trips to Sapporo every now and then. Maybe he'd find a way to bring some of his business there, to give him the excuse to visit. Or he'd simply be direct and tell Michi he wanted to see if they could have more. Take her to that secluded little cabin in the mountains his father had owned, let her best him at skiing, even though he was pretty darned good.

Hot chocolate by the fireplace during the winter. A walk through the stunning Onze Harukayama Lily Garden in the summer. A trip by rope car up Mount Moiwa in the autumn to enjoy the stunning panoramic view of Sapporo's turning colors.

But then his dad had died, and Eric had had to make an emergency trip back home. Corporate jet waiting, he'd been out of the hotel room and out of Michi's life ten minutes after the notification. He'd tried texting, but it had bounced back. Had tried calling, but even in this modern age of technology, that hadn't worked either. Then life had gotten so complicated, and his struggle to keep up with it had turned into an almost never-ending battle.

Unfortunately, Michi had been lost in all that, and by the time his life had settled down enough to get back in touch with her, which was what he'd wanted to do, it had been a year and a half later. Too much time had gone by and he'd been headed in an entirely different direction—one that would never work for Michi as she was so devoted to her practice. So why try to start something with her when he was barely keeping his head above water?

Even though he'd thought about her off and on all that time, it had been easier to shut the door on all possibilities—or as some would call them, hopes and dreams—and move on. As they said, timing was everything, and his was off in the worst kind of way. "Well, you're stuck with this life now," he said to himself on his way back to his desk. "No point in worrying."

Bucky was waiting for him when he got back. Actually pacing the floor like a caged tiger, which put Eric instantly on alert. Nervous people made him nervous. That was something new, as he'd expected nervousness when he'd been a surgeon. But nervousness in business worried him, because to Eric it always meant the worrier knew something he didn't, and that was a bad place to be when you were in the middle of a business deal. "So, how's it been going?" he asked, as Bucky took the seat across the desk from Eric.

"Good," Bucky said, then repeated himself. "Good."

"And I'm assuming you want an answer from me today?"

"Moving along with this deal would be to everyone's advantage," he said. "Money-wise, this is our best chance. If we hesitate any longer, we'll either lose the property altogether or the cost of it will go up."

That sounded just like his father, always answering with a warning and a dire consequence. *If you don't take over the company someday, Eric, do you know how many lives will be changed, and not for the good?* That was one he'd started hearing when he wasn't even ten.

Then there was always the classic, *When you interrupt me like this, it costs money. Losing money may mean losing jobs. Losing jobs means people get hurt. Is that what you want to happen?* In other words, go away, little boy.

But the one that stood out most in Eric's mind was when his father would force him to make a choice, then ridicule him for it. *Are you sure that's what you want, Eric? Have you thought it through? Looked at consequences on both sides? Because from what I'm observing you've made a very poor choice. It's not worthy of you, and what you do reflects on me.*

That had been the day his dad had put warehouse specs and details in front of him and told him to read everything very carefully as the decision whether or not to buy was totally up to him. He'd been eleven and he'd chosen not to buy for what he'd believed were sound reasons: bad location, too old, not accessible enough. His dad had reversed his decision, though, gone ahead and purchased the structure, then lost a ton of money. For years he'd blamed it on Eric for not standing behind his convictions. "You'll never be a good businessman," he'd said.

Well, his dad had been right. He wasn't. At least, not in the way his dad would have wanted.

"I'm going to be honest with you, Bucky. I don't want to be part of the deal as it stands."

Bucky stopped dead in his tracks then stood and stared at Eric. "Seriously? We've been waiting far longer than we should have and after it all, you say no?"

"It's not a good fit." He really didn't want to have this argument, not with Michi taking over all his thoughts now, and he'd hoped that once he'd stated his decision he could simply move on. But Bucky looked like he was gearing up for a fight. His ruddy face was turning redder, his breathing was getting shallow.

"Sorry to disappoint you, but right now I'm looking more at investing in a chain of low-cost medical clinics, and I don't want to get tied up in too many new ventures at once. Unless..." He slid an offer across the desk to Bucky. One that set aside half the acreage for a wildlife habitat. Bucky took one look, then crumpled the paper and threw it in the trash.

"Seriously, Eric? A wildlife habitat on property that valuable? What would your daddy say?"

Eric didn't have to guess. He already knew. "He'd pull it out of my hands and take it over for himself."

"And you're set to go against that?"

"He's dead, Bucky. The company is mine now, and I like wildlife habitats and low-cost medical clinics."

"They're nice, but at what cost? Because they suck money, Eric. They don't make it."

It's not always about making money," Eric defended, ready for this conversation to end and for Bucky to go away. "Sometimes you just have to do the right thing." This was the way it always happened when he didn't do what people expected, just because it was what his dad would have done. The comparisons were always harsh. People made it clear they didn't respect him or his decisions. But none of this was new to him. People had started the accusations when he was young. He'd grown up with the comparisons. He'd gotten used to the ridicule.

Still, sometimes he did wonder what would happen if he did what his dad would have done. Then he'd chalk it up to a lifetime of attempted and failed Daddy-pleasing and move on. Because in the end it didn't matter. His dad hadn't given him credit for anything, ever. Not when the old man had been alive. And now that he was dead… who the hell cared? Still, sometimes old habits squirmed their way back in. But not this deal. Not anymore.

"Your daddy wouldn't have liked this. Not one little bit. He was a smart man who knew how to take almost any property and turn it into a gold mine. Except wildlife preserves and low-cost health clinics. We both know what he would have said about those."

Ah, yes. This was his dad come back to haunt him in the guise of a slick Texas attorney. "I looked at the land, Bucky. Saw how many ranchers we'd have to displace. It was never mentioned in any of the paperwork, but there are nineteen active ranches out there. Nineteen livelihoods. Nineteen people depending on that land."

"But they'll leave when we offer them a fair price, Eric. Everybody has a price, you know. Besides, it's good land. Just far enough away from everything that when people come to the casino they'll probably stay a day or two. And it's close enough to the population base that it won't be too inconvenient. Meaning lots of cash flow. *Cha-ching.*" He gestured as if he was pulling the handle of a slot machine.

This got down to the fundamental difference between his dad and him. His dad's profit had been meant to line his dad's pockets. The profit Eric made went to something different, something better, in his opinion. Buildings and property management were necessary, but so were humanitarian efforts and charities and people in general. And coyotes. He thought about the little coyote pup he'd seen on that land, and wondered what would happen to all the displaced species, both animal and plant life. Would they just be plowed under and forgotten? That thought, more than anything, was the deciding factor. So was Bucky's attitude, to be honest.

"So your intention is to move in, bulldoze everything under and shove aside the lives that get in your way, then build your own version of paradise by the light of a slot machine?"

"Not shove, Eric. Convince. We'll convince them to move on."

"And start over, like it or not."

"Has to be done. Some of those ranches are in the path of progress so they become part of the deal."

"Maybe you think it has to be done, but not by me. That's not the kind of deal to which I want to attach the Hart name." No, his deal was to favor the coyotes and the prickly pear cactus and the ranchers. Preserving posterity, even if that posterity was not his own. The older he got, the more he thought about it.

"Is there anything I can say or do to help you change your mind? Up your percentage of the deal. Build you a custom suite in the complex with everything you could ever want in it? Introduce you to my sister…for God's sake, Eric. Be reasonable here."

"I am being reasonable." It was a sound decision. Possibly the best one he'd made since taking over the company, and he felt good about it. Somehow he thought Michi would approve, and that made him feel even better. Of course, it wasn't the same feeling he'd had when he'd left the operating theater after a good surgery, but in his line of work now it was probably as close as he would get. "I appreciate the opportunity, but it's not for me."

Bucky nodded, but ignored the hand Eric extended to him. "Your daddy wouldn't have missed this opportunity. He was an astute man who knew a good deal when it was presented to him and he always jumped right on it."

"If he were here, I'm sure he'd be flattered by the compliment. But I'm the one who's here now, making the decisions. Not my dad." And for the first time since he'd taken over, he felt like he was on solid footing. Maybe because seeing Michi again had sparked a little optimism he'd been lacking since he'd left medicine. Or maybe he was simply coming into his own. Whatever the case, this time he wasn't living in his dad's shadow, doing what his dad would have done. This was what *he* wanted, and it felt good.

"Your loss." Those were Bucky's final words before he left.

But, it wasn't a loss. Not even close to one. And Eric simply smiled as he sat back down, pulled out his cell-phone, and punched in a number. "You know that piece of property down in Texas? The one they want to turn into a casino oasis? Buy it. Every last inch of it." He listened to the voice on the other end—one of his lawyers. "Yes, I'm aware of the cost. And, no, I don't intend on selling it back to the casino investors at an inflated price. I want the land to remain as it is. I want the people who live on that land to go on living there, with the legal understanding that if they should move, that property will revert to Hart Properties. Oh, and the purpose of that property is to remain a natural habitat. Tie it up so tight that it won't be touched forever. And erect a plaque dedicating it to the coyotes."

On that positive note, and so full of positive energy he felt like he was going to burst, Eric changed out of his suit, bade Natalie good afternoon, exited the building, then took a run down to the park. It was the first time he'd run since he couldn't remember when, and it felt good. Everything felt good. Sure, Michi was a big part of that, but with this Riku somewhere in her life… well, he didn't expect anything to come of him and her. But right now he felt great, and he wasn't going to worry beyond that. He'd made a wise decision, he'd seen Michi again…so far it was turning into a very good day.

\* \* \*

"He's had a good day," Agnes said, handing Riku over to Michi. He was sound asleep, sucking his thumb, looking as angelic as a child could look. "Although I will say he tires a little too easily, which is a concern. But…" Agnes shrugged "… Dr. Kapoor will fix him and all of us can finally breathe a sigh of relief."

"Can you watch him for a little while tonight?"

Agnes arched curious eyebrows but didn't ask.

"OK, I have a date with Eric. I ran into him and—"

Agnes raised her hand to stop her. "Your business, Michi. Entirely your business. Of course I'll watch him. Spending time with Riku is the best part of my life, except for spending time with your uncle."

"I usually put him on a little oxygen at night. That's when he seems to have the most difficulty breathing."

"And we're set up for that. Nothing to worry about."

She loved her aunt's cheery outlook, wished she had some of that herself. Maybe in time. After the surgery. After Riku was on the road to recovery.

After…after…after. That was her life. Everything now came after. But truncus arteriosus, a rare type of heart defect, pushed everything in her life aside. All she had to cling to was *after*. Everything else was a wait-and-see game.

"But I worry anyway," Michi said as she looked down at her sleeping son and tears welled in her eyes. "There are so many questions, Agnes. Should I have had this done earlier, before he was as compromised as he is now? Should I have tried harder to tell Eric when I found out? Maybe seek out his advice? Should I tell him now and leave out the part that Riku's his son? Or should I tell him everything and hope he doesn't retaliate in some way? Because that's what scares me. Would Eric see me as negligent for my choices and go for custody?"

Agnes gave Michi's arm a squeeze. "I know you're still suffering from that incident with the social worker, but she's not Eric and I don't believe he's a vindictive man, Michi. I know him, not very well on a personal level, but what I know about him as a doctor makes me feel confident that Eric will do the right thing after *you* do the right thing."

"Which is tell him."

Agnes shrugged again, then gave her niece a bracing hug. "Have a nice time. And if you want to check on Riku, we'll do a video call."

Agnes's cheerful exterior was only for show. She was every bit as frightened as the rest of Michi's family. Still, with so much concern and support, the guilt Michi carried around was getting heavier because her common sense was right. Eric had to know. Her heart was telling her the very same thing. But it was fear holding her back, and it was a feeling she couldn't carry forever. The burden of it was too massive.

Yet when she thought of Eric's new world, that was where all her debates with herself wavered. Eric lived in a world she didn't understand now. Would Riku fit in there? Would Eric want him to fit in? She didn't know, but that wasn't going to stop her. Not now. After tonight, nothing in her world would ever be the same again. What that world was going to be, though…she wasn't ready to think about that.

Michi spent the next couple of hours sitting at the side of the bed Agnes and Takumi had placed in the spare room, simply watching Riku sleep. She loved doing that.

Tried hard to do that as much as she could every day then, at the end of it when she tucked him in for the night, she kept her vigil long into the night.

Life worked out well despite her busy schedule. She saw very few patients now. Someone else had taken over the majority of her admin work. And her grandmother, a retired pediatrician, took care of Riku when Michi couldn't. Her parents were always on hand as well. So far, she'd never gone outside the family to find someone to care for Riku when she couldn't because her eager family always jumped in first.

She was lucky having so many people who cared. But Eric—did he have anyone? She didn't really know. She should, because Eric's family would also be Riku's family. Surprisingly, this was the first time she'd ever thought of that. Probably because she'd never allowed herself to accept the fact that Eric was a real part of Riku's life.

"Your daddy's a good man," she said, as Riku slowly opened his eyes. "And he won't understand a word you're saying when you start to talk because you'll speak in Japanese and he won't. Which means we may have to teach Daddy to speak our language." Riku didn't say anything, the way he never did, but he did smile, then reach up for her.

"Are you hungry?" she asked him.

Again, he didn't answer, but she always hoped. Just one word would have sent her over the moon with joy. The doctors had told her not to worry because his delay in talking was probably a side effect of his illness. Not in a medical sense, though, but more from having spent most of his life having medical treatment, which had slowed down his development in both speech and physical co-ordination. He did understand her, though. Of that, she was sure, because she could see the look in his eyes when she talked to him. "Uncle Takumi made you some applesauce. Does that sound good?"

Riku sat up and scooted toward the edge of his crib. Once there, he pulled himself to his feet, but it was difficult. He knew what to do, but his body didn't always allow it to happen. But Riku was a fighter. He struggled through, and Michi was so proud of him for that. Her son had a strong will, which would help him with some of the adaptations he'd have to make due to his heart.

"Here, let me help," she said, picking him up and putting him on her hip. "You're getting so big it's hard for Mommy to carry you." Despite his illness, he was big for his age. Was that something he'd inherited from Eric? Eric was tall, broad-shouldered, strong. She'd always known Riku might grow up to be just like his daddy. Maybe even hoped for it. And sometimes she did see Eric in him. In his smile, in the way he observed everything around him. At times she could almost see the two of them together, father and son, so alike yet so different. Her heart warmed when she fantasized them as a family. But afterwards, when her reality returned, along with it came an ache she couldn't describe because that was when she realized that not only did Eric need Riku, Riku needed Eric. And she'd let them both down.

"So, how about we get you something to eat, then we can play some games?" Then she'd go next door to meet his father and hopefully, sometime in the span of these next two hours, figure out a way to make things right for everyone. If that could happen at all.

* * *

"This is nice," Eric said, sliding into the booth alongside her. "It's one of my favorite places to eat. And it's kind of a small world, your uncle owning it."

"If you like Japanese food, this is the place to eat."

"And just like that the fantasy vanishes."

"What do you mean?" she asked.

"It was nice thinking that somehow in this vast universe we were meant to meet again."

Of course, their meeting was no coincidence, but she wasn't ready to admit that. Not yet. "Nice dream, except I'm more rooted in reality."

"Like I said, the fantasy vanishes."

"Do you really believe in fantasies coming true?" she asked him.

"I like to think they do. Haven't really had any proof to back it up, but when I was a surgeon I did witness miracles every day. And fantasies, miracles and wishes are pretty much the same thing. So, what about you? Why so…practical?"

"Because maybe a miracle happens from time to time, or maybe it's not a miracle as much as a statistic, or odds for or against you." She'd seen enough of both to be skeptical. Yet Riku was a miracle. She was firmly convinced of that even though she was skeptical of miracles otherwise. But why was she skeptical? Maybe she'd been let down too many times.

"That's too bad. My dad was like that. The only things he believed in were what he created from a practical perspective. At least, practical to him."

"But isn't what you're doing now based on practicality?"

"I bought two hundred and fifty thousand acres of

desert land this morning to preserve a coyote habitat. It was slated to be a casino, but my concern was where that poor coyote would go once it was forced out of its habitat. And in my father's world there's nothing practical about that."

"What about your world, Eric?"

"It makes sense. Not practical sense, but emotional sense."

"Then you did a good thing, if you're happy with the decision."

He chuckled. "That's not what my advisors are saying. As we speak, they're probably trying to find a way to have me committed to a home for the pathetically sentimental." He scooted just a few inches closer to Michi. Not so close that he was actually touching her but close enough he felt connected, and if anyone looked on, they would assume a connection.

"Why did you leave medicine?" she asked him, as the waiter placed menus on the table. "I mean, I heard that you'd inherited a company, but when you're so good at what you do, the way you were, why give it up unless you've lost your heart for it? And judging from what I came to know at the conference, you weren't the type to lose heart for what you do...*did*."

"It's complicated," he said. "Something to do with family expectations and living up to the stature of a man I didn't particularly care to live up to. Also, I think I got myself caught up in something that was always meant to get me caught up. My dad wanted his progeny to take over where he left off, and in one way or another he prepared me for this my entire life."

"And you like it?"

"I don't dislike it the way I did at first. The people I

work with are good. I'm able to do things I could have never done before."

"Like your wildlife habitat?"

"That, and low-cost medical clinics. I fund various causes—women's health care, several sources devoted to finding cures for cardiac disease, especially in pediatrics. It all works out."

"Then you're happy?"

"I have what I need. To most people that would be happiness, I suppose."

Yet she saw such sadness in his eyes. Sadness and longing. "You're right. It does sound complicated. Do you think you'll ever return to surgery?"

"That's the question I ask myself every day as I put on my custom-tailored, five-thousand-dollar suit and wait for a limo to come pick me up for work."

"Am I detecting some cynicism?"

"More like ambivalence. Sometimes in life you end up doing what you have to do even though it's not what you want to do. I have hundreds of people in my care now who deserve to have the confidence of knowing that when they wake up tomorrow, they'll still have a job, and that they can expect pay raises and excellent working conditions. I sponsor scholarships that put their kids through college and pay for medical benefits that no other company the size of mine can come close to.

"So, while this isn't what I'd originally intended for my life, events and circumstances bring about changes we can't anticipate. What we do with those changes defines us." He stopped and took a breath. "So, how about you? Is your clinic growing the way you'd expected it to?"

"I've had some changes myself," she said, knowing

this was about to become her now-or-never moment. Surprisingly, she wasn't as nervous about it as she'd expected. Something about Eric put her at ease.

"Unexpected ones?"

"Definitely unexpected. But good, because they've taught me to refocus on what's really important. Before when we...well, when we were together for that night, I didn't know what I was about. You were attractive and I wanted you...so I seduced you."

"And you did a damn fine job of it."

"But it was a diversion, Eric. An emotional response that didn't know which emotion to attach itself to."

"Then what you're telling me is that I was a practicality?"

Michi shook her head. "No. You were a reaction. I'd always wanted children, and I'd just been told that wasn't possible, given the severity of my polycystic ovarian syndrome. I was...floundering. Trying to find something to give me some stability. Something that made some sense, even if only for little while, because, trust me, one-night stands are not my normal reaction. But you were so...kind. And I felt so comfortable around you.

"So, I thought that with you I could just have one night that made sense at a time when I was drowning in a whole sea of other things that were making no sense at all. In my twenties, there was plenty of time to start a family. In my thirties, I was stripped of all my options. When we met I just wasn't coping."

It was a lot to divulge, considering no one knew any of this. Not even her family. But these were the things Eric needed to know. Things that might help him understand better.

He reached over and took her hand. "For what it's

worth, I don't think I zeroed in on your vulnerability as much as your sadness. And I understand what sadness can do to a person. I'd seen it in the parents of my patients, even in myself. I wouldn't have taken advantage of you, Michi, if I'd known what you were going through."

"Well, I'm not very good at putting a lot of myself out there for other people to see. No particular reason other than that's who I am. So, what we did…it was what I wanted. Connection. Arms around me. Someone who would make me feel that I wasn't such a failure. And, yes, even though it was just for a few hours. But, other than great sex, which was my escape for a while, that night changed me, Eric. You changed me in ways I never expected could happen. Changes that couldn't happen to the woman who felt like she was failing at all the things that meant the most to her."

"And now?"

He let go of her hand and instead put his arm around her shoulder, and even in that innocent gesture, she understood how Eric had gotten to her in a way no man had ever done before. With him she felt safe. Even a bit optimistic, although that optimism might be short-lived. "Let's just say that work hasn't come first for a very long time, and it never will again. There are more important things, things that shouldn't or couldn't have happened but did."

"You've got my head spinning, Michi, because I don't understand what you're talking about." But it was serious. He could see it in the way her fists were clenched on the tabletop, and the way she avoided looking at him. Was she going to tell him she'd fallen in love that night? That would be nice, because in so many ways, so had he. Except he'd been the one to put it aside for his work, while Michi had stepped away from her work to embrace it, or something like it.

"Sometimes I don't either, Eric. And what I've done…" She took a deep breath. "I've hurt people."

"That's not possible. That's not who you are."

"But it's who I've become."

"Because of me?" he asked.

"Because of me." She twisted sideways and finally looked him straight in the eyes. "I had a baby, Eric."

He blinked, and opened his mouth to speak but closed it again.

"Despite my diagnosis, I had a baby. His name is Riku and he's changed everything in my life."

"Then you're married?" He swallowed hard as he withdrew his arm from her shoulder, pushed himself away from her, then finally braved a look at her hands to check for her wedding ring. But there wasn't one.

"No," she said, almost too quickly. "I'm a single mom."

"If this is what you want, then I should congratulate you. Especially since you didn't think it could happen."

"Don't congratulate me yet. Especially after what I've got to tell you."

A hard knot formed in his stomach. Life had certainly thrown him some curve balls, but… "How old, exactly, is Riku?"

"He's just a few weeks past his second birthday."

"Then that night…" Even he could hear the wobble in his voice with that question.

Michi nodded. "Riku."

"And you didn't tell me?"

"It's complicated, Eric. I always intended to, and even tried to, but other things got in the way."

Right now, he was too stunned to be angry, but he knew that was coming. Could feel it bubbling up inside him. "What things were more important than telling me about my son, Michi?" The boiling anger was rising higher and higher.

"First, there was my pregnancy. It was..." As a passing the server pushed through the door to the kitchen, and for that instant the door was wide open, Michi saw Agnes in there, holding Riku. And Riku looked limp.

A mother's instinct took over, and with no thought about Eric she bolted out of the booth and into the back room. "What's wrong?" she gasped, taking her son out of Agnes's arms.

"Fever, Michi. Too high. It came up quickly, and I was asking Takumi to drive us to the hospital."

"Who needs the hospital?" Eric asked, coming through the door. Immediately, he saw the child in Michi's arms and knew it was his son. "What's his temperature?" he demanded.

"It's one-oh-four," Agnes said, looking at Michi. "And he's beginning to sound congested, so I put him back on his oxygen and upped it a little higher than usual."

"I told him," Michi said as Eric moved to lay his hand on Riku's forehead. Tears streamed down her face as he took Riku into his arms and ran from the restaurant, holding onto his son for dear life.

Running was faster than driving or calling an ambulance, and in those few minutes, when he didn't wait for Michi to catch up, he cursed the world and the universe and Michi for keeping this secret. And even then the anger hadn't boiled up as much as he knew it still would.

Why? Because he had a son who needed him. A son he had fallen in love with at first sight. A son who made him feel every bit the father he'd never expected to be.

"We're going to get you taken care of, Riku," he said as he burst through the emergency room doors and ran straight to the area sectioned off for pediatrics. "Your father will make sure you're taken care of."

"This is my son," he said to the attending who came to put Riku into one of the emergency beds. "Take good care of him." His son, he thought as the doctor carried Riku away. He had a son. And he was a father.

Eric turned as Michi caught up to him, and he saw the tears streaming down her face. Now wasn't the time, he realized. Their son was sick and that stopped everything else in the world. Now he understood what Michi had meant when she'd told him there were things more important than her medical practice. Because now, in his world, there was nothing more important than Riku.

"They'll take good care of him," he said, slipping his hand around her waist and pulling her into him. She needed his support as much as he needed hers right now, because their son was sick. *Their son...*

But soon, very soon, the inevitable reaction would happen. The anger. The frustration. The hurt. All of it. Because yet another person in his life had manipulated him. And it was Michi. The last person he'd ever thought would do that.

Maybe that, above all else, would be the biggest hurt.

# CHAPTER FOUR

HOURS SEEMED LIKE DAYS, and she hadn't been allowed in to see Riku yet. They were still testing him. So, in the waiting room, Michi paced one way while Eric paced another, neither of them speaking. Eric not asking any questions because his anger was as obvious as his fear. And she was offering no explanations or apologies as right now they would fall on deaf ears, and she really needed Eric to hear her. But they were there together and, for the moment, that was the best either of them could do.

It was only after one of the nurses reassured them that Riku was stable but still had another hour of tests ahead that Michi and Eric both decided to go to the cafeteria for a break. As they were standing in line, he to pay for his coffee, she to pay for her tea, she finally broke the silence. "Don't you want to say something? Or ask me any questions?"

He turned to face her. Kept his voice low. Kept the anger on his face in check. "Other than knowing you hid my son from me, what else is there to ask? If I asked why, would you tell me? If I asked if you're sure he's mine, would you try to hide another truth from me?"

"He's yours," she said. "There hasn't been anybody else since we…"

"Great," he said, fishing a couple of bills from his pocket to pay for his coffee, then another couple to cover her tea. "You're capable of telling the truth, if that's what you just told me."

"I've never lied, Eric. I've just never—"

"That's right. You're the one who doesn't put herself out there for others, aren't you? Not even for the father of your baby." He went to a secluded table in a far corner of the cafeteria and sat down. Then stood back up and pulled out a chair for her when Michi caught up to him. Damn old-world manners, he thought. Even for someone who'd done what she'd done.

"It was a bad pregnancy, Eric. I almost lost Riku several times. I was flat on my back for so long, not moving except when necessary, exam after exam, close calls… I spent most of the pregnancy after the first trimester in bed. And while that's no excuse for what I did, or didn't do, you do need to know what was going on with me. My intentions at the start were to let you know. But when it got bad…"

"I'm sorry for that," he said, his voice gentle. "I might not have been able to help, but I would have been there for you if I'd known. I'm not the kind of man who would turn my back on something like this."

"I was confused. Fighting a battle I didn't know how to fight. And after that one night together, remembering how adamant you were about not having any kind of involvement in your life, what was I supposed to do? Take you at your word, which was what I did? Or risk reaching out, only to be rejected? Emotionally, I wasn't up for that, Eric. I was fragile, and I wasn't able to handle any more than I already was."

"I'm sorry for what you went through, Michi. There are no words to express how I feel about that. But no matter what I'd told you, I had a right to know. Don't you understand that? Riku isn't just yours. He's mine, too. You carried my son for nine months, and now, two years later, the only reason I know anything is through a series of coincidences. What if we hadn't had that chance meeting in the coffee shop? Would you have gone back to Japan thinking you could save your secret for another time? Or forever?"

"The coffee shop might have been a coincidence, but I was going to tell you, Eric. I was struggling with how to do it. And, yes, not telling you would have been easier. Especially after making it through a bad pregnancy and hysterectomy, only to find out Riku was so ill. I think at that point I was beyond coping. It was all I could do to get myself from one moment to the next. But it was it was never my intention not to tell you. I just didn't know how or when. And I was scared…"

"Of what?"

"That you'd take him from me. Especially once you knew that he's…" She'd said it too many times, explained it too many times and now, when she most needed to say the words, she couldn't. Because this was the one time that mattered above all others. The time that could affect her and Riku for the rest of their lives.

"He's what, Michi? Tell me. What's going on?"

"Sick, Eric. Riku is really sick, and the real reason I'm here in New York is so he can have surgery. What you saw weren't cold symptoms. They were…" A lump formed in her throat as she struggled with the word. "They were the outward symptoms of his heart defect."

Eric blanched. "What?" he gasped.

Michi shook her head, then bit down hard on her bottom lip to keep herself from crying. "He has…" She drew in a deep breath. "He was diagnosed with truncus arteriosus with a ventricular septal defect. And, yes, I know that's your specialty. But since you couldn't be involved my aunt set it up with the doctor who will be performing the surgery. Dr. Anjali Kapoor."

"You asked her without consulting me first?"

"I've done a lot of things I should have done differently but, yes, I did. Now that you're not practicing, she's considered the best surgeon for Riku's condition, and I was lucky she agreed to do the surgery. With one less of you in the field, she's very busy."

"You let other people help, but not me? Why, Michi? I don't understand what made you think I'd take him away from you."

"I didn't think that…well, not seriously. But I'm so used to protecting him from everything now…"

"Including his father." He sighed. "Did it ever occur to you that my son might need me? That I might have an opinion on his surgery based on how that *was* my specialty when I practiced?"

"But you as good as told me you didn't want anybody in your life. That's all I could think of, Eric, as I went through the steps I had to take to make sure Riku was getting everything he needed. All I knew was that Riku had a mother who would give her life for him and a father who'd said he didn't want to be involved. There's a wide gap in there, and I simply didn't have the emotional stamina I needed to bridge it.

"I tried getting hold of you during my pregnancy and even after Riku was born, but I couldn't, and I didn't have the energy to keep trying. And before you ask why Agnes didn't try…she didn't know you were Riku's father. Not until much later. Not until his doctors had determined he would need surgery. By then…all I can say is I'm sorry. I could have tried harder, but everything I had in me went to Riku and there was nothing left over for anything else."

Eric opened his mouth to say more, but no words came out. He looked so angry and hurt. To find out he had a son, then shortly after to be told his son was ill—her heart did go out to him as the pain she saw on his face was what she'd put there. But it was done, her choices made, and she couldn't go back and change things, not even if she wanted to. "I wish we could have done this better," she said. "I'm sorry you found out about Riku this way."

Eric nodded, but still didn't speak.

"Oh, and in case you're wondering why I didn't have the surgery done earlier, Riku's cardiologist back home advised that since the surgery would entail two different procedures, we should wait until he was a little older, and a little larger. Otherwise I'd have had it done a long time ago. I know it's usually done early on, but I wasn't negligent about this, Eric. He's had good medical care since the day he was born."

Eric walked over to the cafeteria window and looked out on the parking lot. It was not yet morning, but the day shift workers were beginning to appear. Parking their cars, heading into the hospital. Reporting for duty. Business as normal, except for him. Because now nothing was normal. His life had just changed, and he didn't know what to do about it yet. There were no rules or guidelines for this sort of thing. And right now, he was feeling so…lost, like the way he'd always felt after one of his father's rejections. Lost, bewildered, scared. "How bad is he?" he asked on a discouraged sigh. "And don't hold back, Michi. Not this time."

She took a sip of her tea, now cold, and bit her lower lip. "He's a little behind in some of his development like speech, but overall he's been good. It's only been in the last few weeks that I've noticed any real physical changes in him. You know, the intermittent oxygen when needed, a little less energy than before, lack of appetite."

He turned his back to the window to face Michi. "I might not have done anything differently for Riku than you've done, but I could have supported you…assured you that you were doing the right things. So why, Michi? I know you had serious problems, but I still don't understand why you didn't try harder once he was born."

"Why?" She drew in a deep breath. "Why didn't I try harder? Because of you, Eric. You, better than most, know the kind of care that he's required. It's twenty-four seven. You move from one thing to the next without getting a break in between. But I've never minded any of that. Not one minute of it. But you…you didn't want the commitment. No strings attached. Sure, you might have jumped in at the start, but I wasn't convinced you had the long haul in you. Riku's care is the long haul now, and even after his initial surgery, all I could think of was what would happen when you decided it wasn't in you any longer to make the commitment to his care.

"Personally, I didn't need that kind of rejection but, more, Riku didn't need it. He needs people around him he can trust, and he's old enough to make those distinctions. But his daddy…" She shrugged. "The whole situation scared me. You scared me."

"Based on what?"

"Some of the things you said. But mostly your jump from being a surgeon to a property manager. At the seminar you were excited about expanding your practice. I could see it in the way you took in every last detail of physiatry. And I heard it in the questions you asked. Then, in the blink of an eye, you'd gone off in an entirely different direction. Sort of like the way you left me that night. There one minute, then sneaking off into the night the next.

"And you didn't even come to my last class, which told me you were already part of my past. Riku needed stability and I wasn't sure you could give that to him when what I heard from you was how you didn't want the commitment, then afterwards what I saw said the very same thing.

"With Riku, I needed a commitment. Maybe not a marriage or a relationship with me, but somebody who would stand beside me through all of it. But you were hopping from one thing to another, and in that I didn't see a man who would stay there for Riku, no matter what. What I saw, Eric, was a man who would go sneaking off into the night again."

"Did it ever occur to you to give me a chance?"

"It did. But I was…still am overwhelmed and I couldn't add your commitment problem to my problems. And, yes, it hurt leaving you out, but there weren't a lot of options available to me—continue to pursue a man who'd already told me he didn't want a relationship of any kind or concentrate on giving Riku everything he needs. For the sake of my son—our son—I did the right thing. The only thing I could do. Or, at least, the only thing I *thought* I could do. And I'm sorry I hurt you. That was never my intention."

As various workers on the morning shift began to filter into the cafeteria for their coffee, Eric took hold of Michi's hand and led her down the hall to the nearest private room, which happened to be the hospital chapel. Dimly lit and very empty. After they'd seated themselves in the corner of the rear pew, he leaned his head back against the wall and closed his eyes.

"My dad and I always had a difficult relationship," he began. "My mother left when I was five. Walked out the door one day and never came back. I never knew why, and I was forbidden even to speak about it. Meaning, at age five, I knew what rejection felt like. So, raising me was up to the old man, and all he wanted was an heir, someone to take over where he eventually left off. Since I was his only child, that would have been me. Except that wasn't what I wanted. Being a surgeon was. That topic opened up more debates and arguments than I can remember over the years, and since my dad already wasn't a nurturer, and that's putting it mildly, it simply widened the gap between us.

"As a result, I was raised by a lot of people: teachers at the boarding school where he sent me so he wouldn't have to deal with me; any number of hired nannies; the school custodian when Dad forget to take me home for a holiday; the woman who came in twice a week to do laundry. I was up for grabs, basically. Anybody who wanted me for a minute or a day or a week could have me. That was my life when I was a kid. I had a father who didn't love me and, as a result, I was always afraid

I'd turn out just like him. Kids do that, you know. Turn out like their parents."

"Which is why you were so adamantly against relationships?"

"I would never put another child through what I went through. No physical abuse. No deprivation of anything except the thing I wanted the most. So, my no-commitment policy, it protected me, but most of all it protected someone else from me. Someone I might have come to love dearly." He shifted his position, moved over toward Michi until he was just barely touching her. And she didn't pull away. Even that simple gesture gave him the encouragement he needed to tell her more.

"Anyway, prior to coming to your seminar it had probably been three months since I'd had any contact with my dad, which suited me just fine as he was putting more pressure on me to leave medicine and join the company. Since I'd lived with that most of my life, I was pretty well able to shut it out. But there was this little boy inside me who always tried to win his dad's favor, even though he knew it wouldn't happen. Then the little boy turned into a successful man who'd still never received the approval or even the acknowledgement he wanted. At the time of the seminar we were basically estranged. I'd had enough, and I think even he was getting tired of the back and forth.

"But that night—*our night*—I got a text telling me he'd died. No explanation, no nothing. Just the words, Your dad has died. Return home immediately to assume control of Hart Properties. From his lawyer, by the way. For all his money, and all his importance, he was alone in the end. But he still got what he wanted because I did go home and took over where he'd left off.

"At first, I kept telling myself it was temporary, that I'd find someone to replace me then go back to medicine. But the people I interviewed…they all seemed like a different version of my dad. And here was little Eric with an entirely different view of the way things should be. So, I stayed. Resigned my position at the hospital and took over the company, probably to show myself I wasn't my dad. Strange psychology, I know. But parents do shape who their kids turn out to be. Except I had this altruistic view, whereas he was simply about profit and loss."

"I'm sorry," Michi whispered, taking hold of Eric's hand.

"So am I. As much as we didn't get along, he didn't deserve to die alone, but he did. Then the thing I'd always told him I didn't want to happen happened. Everything he owned became mine, including the company… the company that had originally torn us apart. And the first thing I knew, people were counting on me. I controlled their jobs and, essentially in some way, their lives. Hundreds of people. At night, when I'd try to go to bed, I'd see their faces. They needed something from me. Something better than my dad had ever given. Long story short, I gave up me to become a different version of him. And as for the morning I left without saying goodbye… I didn't even realize I'd done that until I was halfway back to New York.

"I intended to call you, but the instant I stepped out of the corporate jet my new life started, and it overwhelmed me for months. There were several times, during that period, when I thought about calling, but I didn't because I thought, *What's the point?* I wasn't the man you'd met in Japan. In fact, much of the time I wasn't even the man I'd always known. And I wasn't happy about any of it, Michi.

"After that night together, like you, I'd thought we could have more. I wasn't sure what it would have been since I was still against ending up in a real relationship. But it was the first time in my life I'd ever allowed that thought in, and for a little while I was hopeful. Then after the text, let's just say that I gave up on anything I might have wanted in order to prove myself to a man who would never know. By the time I'd figured all that out, it was too late to do anything but follow my new course."

"A course that's not being true to who you are? Can that ever make you happy, Eric?"

"Well, you know what they say about not always getting what you want. Only in my case I think I was confused about what I wanted. In the end I realized that, after a lifetime of trying to get it, my dad's approval didn't matter. Not to him and certainly not to me. But by that time, I had too many people dependent on me for so many things that I couldn't simply walk away."

"Sounds like we both went directions we didn't anticipate."

"And I'm glad yours was the better direction," he said. "I'm still angry that you didn't include me, and that's something it's going to take me a while to work through, but you've been a good mother to Riku. And now I want to prove I can be just as good a dad."

Michi brushed back a tear falling down her cheek, and he brushed away the next one with his thumb. "He needs both of us together, you know." And she truly wanted that to come from both of them. But words and sentiments aside, she still wondered if she could count on him in the long term because if he did back away again, she could take the rejection. Riku couldn't, though. And he was her only consideration here. Not herself. Not Eric. Only Riku, and she would fight with everything inside her to protect him, even if that meant fighting Eric.

But he seemed to care. That was what she was counting on, and praying her judgment wasn't being skewed by one night when all her wishes had come true.

# CHAPTER FIVE

HE'D HEARD ALL her words and now he was stuck trying to get himself through the maze of uncertainty so he could figure out what to do next. Not only did he have a son—something that thrilled him to bits—but his son was sick, something that scared him worse than he'd ever been scared in his life. Apart from getting Riku through his illness, could he be a good father to him? A real father? The kind of father he'd never had?

Certainly, he'd never had an example to follow, but loving that little boy could make up for everything he'd lacked in his life, if he got it right. That was the big question. Could he? Michi had been right when she'd reminded him of how he'd said he didn't want involvements. He hadn't, and he always put that out there first. He knew that and, to some extent, had even worked at perfecting it. *Here I am, my terms. Take it or leave it.*

Sure, it protected him. Kept him apart from anything more that could let him down. Yet that had changed the moment he'd found out about Riku. Instant love. Total, complete love for someone he hadn't even properly met.

So, yes, he did understand Michi's reasoning for keeping Riku a secret. To anybody on the outside, looking in, he was a sleight of hand trick. *Here I am but if you take too long to blink, I'll be gone.* But if you were on the inside, looking out…well, who was he kidding? He'd never yet let anybody get close enough to know him on the inside.

Still, to hide his son from him? Sick or not, that little boy was his, and he should have been included in both the good and bad of Riku's life. Not only because he already loved that kid, but because no child deserved to grow up so separated from either of his parents, the way he'd been separated. His dad's reasoning he understood up to a point. But his mother's… That was a wound that had never quite healed, and he didn't want Riku ever to have to deal with that.

OK, so maybe those considerations didn't belong here now, when Riku was on the verge of a major surgery, but there were so many different things to think about. Things that had never before entered his mind. His son's schooling. Would athletics be possible or would Riku be more the studious type? Or maybe an artist or musician? Would he go to university someday, and what would he study? Would he get married? Have a family of his own?

And Michi? What about Michi? He didn't want to hate her. Quite the opposite. But after what she'd done…

Well, one thing was sure. For now, he and Michi would unite for the sake of their son. Getting him through this surgery was the *only* thing that mattered. Everything else could be worked out later. "Is he susceptible to colds?" Eric asked, holding her hand, needing the feel of it in a way that was foreign to him. But Riku was having another scan now and all he could do was wait. It was killing him.

"I don't take him out around too many people because I know his heart condition can suppress his immune system. So, I really can't answer that because he's been pretty sheltered so far."

"And did you choose anyone special to be on the surgical team, or did you leave that up to Dr. Kapoor?" This wasn't right. This conversation should be between two parents who were frightened for their child. Not one parent who was able to show her vulnerability and one who hid behind his medical knowledge. But it was safe there. Someplace he could count on. Someplace that had never let him down when everything else in his world had.

"Really, Eric. That's what you want to talk about? The surgical team?"

"My default, I guess."

"Riku doesn't need a default. He needs a dad. And, yes, you could argue that I've deprived him of that, and you'd be right. But that's not what it's about right now." She broke loose of his hold and walked over to the crib where Riku would be returned shortly. It was midmorning now, and the hospital was in its full daily swing.

"He has a crib at home that's decorated with baby animals. He's particularly fond of the giraffe. So I made a mobile to hang above his crib…all giraffes. Sometimes at night he'll wake me up giggling, and I'll know he's watching that mobile. It makes me feel…safe, hearing that giggle."

She turned around to look at him. "He has a beautiful giggle. When I hear it, I can almost forget what else goes along with it. But he's a normal little boy, Eric. Likes the things all toddlers his age do. And so often, when I look at him, I wonder if he wonders why he's not allowed to do those things. Or, at some point, will he resent me for not allowing him to do the things I know he'd love to do?"

He walked over to the crib but kept his distance as he didn't feel like he had the right to encroach. "Kids are resilient. I used to see that every day. One day they'd be so sick it would break your heart, then later, after surgery, they'd be up and about like nothing had ever been wrong in the first place. For me, that was always the best part. Seeing the way they bounced back."

He drew in a deep breath, resisting the urge to move a couple steps closer then pull her into his arms, but the mixed messages from that would only muddy a dire situation, and Michi didn't need to deal with any more than she already was. "He's not going to hate you. Well, except for when he turns into a teenager and those can be pretty trying years. But when he's mature enough, he will see the sacrifices you've made for him, and he'll come around."

"Not sacrifices," she said, wiping away tears streaming down her face. "Not when you love someone the way I do Riku. Then whatever you do to make their life better, or easier…that's what makes your life better as well."

Damn, she was a good woman. All the attributes he'd thought she had were there in abundance. And, yes, he had every right to be angry. But being angry at Michi… it just wasn't in him. It was all one big, conflicting mess. But watching her suffer, and knowing what she'd given up to take care of their son…it brought out feelings in him he'd never expected. Tender feelings. Caring feelings. Feelings of how he so desperately needed to help her he'd put himself through anything just to be close by.

"When is the surgery scheduled?" he asked, retreating to his safety zone because right now his feelings were too close to the surface and Michi didn't need to deal with them. He was used to doing it on his own. He would manage.

"Dr. Kapoor's lecturing in Dubai right now. If Riku can be put on a normal schedule, it'll be in four days. If it's decided he's an emergency…" She shrugged. "I suppose I should have had a back-up plan, but I didn't."

"Can I take care of that for you?"

"You can't operate, Eric. If you could, you would have been my first choice."

"But there's somebody…my mentor, actually. I'd like to give him a call and see if he'll come in if we need him."

"Do you trust him with your son's life, Eric?"

Eric nodded.

"Then do what you have to do because I trust you to make the right decision. I'm so tired of doing this alone. Mentally exhausted. And I need you, Eric. I need you to make decisions to get Riku through when I'm not capable of doing it any longer. Or even for a moment or two. Yes, any of my family would help. But Riku needs this from his father. And I need what Riku needs."

It wasn't Eric who stepped up to Michi but Michi who stepped up to Eric, and allowed herself to be pulled into his arms. And for the next several minutes they stayed that way. Like a family. Until a nurse poked her head in the door. "Just thought you should know, your little boy will be back in just a few minutes. The scan is over and as soon as the doctor finishes making his notes, he'll accompany Riku back here. Oh, and he's lightly sedated, so I think he'll be sleeping a while."

"I was hoping he'd be awake so you can actually meet him and see just how wonderful he is," Michi said. Something that should have happened before now, but there was no going back, was there? No way to make amends for the pain she'd caused. So, at the moment, all she could do was move forward and keep hoping for a resolution that would benefit all three of them. "Look, Eric. I don't know how he's going to react to you, especially now that he's not feeling well. Like I said, I've sheltered him, so maybe you shouldn't expect too much this first time. Especially if he's groggy."

"Would you rather have me stay away?"

"No. Not at all. I just don't want you to be…disappointed. Or hurt. When he's not feeling well he can be moody."

"I know how to deal with sick children, Michi. I used to be very good at it."

"But this is different, Eric. He's your son and he might not respond to you the way you'd want. I just want you to be aware of that." Because she wanted this first real meeting between father and son to be perfect. It wouldn't make up for what Eric had been deprived of in the past, but it might give him some encouragement for the future if Riku responded well.

Suddenly it struck her that her investment in this situation wasn't just for Riku's sake. It was for Eric's as well. What he wanted, what he needed mattered so much she was surprised she hadn't seen that before now. Maybe it was another way to exclude him? Or maybe it was something more, something where she was afraid of where including Eric might take her.

"Does he know he has a father?"

Michi nodded. "I've mentioned it. Shown him where you worked. Told him what kind of man you are."

"If I speak to him in English, will he understand me?"

This time she shook her head. "We speak Japanese at home. That's what he understands."

"So basically I'll be a stranger who doesn't speak his language, which means there's no real reason for me to see him except that I want to."

"I think he'll know, Eric. Or at least he'll sense your feelings for him."

"I hope so," he said, holding out his hand to her and moving back toward the wall as the nurse wheeled the gurney through the door. She lifted Riku into the crib and began to attach wires, tubes and all manner of other medical equipment no child that age should ever have to know about. "He's doing well," she assured Michi and Eric, then exited the room as the doctor on the case entered.

"Well, the good news is, after comparing previous records to the results of the tests we've just taken, there's been no significant change," reported Dr. Leroy Watson, staff cardiologist. "I've sent everything to Dr. Kapoor and she agrees we should do what we can to keep him stable. Considering his condition, that's still a lot more than the little guy deserves, but I don't want to risk any setbacks." He looked at Eric. "Would you like to look at his test results?"

"I would, except I'm the dad in this one, not the doctor. So I probably shouldn't."

"Well, anyway… I expect he'll sleep the rest of the day. Probably most of the night, too. I'll leave the three of you alone. But if there's anything you need…"

"Thanks, Leroy," Eric said. "For what it's worth, I'm glad you're going to be his hospitalist."

Leroy chuckled. "You should be, since you're the one who requested me."

Michi looked up at Eric. "Seriously?"

"OK, I can't be my son's doctor, and we all know why. But I sure as hell can get the best doctors to look after him."

"And I blush," Leroy said, taking a bow then backing out of the room.

"Without telling me, Eric?"

"Let me contribute something, Michi. You just told me to help you make decisions, and that's what I did. I talked to Leroy, who had an opening, and I jumped on it because he's in high demand. He's good. No, he's damned good and I didn't want to miss the chance to have him take over Riku's normal care. I mean, there's not much else I can do right now except find the best for Riku. So, if you're angry…"

She stepped up to him, stood on tiptoe, and kissed his cheek. "Not angry. Grateful. But obviously still on autopilot for overreacting."

"Overreacting accepted. Overprotective accepted as well. You're the kind of parent Leroy and I love working with."

"Not possible," she said, smiling. "Back in Japan, I made the lives of several of his doctors miserable with my ways. I didn't mean to, but sometimes I couldn't help myself."

He chuckled. "OK, so maybe I'll take back the 'love working with' part and change it to *appreciate* working with. Or *respect* working with. Or *fear* working with. Or run away from totally."

Michi smiled. "All right. I get your point and I'll try hard to do better here. But be warned…"

"Duly noted," he said. "And I'll have Leroy mark in Riku's chart that his mother has an overabundance of overbearing and overprotective tendencies. Will that work for you?"

"I think I'm beginning to understand why you were considered so good. Sure, you had your OR skills, but you top them with your nonsense skills."

"I aim to please, ma'am. I surely do aim to please. And now, on a serious note, will you tell me about him? I want to know everything. His likes, dislikes. Favorite food. What kinds of toys does he play with? His personality. Everything…" Spoken like a man with a desperate need to know.

"Anything you want," she said, reaching into the crib to take hold of Riku's hand.

"We certainly did make a beautiful boy," Eric said, standing back just enough to catch the entire picture of mother and son. "And there are so many things I want to do with him when he's better."

"You said when," she said, choking back the tears that so badly wanted to fall. "You said *when*, not *if*. Everybody has said… Even Dr. Kapoor said if. But you said…" She swallowed hard as the tears fell despite her best effort to hold them back. "I know people don't mean anything by it, but it hurts, Eric. Nobody knows how badly."

"I think I can guess," he said, resisting the urge to pull her into his arms. It might have been the decent thing to do, but he wasn't sure what Michi wanted, or expected of him. And now didn't seem the time to overstep, even though that's what he wanted to do. Pull her into his arms, hold her, reassure her. All mixed feelings, to be sure. Feelings he wasn't yet ready to explore. Not until he had sorted some of his own confusion.

"Michi, I've never seen any of my patients in terms of *if*. It's always *when* because that single, simple word

gives hope, and not just to the parents and family but to
me as well. And because this is my son, I refuse to believe anything but *when*. I want to figure out what kind
of future I'll have with him *when* he's better. I know he'll
have some restrictions, and there'll be another surgery
or two in the future, but he's going to have that future.
That's what I'm going to think no matter what anybody
else says. It's what I have to think. What we both have
to think."

"I want to make us work. Maybe not as a family but
as two adults who love one child…love him more than
anything else in life. And I do want to think in terms
of *when*. I try hard to, but then I get scared, or someone
says something, or, like now, Riku gets sick, and nothing
makes sense. I panic when he sneezes, Eric. Or when he
isn't as responsive as I think he should be.

"I watch every little thing he does and read more into
what I'm seeing than I should. I can't sleep in my own
bed because I have to be in the chair next to his bed. And
I can't turn off the lights at night in case he does something, or something happens to him I can't see. That's
the life I've been living ever since he was born. I miss
more work than I should. I never go out with friends. I
don't even make it to dinner most of the times my family gets together because I don't like Riku being around
so many people. And masks…"

Eric chuckled. "Seriously? You ask people to wear
masks around him?"

"Not my family so much anymore. But when he was
first diagnosed I did. I carried spares in my pockets,
just in case."

"And it was your choice to do it all alone?"

"It was the only thing I knew to do. For me, these past

few years have been a struggle just getting from day to day. I've devoted everything I am to get *him* through. Not me. Him. Which, of course, I made a mess of, didn't I?" She pushed herself back from the crib a little, then looked up at him. Saw a look on his face that broke her heart. "I never meant to hurt you," she said, reaching up to brush his cheek with her hand.

"But you did," he said, his voice sounding so broken it barely escaped him. "And I haven't figured out what to do about that yet, Michi, because there's already been too much pain."

Her stomach churned. She couldn't blame him for what he was feeling, and in so many ways she loved him for trying to hold it back. Most people wouldn't have done that. But, then, Eric wasn't most people. "Eric, since Riku's going to sleep for a while, could we get out of the hospital? I've spent so much time in them, not just working but with Riku, I'd simply like to get out for a few minutes and take a walk. Maybe Agnes will come sit with him while we're gone."

"Do you want me to go ask her?"

Michi shook her head. "No, you stay here with your son. I'll go talk to her and meet you back here in a few minutes."

The night was cool but not cold. Jacket weather, not coat. Michi loved the crispness of it, and the sense that the slight chill brought about new hope. "Thank you," she said to Eric. "It's been so long since I've simply stepped away from everything, I can't even remember when the last time was." She drew in a deep breath of air and let it out slowly. "Maybe three years or more." She laughed. "In fact, I think you were my last step away."

"Then I should be flattered."

"Are you?" she asked.

"More than you could know."

Standing with Eric at the top of the hospital steps, Michi looked at the street down below, to the congestion of traffic and the masses of people walking almost shoulder to shoulder, trying to get to wherever they were going. No one seemed perturbed. In fact, everyone in her view seemed to take whatever came their way in stride. It would be wonderful to live life that way, she thought. Standing in the middle of so many people going so many different ways, and no one seeming to care about the distractions and misdirecting.

"Do you ever have the urge to simply be part of the crowd? Get yourself lost in it for a while and let it sweep you along to wherever it's going?"

"Occasionally. More so now than when I was younger. My structure now is…different."

"But wouldn't it be nice to be on your own for a bit? No cares, no worries. No responsibilities. Especially no responsibilities, except to yourself."

"You do have to take care of yourself sometimes. Give in to the pressure and simply…breathe. And I understand that when you have a child, your child always comes first. But there's room in your life for you as well, Michi. Now that I'm here, I'll make sure you find it whenever you need to."

"I wouldn't really want to be on my own. Not without Riku. But you're right. Sometimes I don't really feel like there's much room for me now in my own life." She looked up at the sky, and through the maze of New York city lights she could see the black sky and a smattering of twinkling stars. "That's what people keep telling me, but…"

Eric chuckled. "But you're stubborn." He took her by the arm and led her down the hospital walkway to the sidewalk. "You always do it your way."

Slow steps, deliberate. Allowing her time to take in the things that had eluded her for so long. She was so keenly aware of his presence she tingled from his touch even through her jacket. "Or not stubborn as much as dedicated, as I would prefer to call it." Across the street, a vendor cart seemed to float in a halo of steam as people lined up to buy whatever was being sold.

"Usually hot coffee, tea, hot cider or hot cocoa," Eric said, as if reading her mind. "Which would you prefer?"

Coffee and tea were everyday. Cider wasn't to her liking. But sipping hot cocoa on a chilly night while walking along the teeming street on the arm of the most handsome man in the crowd…how could she resist that? Moments of fancy or even fanciful romance didn't come along for her too often and she was in the mood for a bit of that now. But only for this one moment in time. That's all she could allow. "Cocoa, please," she said.

"Then let's make that two hot cocoas," he said to the vendor, then looked at Michi. "With or without marshmallows?" he asked.

"Marshmallows. In Japan we have what's called the blooming marshmallow that unfolds as a flower on top of the hot chocolate." She laughed. "Funny. I haven't thought of that in years."

"Then we'll have to make sure Riku has his first blooming marshmallow experience when he's well enough to drink it." Eric handed Michi her paper cup of hot cocoa and pointed to the carriage sitting empty just down the street. "Care for a ride?" he asked.

The horse was white, its tail braided with shiny blue streamers. The carriage was white as well, decorated in the same shades of blue as the horse's tail. "As many times as I've been to New York, I've never done that." And doing it for the first time with Eric seemed perfect. The way everything seemed perfect right now.

"Then I think it's time for your first ride."

"You don't think it's too chilly?"

"You've got your hot cocoa to keep you warm, as well as the blanket the driver will offer us once we get in. And if neither of those work, you've always got me."

Suddenly the image of a snuggle with Eric was all she could think about. And before she could blink, they were in the back of the horse-drawn carriage, its top up, and clopping their way slowly down the road toward Central Park as the coachman in front chattered on merrily about the various buildings and sights they were passing.

To Michi, it felt like she and Eric were stepping back in time to a place where the honking horns didn't exist, and the people on the street were all lovers, walking arm in arm. OK, so maybe she was waxing too romantic, but that was an image that seemed to belong there. To her. To them, as they sat shoulder to shoulder, meandering through Central Park while the soft jostle of the carriage rocking to the gait of the horse, the placid, mesmerizing sound of hooves on pavement turned into just the balm she needed to soothe her soul. And for Michi, in that time, the coachman didn't exist. It was just Eric and her. Her eyes, her senses, her awareness only of him.

"Are you enjoying this?" he asked.

"You don't know how much. If I could make time stop

right here for just a little while…" She smiled at him. "Be careful what you wish for, right?"

"You're allowed a wish for yourself," he said, as the coachman slowed for one of the park entrances.

"Care to get out?" the coachmen asked, turning very slowly in his seat, as if to be unobtrusive. Perhaps that was the instruction given to coachman when they believed they carried lovers. Blend in, make the ride about them, not you. Don't interrupt what appears to be a private moment.

Eric looked over Michi. "We could ride a while longer or take a walk. Your choice."

"I'd love to walk," she said. Hand in hand. Maybe lingering by one of the reflecting ponds, echoing exact images from their edges. Or strolling through one of the many dimly lit tunnels where untold kisses had been stolen or offered up freely. "I've never done that here, after dark. It always seemed so sad, being alone here, maybe the only person without a lover or someone to walk with them."

"Wishes again?" he asked, as he helped her out of the carriage.

"More like observations, I think. And maybe guesses." She'd never had anyone in her life she'd considered a lover. Acquaintances, dates, friends, but no lovers until Eric. And she wasn't considering lover in the sexual sense as much as an intimate sense. In her life, Eric was the only man she'd ever felt close to.

After handing the coachman a generous tip, he took hold of Michi's hand and pulled her over to the trail, then led her to the top of the steps leading down to the reflecting pond, where the twinkling stars above seemed to join with the water as sparkling shards. Champagne glasses.

Pure crystal. Diamonds. Eric simply stood there a moment, looking down at her. "Someone like you should never be alone here, Michi," he finally said.

"And that would be your wish?" she asked him.

"No, this would be." He stood, legs braced to receive her weight, and the chill of the night air, as if by magic, wove a spell around them, binding them together to seek the warmth they each had to offer. Her arm, pressed to his, burnt like a slow, smoldering ember, piercing the layers of his jacket and shirt and on through the rest of him, like he was mere air, powerless to stop the burning of it. Not that he would, even if he could. "You know, we always do our best kissing at night," he said, his voice raspy with desire.

"We've done our only *real* kissing at night," she replied.

"A nice habit to repeat." Eric shifted slightly and for a moment Michi wavered, off balance. But he caught her quickly, pulling her into his arms then bending his face to meet hers. Her dark eyes were caught in a moment of indecision. Should she? Shouldn't she? But the questions were hers to answer, not his. "If that's the kind of habit you like," he said, his lips only a heartbeat away from hers.

"Habits can be good," she said. "So can spontaneity."

"Either or," he said as his lips met hers, and his grip on her tightened, pulling her into him even more while she pressed herself to him with the same eagerness.

The tip of his tongue brushed hers and she opened to let him in as he welcomed the urgency that sent a wildfire racing through every nerve, every sinew of his body. It was Eric who was left weak in the knees, overcome by sheer want for her. It was also Eric who held onto her for dear life. That at first frightened Michi, as she tensed up and backed ever so slightly away from him.

"It's all right," he said. "Just relax and listen to your heart." He chuckled. "Even if it's telling you something entirely different from what your head is saying. Which it probably is if what I'm feeling is anything close to what you're feeling."

"But I don't know how to make my head stop," she said, glancing over at the group of people walking around them, giving them a wide berth. Laughing quietly as if they knew something she didn't. "As much as I'd like it to sometimes. But it's like I can't shut down. I'm always on alert. My mind going in so many directions. Sometimes I wish time would slow down or simply stop long enough to let me catch my breath before I have to move on to the next challenge."

"As much as we'd like it to, time doesn't stand still. Unfortunately, you must play its game as it will never play yours. And its game is sometimes cruel. I'm sorry that's the case for you, that you're not able to enjoy all the moments given you, especially with Riku. But soon, after the surgery…."

"I hope so," she said, trying to hide the look in her eyes, which she knew would betray her need. But she'd fought the battle to hold everything back from everyone for so long that just this once she wanted to let go. Let her vulnerability take over. Lean on someone else… Eric. "Because doing this alone…"

In the catch of a breath he took her lips, his late-in-the-day beard rough against her skin. A faint moan escaped Michi's lips and he could feel her resistance begin to melt away, causing the level of his heat to rise, to burn in his chest, his face, his lips, everywhere. It was like his will had surrendered to hers, getting itself tangled in her hesitancy. Wanting more yet fearing more would send her skittering away. "I, um…" he said, backing away. "Care to go ice skating?"

Michi blinked hard, looking up at him in disbelief. "Ice skating?" she asked.

He confirmed her question with a nod.

"Why?" she asked.

"It's safe. And right now I really need safe."

He needed to be safe while she was willing to take the risk. Well, she deserved that, didn't she? Probably should have seen it coming. Michi laughed, not because it was funny but because of the sheer frustration building up inside her. "Habitually or spontaneously?"

"Maybe a little bit of both, where you're concerned."

"So, do they rent skates here?" she asked, holding her hand out to take his. As athletic as he was, or used to be, Eric's skating was over in less than five minutes. No tumbles to the ice, but he was getting pathetically close to it, and he wanted to look better than that. For Michi. He didn't give a damn about the other hundred skaters on the ice, all in their various stages of taking their own tumbles. All except for Michi. She was graceful. Like a swan. Floating over the ice, casting a spell that made her appear to glide above it. And the smile on her face… In this moment, she had no cares, no worries. She was simply there, wrapping herself in the bliss of pure abandon, no thought of the world that would come crashing back soon enough.

Despite their problems, if he hadn't fallen a little in love with her before, he surely would have now, watching the pure magic she spun over everything. Including him. After nearly ten minutes of indulging himself in watching her, he took to the ice again, catching up to her not as quickly as he would have liked. She stopped when he finally did and smiled. "I'm out of shape," she said, barely winded.

"If that's what you consider out of shape, I'd love to see what you consider *in* shape."

"You did," she said, holding out her hand to him. "Here, let's do this together."

"I'll hold you back," he warned, knowing that nothing in Michi's life should ever hold her back from anything she wanted.

"Maybe I'll hold you back."

He shook his head. But didn't say a word. Instead, he took hold of her hand, and in mere moments they were sailing over the ice together, smoothly, effortlessly. The way he wanted their lives to be. Until…

Michi looked down at him, sprawled flat, staring up at the sky. Then laughed. "One of life's little bumps," she said, as he refused her offer to help him back up. So instead she took out her phone and snapped a photo.

"Seriously?" he asked, once he was up, brushing ice crystals off his back side.

"For Riku. To put in the scrapbook of his life." She winked. "Or maybe in the scrapbook of mine. You're not there yet, you know."

"And this is where you want me to start?"

"This is absolutely where I want me to start. Foibles, falls and all."

# CHAPTER SIX

AN HOUR AFTER the ice rink had closed, they were back
to life as normal, and Michi felt herself go weak in the
knees with the latest news. But before she tumbled to
the floor, Eric put a steadying arm around her like it
was simply something he always did. "You OK?" he
whispered to her.

She nodded. "It's not easy." But Eric did make it easier and for that she was grateful.

"As you know, it's all part of the defect he has," Leroy
continued, holding out a bottle of water for Michi without missing a beat. "But oxygen's easy enough to sup-
plement and I've ordered blood gases drawn, so until we
know more…" He looked at Eric. "Wish I could do better. But I think his surgery needs to be moved up. That's
your decision, of course. Oh, and I've made Dr. Kapoor
aware of the downturn in his condition."

"Minor downturn," Michi challenged. In Riku's life
there were upturns and downturns. A problem with his
oxygen levels was only one of so many things she had
to monitor. She looked at Eric. "So, about your back-up
plan…"

"And this is where I leave the two of you to your
discussions." With that, Dr. Leroy Watson prepared

for one of his well-known grand gesture departures by kissing Michi's hand. "Call me if you have questions. We'll make sure there's an OR available when you decide what to do."

Amidst the strife, Michi did smile. "Were you ever that bold when you were practicing?" she asked. "Because I like his form."

"For me, bold was stepping out from behind my mask. Despite his demeanor, Leroy is as good as they get. A good old country GP trapped in a big-city hospital."

"Well, for what it's worth, the little personal touch makes a difference."

She stood there for a moment, looking at Riku, who was now under an oxygen tent. He was sleeping peacefully, no stress or pain showing on his face. "He's a fighter, Eric," she said, biting her lower lip. "But how long can a person fight before it just wears them down too much?"

He slid his arm around her shoulder and pulled her into him. "It's time, Michi."

She swallowed hard and nodded. "I suppose I knew that when Agnes called us to come back. Riku's ready, and so am I." She looked up at him. "What about you? Because this is about you, too."

"I want my son healthy. Dr. Kapoor would have been a good choice, but I can have Henry Johnston here inside three hours."

"And he's your back-up plan?"

"My mentor. A man I'd trust with the life of my son."

"Then get him here. I know he'll want to run tests first, so the sooner the better. OK?"

This time Eric was the one to swallow hard and nod.

"I'll have the corporate jet off the ground as soon as Henry's ready to fly."

"It's the right thing, isn't it?"

"For all of us, Michi."

Michi was taking it all in, and she understood everything that went on in the next little while. Eric's friend was getting himself ready to come to New York. More tests were being ordered. Agnes was co-ordinating with the surgery department. Her parents were on their way over from Japan. There was a flurry of activity suddenly. But watching her baby sleep, it was like she was floating over and above all this and looking down on Riku, seeing him as a perfectly normal, healthy child. She was pushing him on a baby swing. Helping him build sand castles. Sailing balsa boats with him on the pond. Feeding ducks. Going barefoot in the grass.

"Did you hear me, Michi?" Agnes asked.

She heard her name and blinked herself back to reality only to find Eric holding her hand now. "What?" she asked.

"Dr. Watson has written the order to move him to the pediatric intensive care unit until we get the surgical arrangements made. As a precaution, though. Only as a precaution."

"Then I'm glad he's going to have twenty-four-hour care for a while." She looked at Eric, who was simply standing off by himself, staring out the window now. "It's a good thing, isn't it, Eric?"

He sucked in a shuddering breath. "It's another cog in the wheel. First the PICU, then the surgery, then the road to recovery. So, yes, it's a good thing."

She studied him for a moment, her heart aching for the pain he was experiencing. And it was she who went to his side, took his hand, and simply stood with him as the transport technicians and nurses prepared Riku for his next big move.

"I've always known this moment would come. Of course, I've wanted to delay it. I know about the procedure, what it involves. Watched videos, studied every movement a good surgeon should make. Considered every way it could go wrong, and every way it could go right. All preparing me for what will be happening shortly. I can quote you statistics, I can quote you long-term goals for children with Riku's heart defect. Successes. Failures. If it's out there, I've read it, hoping that when the time came I would be ready. But I'm not." She sniffed back a tear.

"Knowing what I know doesn't make things easier, and I can't even begin to imagine what you're going through, being the best in the world at this procedure yet standing aside feeling virtually helpless. And that's what you're feeling, Eric, because that's what I'm feeling. All the medical knowledge in the world and none of it will help our little boy."

"The first time I performed the procedure, it was the best feeling in the world, giving normalcy to a young life that had seen very little of it. Everybody told me the first one was the best and after that it all becomes routine. But it never was. For me, there was always a thrill seeing blood coursing through a tiny body the way it should. Seeing a sick child become vibrant in almost the blink of an eye. Knowing that in a very short time that child would be living a normal life, doing normal things. Experiencing life in a way he or she never had before. And to be part of that…"

"Didn't it kill you, walking away from it all?"

"It did. I used to love getting up in the morning knowing my little bit of effort that day could change a life. Then, when all that stopped, I still got up in the morning, but there was nothing to love. At least, not the way I loved being a surgeon." He chuckled bitterly.

"So, here I am on the other end of it now, and the only thing I can think is I wish to God I could be the one to do this. It's like my not doing this is letting him down. Funny, the things we think about in a crisis. I know Henry is the best possible surgeon we can get. I know this hospital has the very best in all the latest technology to make this a huge success and help Riku along in his progress. But I still feel like such a damn failure."

They stepped aside as Riku's bed, along with his unplugged monitoring equipment, was rolled to the door. "You're not a failure, Eric. How can you be, when you were never even given the chance to know your son? Or to succeed at anything with him? And I'm so, so sorry for that."

"Well, regrets don't really get us anywhere, do they?" he said, taking hold of her hand and walking out the door with her, then to the elevator and to the pediatric intensive care unit, where Riku was being settled in.

He was still sleeping, thankfully breathing easily. For that, Michi was grateful. It was a good sign. And she was grateful to lean on Eric for support. That was also a good sign. And soon, maybe very soon, they could face happy prospects and talk about being a family. That was what she had to keep in mind. They were a family now, in some fashion or form, and Riku made that possible.

The rooftop garden was lush, and much larger than he remembered it being when he'd worked here. It was mostly planted with autumn vegetables now—squash, a few late tomatoes, kale, carrots, beets, second-harvest lettuce. All the right ingredients for a salad. But it was a teaching area, a place to train children about nutrition and re-acquaint adults with wholesome foods they might have forgotten. Eric used to take his breaks here, come outside to get away from the hospital atmosphere and the incessant worry of the operating room, and simply think. Or, in some cases, try not to think. Today it was a little bit of both.

"Someone's put a lot of effort into expanding it," he said to Michi, who was sitting on the garden wall, sipping hot tea. They'd spent the night in Riku's room, neither of them sleeping, and now, in what most would consider the still wee hours, the final prep for surgery was underway. Henry was here, ordering the tests he wanted, even though many were repeats of what had already been done. But he was thorough and, with Riku's life in his hands, Eric was glad for that.

"That would be my aunt, although she doesn't want anybody to know it. She started this garden as a retreat just for frazzled doctors, and over the course it turned into something significant. I've done the same at my parents' hospital, and it's amazing the way children respond when they're given the opportunity to learn then invest that knowledge in something they can see growing. Riku loves the garden. When the weather's good, I take him there as often as I can."

"Does he eat the vegetables?"

"Sometimes. But only if he picks them. That's the part he loves best, I think. Finding a little cherry tomato, plucking it from the vine then eating it as his reward. He likes sweet red peppers, too. I think it's all about the color, because if he doesn't go for something red, orange is his next favorite. Except carrots. He hates carrots. But he loves sweet potatoes. So, if he finds one, he gets so excited when we take it home and I cook it up for him. Sweeten it a little, then sprinkle on a bit of cinnamon and he's in heaven. But you should have seen him the time he dug up a radish. Not sure who planted them, or why, but he loved it because it was red, and he fussed until I let him take a bite. Then it was like his whole world turned upside down in one little bite."

"What happened?" Eric asked.

Michi pulled her phone from her pocket and searched for a video. The one where Riku was having a bit of a temper tantrum, angry at the radish, looking at it like he couldn't believe it had betrayed him. Then finally trying to rebury it in the dirt. "He has a temper some-times," she said, laughing at a video she had laughed at a hundred times before.

"Can't blame him, expecting something to be one way only to find out you're entirely wrong. I'd have buried it back in the dirt, too."

"He's going to love having you as a father," she said.

"And that doesn't scare you?"

"Of course it does. Turning control of my son over to anyone scares me. But for the first time I see Riku's future and I finally understand there must be more than me in it. A sick baby needs his mom, but a rambunc-tious toddler, which is what he's going to be, needs more than that."

"Michi, I'm not the sort who'll get tangled up in the parent thing for a while then back off it. I know that's what you're afraid of because all you've seen of me is how I back off. From surgery. From one night we both know should have been more. I keep thinking if I'd only woken you up and told you why I had to go we might not be where we are now. And I'm not talking about Riku. I mean, maybe you would have trusted me more when you found out you were pregnant, even come to me for support.

"But what you saw was a man who was always backing out the door. And while that's not my nature, it's all you had to go by. So, I do understand your doubts about me.

"But, please, don't assume that I'll back out the door once I've had enough of being a father. I'll admit it scares me. I don't have a very good example to follow. But if love counts for anything, I do love that little boy with all my heart."

"It was never about you being his father, Eric. It was about you deciding you didn't want to be his father. I didn't want my son starting off his life being rejected, and I wasn't sure you wouldn't do that."

"What do you think now?"

"I think you mean what you say."

"But?"

"But I need to take this one step at a time. I'm not going to keep you away from your son, but I don't know how we're going to work out the details yet. And right now I can't think about that."

"Fair enough," he said. "But just so you know, I'm in this all the way, Michi. Not just for Riku but for you."

"That's what I want. I really do. But, like I said, now's not the time for this to be happening. I can't deal with more than I already am. And in the meantime, I have a toddler to get ready for the day, even though the day is about more pre-surgery tests. We have this little ritual every morning, if you'd care to be part of it."

"Are you sure you want me there? Or if Riku would want me there? Because as much as I want to be part of everything, I also don't want to disrupt his life, especially in the things he's come to count on."

"Maybe it's time to let him see how he can count on you."

"So, what's this morning routine?" he asked.

"After the normal bath, breakfast things, we do 'The Wheels on the Bus.' Do you know that song?"

"In English?"

She shook her head, laughing. "Not unless you teach him the English version. But now it's all about the Japanese."

"And I'll look silly, not knowing it."

"Maybe if you just do the hand gestures while I sing."

"Only if I can teach him 'Mary Had a Little Lamb.'"

"He already knows that. In Japanese."

"'Twinkle Twinkle, Little Star'?"

"In Japanese."

"How about 'The Poor Father Who Couldn't Speak Japanese'? Does he know that song?"

"Not yet. But give him time. He'll figure it out."

"That's what I was afraid of."

"So, are you in or out?"

"Where Riku's concerned, you don't have to ask. And the title of that song in English is 'I'll Be There.'"

"I hope so, Eric. I really hope so."

"Would you like a glass of water or maybe a cup of tea?"

Michi was sitting in the rocking chair next to the crib, holding Riku and singing a quiet song to him while Eric put away the baby lotion and bathing supplies. He almost hated to disturb that moment, it was so beautiful, but Michi wasn't taking care of herself. And as this was, essentially, his first time with his son, he was nervous, and he hoped Riku wouldn't sense that.

"I would love some tea, but I think I'd like to go get it for myself while you sit here with him."

It was still early morning, but activities were picking up. Doctors on rounds. Nurses starting their assigned duties. Dietary bringing food, not so much for the tiny patients but for the parents who sat vigil and didn't take care of themselves. Parents like Michi, who looked so tired and pale as the morning light peeked through the blinds and betrayed her exhaustion. She'd borne this burden for so long alone, it was showing on her. Yet she wouldn't stop, not for a minute. Wouldn't even slow down. "Are you OK to do that? You look…"

"Tired?" she asked. "I've been tired for a while now. And there's only one cure." She scooted to the edge of the chair and gestured Eric over to her. "He's not a very sound sleeper, so don't worry if you wake him. He sleeps when his body tells him it's time."

"And your body?" he asked, lifting Riku gently into his arms, then stepping aside as Michi stood up.

"As the commercial on television says, it keeps on ticking. I'm fine, Eric. I appreciate your concern, but I've learned how to get through almost anything." She headed to the door. "Can I bring you anything?"

"I don't need anything, but you do, so why don't you go find a place to sleep for a while?"

"I… I don't sleep well if I'm not near Riku. And I really do want to be here when Henry comes back with the test results."

"Well, go do what you need to do, but don't worry. I'm here. Riku will be fine."

"I know that," she said, smiling. "Just be patient with me for a little while. It's difficult adjusting to having one more person involved, and that's my problem to overcome. Not yours."

Riku opened his eyes and looked up at Eric, stared at him for a moment, then snuggled in against his chest. "We'll work it out, Michi. But you do need to take care of yourself. So, go find a quiet place to sleep, and I'll call you when we know something. Doctor's orders," he said, smiling.

"Thank you, Doctor. You're too good. You know that, don't you?"

"I hope I come someplace close to that," he said. "Maybe in time I will. Oh, and thank you for the father-son time."

She took one long look, smiled, then turned and walked away. She was a good mother to Riku. The best. No mother could have given more and he was grateful for that. And maybe somewhere inside that gratitude he would find the forgiveness she needed. Because the more he saw of her, and the more he saw her devotion, the more he was beginning to understand what a rough situation she'd been in almost from the moment they'd slept together.

The fight in her spirit…that was certainly new to him. So was the fierceness with which she took care of their son. While there'd been a time when he'd thought he could fall in love, what he was feeling now was admiration and even pride. Michi was everything he'd thought he'd loved, and so much more.

"You have a pretty great mother," he said to Riku,

who was staring up at him. "But in your own way I'm sure you already know that. What I'm hoping is that, in time, you'll also come to realize you have a pretty great dad, because that's what I intend to be to you. Everything that my father wasn't to me. I promise you that, Riku. However this works out, I'll be a part of your life." A substantial part, he hoped.

"So, what do we do now? Do you go back to sleep while your daddy sits here and rocks you? Or do we have a man-to-man talk? Your choice, little man. Because anything you want to do, your daddy wants to be part of it."

Riku's response was to squirm in Eric's arms, then mumble a couple of words Eric didn't understand. "What's that? You want your daddy to teach you how to play baseball? When you're older and you understand how to moderate yourself in your activities, I can certainly do that. And teach you to swim. Maybe we'll go camping. Do you think you'll love nature? It sure is a beautiful world out there now that you're in it."

Tears welled up in Eric's eyes as Riku smiled at him. Such a beautiful smile. Such a beautiful boy. An old song came to mind, one he remembered his mother singing. Something about baby resting his head close to mommy or daddy's heart, never to part… And, as he sang the song quietly, the words rang so true because he wouldn't part, not from Riku.

Outside, in the hall, standing just to the side of the door so he wouldn't see her, tears streamed down Michi's face. The song Eric was trying to recall was the song Riku loved the most. "Baby Mine." Eric was going to be a wonderful father to Riku. She sniffled back more tears then headed off to find a place to sleep. For the first time in ever so long she knew she would. Riku was safe with Eric and Eric would give his life for his son. Of that, she had no doubt.

"I put him back in his crib about an hour ago," Eric said. He was leaning on the hall wall outside Riku's room so as not to waken him. "We talked for about an hour, then he finally went back to sleep. And you?"

"Two blissful hours. Thank you."

"We're in this together, you know. When you need to sleep, or simply get away for a little while, I'll stay with him if that's what you want." She looked rested, but not enough, and if he could, he would have taken her back to his house, put her to bed, maybe gone to bed with her simply to hold her, and let her sleep as long as she needed. But Michi wasn't going to do that, and he understood the reason. Even two hours with his son made him realize there were so many responsibilities ahead—ones he didn't know about, ones his father had never taken seriously with him. And being there when your child was sick was one of the most important.

"I appreciate that, but you've got to understand it's hard letting go. Earlier…that was the first time I've ever walked away from him and left him in the hands of someone other than my family."

"But I'm Riku's family."

"I know. And I think Riku knows as well. But it's still difficult for me. So, any test results yet?"

"I just talked to Henry, as a matter of fact, and he'll be here shortly to discuss options with us."

"What kind of options?" she asked, her voice now on the edge of panic. "I thought at this point we just do the surgery."

"Well, Henry has his ways. He's very methodical." He looked into Riku's room and his gaze went immediately to the monitors. Old habits. "He's on an up and down curve right now. That's why he's on the infant cannula for oxygen now instead of being in the tent. He's showing improvement, Michi, which is a good thing, especially with surgery coming up so soon."

"I was hoping you'd tell me my miracle baby had experienced some kind of miracle cure."

"That's what the surgery is. And once you finally get to meet Henry, I think you'll be a lot more confident."

"If he's anything like Leroy Watson, I'm sure that will make me feel better."

"So, you like your men bold?"

"I knew a bold man once."

"And?"

"And he became a terrific father. Story still in progress."

"You mean the part where you stood out in the hall for fifteen minutes, listening to my pathetic attempt at a lullaby."

"Very bold," she said.

"Very bad," he responded. "And I think the only reason he went to sleep so easily was so he wouldn't have to listen to me."

"Or because he felt safe. 'Baby of mine.' That's his favorite, Eric."

"My mother used to sing it," he said. "It's one of the few things I remember about her, to be honest. I think the song made me feel…"

"Safe, the way it makes Riku feel. You have a good fathering instinct. I know you don't trust that yet, but it's there."

"How about we go back into the room, take our respective recliners and wait for Henry?"

As the sun peeked in through the blinds, it was Eric who dozed off while Michi stayed awake, marveling at how right this felt. Her two men sleeping while she kept watch over them. Except for the circumstances, it would have almost been perfect.

# CHAPTER SEVEN

"I CAN'T BELIEVE it's so late," Eric said, stretching his back.

"It's ten," she said.

"I'm assuming in the morning." This was the part about being a surgeon he didn't miss. The off-on schedule. Sleep for an hour or two. Operate. Do rounds. Doze. Back at it. It almost felt like he'd never left his practice because there'd been days where he literally hadn't known if he'd been waking up at night or during the day. Loss of orientation was one of the hazards of the profession. Back then. Not now. His day, his company, his people carried on whether he was there or sleeping in at home. Which he didn't do...force of habit. But the difference was that in one place he'd been essential, in another place he wasn't so much.

"In the morning, and Henry stopped in a little while ago. He didn't want to disturb your sleep, so he'll be back as soon as I text him." She handed him a cup of coffee and pointed to a plate with pastries. "Courtesy of my uncle. He sent them over earlier and said he'll bring us a proper meal a little later."

"So, you didn't discuss..." He stifled a yawn as he scooted toward the edge of the recliner.

"No. I thought whatever he had to say was something we both should hear. Which is why I asked him to come back."

Pushing himself up, he went to Riku's crib and looked down, expecting to see him sleeping. But Riku was wide awake, smiling. "Is he always happy in the morning?" he asked, turning to take the coffee.

"Always."

"Then he must get that from you because I hate mornings. Always have."

"Even when you were operating?"

"I functioned, and I made sure I was ready for it, but I didn't start my surgical schedule until eleven unless it was an emergency or I was overbooked. Came in around eight, caught up on charts for an hour, went on morning rounds with my residents, visited the family of my surgical patient, and by the time I'd done all that I was ready to operate. And, yes, you now know my deepest secret." He turned to Riku. "Your daddy doesn't do mornings very well, but I'll bet your mommy does."

"By this time, Riku and I are both ready to face the day, and if it's a nice morning we may already be back from a walk in the park. Oh, and I may have gotten in an hour of tutoring by now."

"Well, in my life now I'm already at work, Natalie has been yammering on about something I don't really care about for at least twenty minutes, and there are anywhere from three to five empty coffee cups on my desk." He walked over to the table next to Michi's recliner and selected a pastry—cream cheese. "Going out in the field isn't so bad. In fact, I like it, exploring old buildings or land. Those are the good days. The bad ones keep me at my desk or tie me up in meetings. I don't like being sedentary."

"Even with his condition and limitations, I try to make sure Riku isn't sedentary. Partly because he needs the mental stimulation but also because I'm preparing him for the future when he'll be able to resume normal activities…up to a point." She bent over the crib, rearranged a few tubes, and picked him up and simply held him to her chest. "When I was pregnant, and spending so much time in bed, I read every book I could on raising a baby. There are so many authorities, so many opinions. But in the end none of the so-called experts told you what to do if your child was sick. So, for me it's always been about using common sense."

"Maybe you should write a book," he suggested.

"Or we could, together. You from the medical perspective on raising a sick child, me from the emotional or mothering perspective."

"Which would suggest a relationship of some kind," he said, smiling. "Which means you'd write it then add my name as an afterthought?"

Michi blushed. "I suppose I deserve that, don't I?" She sat down in the rocker next to the crib, taking care not to jostle or loosen any of Riku's tubes or wires. She repositioned the oxygen cannula under his nose, and taped it back into place. "After what I've done."

Eric picked up a pineapple pastry and offered it to her, but she shook her head and looked down at Riku, as if he was the reason she couldn't or wouldn't eat. "Look, Michi, it's over. We can't go back. What I lost is lost, but I won't be put in that spot again. I won't allow it but, more than that, I don't believe you will allow it either. So from now on it's forward. No looking back. No anger. No guilt. None of that helps any of us."

"Why are you so kind to me?" she asked.

"Because that bundle in your arms is the best thing that's ever happened to me. We both created the mess… me with what you perceived me to be. And in some ways, my not sticking to anything for long does fit. Maybe not as much as you think. But it's what I projected, which is why I do understand why you weren't as keen to find me as you might have been otherwise."

"And my part of the mess?"

"Believing that you should tackle everything in life on your own. Independence is good, and I hope Riku gets that from you. But sometimes the struggles are too tough to face alone, and I don't think you know how to deal with that. Maybe you feel a little overshadowed because you come from such a strong family and you don't believe you measure up. Maybe your whole ordeal clouded your perspective a bit. I don't know what it is, but I do know that you're afraid to let a little of Riku go because the biggest fear you have is that in letting go you might also fail him. Or maybe someone else might see what you really fear."

"What do you mean, what I really fear?"

"I've spent a lot of hours trying to put together the pieces of your puzzle, Michi, and it all goes together except that one piece right in the middle. It's missing. And I think that's the piece, once put in place, that will finally tell me, and maybe even yourself, the real reason you're so protective."

"Because he's sick."

Eric shook his head. "Maybe that's what you're telling yourself, maybe that's what you even believe. But there's something else, Michi. Something you're not telling me, and maybe not even admitting to yourself."

"I wouldn't hurt him or do anything that would cause him any problems, Eric."

"Except maybe hide behind him?"

She blinked hard, then shut her eyes for a moment. "Is that what it looks like to you? That I hide behind him?" She opened her eyes slowly and look up at Eric. "Because I thought I put him before me. At least, I try to do that."

"And you do, Michi. Beautifully." He knelt beside the cradle and took Riku by the hand. Riku responded by giggling and squirming.

"I think he wants to be held by Daddy right now."

"Because he and Daddy swap stories. I tell him about all the mischief I got myself into when I wasn't much older than he is. And he tells me all the mischief he has planned for his future. Oh, and he really wants to learn how to play soccer. I was holding out for baseball, but Riku definitely prefers soccer."

Michi lifted him over to Eric, then stood to allow Eric to take the rocking chair. "I don't suppose I've ever heard Riku talk that much."

"He and I have this special language. You know, a father-son thing."

"Well, when he does start to talk, I can't even imagine the things he'll have to say since he takes it all in." Even now, Riku was fascinated watching the blue light on the cardiac monitor flash off and on.

Rather than cradling Riku the way Michi did, Eric sat him up more and let him lean into his own chest and thrash about a bit until he found his own comfortable spot. One where he could continue watching the machines. "Oh, and he wants a pony, just in case you didn't know that."

Michi laughed. "He told you that, too?"

"Well, not in so many words, but when I asked him if he'd like a pony when he's a little older, his eyes sure lit up."

"You're going to spoil him, aren't you, Eric?"

"No. But I'm going to give him the kind of life my dad never gave me. And… I never had a pony."

"So, when do you buy him…?"

"Excuse me. I hate to interrupt," Henry said, 'but I've got some prep work to do before Riku's surgery tomorrow, as well as a long list of things my wife wants me to bring back from the city. So…"

"It's scheduled for tomorrow?" Michi asked, as her heart leapt to her throat.

"In the morning, first thing."

Her head started spinning, and her breaths were catching long before they reached her throat. "I suppose that's good," she said, looking down at Eric for support. "Eric?"

Eric nodded. "So, was there anything remarkably different on the last set of tests you took?"

"The overall picture is slightly less than it was before. Nothing to be alarmed about, but the gradual decline isn't going to stop. I did talk at length to Dr. Kapoor, who agrees we should go ahead with this. She'll be on her way back, but she doesn't want us to wait for her."

"So, this time tomorrow Riku will be…"

"In the middle of open-heart surgery," Henry said, stepping forward to take a pastry. "I'm on my way to Supply to make sure we have everything we'll need, and back-ups just in case. Then I'm going to have a look at the OR to familiarize myself with it. And after that, I've got to go in search of…" he pulled a handwritten list from his pocket, and read "'L'Amour de La Nuit Parisienne.'"

"She has good taste," Michi said. "Make sure you get the *eau de parfum* rather than the *eau de toilette*. Costs more, but worth it."

"You wouldn't happen to know what a *minaudière* is, would you? She wants one in black, with beads or crystals. But my question is one what?"

"It's a purse, Henry," Michi said. "There are plenty of specialty handbag outlets in Manhattan, so look online."

"And I can find the perfume…?"

"At a perfumery. Again, look online for an address."

Henry chuckled. "We've been married thirty-three years and I still don't know what she's all about. But it's a good life." He looked at Eric, who was still holding a dozing Riku. "Especially if you can find a woman who knows what a *minaudière* is. Anyway, I've written a couple of orders for Riku, nothing drastic. And I'd like him to sleep as much as he can for the rest of the day. Both of you look like a nap might be in line as well." He held up his cellphone. "Call, text about any little thing. The last few hours leading up to the surgery are the toughest, so my suggestion would be to get yourself out of this room while he's sleeping, clear your head, and brace yourselves for tomorrow. It's going to be a rough day for both of you."

As if on cue, Takumi appeared in the room with a tray full of food. Various breads, fruits, yogurts, fresh juice. "Breakfast is served," he said, as Henry took a look at the abundance of food and shrugged. "If only I didn't have to go find that *minaudière*."

"Boutique Blanchfleur over on…" Takumi set the

tray on the table then backed away. "Over near Godfrey Street and James Martin Circle."

"Well, it looks like my day is planned," Henry said, moving backwards toward the door. "So, like I said, call, text, whatever. And I'll let you know more later about the exact schedule for the morning."

Then he was gone. Takumi followed. And it was just the three of them again. A little family. Everything she'd ever wanted. Michi sat down in the recliner nearest Eric, kicked her footrest up, and sighed. Nothing was right in her world, yet the hopelessness she always lived with didn't seem as heavy right now. Even with tomorrow morning approaching faster than she wanted. "Do you mind if I close my eyes for a few minutes?" she asked.

Before Eric could respond, her eyes dropped shut, and her breathing evened out.

"You know you've got the best mommy in the world," he said to Riku, who was also nodding in and out. "So, it's up to the two of us now to figure out how to turn this into a real family."

He rocked Riku for a while longer, then put him back in the crib, sat down in the recliner next to Michi, and within just a few seconds all three of them were sleeping.

"I guess it was bad form having two sleeping doctors in the room while they were getting ready for their afternoon duties," Michi said, yawning and stretching as she leaned on the wall outside the door to Riku's room. "Or maybe we got kicked out because you were snoring too loudly." It was a little past noon now, and while a couple of hours of sleep didn't feel like much to most people, to Michi they were heaven sent. Two hours with no spotty waking every time Riku made a noise. Two hours away from her worries.

"You're the snorer," Eric said, standing next to her, stretching his muscles much the way a runner would do before a marathon. "Not me."

"Prove it," she challenged.

"How?"

She laughed. "You're the clever one. I'll leave that up to you."

"Let's see. The last person I slept with before sleeping with you in there was…you. So, will you be my witness?"

"I would except I don't sleep and tell. And I don't snore." She knew he was teasing her, and she enjoyed the lightness for a change. God knew, there hadn't been much of that in her life lately.

"Well, we might have to discuss this further in the future. But in the meantime, I need to go find someplace to take a shower, get myself in better shape or next time Riku wakes up he won't want to claim me."

"Actually, the stubble looks good. I like a man who's not quite clean-shaven."

"Then you must love me," he said, blushing immediately. "Not that I mean in love, but…"

"Don't worry about it," she said. "I know what you meant." Part of her wished he'd meant it differently, though.

She turned around to look at her reflection in the window to Riku's room and she looked pretty bad herself. Hair so mussed she wasn't sure it could ever be made right again. Wrinkled clothes. And while she wasn't actually slumping, it was an image that would have fit.

"Well, maybe I could borrow some scrubs and find a shower somewhere myself."

"With me?" he teased, grinning at her.

"You wish." Smiling, Michi shook her head as she pushed herself off the wall and headed down the hall to the nurses' station to beg anything she could get to help her tidy up. Eric wasn't far behind, on the same mission, and when he stood next to her at the desk, waiting for the clerk to bring them soap, shampoo, towels and scrub uniforms, he was so close their arms touched.

It sent a shiver up her spine, and it surprised her that she could react to him so quickly. She had that night. But those had been different circumstances. And now…she wasn't prepared for this. The timing was so wrong. The situation so dire, yet even in the aftermath of something so innocent, she could still feel the shivers.

"I'd, um…" She shut her eyes, trying to get her mind back on track. "I'd thought about having the surgery done back home," she said, opening her eyes but avoiding looking into his. "I'm glad he's here, though. Glad that this time tomorrow he'll be through the worst of it."

"Why didn't you go through with it there?"

"Because of you. Even though I knew you couldn't be involved, I felt better knowing you were near."

"Would you have let him go into surgery without telling me?"

She shook her head. "I know you said no looking back, but for all I've done I wouldn't have done that. Not to either you or Riku. And I'm not lying to you, Eric. For everything I've done, I've never lied."

He took her hand in his as they waited. "I know that." Then he nudged into her a little harder and finally put his arm around her shoulder, pulling her against him.

She didn't protest, didn't even try to move away, because she could feel his strength soaking into her pores. His was the strength she needed, even if she hadn't realized that until now.

Giving in to it even more, Michi leaned her head back against Eric's shoulder. "I'm so tired," she said on a sigh. "Too tired to think or move. Not even sure I've got enough left in me to breathe on my own. And this is something sleep won't fix. I'm glad you're here, and I'm glad we're not fighting."

He brought his other arm up and fully wrapped her into him. "I'm glad I'm here too, Michi. And that we're not fighting. But later, when everything has settled down, we really do need to figure this out. How I'm going to be involved in his life. Expectations that I have for him…and I do have them. There are a lot of things to straighten out when…"

She froze. Her body tensed, even though she didn't want it to. But the fears never totally went away, and when he talked about what he wanted, the floodgates always opened. It was a natural reaction. Especially now, after seeing how Eric was with Riku. But this was something she couldn't help. Something she couldn't overcome…at least, not yet. So, she pulled away from him. Or tried.

But Eric wouldn't let her go. He held onto her, perhaps because he needed the feel of her almost as much as she needed the feel of him. "He's going back to Sapporo when he's better, Eric," she said, her voice so tentative she barely recognized it. "To his home. That's always been the plan. He needs to be there…in a place he knows."

"As he should. I'm not taking him from you, Michi,

and I don't know what it will take for me to convince you that I want what's best for both of you. I'm not looking for custody. Not looking to infringe in any way. But I do want my place in his life and I think we both need to figure out how that's going to happen."

"I don't want to be on the defensive," she said. "Always scared that something will happen, that someone will try to take him from me."

"You mean me?"

She nodded. "And the social workers at the hospital." She stepped away from the desk, then walked down the hall to a private consultation room. Eric followed her in and shut the door. He led her to a chair and she sat, but only on the edge. "That other piece of the puzzle…it comes back to haunt me in so many ways. And maybe I should have told you sooner, but this isn't easy to talk about."

"If you can't, then…"

"No, I have to. My sins are never about lying but always about omission. You need to know what drives my constant fear that someone will take Riku from me." She shut her eyes for a moment, as if she was trying to convince herself to go on. This was very difficult for her. It showed on her body, in her face, in the way she wrung her hands.

"Take your time," he said gently.

"That's one of the problems. I've already taken too much time." She let out a long, weary sigh. "And please, after you hear what I say, don't judge me. I've already done enough of that for the two of us."

"What is it, Michi?"

"They thought I wasn't fit. That somehow my lifestyle during my pregnancy had caused his heart defect."

"What?"

"They accused me of taking drugs."

"Who?"

"The social workers at the hospital."

Eric blinked hard. "But you were sick. How could these people…" He balled his hands into fists. "I don't understand."

"I took blood thinner shots. They're approved for pregnancy, very safe, and clotting was a huge concern for me right from the start. Three times before, when I've tried to have a baby, I've thrown a clot that terminated the pregnancy. So, for me the shots were vital once I knew I was pregnant."

"But how did the social workers…and at your parents' hospital. Didn't they know you?"

"I wasn't going through anybody at my parents' hospital. I was going someplace where nobody knew me, afraid that if people knew what I'd done, it would bring shame to my parents. And before you say anything, yes, that's an old way. Very traditional, but I respect my parents' sense of tradition. People aren't so concerned about those things any more. But I was trying to save face, so I went elsewhere."

"Still, the jump from blood thinner to drugs…how?"

"I taught one more seminar after you left. I was very early into pregnancy, not really unwell but experiencing the usual things. Morning sickness, vomiting. Anyway, one of my students, a social worker in the hospital where I was going for care, caught me retching in the bathroom and made the off-handed comment that the first trimester was the worst. So far I hadn't told anybody I was pregnant, but since she'd already guessed, we talked about it for a bit. Nothing serious. Mostly about the four children she'd had, and her morning sickness, how many hours of labor, that sort of thing. And as it was the last day of the seminar and I knew I'd never see her again, I didn't mind opening up. She seemed very nice.

"Anyway, later I went to take my shot, and she walked in. I didn't think anything of it. You know, hike up the shirt, swab the belly, take the shot. She asked if I was diabetic, and I told her no. Since my condition was none of her business, I didn't say anything else, which left her believing I was...taking some kind of drug."

"OK, that makes a little sense. Not much, but I can understand how someone who works in the medical system but who isn't medical could get confused. But how did it progress to the point where you were being called unfit?"

Michi shook her head. "Because I told her who I was seeing when we had that chat, she called my doctor and reported what she'd seen...me shooting up drugs. Except my doctor was off on holiday, so one of the associates took the call and simply filed the paperwork to put me under investigation. Nobody even asked me, Eric. I swear... I had no idea all this was going on.

"So, when my condition started to go bad, my own doctor hospitalized me for some tests, and I suppose my admittance sent up some kind of red flag. Another social worker came, told me she'd been advised that I was potentially harming my baby, and you can guess the rest. For a little while I was put in protective custody, pending further investigation. Literally arrested and charged with a crime. And later, even though my doctor straightened it out, and the arrest was erased from the books, the red flag never came down and I lived under this scrutiny, and stigma.

"I realize they were doing what they thought best, but there I was, fighting to keep my child, getting sicker and sicker, and the whole suspicion that I could be causing my problems... I was labeled as having Munchausen syndrome, Eric. You know, where I was hurting myself, or by proxy hurting my unborn child, to get attention. And I was mandated for psychiatric counseling."

"That's ridiculous. How can taking a blood thinner elevate to psychiatric counseling?"

"It was wrong, but it happened. And my psychiatrist, once she understood the situation, was fighting for me. But once the word is whispered, you can't take it back. I was being called a threat to my unborn child, and it was only after I finally told my dad what was happening that he stepped in and, well, long story short, I spent the rest of my pregnancy in his hospital, under the care of another high-risk obstetrician. But it all came back when Riku was born sick. The threats to take him from me. To declare me unfit to be a mother.

"Words, Eric. Once they're spoken you can't un-speak them. Accusations are the same way. Once they're made, if people believe them, they're not inclined to be talked out of what they think they know."

"And you couldn't tell me this?"

"I couldn't. Even now, aren't you wondering if what they said is true? There were so many problems with me, with Riku... Don't I look like I could be complicit in some way?"

"No!" he said, fighting to remain calm. "That's not you."

"Even after I made a rather controversial decision to delay his surgery when, traditionally, it's done when the child is much younger?"

"Under your doctor's advisement, Michi."

"My family and all my doctors stood behind me, Eric. But one person who misunderstood something she saw almost cost me my son. It was a tiny, tiny snowball that avalanched. And because I'd lost pregnancies in the past, all I knew was that I had to withdraw from everything to give Riku a fighting chance to get into the world. So, while I was being threatened, and even watched, I simply shut my eyes to everything, including you, and the only thing I allowed in my mind was my baby. So, it's not fierce independence you saw as much as abject fear. And it damaged me. I don't trust. I'm always afraid that something I'll do will cause more problems."

"Are you getting help, Michi?" he asked, kneeling next to her and taking her hand.

"I have. And I will again when I go back home. But the stigma of it all, Eric... I can't deal with it and be there for Riku. I know I overcompensate by being protective, but what if I take him out on a chilly day, and someone thinks he's not dressed warmly enough? Or what if they see him without his oxygen and don't know he's allowed to be off it from time to time?" She swatted back tears.

"What if I came here and told you that you have a son you never knew about, that he's sick, that I went against traditional advice on when the surgery should be done and did what I believed to be right? Maybe to you it would make sense. But to someone else like the social worker who saw me take my blood thinner and had me arrested for it? That's why I'm scared all the time, Eric. They labeled me with a syndrome I don't have, accused me of things I didn't do and I'm always afraid that there's going to be a third round, and this one I'll lose."

"I wish I'd known," he said.

"Then what? You'd start watching me, too?"

"I don't even know what to say because if I didn't know you, I might have. Or you might have, if you suspected abuse in one of your patients." He sighed heavily. "I'm so sorry. But you're not in this alone. None of it. And for what it's worth, I know there's nothing about you that's unfit. I trust that, Michi. Trust it and believe it. And I'll go to the mat for you if that's what I have to do to make it right."

"Thank you," she said, then leaned forward and fell into his arms and sobbed. And for the next half-hour neither of them spoke. There were no words to say. Only emotion, and deep, deep pain. For both of them.

"Do you think they've had enough time to get everything set for the afternoon?" she asked, knowing her face was swollen now, which would only make her look worse than she had before. "I need to hold him. Or sit next to him. Whatever he's up to tolerating."

"Let's give them a few more minutes. The nurses here are thorough. They're going to take care of Riku the way you would. And it's only been a little over half an hour."

Thirty-plus minutes that seemed like forever. Like when she was a child and one of her parents would tell her to wait a few minutes for something—to open a gift or have a piece of birthday cake. So much of that little girl was still in her—the one who was always impatient to make things happen. Probably because everything behind her now still scared her and her only hope was going forward as fast as she could to get away from it.

"When I was a little girl, I always knew I was going to grow up to be a doctor. It was the life I lived because of my parents, the only life I knew. And even when I was young, I understood how what they did was important. Sometimes one or the other would take me to work with them, and I'd see all the looks of admiration people would give them. It made me proud to be their daughter, to be part of something that made such a huge difference in the lives of so many people.

"So that was always set for me. There was never a time that I didn't want to be a doctor."

"Was being a physiatrist something you always wanted?" he asked.

Michi laughed. "No. That came when I was in medical school, and I saw the difference that could be made in a group of people who might not have anywhere else to turn. Part of our practice deals with helping people overcome the disabilities they've received from strokes or accidents. Apart from the therapy they need, we offer them lifestyle, and changes that can make an overall difference in quality-of-life issues. So maybe we can't get someone out of a wheelchair, but we can teach them to live their life to the fullest with their other capabilities.

"Modern medicine doesn't always know what to do with those who don't make a full recovery but recover enough to get back to life. So, when I saw that happening, I knew that was what I wanted to do. For me, it's exciting knowing I can be part of something so life-changing, so important."

"But there are medical consequences, aren't there?"

"Of course there are. The people who come to me are injured or physically broken. They need modern medicine to help them get along. Therapy, medications...you name it. In my case, I specialize in athletes. One of my partners is all about stroke recovery. Another is about degenerative disease processes like arthritis and neuromuscular diseases. We have a pediatric specialist, who will work with Riku when the time comes, and someone who specializes in teenagers."

She paused and smiled. There were times when she thought she'd moved so far away from her world that she'd never get back to it, not fully. But something about Eric gave her optimism, and she truly hoped he could find his way back to his real world as well. That was where he was happiest and she did so want him to be happy. "People survive injuries and conditions that not so long ago would have killed them. My job, as a doctor, is to teach them how to survive through any means we have available."

"You wouldn't have had the patience to be a surgeon, would you?"

She laughed. "You noticed that in me? Because you're right. I like results I can see and patients I can form a long-term bond with. As a surgeon, you don't get to have that. Your patients get fixed, and you're only allowed to see the tip of the iceberg with that. Sure, you may have follow-up appointments, but those don't last long. And your bond is only for that short period of time that child is your patient. Then there's another child, another temporary bond.

"My patients stay. And I like that because I love watching progress over the long term. So, no, I couldn't have done what you did. You save a child and you take the front spot as the hero. I teach a patient with ankylosing spondylitis a better way to sleep to give him pain relief over the long term, and there's no one in the hall outside their hospital room giving me a hero's accolades. But that's OK because if my patient does sleep better because of me, I'm happy."

"Well, your seminar was an eye-opener for me. I was actually considering bringing a physiatrist into my practice for a little while. I'd even decided to talk to you about coming over to set it up for me. But we all know how that turned out, don't we?"

"Unfortunately," she said, smiling as she thought of Riku getting to the point where physiatry would benefit him. She'd never thought that far ahead before. But now the future was creeping in and she didn't want to stop it.

"So, his name. Why did you decide on Riku?"

"First, because it's a traditional name. Depending on how it's spelled in Japanese, it can mean several things. The way I spell it, it means enduring for a long time. I suppose I needed that reassurance, given the difficulties he had at birth."

"Does he have another name?"

"Like what you would consider a middle name? You do know that in Japan we don't use middle names. Even our documents such as passports and family registries have no place to write a middle name. But because Riku is half-yours, out of respect for your culture I did give him a middle name. It's Haru, spelled to mean eternal treasure. Because that's what he is. My eternal treasure."

"Riku Haru... Sato?"

"Yes, Sato."

"It's strong. The way he will be after his surgeries."

"I'm surprised you don't want to get your name in there somewhere. Isn't that a tradition, to give the first-born son part or all of the father's name?"

"It is, and I'm actually the fourth Eric Alexander Hart in line. And, no, Riku doesn't need my name. There's no thought to it. And his name...it's all about thought and love. It's a good name, Michi. A very good name."

She was glad, because for a little while she'd thought about calling Riku Eric. But that had changed when she'd first set eyes on her baby and had known he needed something from her tradition. Something that would give him a strong identity later in his life. And to her, his name promised a life beyond his illness.

"I really do need to get back to him," she said, twisting in Eric's arms to pull herself away from him. As she pushed away, though, a tingle of dizziness washed over her, probably from worry or a lack of sleep or eating. She wasn't worried, because whatever had caused it would go away once she was back sitting next to Riku's bed. But another step brought on even more spinning, and Michi reached out to Eric to take hold of his arm to steady himself. "Maybe I should have eaten something after all," she said, shutting her eyes to let the wobbly floor around her settle down. "One of those pastries earlier."

"Michi, are you OK?" Eric took a firm hold of her arm and held tight as she reached for the wall to hold herself up.

But the tightness in her chest was barely allowing her to breathe. "Just tired," she said, trying to regain her bearings. "I wasn't expecting any of this. Even though I knew the surgery had to happen, I never really admitted it to myself, and now that it's so close…" She went to turn around but instead staggered into him. "Maybe after we're sure Riku's going to be OK, you can sit with him while I go find something to eat." His gentle hand on her arm caused another shiver, but this time it was from the awareness of how close they were standing, of how she could hear his every breath and almost feel the beat of his heart.

"Maybe I should carry you," he said, his voice so low it nearly blended with the night.

"You offered to do that once before. Remember?" Their night together, when he'd offered to carry her to his room. It had been a romantic gesture, but as unnecessary then as it was now. "But, no, I don't want to be carried. I'm perfectly capable of getting there on my own." Yet maybe with some of his help. "I may be a little dizzy, but it's nothing that requires a knight in shining armor to come to the rescue. I just need to go back to Riku. Make sure his favorite teddy bear is tucked in bed with him."

He nudged her chin up with his thumb. "What you need is to follow doctor's orders, and this doctor is prescribing a knight in shining armor, even if only for a little while. You need someone to take care of you so that when he needs you, you're up to taking care of Riku."

"But I don't want to be carried," she said, looking into his eyes. "No one's ever had to do that for me, and now's not the time to see if what happens in the romance novels really works. You know, the hero whisks her into his arms, carries her off, and all is well. That's not my story, Eric. Mine's where I do everything I can to get from day to day. That's the way it's been for a long time now."

"Maybe you don't need someone to carry you in the literal sense," he continued, "but in the sense that even *you* need to give in and let someone take care of you from time to time."

"Even after what I've done to you?"

"Even after what you've done to me. But also, even after what's been done to you. Your needs count, Michi. You've taken so much of the bad for so long I think you may have forgotten there's good out there for you, too."

"It is. My parents, my brother…the rest of my family."

"I'm part of that family, you know. Maybe not in the way most people would consider it. But we all have one thing in common…wanting the best for Riku. And for you. And if that means me having to pick you up and throw you over my shoulder…"

Michi stepped back from the door then turned to face him, stood on her toes and kissed him on the cheek. "Thank you for listening," she said. "And caring. You make things easier."

His gaze locked in on Michi's face, taking in the vulnerability in her eyes, the fear in her face. "I hope to make them better as well," he said, realizing he was as caught in her spell as he had been that one night they'd had together. He'd wanted her like he'd wanted no other woman before, and no one had come close to filling that need in him after her. Her intellect, her determination, her sense of duty…and her beauty. One look at her had told him he was way out of her league. Women like that didn't happen in his life, so he'd walked away from it with regrets, knowing it was only a fantasy. This time he wasn't walking away from it.

"Michi," he said, as she turned away to finally leave. "What about you? Do you want to work on making things better between us…not just for Riku but for us?"

"I do, but…"

"But you still don't trust me enough?"

She shook her head. "No, I do trust you. But I don't want to be divided. Not right now. Not when Riku needs all of me." She brushed her hand across his cheek. "Everything is so tentative, and I'm just…just not in that space. But I want to be, Eric. I promise, I want to be, and I hope you'll be patient with me for a while because, right now, Riku comes first."

"I understand," he said, helpless to back away from her, from them... But her words gave him hope, and that was all he needed for now. A little hope, a vision of the future filling him with desires and wild thoughts of things he'd never imagined for himself. So, with a gentle hold, he cupped the back of her neck and kissed her deeply, possessive in his touch yet still tentative.

Was this taking advantage of her now that she was so defenseless because of a situation neither of them could control? Or did she need his toughness the way he needed hers? "Should we stop?" he asked, twining his fingers through her silky hair.

She didn't answer right away, which he feared *was* her answer. But then suddenly Michi's body melded to his with an answering moan, and she offered up her mouth in a ravaging need he understood. Desire overtook him with a searing shudder, then took hold of his conscience. And it felt like a dagger piercing his heart when common sense finally returned, and he gripped her arms and pushed her back, his breaths so labored he feared he would be overtaken by lightheadedness.

"As much as I hate to say this, we can't do this because neither one of us can know what it is. Not in a real sense." He dropped his hold on her and stepped back. "And trust me, if circumstances were different, I wouldn't be walking away from this. Not this time. But we've got to take it slowly right now, to see what's there after Riku has recovered. Anything else could hurt all three of us. So, I'm sorry, Michi. I should never have started this. Will you forgive me?"

"I did before," she said, then turned away from him

and finally left the waiting room. Her steps down the hall, as he watched from the doorway, were slow, though. And he wondered if he'd made her cry. God help him, that was the last thing he'd wanted to do.

# CHAPTER EIGHT

THE DAY DRAGGED BY with surgical prep and adjustments to the various equipment and tubes Riku was hooked to. Michi spent a good bit of the rest of the day with her family, especially her parents, who'd flown in from Japan, while he caught up on work, not going into the office but doing it by phone. Then the night turned into one of the longest of his life. Maybe even *the* longest.

Riku was sleeping soundly now, and even though it was early, he and Michi took to their respective recliner chairs, made themselves comfortable, and didn't sleep. He'd offered to split the night with her, staying awake for half of it while she slept, then switching around. But she'd declined, claiming she was too wound up to sleep.

Truth was, he was wound pretty tight himself. So, there they'd sat, hour upon hour, quietly, so as not to waken Riku. He'd stared at the ceiling most of the time. And whenever he'd glanced over at Michi, she'd been watching Riku. He wanted to talk to her, or hold her or do something, but she wasn't going to leave Riku's side, and to stay there meant being extra quiet.

Once, when Riku stirred and set off an alarm, they both practically jumped to get to his bedside, but she was faster. More practice, he supposed. Thankfully, it was nothing. Riku had tried turning, causing one of his wires to come loose, tangling his chubby little fist in it. Michi took care of it, of course, then settled back into her chair once Riku had gone to sleep again.

"Am I of any use here?" he whispered.

"It's nice to have someone to back me up," she said. "Makes me feel less alone. And I think he needs you to be here. But if you have other things to do..."

"No, everything's under control," he said, hoping that was the case. Right now, the corporate part of his life was so distant, so unimportant he didn't even want to think about it. And for all the good his afternoon efforts had been toward answering correspondence and emails, after Natalie had brought him his computer, he simply wasn't in the mood.

Here he was with all the money anyone could ever hope for, and all the resources, but none of that was doing Riku any good. It was funny how his dad had always counted on money as the means to fix everything, yet what was required now was a skill he had but couldn't use. It made him feel so damned helpless. "But if you don't mind, I'm going to go stretch my legs. Can I bring you anything?" he asked on his way to the hall. He was restless. Needed some space. Time to think. Early morning activity had already picked up in the hall the same way it had the day before. Doctors were making rounds, nurses were getting patients up and started for the day, parents who'd stayed over were emerging from patient rooms or wherever they'd slept, looking for coffee.

Soon they would come for Riku. That was what scared him more than he cared to admit. And even though he knew the procedure step by step, that didn't settle him.

"I'm good," she whispered, not taking her eyes off Riku. "Maybe after they take him in, I'll go get something, perhaps leave the hospital for a bit to clear my head. I'm not sure I can be here while…"

She was feeling the things he was at the moment. Fear, anxiety, the need to grab Riku and run someplace far from here where he would be safe and happy and healthy. "Just text me if you hear anything."

She nodded then shut her eyes, retreating into a world where children didn't need surgery and parents lived happily ever after.

Eric had been gone an hour now, and while she wasn't worried about it, she did wonder when he was coming back. As the minutes ticked off the clock, and Riku was getting closer and closer to the surgery, she was finding herself so edgy she couldn't concentrate. More than that, she'd begun doubting every little thing she did. Even changing Riku's diaper had set her off in a panic because if things didn't go as planned, and if the unspeakable did happen, something as simple as a diaper change would hold such incredibly strong memories. And not good ones.

Michi desperately wanted her memories to be good. Part of those memories included Eric and how amazing he was with Riku. He was a natural. His instincts were perfect, and not only because he'd chosen a career helping sick children. His instincts were the right ones for being a great dad.

And he was being so good to her, too. Even though he had every right to be angry, and even hate her. In fact, he was so good, now she was thinking about Eric, there were tears running down her cheeks for all the things they might have been, and all the things she'd done to make sure none of that would ever happen.

"Why?" she whispered, as she watched her son. "Why am I so afraid of letting him in?"

Once she'd believed it was because he might take Riku from her if he believed her unfit. But he didn't, and he had proved that over and over. Even after she'd told him how they'd tried to claim she was trying to harm her baby even before he was born, Eric didn't believe that. He hadn't even come close to believing it.

So, what was it she was feeling, that constant undertow of something trying to drag her along, trying to get her from place to place? Could her feelings for Eric be deeper than she'd intended to allow? Not just caring for him as Riku's father but perhaps falling a little in love herself? It wasn't out of the question and there were times the urge was so strong it almost overtook her. Admittedly, her timing was bad. But not her intention.

Michi stood, then leaned over the rails of the crib to straighten Riku's blankets and check to make sure he was doing as well as could be expected. The monitors everywhere told her he was, but she had to touch him, feel his soft skin, lay her hand across his chest for a moment to feel the rise and fall of it. To love someone this much scared her. It had scared her from the moment she'd known she was carrying him. Because love was such a huge responsibility, and there were so many ways to let someone down inside it.

Tears streaked down her cheeks again, but as she stepped away from the crib, she stepped backwards into Eric's arms. And he held her, and let her cry quietly on his shoulder for what seemed an eternity. Her body was racked with sobs, but she didn't want to move, couldn't move, and for the first time in so long she couldn't even remember she felt a faint glimmer of hope that everything would be fine.

"I'm sorry," she whispered, sniffling. "I don't usually cry this much. But with everything that's going on, it's like I can't turn it off."

He handed her a tissue and led her away from the crib. But not too far away because he understood her need to be there. "It gets overwhelming sometimes," she said. "And frustrating, with all this waiting." He was still holding her, but not as tightly. And she liked being where she was. Eric made things right. Feeling his physical presence, knowing that no matter what she'd done she had his support...

"And while everybody in my family is so supportive, they haven't been through anything like this, so they can't fully understand. And sometimes I feel so alone I don't know what to do. Sometimes I'd like to be weak for a little while, so I can turn my pain over to someone else for a few minutes until I can regroup and start it all over again." She sniffled. "Being independent isn't always so easy, you know."

"Why try so hard at it?"

"Because I've invested so much into my work I've let the whole personal side of my life go. Meeting you, then having that night...that was the first time I ever let myself go, Eric, and simply enjoy something—you—because I wanted to. I've always felt like I had to compete with my entire family to be as successful as they are. And sometimes that was just so difficult. I've always felt insignificant when everything else around me exuded success. Then when they accused me of Munchausen's, even though I knew they were wrong, I doubted myself. Not in that I'd ever do anything to harm my baby, because I wouldn't. But I wondered what kind of outward appearance I projected that would make people think of me in such a way."

"That was the pressure getting to you, Michi, the pressure you put on yourself. The people who know you don't see the things in you that you see."

"There was always a lot of pressure on me to uphold the family reputation," she conceded. "My parents are wonderful, don't get me wrong. But look at them. Look at what they've done together. Growing up knowing the same is expected of you isn't easy, which is why I've always kept to myself, for fear I'd be called out as a fraud. And here, in this crib, is the proof of that. As much as I've loved him from the start, I was doubted. My love was doubted. My need to protect my baby was doubted.

"I love my career, Eric. Love building my clinic. But I also love being a mother more than anything, and when I look at Riku I'm aware that everything I've built myself to be is just a façade. The only thing that matters is my son. And without him…who am I?"

"You're who you always were, Michi. Riku doesn't change that. In fact, when we were together in Japan I didn't even consider that you were truly approachable. You held yourself back. I knew there was more, could almost see it surface, but you didn't let it. And now, as I see you with Riku, I see that same bright, hard-working woman, but through a gentler focus. Riku brings out the best in you and I don't think you ever had that opportunity before because you were so busy trying to be the person you believed your family wanted you to be.

As Shakespeare's Polonius said, *'To thine own self be true.'* I think this is the first time you're allowing yourself to do that."

"Well, it's not easy."

He chuckled. "It gets easier with help."

She reached up and stroked his cheek. "You're such a good man, Eric. You didn't deserve a disaster like me in your life."

"But without you I wouldn't have Riku. And I'll admit it was love at first sight with him." Maybe with her, too. Definitely a little. But maybe more than he was ready to admit. "So, can you tell me about him?" Eric laughed. "You promised to, but we didn't get around to it. We can stand in the hall just to get you out of the room for a while, but you can still see him, if that's what you'd prefer. Or we can do anything or go anyplace as long as you tell me about Riku. I need to know more about my son before his surgery. You know…what makes him laugh besides giraffes? What piques his interest? What he doesn't like other than radishes. What is he like?"

She followed Eric to the door of the hospital room, then stepped out and found the place where everything in the entire room was visible to her. "First, he's always happy. He laughs and smiles all the time. Even when he's sick sometimes. It's like he knows that's what he was put here on earth to be and he tries his best to do it. Also, besides *your* studious look, which he gets when he's trying to figure out something new to him, he also has your smile. And when he's feeling good, he's very vocal, not so much in words as in sounds."

She smiled. "But he understands what I say, because he's smart, Eric. Sometimes it's hard to see it because so often he doesn't feel well, but on his good days I love watching how methodical he is. He's definitely going to grow up to be a thinker like you."

"Well, for sure, he's a fighter. Like you, Michi. I've watched him play, watched the way he deals with all these things attached to him now, and he fights his way through, meaning he's one tough little kid. Tough, like his mom."

"Is that a good thing?" she asked.

"It's called determination and, yes, it's a very good thing."

"Then maybe he's the best of both of us." She stepped inside the door a little more, then held out her hand to Eric. "Look at him." she said, as Eric took her hand and stepped to her side. "He's not asleep. He's studying the cardiac monitor. I wonder what his two-year-old mind is thinking about it?"

"How to take it apart and put it back together, probably." He chuckled. "Like me, in surgery."

"Then maybe he'll be a surgeon."

"Or an engineer. Or a mechanic. Or anything he wants to be."

Eric's unbridled enthusiasm filled her with so much hope for Riku's future. This was the first time she'd ever really allowed herself to feel optimistic about his future, and she owed this to Eric. Where all she saw was illness, all he saw was potential. Which made her happy beyond belief.

"I want him to get better so badly, and I can visualize all the things we'll do, but sometimes it's so hard to see it. Sometimes those images just aren't in my head, which makes me feel like I'm letting him down." This was the first time she'd ever said that to anyone. But it was true. Her inability to always see a bright future ahead made her feel like she was a bad mother.

Eric slipped his arm around her waist—something that had become so normal for them. "In a sense, his illness has also become his normal. You expect that, and you anticipate all the things that could happen as a result. But thinking in other terms, terms that have nothing to do with his heart, frightens you because you're not prepared to go off in another direction, or deal with something else that might come up. You're afraid you can't handle that. Like including his father in his life."

She nodded. "It's been easier to avoid the things that scare me rather than face them head on, and what I thought you might do scared me."

"Even now?" he asked.

Before she could answer, the heart monitor alarm went off, and Michi and Eric ran to his bedside. Eric studied the rhythm tracing across the monitor screen while Michi repositioned Riku for better access to his chest. Then they were pushed away from the room as several nurses and a couple of doctors rushed in.

"This has been my life, Eric. Complications, over and over. I can't…" She choked, then cleared her throat. "I can't keep on doing this. Not for Riku's sake, not for my own. Being strong… I can't even pretend any longer." She looked up at him as they walked to the waiting room at the end of the hall…the one where her family wasn't gathered. The one where they could be alone.

"You don't have to pretend anything, Michi. The people who matter know who you are and what you're going through. All the support you want is there when you need it. And here…" He opened his arms to her. "For the rest of your life."

She fell into his open arms and stayed there, letting him hold her, loving his comfort. Loving him. Until there was a knock at the door and Henry's entrance signaled the beginning of the next phase.

"It's time," Henry said. "Everything's ready, the OR is prepped, I have a good surgical team, and Dr. Kapoor is on her way, even though she won't get here in time. So…"

"How long?" Eric asked.

"Inside the hour. But you still have some time to be with him before we take him down to surgery."

Michi swallowed hard. Looked at Eric, who had tears in his eyes. Then she looked into the faces of her family, who'd followed Henry to find them, but didn't see in any of them what she saw in Eric—a love greater than anything she'd ever seen before.

"I'd like to scrub in, Henry. If that's all right with you. Just to be with Riku. That's all."

Henry nodded, then smiled. "I never assumed you wouldn't."

Then the furor began. People everywhere in Riku's room, doing various jobs. Changing his clothes, adjusting his medicines, removing old wires and replacing them with new ones. More leads on his chest. Medication adjustments. In the hall outside, Michi and Eric watched as ten people surrounded Riku's bed, practically swallowing him up in all the activity. And all she wanted was to hold him. "I'm glad you're going in with him," she said. "He needs you there."

"There's nothing I can really do, but it felt like I had to be there anyway."

"Because you're a surgeon, Eric." She looked up at

him. "That hasn't changed. And I hope you realize that before you're gone from it so long you can't go back."

"Do you think I'll go back?" he asked her.

"I think that once we're through this and Riku is recovering nicely, you'll have an overwhelming need to stay close to the things that make you happiest in life. At least, that's what I'm hoping for myself. And I think we're a lot alike in that. If surgery is what makes you happiest…"

Choosing what made him happiest. Becoming a doctor might have been the only time he'd ever done that. In a way, it was an odd concept but a good one.

"*'Medice, cura te ipsum,'*" Eric said. *Physician, heal thyself.* A saying from a Greek proverb.

His whole body ached because he'd probably slept badly in a chair much too small for him, but he was doing what he always did before he performed a procedure… he called it warming up his surgeon's mind. Going over, in his head, the procedure. Step by step. Looking at it from every angle, anticipating the problems, listing all the things that could go wrong and gearing up to correct them if they did. Here, in his pre-surgery shower, that was what he always did, and even though he had no authority in the OR this time, the habit was still there.

"I could, um…after the surgery is over and we get into that waiting phase of recovery," Michi said, mustering all the optimism she could, now that the surgery was mere minutes away, "I could stay awake and wait if you need to take a nap. You look exhausted."

"Probably because I am," he said, from the shower.

He was inside, while she was standing outside, leaning on the wall, waiting for him to emerge.

"But you'll be okay to be in surgery with him?" The room was steamy and warm, but not too warm that she was working up a sweat, as all she could feel now was the stark, cold chill of fear.

"I'll be fine," he said, finally stepping out, bare-chested, barefoot, with a towel wrapped around his middle.

He was a good-looking man, she thought. Even now, when everything she had was focused on Riku, she did take a moment to admire what she had in front of her. The memory had always been vivid. Eric was as beautiful physically as any man she'd ever seen. Now, and then. "But if you start to get too tired…" she said, as he grabbed a pair of clean scrubs off the hook near the shower and began to drop his towel to the floor.

Even though he wasn't modest, hadn't been that night, didn't seem to be now, she spun around to allow him a modicum of privacy, and to allow herself to think about something other than the physical man.

Eric chuckled. "We made a baby together. You don't have to be shy."

"Well, you're certainly not. But I… I need to keep my thoughts focused on Riku."

"And I would distract you?"

"Everything would distract me, Eric. Right now, I don't want to think about what I have to think about, and any distraction will do. Which is why I can't be distracted."

"But I'm not just any distraction, Michi." He took hold of her shoulder and pulled her around straight into his arms, straight into his bare chest, where she buried her head and shut her eyes. Thankfully, his scrub pants were on, but his feet were still bare, and his hair dripped water down the side of her face. "We're going to get through this," he said, holding her tight. "And on the other side, when Riku's better, we'll figure out what we are, and who we are."

She looked up at him. "It's like I'm not even here, Eric. I am, yet I'm someplace else where none of this is necessary. If something happens in there, if there are decisions...you do that, Eric. Please, do what's right for Riku. I've already told Henry to allow you to make the decisions, if that becomes necessary."

"Why?" he asked, his voice thick.

"Because this is what you do, who you are. Because I trust you with your son's life. Because I believe you would trade places with him if you could."

"I would," he said. "I would take his place in a heart-beat..."

"Which is why I trust you with his life. His life is part of your life now, and you'll do the right thing." She stepped back, grabbed the scrub shirt from the hook on the wall and handed it to him. "And I believe surgery generally requires shoes, too." She braved a smile that lasted mere seconds, then disappeared.

Deep in her heart she truly did know Eric loved Riku. It wasn't the kind of love that came of getting to know someone, or a love born of familiarity. It was the love of a parent. The same love she felt. And her heart skipped a beat when she realized this. Eric was such a good man. Easy to love. And she'd already fallen. So many ways to love. Her life was blessed with them. "So, you'd better get them on and get out there. The most important person in your life needs his daddy now."

Michi turned away immediately, trying to regain control. But that wasn't going to happen until Eric came out of surgery and told her himself that Riku had come through like a champ. "Take care of him in there," she said, on her way to the door. "Take care of our son, Eric."

Then she stepped into the hall, looked right and left for someplace to go to have the good, hard cry she needed before she walked the hall to surgery holding her son's hand. As it turned out, that cry came in an empty utility closet just outside the hall to the suite of operating rooms. And there she sobbed until her throat hurt and her eyes were swollen. Ten minutes later, when she stepped into the hall, Eric was standing there with a tissue and a bottle of water for her. Smiling, not questioning.

"It's time," was all he said. Then he took her hand and led her back to Riku's room, now vacated by all the techs and nurses, where Riku was already getting groggy from his pre-surgery IV induction of a medicine that would have him well asleep even before he got to the OR.

Then came the surgical nurses, ready to move him. So Michi took hold of Riku's right hand, while Eric took hold of his left and, for the first time, they walked together as a family of three. Riku in his bed, with his parents on either side while he slept, unaware that his world was about to be changed drastically.

All too soon, they were at the surgery entrance where Eric would go on with Riku and she would go to her parents to wait. "Mommy loves you," she said, bending down to kiss him. "And when you wake up, she'll be right there with you."

Eric didn't say a word as they pushed through the doors and left Michi behind, standing at the window, looking in as he and Riku turned the corner to the operating room assigned to Riku's surgery. He took one look over his shoulder as he turned that corner, and tried to manage a supportive smile for Michi. Then he went to the scrub room for that part of the prep, while Riku was wheeled into the actual operating room.

And Michi… She'd made it mere steps away from the door when she gave out, leaned against the wall and slid silently to the floor. Not crying. Not reacting. Not… anything. Too numb. That was where Agnes found her and helped her to a private waiting room and into the arms of her family.

But it was Eric's arms she needed. And it was in Eric's arms she'd be when this day was over and Riku was asleep, and closer to being healthy than he'd ever been before. Her little family. That was what she wanted them to be. And it became part of the dream of her heart. Eric and Riku and her together…all of them healthy and safe. And so loved. That was the full dream of her heart now. The only one.

The clock simply wouldn't move. It seemed like every time she looked up it, it was at the same place it had been the time before. How long had it been so far? Over three hours?

"He's good," Eric assured her. He'd left the OR when Dr. Kapoor had arrived to assist, and the OR had got too crowded. "These things take time, and you can't always predict what's going to come up along the way. But that doesn't mean anything's wrong." They were alone again. She'd sat with her parents for the first two hours but in their worry they'd seemed…clingy. She didn't want clingy. Wasn't able to tolerate it, even from her family. So, she'd returned to the private waiting room where she and Eric had talked hours ago and shut herself in, wanting to hide herself away from everything. Eric had joined her only moments later, making her realize it wasn't being alone that she wanted. It was being with Eric that meant everything.

"And nothing's going wrong?"

"You've got Henry and Anjali in there. The best tag team in the world, in my opinion. They're not going to miss anything, Michi. They're not going to let anything happen."

"I wish it could be you," she said.

"If you mean on the table, with my chest cracked, so do I. If you mean performing the surgery…" He held out his shaky hands. "Not with these."

She laughed as she took both his hands in hers. "I guess even the best have their lesser moments," she said, settling back on the sofa with him. Ten minutes later she urged him to his feet. "I need to go someplace to breathe. These walls are beginning to close in and if I don't get out of here, I'm going to literally start climbing them. Want to come with me?" she asked, holding her hand out to him. "Maybe go up to the roof garden. It's a good place to think. And be within running distance when he's out of surgery."

Five minutes later, after stopping at the OR desk to let the nurse know where they'd be, Michi and Eric pushed through the door to the garden and stepped outside. It was a beautiful autumn afternoon. The temperature was perfect, but the skies threatened rain. For a moment she felt…peaceful. "This is nice," she said, shutting her eyes simply to enjoy a bit of communing with everything surrounding her. "Back home, I don't have any kind of garden with my condo, so I always enjoy my version of this. Simple things. Plants and sky. And in my hospital garden a little water feature with a foot bridge, lined by cherry trees and bamboo."

Stepping closer to Eric, she laid her hand in the small of his back, not to massage but merely to let him feel her presence, and take whatever strength she had to give. Because he looked exhausted. Strung out. In emotional agony. "Is there anything you want to tell me?" she asked.

"Like I said, Riku's holding his own." Eric turned to look at her. "It's me who's not doing so well. When it's a child you don't know, it's difficult enough, but when it's your own child…" He took in a deep breath, then it was she who pulled him into her arms for a change. She who held him. She who felt his tears on her shoulder.

They stood that way for several minutes before he straightened up, scrubbed his face with his hand and took in a deep breath. "I was doing just fine, staying objective. Until his chest was open and it was my son's tiny heart I saw beating in there. I'm just glad he wasn't awake to see what a mess his old man was."

"But you stayed."

"Because I had to. There wasn't another choice. That was my boy…our boy. This was the first real thing I've been able to do for him and I wasn't going to let him down. It's also when I realized that I'm not my old man, that I don't turn my back on the people who should mean the most to me or, in this case, the child who does mean the most to me. My dad would have walked out. Come back later to see how it turned out. But I'm not my dad."

"You're certainly not," she said, sidling up to him so their arms touched, then eventually leaning against his chest as his arm slipped around her shoulder. "You're certainly not." A tear trickled out of the corner of her eye and blotted itself against Eric's green scrub shirt, leaving its presence there in a damp circle above his heart. "So Henry repaired the truncus?"

"He did, and when I left he was working on the valve to fix some regurgitation that wasn't diagnosed before. That's probably what they're doing now...the surgical creation of a tricuspid truncal valve. In the cases where I've done it, it seems to provide the best outcome."

"You gave them permission for that?" she asked. "Because it wasn't mentioned in the surgical risks that were addressed."

"I did give permission. There are other ways to go about the repair, but in my experience this was the best and will serve Riku better in the years ahead. Should I have spoken to you first?" he asked.

Michi shook her head. "I told you I trusted you to make the right decisions. I'm glad you were there to do that." She pulled back and looked into his eyes. "I trust *you*, Eric. And maybe that's been slow to happen, but it's happened in a huge way. It makes me feel better. Gives me hope I haven't had...ever, simply letting go and trusting. It's easy to be overprotective and not so easy to let someone else in. But I want you in, Eric. I don't think either of us is in a position to know how yet, but just know I do want you in."

Eric nodded, and pulled her even closer. "You've done a very good job taking care of him, and I don't blame you for being overprotective. I would have been, too. And I do want to be in. In his life, in yours... We'll figure it out when the time's right."

# CHAPTER NINE

"Eric," Agnes said, stepping out into the garden, interrupting the solitude there. "Michi. I need to talk to both of you."

Eric swallowed hard. This was the part he always hated. The part where either he would step out of surgery to break the bad news, or one of his surgical associates would do it. Judging from Michi's still relaxed body in his arms, she hadn't figured it out yet. But she would.

"Just say it," he said. Too many doctors beat around the bush. He wasn't in the mood for that. He wanted to know what was going wrong, and he wanted to know now. If only he could shield Michi from it. But he couldn't.

"Say what?" Michi asked.

"We haven't succeeded in getting him off the machine." Agnes stepped closer to Michi, but Michi squeezed herself tighter into Eric's arms as if pulling away from Agnes was pulling away from the truth. And getting closer to Eric was getting closer to the only person who could make her feel better right now. "Henry sent me to tell you."

"Which means?" she asked, even though she knew.

"Which means it's going to take a while longer than we expected."

"Any arrhythmias?" Eric asked.

"No, and no excessive bleeding either. He's doing well overall, but he just doesn't want to come off bypass yet. Thought you'd want to know why the delay."

Michi looked at Eric for an explanation. "Is there anything that should be done?" she asked him.

"Trust the man who trusts the surgeon. If Henry's not upset by this—and I'm assuming he's not or he would have called for me—then I'm not."

"Then I'm not either," she said, trying to muster a brave smile that simply wouldn't come.

"Anyway, I'll keep you informed," Agnes said, heading back to the door. "Oh, and, Michi, you've been cleared to sit with Riku in Recovery for a little while. Someone will give you a fifteen-minute warning when the nurses decide it's appropriate."

She nodded her gratitude then went to the ledge surrounding the garden and looked out over the afternoon activity down below. "Down there, everything is so normal. People living their lives the way they were meant to. And us, up here, our lives stalled or even stopped. It doesn't seem fair, does it?"

"Usually, it's not. But we muddle through, don't we? Because, if we don't, what's the alternative?" While he'd always felt cheated and frustrated that he'd left his surgical practice to take up his father's dream, this was the first time he'd actually felt guilty. It was an odd reaction, and it surprised him, and it was also the first time he'd seriously wondered if he could go back to the life he wanted and not the one expected of him. He'd always thought of changing his path as permanent but, as he was discovering, there were unanticipated twists and turns that made life different. And better. But to be a surgeon again... "How about I go talk to Henry, then let you know exactly what's going on?"

"Would you, Eric?"

"Meet me back here in thirty?"

"Can you make that twenty?" she asked.

She looked up at him, then nodded. "Tell him I love him, Eric. Please, tell Riku."

"I will," he said, his voice raspy. "I promise, I will."

Michi was concerned but not upset as she sat outside alone, her back to the garden wall. There was still plenty of light left in the day and, optimistically, by the time it was dark, Riku would be settled in his PICU bed, and all the worries of the world would be long over. It had been nearly twenty minutes already, and she was ready for Eric to return now that she had her second wind and her nerves weren't quite so on edge.

"Want some company?" he asked, coming up to her, handing her a bottle of water and a tissue, pre-emptively.

She nodded, choking back her tears then dabbing her eyes with the tissue. "How is he?"

"He's fine. On his way to Recovery." He slid down the wall next to her and pulled her into his arms. "They want about thirty minutes to get him settled in then you can see him. Henry's anticipating about two, maybe three hours in Recovery then back to the PICU. He's good, Michi. Strong. Everything that should be taking place now is taking place. He's breathing on his own. His vitals are normal. His heart is beating the way it should, and nothing but normal is showing up in the EKG tracing. It's everything we could have asked for."

"And the bypass machine?" she asked.

"Everything good there, too. It took him a little longer to come off than it usually does, but there really wasn't a reason. Just one of those things."

She leaned over against Eric and lowered her head to his shoulder. It was a safe place to be. A place she trusted with a man she loved. "So now we wait?"

"Yes. And maybe bask in the moment. He sailed through and he's good. I really want to stay in this place for a little while and just be grateful."

"Thank you," she said, wiping back her tears and sniffling.

"Thank you," he said on a deep sigh.

"For what?"

"For Riku. Thank you for Riku."

Michi nodded as words failed her then she collapsed into Eric's arms. "I don't even know what to think," she said. "It's been so long…"

"Then don't think. Merely enjoy the moment. He came through it, Michi. We all came through it."

Light rain was beginning to trickle down when he took her in his arms. They were still sitting on the cement, caught somewhere between the happiness of the moment and the pent-up emotions that no longer needed to be trapped. Riku was on the good side now, the place that made all the difference in the world, and all she wanted was to sit here, getting wet, and feel Eric's arms around her.

"Are you sure we shouldn't go in?" he asked.

"Not just yet. I don't want to share this moment. It's ours, Eric. Only ours. And a little water can't take it away from us, but the people on the other side of the garden door can. If you don't mind sitting here with me for a little while longer." She tilted her face to the sky and let the gentle rain wash over her. "It's funny. I wasn't sure what I'd do at this moment. I had fantasies of jumping up and down or simply crying. But what I want to do… The only thing I can see myself doing is…"

Eric chuckled. "What?"

Michi twisted in his arms to see the glorious rain streaming down his face. "Kissing you."

"Would that be a kiss of gratitude or relief?"

"No," she said, feeling so light she was afraid the churning of the air around her might pick her up and blow her out of this dream. But it wasn't a dream. For the first time it wasn't a dream. "And after the kiss I want you to allow me the chance to tell you that I love you more than I have ever imagined that I could love anybody. It's not going to be simple, and I don't even know how you feel about me, but that doesn't matter, Eric. After you kiss me, I'm going to tell you I love you."

"Then I suppose I should get to that kiss," he said, taking her face between his hands. "Because I like the sound of what comes next." With that, he pressed his mouth to hers. Gently. Ever so gently. It wasn't the kiss of lust or urgency but one of something deeper, of pure need that exceeded the physical.

It was Michi who parted Eric's lips, seeking more than either of them expected. Tongue touching tongue, breathing in rhythm with one another… She wasn't forceful either. More like she simply needed to be there, doing what they were doing, drawing from each other, giving to each other.

She giggled and pulled back when the water from his wet hair dripped to her nose. Then threw her arms around his neck and drew him back into the kiss. But this time it was deeper. A kiss that could lead elsewhere and might have had her cellphone not dinged a text message. "Maybe this is it," she said anxiously as she pulled it from her pocket, while Eric shielded it from the rain.

The message from Agnes was simple. One word. Ready. And that was all it took to catapult Michi to her feet while Eric still sat there on the wet cement. She held out a hand to help him up, and when he rose to his feet he scooped her up into his arms and spun around, both of them laughing and crying. "We did it," she said, feeling like a child let out to play for the first time in her life. The way Riku would soon feel. "We really did it, Eric."

"And…"

She laughed. "Do you really want to hear the words?"

"I do," he said, smiling.

"I do, too." She drew in a deep breath and shouted as loudly as she could, "I love you, Eric Hart." It was improbable, maybe even impossible, but at that moment she needed to say it as much as he needed to hear it. Then, like everything else between them, they'd tuck it away and work out the details later.

"And I love you, too," he said, a little more quietly. Then kissed her as he lowered her to the ground. "Now, go dry yourself off and get to Recovery. Someone there needs you."

"Someone right here needs you," she said, sliding her hand from his as she walked away. "And, yes, I know. We'll sort that along with everything we'll be sorting. But… I just needed to say it. Something I haven't been good at doing."

"And I needed to hear it." He pointed to the door. "Now go. Before I really do pick you up and carry you."

She did go, smiling all the way down to the dressing room to find dry scrubs, then all the way to Recovery. For the first time since that night with Eric, she felt like there was something to hold onto. She needed that in her life. She truly needed that, and Eric was the only one who made her feel that way. She hoped, after the craziness of the past several minutes, that it didn't wash away with the rain.

It was like the weight of the world had finally caught up to him and crushed him beneath its ugly shell. He was physically tired, emotionally drained, and he had no one to turn to but Michi. Yet as he watched her walk toward the recovery room he was so proud of the strength she was exuding. She'd been through so much more than he had, and for so much longer. But she wasn't broken. Tired. Worn down. But so strong. And it was from her strength that he was finding his own.

"Your kid's a fighter," Henry said, putting his arm around Eric's shoulder.

"He gets it from his mom," Eric commented, his eyes still focused on Michi until she disappeared into the recovery room.

"I know it's none of my business, but what happens now?" Henry asked. "And I'm only concerned because he's my patient."

"You're concerned because you're nosy, you old buzzard," Eric said, chuckling.

"Some of that, too."

"Eventually, when he's ready to travel, he'll go home to Sapporo. He has good doctors there so I don't think his health is a concern. And when the next surgery is up, well…maybe you again."

"Then you'll fly me to Japan on that fancy plane of yours?"

"If that's what it takes."

"Will you be living there, too, Eric?"

"Michi and I get to a certain point then we don't go any further. As in making plans for what happens next. So, I don't know where I'll be. Probably either going to or coming from Japan."

"Consider staying, Eric. Be with your family there. Maybe get back to surgery."

Eric turned to face his mentor. "Sounds simple, doesn't it?"

"It can be, if that's what you want. Hell, I never thought I'd leave Texas, but look at me now. All small-town New York because the woman I love was worth the change. Anyway, I'm going to have Riku brought back to the PICU as soon as possible so you and Michi can both sit with him. But it's probably going to be three hours, according to hospital protocol. So go rest up. You've got some pretty important daddying to do. Oh, and you're welcome in Recovery, too."

Eric shook his head. "She needs this."

"Well, whatever suits you. See you in a while, when he's back in PICU."

The minutes with Riku flew by then suddenly she was alone in the hall, walking back to the waiting room to find Eric. Riku was still sleeping, and he looked so tiny and fragile against all the machines surrounding him. But his heart tracing looked good. Better than she'd ever seen it. And the blue tinging around his lips these past few weeks had pinked up nicely, as had his fingernail beds. Meaning his heart was working the way it should and his body was no longer being robbed of oxygen.

It was all good, and she couldn't wait to find Eric, wondering if their earlier celebration could be continued, or perhaps had it been a one-off? A reaction to the moment, to the joy, to the relief? So much of this was because of him, and there weren't enough ways in the world to give him the thanks he deserved.

But would he even want to see her now? Especially after the way she'd been so giddy in the garden, saying things she otherwise might not have said, doing things she might otherwise not have done? Well, there was only one way to find out, wasn't there? Go find Eric and simply ask if there was another step for them to take together. Something that would lead to another step, then another…she hoped.

"Isn't Eric here?" she asked her mother, who was sitting near the window in the waiting room.

"He stopped by for a couple of minutes, told us more detail about how the surgery had gone. We thought he'd stay with us, of course, but obviously he didn't. I don't think he knows where he belongs, Michi."

Of course he didn't. She'd never given him the opportunity. Never given him the chance to find out. Or the support he needed as badly as she did. Everyone in Riku's life had their defined place. Everyone but Eric who, while he wore the title of father, was still unsure of where it got him. Did he think that now the surgery was over, he was no longer needed? How could he feel anything but that, when she'd been the one to do that to him?

"I, um… I'm going to take a walk," she said. "Riku's

going to be in Recovery for a while longer and I'd really like to get out of here for a bit. They'll text me when he's ready to go to PICU, and I'll be back for that." And while the cafeteria wasn't necessarily her destination, she headed in that direction, hoping to find Eric there. Texting him as she walked.

Where are you?

Lobby. Waiting for my driver. Going home for a while.

May I come with you?

She was not sure why she responded that way but being with Eric was the only thing that made sense. So, she waited for his rather prolonged response before she took another step in any direction.

Sure. Waiting in lobby.

She was positive that his hesitancy in responding right away was because he wasn't sure what to do. And the lack of enthusiasm in his response probably indicated the same. But she was not going to be deterred. They'd put off everything until after Riku's surgery, and now it was after Riku's surgery, which meant it was time to see what they had together in all this. It might not be easy, and it might be heartbreaking, but she'd done a bad thing by Eric once before, and she wasn't going to do that again.

"That white stretch out there is yours?" she asked, stepping up behind him.

"Technically, it belongs to the company, but since I own the company…"

She took hold of his arm. "Care to give me the grand tour? I've never been in a car like that before."

Eric chuckled as he led her out the door. "Let's see, tires, doors, seats inside. And William. When he retired from the company, he wasn't ready to call it quits so I took him on as driver, estate handyman, gardener, whatever. He lives in the guesthouse and he's grateful that even at his age he still has a purpose."

"We all need a purpose, Eric," she said, climbing into the back seat and dropping down into the buttery white leather. "But sometimes finding the right purpose is difficult. Sometimes it takes a few misfires to get it right."

The sky was clear, the rain long gone, and the night was decidedly colder than previous nights. Which meant winter was setting in. And this winter she had plans for Riku. Nothing strenuous, nothing outside except some easy sledding on a very limited basis. Still, for the first time ever she had plans that would happen. Something to look forward to and get excited about. Something so tangible she could almost feel it right now. Before today, all plans had been subject to change, or had disappeared altogether. But not anymore. This was the first time she felt free enough to think forward. "So, you live in the city?"

"Secluded area. Not central but nice."

"Let me guess. Passed down from generation to generation."

"To Riku, when it's time." He settled in across from her and sighed. "Oh, and for what it's worth, white isn't the color I would have chosen. Neither was a stretch. But…"

"It was passed down to you with everything else."

"And Riku can have it right now if he wants it. Personally, I prefer my SUV. But sometimes a Hart has to be a Hart."

"Why tonight?" she asked him.

"Long-range plans involved. And that includes the whole Hart legacy. It only seems proper that it all begins in the Hart stretch."

They drove several blocks before they cut out of midtown and headed for the mansion. This was really the first time Michi had ever explored Manhattan by night, and it was beautiful. Everything she'd imagined. All the magnificent buildings with all their magnificent light. "Would you believe I've never been up the Empire State Building? I think I'd like to go on a clear night, so I could look out on all the lights for miles."

"Then we'll do that. And as Hart Properties has a helicopter, maybe you'd like a ride over the city at night as well. Best view in town, in my opinion."

"Are you a pilot?" she asked.

"As a matter of fact, I am."

"Then you could take us."

"Or I could have the company pilot take us so we could snuggle up in the back seat."

She smiled at the suggestion. "I like that. Bring a blanket, bring a Thermos of hot chocolate."

He chuckled. "Except the chopper is heated, and it's equipped with a coffeemaker, which can easily convert to hot chocolate."

Michi laughed. "You really do know how to spoil the romantic moment, don't you?"

"Old habits that haven't died, I suppose."

"Could we work through them together?" This wasn't

what she'd intended to talk about. At least not now. But she'd declared her intentions without anything back from him. So, she had to know if she was kidding herself, that maybe he was still angry and wouldn't get over it. Or if he was ready to move on, as he'd hinted.

Unfortunately, before he had time to respond, the car had come to a stop outside a virtual castle, and the driver was already opening the door for her to exit. She stepped out, trying not to gawk too much or, at least, with her mouth hanging open, waited for Eric to come from the other side, then took hold of his arm and let him lead her into the most magnificent foyer she'd ever seen. One that belonged on the pages of an architectural journal.

"This isn't what I pictured," she said. Everything was in grand style from the massive pendant lights at the entry to the marble staircase inside the hall. Even the ebony grand piano in the music room off to the side of the entry, the mahogany antique Chippendale chairs sitting across from it, and the heirloom Persian rug upon which everything sat. "It's so…"

"Ostentatious," he supplied.

"Maybe. But beautiful. Like in a museum."

"Or a mausoleum. My dad never let me come in here. I was restricted to my bedroom, my playroom and the kitchen. Occasionally the dining room, when he didn't want to eat alone. Which was hardly ever."

"Too bad, because beauty like this should be enjoyed. Not restricted. Who did the decorating?" she asked, as she brushed her fingers lightly over a sofa table behind the massive empire sofa sitting off to the side of the room.

"A couple of great-grandmothers back, so I'm told. The Hart family has always been larger than life, and their lifestyle was part of it."

"But not your lifestyle?"

"I prefer to keep things simple."

"Yet look at all this. I can't even picture you rambling around through all the halls here, let alone living in them."

He chuckled. "I don't. Pretty much I live in the same area I always have. My bedroom, changed to fit a man rather than a boy. My playroom changed into an office. And the kitchen, where I usually stand over the sink to eat, when I eat here. Which is hardly ever, since I'm more of a grab-bag-and-go kind of a guy."

"Fast food?"

He shook his head. "Top restaurants are more than happy to put a decent meal in a bag for me to take away."

"Well, I'd like to say I'm getting mixed signals on your lifestyle, but I'm not."

"Because pathetic isn't a mixed signal," he said.

"Well, if this was the house I had to come home to, I'd probably live the way you do. All this is good for show, but when it comes to living, I like livable. Someplace where I'm comfortable. A house where, if I break a vase, I can replace it rather than have to claim it on my insurance." She turned back to Eric. "Are you happy here, Eric? I guess that's what's important, isn't it? Being happy where you are?"

"I've never really thought about it. This house exists, and I exist inside it." He sat down at the piano and opened the lid over the keyboard. Then played a perfect arpeggio with the fingers of a perfected pianist. Or a perfected surgeon.

"That's beautiful," she said. "What comes after it?"

"Anything you want. Maybe an old Beatles tune?" With that, he launched into one of the oldest. Then transitioned into Chopin. "A nocturne is always good, too." Then a show tune, followed by several fragmented jazz chords, ending in part of Beethoven's "Ode to Joy" from his ninth symphony. "It's a matter of mood, I suppose."

"And what's your mood?" she asked, taking her place behind him then leaning over and, with one finger, playing a simple melody that sounded Japanese. And haunting. "It's called 'Takeda Lullaby.' My grandmother used to sing it to me. It's an old cradle song sung by bura-kumin, a group who were outcasts because of their occupations, like undertakers, butchers or tanners. They were deemed tainted by the old society because of who they were."

"And you sing this to Riku?"

"It's one of his favorites. Makes him smile. It talks about rising above adversity to a higher life."

"I think my mood might be like Riku's when he hears this. Not because of the song as much as the way you make me happy."

She changed her tune to the old Shaker hymn "'Tis a Gift to Be Simple" and Eric chuckled.

"Simplicity hasn't ever been anything I've had much to do with in my life," he said.

"Have you ever wished for it?" she asked, as she sat down next to him and continued playing, but with both hands.

"Most of my life. Closest I ever got was when I was in university, but even then, instead of living in the dorm room the way most students did, my dad bought me an elaborate townhouse off-campus."

"And you turned it down, of course, in search of the simpler."

He chuckled. "No, I kept it. But I did turn down the chauffeur and maid that came with it."

"You accept your wealth quite well," she said, lifting her hands from the keys. They were sitting much too close together, side pressed to side. But it felt so good, so natural that she didn't want to move. Not yet. "Have you ever considered donating your house and all its antiques to a museum and going back to your townhouse days?"

"I have, but something always stops me when I get close to going through with it."

"What?" she asked.

"My sense of family, I suppose. My dad wasn't that great, but there have been other Harts here who weren't him. I remember my grandmother sitting in her room, crocheting. Actually, I remember seeing a picture of her there. She was gone long before my time, but in the photo…she looked so happy. So contented. Getting rid of this house would be getting rid of that. Or maybe the image of another Hart in another photo I've yet to find. So I stay. Keep the part of it I want and leave the rest of it to its posterity. Which probably makes no sense whatsoever. But Riku's now part of that, so the choices will one day be his to make. Or, like me, not make."

Michi stretched her neck and sighed. "It's hard to think that my son belongs to all this. My family is of means, but not on this scale." She stretched her neck again, then laughed. "Too many hard chairs and strange beds lately."

With that, Eric left the bench then took his place behind her and began to massage. "I know this is part of what you do, and I'm sure I'm not nearly as good at it, so guide me if I go wrong here."

She let out a contented sigh. "Trust me. What you're

doing is perfect." So perfect, she leaned her head back against him, took in another deep breath and relaxed. This was a touch she wished could be only for her. But that was merely a dream. The reality was that all too soon she would return to her reality and the ache would return, and everything inside that was relaxed now would only tense up again. But for the moment...

"A little to the right," she said, almost on a moan. "And harder. I can take more pressure. And your thumbs...pure heaven."

"I think that's the first time anybody's complimented me on my thumbs."

"Oh, I think you have a whole lot of body parts to compliment. Remember, I saw them." And behind her shut eyes she was seeing them again.

His massage deepened a bit. "I remember," he said, sighing. "I do remember."

"I think we should stop," she said. Wishing that weren't the case.

"Afraid we could turn this into our second night?"

If only he knew how much she wanted that. Tonight. Right now. Even on the Persian rug. But she couldn't. If they were to happen again, and she truly hoped they would, it had to be perfect. And with everything resolved. Not now, though, as nothing was perfect, and nothing was resolved. Because if ever they were to be together again, she could not bear him leaving her yet another time. Still nothing guaranteed that he would stay. "Yes," she said simply, even though she didn't pull away from him as she might have at one time. Instead, she let him continue his massage as she continued her daydream. For now, anyway. Then, maybe later on...

# CHAPTER TEN

MORNING CAME SLOWLY, and the aches and pains from sleeping in the recliner next to Riku's bed were testament to that. Her frame was small, and it felt like the chair had mangled her. She looked over at the next recliner, surprised to find Eric there. He must have come back sometime in the night, even though he hadn't said a word to her one way or another what he would do.

The night had gone so…well, not wrong as much as off track. There'd been so many things she'd wanted to say, wanted to find out and talk about. But the proximity was driving them past the point of normal conversation to a place neither of them wanted to go. Not yet. So she'd returned by cab, made sure everything was as good as it could be in Riku's world, then reread the text from Eric that told her he'd see her first thing in the morning.

Twice after that he'd texted her the sweetest goodnights. So sweet she'd nodded off with a smile on her face. And now here was morning, and she was seeing him first thing, as he'd promised. The excitement of having him there with her caused her heart to do a little flip-flop. Maybe soon they'd be able to wake up the normal way. Wrapped in each other's arms. Glad to be there. Mussed from the night yet ready to make love in the morning.

"Did I miss something?" he asked, his eyes half-shut, waking up about thirty minutes after Michi did.

"Apparently I did—when you came in."

"Didn't want to disturb you, you were sleeping so peacefully. Except for that snore, of course." He looked out the corner of his eye at her. "You must have been tired because it was really loud."

"I don't snore," she insisted behind a giggle.

He scratched his head. "Must have been a distant fog horn." He chuckled and wiggled his phone in her face. "It records. Just sayin'."

"You wouldn't dare," she said, snatching it out of his hand.

"Try me and see."

"Why, that almost sounds like a proposition of some sort."

Eric blushed and didn't say a word, which disappointed her. She like their lighter moments. Liked enjoying his humor, liked laughing with him. But their conversation was getting dangerously close to a place he obviously didn't want to go, so she changed the subject. "He'll need a morning bath…just a sponge off. Clean clothes. Breakfast. You're welcome to do any or all of it. Or none of it. But, personally, I find his morning routine a great bonding time."

She wasn't sure what to make of Eric's switch in attitude. He changed back and forth so often she wasn't sure what he really wanted. Time would tell, she supposed. And, as of now, she faced two months of it in New York before Riku would be able to fly home.

Eric finally stood, stretched, and went to the side of

the crib. His first action wasn't to assess Riku like a doctor, the way Michi thought he would. No, it was to hold out his index finger to Riku, who immediately grabbed hold. "It gives them confidence," he said, holding out his other index finger to Michi. "Glad I didn't bother you last night because you were sleeping so soundly and peacefully. I tried hard to be as quiet as I could."

"I wasn't sure if you'd come."

"I wasn't sure if you'd want me. But I had to come, Michi. Had to take the risk because you and Riku are... everything."

"I gave our situation some thought, Eric. Where your place should be with Riku, where my place should be with you, and yours with me."

"And?"

"And I wonder why we're both so afraid to come right out and admit what we want. Is it because I was accused of trying to harm Riku, or because you were rejected by your father? These things shouldn't shape us, Eric. We shouldn't allow them to, yet they keep coming back to haunt us, don't they? Me afraid you'll see something in me that makes me look like a bad mother. You afraid you'll turn out like your father."

Offering his finger was the first overture he'd made since sometime yesterday—she was too tired to remember when—and she was glad of it. It didn't mean much, but it was a start. So, as she stood there holding on, she felt the connection, and there was nothing tentative or tenuous about it. The three of them...they were a family. Did Eric feel it, too? "He wants to be picked up and held. Doesn't understand why his mommy won't do that since he counts on her for it."

"With all the children I've worked with—the tiny

ones, the very young ones—I've always wondered what they think when their world is taken away from them and replaced with all this. You know it's got to scare them to death, but kids are such mighty warriors. They're better at accepting the difficulties than most adults are."

"And Riku is the mightiest," she said, allowing Riku to take hold of her finger, somehow creating a complete bond between the three of them. "I just wish…"

"What?"

"That there was some way through this that wasn't so awkward."

"Everything worthwhile takes time."

"You always make things seem so simple."

"Trust me, they're not." He picked up a soft blue baby cloth and washed areas of Riku that were exposed, then blotted Riku's hair dry. "Especially when you're on the outside, looking in."

"Like you are?"

"Like I am."

She picked up a clean hospital blanket and covered Riku after Eric managed to get him into a small hospital gown. Poor Riku, he looked so frail it broke her heart. So did Eric. But that would change for all of them. Riku would reach his normal weight, gain some strength, and move on like none of this had ever happened to him. She, on the other hand, wouldn't forget so easily. Neither would Eric, judging from the way he looked at Riku.

"He does resemble you, you know. In his eyes. He has kind eyes. And his smile. While he doesn't do it so often, he always reminds me of you when he does.

And look at those long fingers…the fingers of a surgeon, perhaps?"

"Or someone who will, eventually, inherit Hart Properties."

"I suppose I never thought of that."

"Well, in my experience, we show him a world full of options and let him decide for himself."

"Because of your dad?"

He shook his head. "No. Because I'm Riku's dad and I want him to have the life he wants, not the life I want for him."

"What about you? What about the life you want?"

"I think I might be in transition again."

"Really? Does that include going back to surgery?"

"It might."

She was so excited she wanted to jump up and down but, instead, she grabbed him and planted a fast, hard kiss on his lips. "That's where you belong, you know. And if there's anything I can do to help you with this… Eric, I'm so happy for you."

"It's not final," he said, trying not to sound too downbeat, at least until he'd talked to hospital admin to see if they'd take him back or not. "Right now I'm just enquiring. And there's the corporation to consider. I've got to put it in competent hands. So…"

"So, if you want it, you'll make it work. You know, what Polonius said."

"What Polonius said." He adjusted the IV tube running to Riku's arm, and by that time Riku was already half-asleep. "Maybe we should go?"

"But he really wants to get out of the crib," Michi told

Eric. "And after the doctors make their rounds, maybe I'll be able to do that?"

"Not yet. Riku's got a long recovery period ahead of him, and this is where we all really need to play by the rules. That includes me."

She spun to face him. "Sometimes I hate rules. I wonder who made the rules. Maybe I should go talk to them."

Eric laughed. "Actually, in this hospital, when it comes to pediatric cardiac surgery, I made the rules."

"Seriously? You made rules that hold me back from my son?"

"Seriously," he said, smiling.

"Then maybe you need to go back to being a surgeon just so you can change those rules or modify the penalty if I choose to break them. Because that's what I'm going to do, Eric. Break your rules."

"Somehow I never thought you wouldn't." He bent down, picked up a very squiggly Riku and placed him in Michi's arms. "And if anybody catches you, I'll deny everything."

"Except holding him right after I do. You're not going to deny yourself that, are you? So, while we're breaking the rules, let's talk about you and me."

"Are you sure you're ready for that?" he asked.

"No. But I'm not sure I'm not ready." She sat in the rocking chair, held Riku close to her chest, and started to rock. "So, where do we begin?"

An hour later, they were still talking, but Eric was the one in the chair holding Riku now. "I don't want to be the dad who's always on the plane, Michi. I want to be the one who's always there."

"Which would have me living in New York. Especially if you go back to the hospital."

"But you don't want to live in New York, do you?"

"Because I have family in Sapporo, Eric. Riku needs them, and I need them."

"And I have no family here."

"I don't want to hurt you again, which is why we have to do this now, before we both go jumping off in wrong directions once more. We have a son in the balance and what we do will always be a part of him. The directions we take, the attempts to be inclusive. Personally, I can give up my medical practice just like that." She snapped her fingers. "And if keeping Riku with his father means relocating to New York, I can do that as well."

"But you don't want to."

"Personally, no. I don't. But for Riku…"

"Would you want me in Japan, Michi? You've come up with ideas, but none have me moving to Japan."

"Because your life is here. Your company, your surgical practice, that mansion. It's a big life, Eric. One you won't have in Japan. And I don't know if that will make you happy. You may think so right now, but what happens in four or five years when you have second thoughts? Or your company needs you again? How do you manage that?"

"If I'm happy where I am, there's nothing to manage. That's all I want for the three of us, Michi. Someplace to be happy, and not necessarily someplace in a geographical place as much as emotional one. For me, it's not about what surrounds me. For you, it is…namely, your family."

"You'd move to Japan for my family?"

"No, for *my* family."

Michi nodded, because she had nothing to say. They'd

talked this out until there were no more words to speak. It was difficult, wanting the same thing yet not knowing how to come around to get it. She wanted what was best for him. He for her. And both of them wanted everything good for Riku. So it should have been an easy thing to figure out. But it wasn't, and she was frustrated. "Look, I'm going to take a walk and clear my mind. I'll be back in a few."

But her walk took her no farther than right around the corner, where she stopped and leaned against the wall. And that was where she waged her own mental battle. She loved Eric. She wanted to spend her life with him. She was willing to move to New York for him. And he… loved her on that same level, with the same arguments. The problem was, there was no middle ground here. And they desperately needed middle ground. Something that would build the bridge that would truly carry one to the other. Something other than Riku.

"Do you love me, Eric?" she asked, walking back into the room. Riku was back in his crib now, and Eric was standing at the window, gazing out at the sky. "I know you said you do, but do you really?"

"I fail at love, Michi."

"How?"

"I have women who want me for my money, for my looks, my prestige. But no one who's ever wanted me for me. It's a fact of my life, and for me to tell you I love you would always make you wonder where and when I'll mess it up. Can I stay with it? Forget my past? Move on? Be what I want to be and not what I've always been?"

"Your father?"

"My father. His father. It's all the same."

"Which seals Riku to that destiny."

"No. We can't let that happen."

"But if it's a family predisposition, as you seem to think, how can we stop it? How can we keep him from falling into that same line? Because, according to your logic, he will. It's inevitable."

He turned to face her. "We keep him from falling into that line by being the parents he needs us to be. Not by being the parents we think we should or should not be."

"And we can do that in a barge or a warehouse flat in Hackney in London, if that's the compromise you want to make to keep us together as a family. The where and how don't matter. But the three of us being together does. When I told you I love you, I meant it. It's been growing, and we haven't exactly had normal time to develop it. But you feel that way about me, too, don't you?" she asked.

"Seriously, Hackney? I wouldn't have expected that of you."

"What do you expect of me, Eric?"

"I don't suppose I know, other than the part where, yes, I do love you, and also that you're the best mom…or mum if we move to London, any child could ever have."

"And there is our start."

"Well, when you make it sound so simple…"

"But it is simple, Eric. We start with what we have and build on that. No couple ever starts out with every-thing. We have some communication problems. And, yes, some of the past may come back from time to time. But we have Riku, which makes us the luckiest couple in the world. And while he can't be our starting place, he can be our inspiration that when we're good together, we can do great things. We already have."

"And the lady hits one out of the park," he said, smiling.

"Because the lady needs to know."

"Then I'll be honest. I want this, and I need it. And I'm willing to do whatever it takes to make it work, including living on a barge, if that's what works for us. I do love you, Michi, but is that enough? Because, believe it or not, my needs are about as simple as they come.

"I don't want the grand lifestyle. Don't want the things that were important to my father, but I'm always going to live with the fear that I might turn into him. You've got to know that because that fear can cloud my judgment. It did when I wanted to reach out to you so many times in the past. And it's a battle I can't fight alone because I don't see it in myself. Or maybe I always see it in myself, even when it's not there."

"I can fight the battle with you. If you fight the one with me that makes me want to tackle the world alone. I used to think I could do it, but it's hard, and it wears me down. But what happens when I hit my stride again? Because I don't want to push you away like I did before. I want to keep you close, where you belong. What if I can't do that, though?"

"Then you turn to me."

"It really is a big leap for both of us, isn't it?" she asked.

"Maybe if we simply hold hands and walk to the edge of the cliff together…"

"It's a long way down if we mess up."

He chuckled. "I can handle heights if you can because I love you, Michiko Sato."

"And I love you, Eric Hart."

"But, seriously, a barge in Hackney? Maybe we could compromise on a warehouse flat overlooking someone's docked barge."

"You don't like water?" she asked him.

"Actually, I own this yacht…"

"Seriously, a real yacht?"

"Well, a yacht and a sailboat."

"Anything else?"

"Some camels, a few windmills, a lake, a couple of Monets, an Indy race team, a football team…" He smiled. "An old bicycle I used when I was a kid that I'd love to fix up for Riku when he's old enough. Oh, and a pony."

"You own a pony?"

"Not yet, but every kid needs one, don't you think? And if you play your cards right, I might get you one, too."

"And what do I have to do to get this pony?"

"Just love me."

"I do. From the first moment I laid eyes on you. Then after you gave me my miracle…"

"Then if you love me, will you live with me in…?" He grinned. "Not Hackney."

"New York?"

He shook his head. "In the mountains outside Sapporo there's a beautiful little cabin that needs happiness and life breathed back into it. It backs into the most beautiful area in which to ski, a nice trip for the weekend in the winter. A beautiful place to be in the autumn. I want Riku to know that place. To know us as a family in that place. It's part of his heritage, Michi. And it'll be a great place to kick back and let him teach me to speak Japanese."

"Are you sure?"

"Earlier, when I was still a doctor with hopes and dreams, and I'd just met you, I'd wondered if we could be more than a one-night stand. You were this amazing, smart lady who knew her place in the world. And you had so much passion for your medical practice. People respected you. I saw that in the way everyone responded to you at the seminar. And here I was, this loner who might have been good at his job but who wasn't very good at life, hoping that things could take a different turn. Maybe even with you.

"But the turn I got… I don't want to manage the company, Michi. I do my best because that's who I am, but I'd rather be back in surgery. I'd rather be happy in my life and planning a future for the three of us as a family. So, yes, I'm sure. Will you marry me? You and Riku are the only important parts of my life and I don't want to lose you."

"If you want me in your life," she said. "Knowing better than anyone else what a mess I can make of things."

"Not a mess, Michi. Just a temporary misdirection. And I do love you. No one's compared since I met you. And keep in mind this deal comes with a pony."

"Ah, yes, the marriage proposal sealed with a pony. We need to have a serious talk about romance, Eric."

"How about you show me romance, instead of telling me about it? I'm a quick learner."

"I know you are, Dr. Hart. I know you are." Michi wrapped her arms around Eric's neck and whispered, "Lesson one, hospital-appropriate and baby-approved." They both looked down at Riku, who was sitting up watching them. And smiling. Michi's heart suddenly filled until it was almost on the verge of overflowing. She'd gone from being the woman who'd thought she could never have her heart's desire to the one who had a lifetime full of it ahead of her. Two men in her life. A little one and a big one.

Yes, she had everything. And she didn't even need a pony. "So, tell me about that yacht," she said, smiling up at him. "I've always had this desire…"

"Any other secret desires I should know about?" he asked, lowering his mouth to hers.

She snaked her arms around his neck and pulled his face all the way down. "Plenty. And you've got the rest of your life to discover them."

# EPILOGUE

ERIC PACED THE floor nervously, as any expectant father would do. Along with him his father-in-law, Agnes, his mother-in-law and Michi. Oh, and Riku. This adoption was a family affair, and what a family it was. Everything he'd always wanted and had never thought he'd have.

"She's almost here," Tamiko Tanaka, their adoption attorney, advised. "Dr. Benedict is bringing her here straight from the airplane, and I've been informed that Mali is doing very well."

Dr. Arlo Benedict, his estranged half-brother. The one he wanted to embrace as family for the first time. The one who'd found Mali and had thought he and Michi might be the perfect parents. He didn't know Arlo yet, but he would. That was a priority, and not one to be put off.

He and Michi had been to Thailand twice to visit Mali since Arlo had first called. She was a beautiful child, full of life. Two years younger than Riku, which meant that they would have their hands full with Riku, now four, and Mali, just turned two. Their decision to adopt had happened almost at the same time they'd married in the hospital chapel, a week before Riku had been released. And now, two years later, it was coming true.

"You do realize that in addition to speaking Japanese and English, you're now going to have to learn enough Thai to get Mali through until she understands the other languages we use?" Michi asked. Basically, a mixture of Japanese and English. "And you're going to owe your brother big time for making the arrangements."

Mali had been an orphan, raised in a communal refuge for wounded elephants in a compound near the village where Arlo lived and worked as the village doctor. She'd simply been abandoned there, probably on the assumption that someone there would look after her, maybe teach her to work with the elephants when she was old enough.

Six weeks ago, after Arlo had asked him if he and Michi wanted to adopt, they'd flown down there twice, and now, almost in the blink of an eye…another miracle child. Life couldn't have been any better. Getting Mali, beginning the road to being a better brother to Arlo, the son his mother had had after she'd abandoned Eric. He wanted that. Wanted the family ties in a way he never had before. And it was beginning to happen.

"Chinatsu called, wishing us well," Michi said, fighting to hold onto Riku. He wanted to run down the airport corridor so he could greet his new sister. And, yes, he could run now. And play light outdoor games. He swam, too. Like a fish.

"She's buying up a rather sizeable chunk of Wyoming, she tells me." He'd hired her to run Hart Properties. She was eminently qualified as a businesswoman and had the same sensibilities he had. So, he'd had no qualms when Michi had suggested her cousin as his replacement.

Maybe she wasn't technically part of the Hart family, but she loved her job, and the company was, once again, in good hands, while his hands were where they belonged, performing pediatric cardiac surgery. Life was better than he'd ever imagined it could be and now that he knew what the support of a good family meant, he was no longer sad for what he'd missed but happy for what he'd gained.

"She's turning it into one of your wildlife preserves. Not your dad's first choice, I would think," Michi said.

Eric gave his wife a playful nudge. "Well, I'm not my dad."

"My sister?" Riku asked, pointing to a long-haired man in outdoor gear headed in their direction, carrying a bundle in a blanket. "Mali," Riku pronounced very deliberately.

"Mali and Uncle Arlo. Can you say Uncle Arlo?" Riku looked up at his dad like Eric had gone crazy, then started tugging at his hand, trying to lead him the direction of Mali. "Are you ready to share your toys with her?" Eric asked, trying to hold him back.

Riku contemplated the words for a moment, then grinned and gave his dad a big thumbs-up.

"Then I say let's go meet your new sister." And, hand in hand, the expanding family walked toward the new Hart member. Eric with tissues in his pocket for Michi, of course. And Michi sniffling well before she took her new daughter into her arms.

"Look what we've done," she whispered to Eric, just before Mali was handed to her. "Just look at what we've done."

He did. Every day. And there was never a moment he wasn't amazed by all the miracles it had taken to get them to this place. His place. His family. The prospect of finally getting to know his brother. And, most of all, having Michi in his life. All of them true miracles indeed.

\* \* \* \* \*

# FROM MIDWIFE
# TO MUMMY

**DEANNE ANDERS**

**MILLS & BOON**

This book is dedicated to my parents,
Rev. and Mrs. J. A. Atkison, who loved and supported
me and made sure I always knew I belonged.

And to Lucretia Lee, R.N.
The best Labor and Delivery nurse I ever had the
privilege to work with. I can never thank you enough
for the gift of your mentorship.

And to Theresa Lee.
While you might not be my sister by blood or adoption,
you will always be my sister of my heart.

# CHAPTER ONE

DIM LIGHTS AND the sound of soft waves crashing against the shore had created an atmosphere of a calm retreat, but midwife Lana Sanders knew that her patient had long passed the point of caring.

"You're doing great," Lana said as she coached Kim through another contraction and watched the fetal monitor. She watched the fetal heart-rate accelerate, then come down to its baseline. So far this had been a perfect labor.

"You're going to be late," Jeannie whispered to Lana as she arranged the delivery table.

"It won't be long now," Lana said, as much to reassure the labor and delivery nurse as well as her patient.

"Push. *Now.*" Kim ground out.

"Wait, I've got to get the camera!" Kim's husband Tom called out as he turned his back and started going through a duffle bag laid upon the bedside table.

*"Wait?"* said Kim. Her voice rose an octave and took on that gravelly sound that only a woman in transition, or one possessed, could reach. "What have you been doing all this time?"

"It's okay, Tom, we have a couple minutes," Lana said.

A deep growl escaped from Kim.

"Okay, maybe we don't," Lana said as she watched a circle of dark wet curls crown.

She positioned the delivery table so that it would be within easy reach, then undraped it, letting the protective covering fall to the floor.

"Kim, we've done this before, right?" Lana waited till she had Kim's attention. "The baby's starting to crown so whenever you're ready go ahead and push."

"Now!" said Kim, then took a fast breath.

Tom rushed to his wife's side and helped her get into position as she curled her body and pushed down. Lana watched as the couple worked together for their child. Kim's face was flushed and glowing with color as she concentrated on nothing but this moment—the moment she would bring a new life into the world. It was both beautiful and heart-wrenching for Lana to watch this miracle.

"Take another breath," Lana said. "Is the contraction gone?"

"No," Kim said, before she took a deep breath then returned to pushing.

"Okay, Kim, I need you to listen to me," Lana said.

She waited as Kim looked up at her.

"Next push we're going to have a baby, okay?" Lana watched as both excitement and fear filled her patient's tired eyes. "You can do this. I promise."

Kim nodded her head and grabbed Tom's hand as she positioned herself again, then pushed.

Seconds later a screaming, squirming baby boy was delivered. Lana carefully suctioned the baby's mouth, then handed Kim her new baby and watched as the experienced mom caught him close against her body, putting him skin to skin to keep him warm while Jeannie dried him off with some fluffy towels. She clamped then cut the umbilical cord that had been the baby's lifeline. Seeing both mom and baby meeting for the first time, she was amazed, as always, by the miracle of life that she was blessed to witness.

"You did wonderfully," Lana told Kim.

Lana delivered the placenta, then made sure her patient's bleeding was controlled. A quick glance at the clock above the bed had her suddenly feeling a sense of panic. She had to get out of the hospital in the next twenty minutes or she was never going to make it to court on time.

She gave the new mom a hug, then posed for a picture with the rest of the Callahan family once they were allowed in the room. She headed to the nurses' lounge for a quick change of clothes, then headed out of the hospital. This was going to be one of the most important days of her life. Today she would officially become a new mom herself—something that until a year and a half ago she had thought would never happen.

There was no way she was going to be late.

Lana white-knuckled her way through the nightmare of Miami traffic. The multiple lanes all seemed to be going nowhere, and Lana was short on both time and patience. For the first time she was scared she really was going to miss her appointment with the judge who would be finalizing Maggie's adoption.

The thought of her sweet, adorable little toddler had her taking a deep breath and relaxing. It would be okay. She was cutting it close, but she would make it. After over twelve months of social workers' visits and court appearances, there was no way fate would fail her now.

It had been fate that had brought the little girl into her life, after Lana had just happened to take on her young mother as a patient. When Chloe had later decided she couldn't handle the responsibility of a new baby and showed up on her doorstep, handing Lana the child along with a notarized letter saying she wanted Lana to adopt her, it had been nothing short of a miracle.

A lane opened up to her right and she swung into it and followed it to the next exit. Fifteen minutes later she made it to the judge's chamber where her appearance was scheduled to be. She was surprised to see that neither her lawyer nor her babysitter and Maggie were outside the room, waiting for her. She had texted both of them to let them know she was going to cut it close.

A note on the door explained that there had been a change in where the session would be held. Lana rushed down the hall to the courtroom. As she reached for the handle of the door a large hand reached around her.

"Let me," said a male voice in a slow drawl that almost curled her toes.

Lana turned and followed the outstretched arm up to the man behind it. The sight of coal-black hair curling around an angular face with a pair of deep blue eyes was startling. Forgetting that she was blocking the door, she let her gaze continue down the tailored black suit to the pointed toes of black leather cowboy boots peeking from beneath his pants leg.

A cowboy in Miami?

The thought had Lana smiling as she looked up at the handsome man and with a quick "Thank you" continued into the courtroom.

A frantic Amanda waved at her from the front of the courtroom, where she and Lana's lawyer Nathan had taken their seats. As soon as Maggie got a look at Lana the toddler started protesting. She wanted to get down and see her "mama" right then.

Amanda had dressed her in the new pink sundress Lana had recently bought, and with her dark curls and big deep blue eyes she looked like a china doll come to life. Lana reached over and took her little girl. She gave her a big tight hug that had Maggie giggling and squirming in her lap.

"Why the change to the courtroom?" she asked Nathan as she scooted into the seat next to him.

"Shh…" Nathan whispered back as he studied some of the papers in his hand.

Amanda looked at the two of them, then shrugged her shoulders, letting Lana know that she didn't have a clue about what was going on.

Nathan was always a little uptight-looking, which Lana put down to his job in family law. She knew that sometimes his cases were very stressful, with emotions riding high, but there was something about the way he was studying the papers in his hands that told her something was wrong.

Suddenly her heart kicked into panic mode. It was the same feeling she had when she woke up in the middle of her repeated nightmare about Chloe showing up at her door and telling her that she had changed her mind. That she didn't think Lana would be a good enough mother for Maggie and she was taking her away. Taking the little girl Lana had fostered since she was six weeks old. Taking her far away to somewhere Lana would never see her again.

It was the same nightmare she'd had for months now, but after today it would surely go away. Once the adoption was final Lana would be Maggie's mother, just as if she had given birth to her. There would be no way anyone would be able to take her away then.

As Judge Hamilton entered the courtroom everyone rose, then sat when the bailiff indicated. Taking a second to look around the courtroom, Lana noted that the social worker, Ms. Nelson from the Florida Department of Children and Families, who had been handling her case, was seated on the right at the front of the courtroom. She watched as the older woman handed the bailiff some papers that were then given to the judge.

Apprehension sent a shiver down her back. Lana looked at her lawyer again, to see his attention glued to the judge, who was now reading over the documents the social worker had presented to him.

"This is the hearing for the final placement of the child known here as Maggie. I know that Maggie has been fostered with Ms. Sanders since…" Judge Hamilton paused as he read the documents in front of him "…since she was six weeks old, and that the child's biological mother personally requested that Ms. Sanders be allowed to adopt her daughter."

The judge looked up and gave Lana a smile. Lana felt the tension ease and relaxed back into her seat. Judge Hamilton had always been encouraging in her quest to adopt Maggie. She knew her case was in good hands as long as he was on the bench.

"Ms. Sanders has been forthcoming in all the demands the court has placed on her, and she has met every requirement that the Department of Children and Families demands."

Judge Hamilton once more picked up the documents.

This was it—finally he would say the words she had been waiting for and Maggie would be all hers.

"To be clear, this was to have been the last hearing and the adoption was to have become final today."

*Was* to have become final? Were they going to make her jump through another hoop today?

"Ms. Nelson, you have indicated in your request to postpone the adoption that you have some new information that needs to be considered. Is that correct?"

Lana watched the social worker as she rose and walked to the front of the court room. Glancing at her lawyer for some sign as to what was happening, she noted that there was no look of surprise in his eyes as he watched the judge and the social worker quietly discussing the new documents she had handed him. When Nathan turned and took Lana's hands his look of concern pierced her heart.

Only something truly wrong would cause that kind of reaction in Nathan.

Amanda reached for her other hand and, looking at her, Lana saw the fear that she knew mirrored her own. Maggie, thinking this was a game in which she was not included, pulled at the adults' hands and started babbling in her sweet baby voice.

Lana released her hold on the others and wrapped her arms around her little girl. Okay, so there was another delay. There had been several over the last year. They had managed to clear each hurdle to get to this point, and if there was something else the court wanted from her she could handle it.

"It has come to the court's attention that there is a new petition to stop this adoption by someone who claims to be a family member—a brother of the biological father," Judge Hamilton stated.

Lana's heart stuttered for a moment, then raced forward at a speed that had a gasp escaping into the quiet court room. She pressed Maggie closer to her chest as she felt the adrenaline rush hit her, telling her either to run or prepare to fight. She clasped Maggie tightly, needing to feel the reassurance that only physically holding her child in her arms could give her.

"Is the person petitioning the court present?" the judge asked.

Lana watched her nightmare play out in front of her as the cowboy she'd seen earlier rose to his feet.

"I'm Trent Montgomery, Judge Hamilton, and I have reason to believe that I'm Maggie's uncle."

Trent walked into the small room at the side of the courtroom and took a seat at the small rickety table. Across the table sat the young woman he had met going into the courtroom—the woman he now knew as Lana Sanders.

He was surprised he hadn't recognized her from the picture he had found among the items his brother had had when he was taken to the hospital. Of course the young woman pictured smiling at the toddler whose hand she held looked young and carefree, with her hair flying all around her face as a breeze blew through the blond strands, while the woman he had opened the door for was all business, in her tailored skirt and blouse and her hair pulled back in some sort of clip.

Now the woman had let her hair down in more than one way, and her bright green eyes shot daggers at him as she talked with an older woman with steel-gray hair and eyes to match. He had no doubt that at that moment she wanted nothing more than to come over to the table where he sat.

Not that he didn't understand the kind of anger she was feeling. When his brother's lawyer had contacted him about the child he had wanted to hit something—anything—just to be able to take out the anger he'd felt at his brother. How could his brother have kept it from him that he had a little girl?

The lawyer had stated that Michael hadn't believed the contents of the letter he had received from his ex-girlfriend. But when the private detective he had hired had brought back pictures of a smiling toddler with coal-black ringlets and bright blue eyes, he'd known that the child was his.

After the lawyer had read Michael's will, and left some pictures of the child, Trent had come to the same conclusion as his brother. The child could only be a Montgomery. Another Montgomery child that had been abandoned.

He'd looked at those pictures a lot during the last two weeks, as he had tried to decide what to do about the child. She looked happy, smiling at the pretty blond woman, who smiled back with a love that seemed to pour out of the picture.

Why would he want to take this child away from this woman who appeared to love her? And what did he know about raising a little girl? Sitting there across from a woman who plainly wished a hole would open up and swallow him, he wondered for the hundredth time why he'd uprooted his life to come somewhere he didn't want to be and where he certainly didn't have a clue about what he was doing.

But he would go through with it. Because his brother

had asked him to take care of this child if something happened to him. And because the little girl was a Montgomery, and that made her his responsibility.

He had failed to keep his brother safe from his father's destructive influence, but he wouldn't fail this child. On paper, Lana Sanders looked like the perfect mom, but Trent knew better than to believe everything he read. He would protect Michael's child as he should have protected Michael.

Once the court awarded him custody of his niece he would pack up and head back to Houston, where he belonged. Somehow he would have to find a way to make things work till then.

"Lana, I want to tell you first that I know this isn't going to be easy for you. You've been taking care of Maggie for months now, and I know you love her very much. Second, you need to know that the court has to consider any interest the biological family has in Maggie." Ms. Nelson the social worker stated. "I've seen the letter they have from Chloe, telling Mr. Montgomery's brother about her pregnancy. And then, of course, there's the resemblance that none of us can deny."

"And where was this biological family when she was six weeks old with no one to take care of her?" Lana spat out.

She looked across the table at the man who had been sitting quietly as she had questioned the social worker. Those blue eyes that she had found so appealing earlier now seemed ice-cold as they followed her every movement. He might as well just be an onlooker into this catastrophe he had orchestrated. Her life had suddenly been turned upside down, and he acted as if this was just another meeting for him to attend. As if he had no interest at all in the outcome.

But then he shouldn't have any interest in her and Maggie's life. He shouldn't even be here.

The pain of her nails biting into her hands had her uncurling her fingers. So far she had managed to rein in her temper. Now, running her hands through her hair, she pushed it back from her face and wished she had left it up in the clip. She could feel the heat of anger in her face and she knew the sight of her reddened face and scattered hair couldn't be a pretty picture.

She would have to get herself under control before she reached panic mode. That was not something she wanted either of these two people in the room to see. Taking a deep, steady breath, she willed her body to relax. Turning back toward the social worker, she pleaded her case once more.

"What about when she was just born and she was going through withdrawal? Was there anybody from this so-called family interested in Maggie then?" Lana said, glad that she no longer heard a tremor in her voice.

"I'm sorry," Trent said. "I wasn't aware of the child until a couple of weeks ago. If I had known I would have seen to it that my brother was here when she was born."

"And where is this brother of yours, huh? Why is it that you're here without him?" Lana asked. "If he's Maggie's father why isn't he here?"

Lana watched the man she had earlier thought of as cold turn glacial.

"My brother passed away three weeks ago."

The shock of the statement stunned her into silence. The man who was supposed to be Maggie's biological father was *dead*? She stared at the man sitting across from her, who had shown no emotion while discussing his brother's death. He was just full of bombshells, wasn't he?

"So why are you here? Why are you so interested in Maggie's life when apparently your brother had no interest at all?" Lana asked.

Turning toward the social worker, she noticed that the older woman had shown no reaction to this new information. Realizing that Ms. Nelson must already know about the death of the supposed biological father, she felt the relief of earlier fade.

"There is no way you can expect me to give Maggie up to a man who isn't even her father. It's one thing to consider the father's rights, but this man is a stranger to Maggie. You have to see that Maggie is better off in a home where she feels safe and loved. That's why Chloe didn't take her. Why she left her with me. She wanted to make sure Maggie would always be in a stable home. She didn't want to ever have to worry that her baby was not being properly taken care of," she said as tears spilled from her eyes.

*No way.* No way would she let them take Maggie.

"We're not making any changes as far as Maggie is concerned until we investigate the situation, Lana," the social worker said as she took Lana's hand and squeezed. "The first thing we'll do is have a DNA test done on both Maggie and Mr. Montgomery."

"I'll give you the information you need to contact me," Trent volunteered.

"Thank you," the social worker responded. "And your lawyer has given us the information you have in relation to your brother's alleged paternity."

"And, having given you that information, I would

like you to consider allowing me some visitation with the child," Trent said.

"'The child' has a name. It's Maggie. And why should I let you anywhere near her?" Lana asked.

"It's your decision at this time, Lana, but we do have good reason to think that Mr. Montgomery's brother was Maggie's father," said Ms. Nelson. "And if the DNA tests come back to show Mr. Montgomery as being her uncle, he will be able to ask for visitation while the court decides on custody."

Lana looked at the man across from her. Cool blue eyes watched her from beneath thick dark lashes. She'd seen that calculating look before, only then it had been on the face of a toddler trying to figure out how to get another cookie after she had eaten her limit.

There was no denying the similarities this man shared with Maggie. And she feared that the DNA test would only confirm what her eyes were telling her now. Chloe had never said much about Maggie's father, but she had said she'd written him a letter telling him she was pregnant when she hadn't been able to get him to answer her calls. She had listed Maggie's father as "unknown" on the birth certificate when she hadn't heard anything from him, and she had refused to discuss him any further with Lana.

Lana rubbed at the tight knot she felt forming at the back of her neck. How could this day have gone so wrong? She was suddenly bone-tired. She knew she had to accept the fact that this fight wouldn't be won here today.

"I'll consider it," Lana said. "But if I agree, I will be present at all times."

"Thank you," Trent said.

"About the DNA, Mr. Montgomery... I'm sure your lawyer has made you aware that the results when testing for an aunt or uncle of a child will not be definitive. It will give us more of a likely match than proof of a biological relationship."

"Actually, it's *Dr.* Montgomery, Ms. Nelson. But please call me Trent."

For a moment Lana thought her brain would explode at this new piece of information. While she knew the court wouldn't show any prejudice as far as financial circumstances were concerned, it would surely still consider if a child's needs could be met. What if they felt that this Dr. Montgomery could provide better for Maggie?

"I'll contact you both after we receive the DNA results and set up another appointment," Ms. Nelson continued as she stood, letting Lana know that there wasn't anything else to be said today.

Lana stepped out of the room and drew her keys out of her purse with trembling hands. She was glad she had sent Maggie home with Amanda instead of having them wait for her. She would have to use the time it would take her to get home to get herself together.

Thank goodness she had found Amanda, a medical student, while she had been looking for a roommate. With Amanda able to fill in as babysitter in exchange for rent, she had the extra help that a single parent needed.

She'd go home and get Maggie into bed, call Nathan to see what her options were, and then she would come up with a plan. Dr. Trent Montgomery might think that he had everything going his way, but they said possession was nine-tenths of the law and right now Maggie was hers.

Lana had only been fifteen when she had beaten the

cancer that had been growing in her body. She'd lived through chemo and radiation treatment. She'd stumbled a bit when she had learned that the treatments that had saved her life had destroyed her dreams of having children, but she had managed to keep going even though she'd been hurting.

She was a fighter and she didn't give up. And she was about to make a certain cowboy wish he had never left Texas.

# CHAPTER TWO

LANA WALKED OUT of LDR Four and headed for the OB nurses' lounge. The delivery had been complicated, due to the size of the baby boy, and the new mom had needed extra reassurance that everything was fine with both her and her baby. Now she would have to hurry back to the office as soon as she'd finished signing off on her orders.

She could hear the whispers and laughter of the nurses as she turned the corner of the nurses' station. There had to be some new rumor spreading through the hospital, because she noted that everyone was gathered around Kat, the queen of hospital gossip. Usually she would have paused to hear what the newest bit of gossip was, but today she didn't have time.

As soon as her paperwork was completed she changed out of her scrubs and headed back to her office. She didn't want to leave her patients waiting any longer. Irate pregnant women could be downright scary, and her staff could only appease them with promises of her return for so long.

John Lincoln, one of the pediatricians employed by the hospital working the obstetric hall, waved from the nursery hallway as she passed. A few seconds later she heard her name called and turned to find John was following her, with another man dressed in the hospital's light blue scrubs beside him.

Lana stopped and stared at the two men even as she shook her head in denial. There was no way this could be happening to her.

"Hey, Lana," John said as he approached. "This is Dr. Trent Montgomery. He's taken the *locum tenen* position we've had open since Dr. Lee left."

"We've met," Lana said as she turned toward Trent. "What are *you* doing here?"

"As John just told you, Ms. Sanders, I've accepted a temporary job with the pediatric department," Trent said. "I'm looking forward to the two of us working together."

Work with the person who was trying to take Maggie away from her? No way was *that* going to happen.

"But why? Why are you here?" Lana asked.

John looked at Lana, then back at Trent with a frown. "I take it you two know each other?" John asked.

"We've met." Lana said as she moved to one side of the hall to let a nurse pushing a patient in a wheelchair pass.

She noticed the look the nurse gave this new doctor in town. Yeah, she hated to admit it, but he was something to look at. Even with his high-dollar suit and cowboy boots gone he looked good. The pastel color of the cotton scrubs should have dimmed some of that masculine power that he threw off, but instead it seemed to amplify the hardness of the body they covered.

There would be a swarm of women circling around him as if he was roadkill as soon as they got a good look at him. And she would just leave them to it. Because no matter how good he looked she didn't want him anywhere near her and Maggie. Why was he doing this to her? Her life was stressful enough without him in *her* hospital, where she would be running into him all the time.

Crossing her arms, she leaned against the wall. There was no way she was going to let him know how rattled he made her. She didn't care how sexy he looked standing there, she was going to let him know exactly how she felt about this ploy of his. Because that had to be what this was—just one more way to intimidate her into giving up Maggie.

But it wouldn't work, she was tougher than that. She would not let him get to her. There was too much at stake here. She had too much to lose to let a hard-bodied, hard-headed man get the best of her. She'd play his game if that was what it took to beat him.

"I'll catch up with you in the lounge," Trent said to John.

Lana waited till John was out of hearing range before asking the question that was burning her tongue. "What do you think you're doing here, Dr. Montgomery?" she asked. "Why aren't you back in Houston?"

Lana watched him take in her knowledge of that piece of information. Yeah, she'd done a little online stalking and it had paid off.

She'd found out that he worked in one of the largest women and children's hospitals in Houston as a pediatrician, for Pete's sake. Why he worked as a doctor at all, when he came from a family loaded with oil money, she didn't understand.

After seeing several pictures of him at different social affairs, all with a different beautiful woman on his arm, she had thought her heart would stop when she'd found an article that listed him as one of Houston's most eligible bachelors and had seen what was listed as his estimated net worth.

After that she had read everything the internet had on him, looking for something—anything—to use against him. But she hadn't found anything, and with every article her fear of losing Maggie had increased.

And apparently all the while she had been checking him out, he had been checking her out too. Because even if he had a good reason for leaving the hospital in Houston, the fact that he'd shown up at the hospital where she practiced out of all the hospitals in Miami meant he'd done his research. Or paid someone else to do it.

Wasn't that what the rich did? Hired someone else to do all the dirty work for them? There were no coincidences with men like Trent Montgomery. No, he had an agenda in coming here, and she would find out what it was one way or the other.

"After my lawyer informed me that the courts would look favorably on me being within their district, I took leave from my job in Houston. Also, it made sense that it would be easier to work with you as far as visitation goes if I was living in the area. A temporary position opened up here, so I inquired and was offered the position."

As if the pediatric department was going to turn down a qualified pediatrician who had graduated from Emory and done a residency in neonatology when they were so short on staff.

"Besides, Miami is a beautiful city," he said as he moved closer, leaning in toward her as a group of staff members came down the hall. "Who *wouldn't* want to live here?"

She knew better than to let his look of innocence fool her, and she certainly wasn't going to let the fact that his body was now only inches away affect her.

"What did you tell the interviewers?" she continued, as she tried to ignore her speeding heartbeat. She hadn't discussed her court appearance with anyone at work—had just told those who'd asked that there had been a small delay in the paperwork at the court.

"I told them I had an interest in the position due to some business I had here in Miami," Trent said as he moved back a few inches. "I don't see why the hospital should have any concern for our private affairs."

Realizing she had been holding her breath, Lana let her lungs expand fully. The racing of her heart let her know she was allowing this man to get to her, and that wasn't acceptable. She would have to stop letting him intimidate her.

"And I'm supposed to believe that you just happened to end up at the same hospital where I work?"

Trent shrugged a shoulder, then gave her a smile that set her teeth on edge. This was a man who not only knew he was charming, but also knew how to use it to his advantage.

"That's what I thought," Lana said as she moved once more to let one of the unit nurses pass.

The fact that it was the same brunette nurse who had walked by earlier didn't surprise her. Word had clearly already gotten out that there was a new male doctor on the unit, and the fact that he was sexy as hell meant that he would be getting even more attention than usual.

Soon the fact that she knew the new doc would come to the attention of the staff. And that was something that she didn't want to deal with right now.

\* \* \*

Trent watched Lana as she stomped off, then stopped to pull a ringing phone from her pocket and answer it. He'd known she'd be angry when she found out he'd obtained a job at the hospital she worked at, and he couldn't blame her. What had surprised him was his reaction to her anger. The woman was as feisty as a wild filly, and reluctantly he had to admit that he'd found it entertaining and even a little arousing to watch her spit and sputter as she reached her boiling point with him.

And that was the strangest thing. Normally the sight of a woman's anger sent him running in the opposite direction. He'd seen enough of his mother's tantrums with his father to know he didn't want any part of that in his life. But this woman's anger was different. It was hot and furious, but at the same time it was controlled and non-threatening.

And she was sure something to see when her green eyes started to spark lightning strikes at him.

The woman would have his head if she knew that while she'd been doing all that ranting and raving he'd been thinking about how cute she was, trying to intimidate him with her five and a half feet against his six-feet-two-inch self.

The insistent screech of the beeper attached to his scrub bottoms went off and he read a message from the ER, concerning a preterm imminent delivery coming in.

"Which way to the ER?" he asked Lana as she ended her call.

For a second she just stared at him. Then, shaking her head, she turned down another hallway. "Come on, I'll show you," she said, not looking back to see if he was following her.

"There's a thirty-three-week antepartum coming in by ambulance," he said when he caught up with her.

"She's thirty-four weeks and six days. That was her husband on the phone," she said.

He knew those six days could make a big difference in the outcome of the delivery.

"Your patient?" he asked as they boarded an empty elevator to the bottom floor.

"Her name is Taylor. Her husband Dean says that her water suddenly broke and contractions started immediately. She has a history of preterm delivery and was on bedrest."

"How early were her other deliveries?"

"She's only had one. Her son Phillip was born at thirty-six weeks."

Trent waited for Lana to leave the elevator, then followed her through the double doors leading into the emergency room. Multiple glass-doored rooms opened up from what looked like the hub of the department, where nurses and doctors could be seen in front of monitors and answering phones.

"This way," Lana said as she turned left. "The department is basically set up with the trauma rooms on this end and the less urgent patients on the other."

She stopped in front of a large monitor set up at the end of the hallway then preceded into a room labeled Trauma Four.

As he entered the large room he noted the baby-warming unit set up in the corner, and the nurses around them opening up the delivery set on a stand near an empty stretcher.

He grabbed Lana's arm and moved her back as a couple of emergency responders pushed a stretcher into the room, holding a pregnant woman panting and gripping the hands of the female responder.

As he gowned and gloved up he listened as the other responder gave his report to the room. "Spontaneous rupture of membranes twenty minutes ago with contractions starting immediately. Contractions now every two minutes. Vital signs with blood pressure elevated and heart-rate tachy at one-twenty."

He watched as Lana, also gowned and gloved, helped move the patient to the trauma bed then immediately did a vaginal exam, all the time talking to her patient in a calm voice.

"Is there time to move her upstairs?" he asked. He knew everyone would feel better if they could do the delivery on the obstetric unit.

"Nope," Lana said. "This one is coming right now."

A young nurse he was sure he had been introduced to earlier as belonging to the NICU team laid a blanket over his arms and he moved over to where Lana stood.

A breath later and Lana was holding out a small baby for the sobbing mother to see, then reaching for clamps and scissors as she made fast work of freeing the baby from its cord.

Rubbing its back to stimulate a cry, she turned toward him. Pausing for a second, she gave him an assessing look, then with a hesitant nod she handed the baby girl to him.

He took over from where Lana had stopped, and rubbed the baby's back as he did his assessment. A small cry started as he reached the warmer, and had turned into a howl by the time he laid her down.

The whole room broke out in cheers. He looked back

to where Lana was comforting the new mom and saw big smiles on both their faces.

"Sounds like she has a good set of lungs to me," he said.

He waited for the nurses to bundle her up, then brought the squalling baby to its mother and introduced himself.

"She's a little early, so I'd like to take her up to the nursery to observe her a little closer, but I'll get her back to you as soon as possible."

"But she's going to be okay?" the new mother asked.

"Her color looks good…she's going to get a seven and an eight on her Apgar. She was a bit slow starting up, but she's got the hang of it now, I'd say."

"As soon as you're ready I'll take you up to her," Lana told Taylor.

Trent laid the baby in the transport crib—she had calmed down some once she had been swaddled into a striped pink blanket—and followed the assigned nurse up to the nursery.

Considering everything that might have happened, he and Lana had managed to keep their personal issues out their jobs, thought Trent. He'd consider that a win for now.

He had no explanation for the way he responded to this woman. Since their first meeting thoughts of her had filled his mind, along with a deep pang of guilt at being the one who would to separate her from the little girl he could see she loved very much. But his agenda was set and nothing could change it now. He'd take care of his niece, just as his brother had asked him to, and he'd find a way to work with this midwife without everything around them exploding, while at the same time using the opportunity to find out everything he might be able to use in the custody battle.

He had to stop this adoption from going through. He wouldn't let his father ruin his niece's life the way he had ruined his brother's and mother's. He would protect her from his father no matter what it took, and once he had custody of his niece his brother's will would make sure his old man never had the power to hurt anyone again.

Lana took her place at Ms. Nelson's desk and waited for the social worker to finish her phone call. For once she had made it early for an appointment, and she planned on taking advantage of the time she had before Trent arrived.

Why the social worker felt it necessary for the two of them to meet together with her she didn't understand. The man rubbed her the wrong way, and she had spent the last few days doing her best to avoid him at the hospital, but there had been no way to get out of this meeting.

She would have to keep control of her temper, no matter how hard it was to stay in control when Trent Montgomery was in the room. Making a good impression with the social worker was too important. And, while her lawyer had given her his opinion of Trent's case for custody, she knew that a lot of the custody decision would be based on the social worker's investigation.

"Sorry about that, Lana," said Karen Nelson as she hung up the phone. "It's been a busy day today. I know this might sound cold, with your situation, but I just wish every child had two adults like you and Mr. Montgomery wanting them."

"That bad?" Lana asked.

She knew that there were a lot of children in foster

homes who would never be adopted. She had seen it in her practice as a midwife, when one of her patients might give birth to a child she couldn't take care of and the child would go into the system. Then the mother wouldn't agree to give up her rights to the child, making it impossible for the child to be adopted, so they just continued to stay in the foster system year after year.

Thankfully Chloe had made it clear in her notarized letter, and later in her correspondence with the court, that she wanted Maggie to be adopted. If only more mothers like her could see that they wouldn't be letting their children down but instead opening up a better option for them.

"Yeah," the social worker said as she finger-combed the back of her hair, took a deep breath and then seemed to reset herself back into work mode as she started going through the files on her desk.

Not for the first time Lana wondered why someone would ever go into social work—especially in Children and Families. The pressure to ensure the safety of all the children they were responsible for must be mind-boggling.

"While we wait for Dr. Montgomery to arrive let's talk about how *you're* doing. I know this isn't easy for you. Are you hanging in there okay?"

"I know you're right about Maggie being a lucky little girl. I get that," Lana said, "but how much harm will come to her if she's taken away from the only home she's ever known and placed with a stranger? She's been through so much already."

"I'm her uncle—not a stranger. And surely you can see the advantages of a child being raised among her biological family?" Trent said as he stared down at Lana.

"She's not even two. She's not really interested in your stock portfolio," Lana said.

How had she let him sneak up on her like that?

"Dr. Montgomery—" the social worker started.

"Ma'am," Trent said as he tipped his big cowboy hat before sitting down beside her. "Please, call me Trent."

Lana watched as he gave the woman what she had overheard one of the nurses call his "killer" smile. He was such a suck-up.

"Trent, please take a seat."

The social worker's smile beamed back at Trent, causing Lana to knot her hands into fists in her lap when what she really wanted to do was wrap them around the man's neck.

"I was just telling Lana that I know this is not easy for her. It must be hard for you too, having just lost your brother and now moving to Miami on such short notice. I was surprised when your lawyer notified me that you were relocating temporarily. I'm sure this has disrupted your life. You must have been very close to your brother to be willing to make these changes."

Lana saw the smile on his face tighten. She didn't have any doubt that there was a story there. Had there been trouble between the brothers? Was there something she could use?

"With my brother gone, I feel that it is my responsibility to make sure his daughter is taken care of," Trent said, and then he turned in his chair toward Lana. "That's what families are for. Wouldn't you agree, Lana?"

Lana looked into Trent's eyes. Somehow he had managed to turn the tables on her, making any protest she might come up with seem heartless and uncaring. Well, two could play that game.

"Yes, families *are* important. That's why I've decided to agree to you spending some time with Maggie," Lana said, and she watched Trent to see his reaction to this piece of news.

She'd thought her lawyer crazy when he'd advised her to consider the visitation, but after he had explained that it would be a way to show the courts that she was willing to allow Maggie to see her biological family after the adoption it had made sense. She was willing to do whatever was necessary to keep her little girl—even if it meant spending time with an irritating cowboy.

"That sounds great, Lana. I'm so glad that the two of you are working together so well," Ms. Nelson said. "The reason I asked for this meeting was so that we could discuss where we go from here. I know the two of you are on different sides in this case, but I want you both to remember the most important thing to consider here is Maggie and her wellbeing."

"Of course," Lana said, and then looked over at Trent.

"Certainly, Ms. Nelson," Trent said.

Lana watched the corners of Trent's mouth twitch, as if trying to hold back a smile. Why did she suddenly feel she had fallen into a trap? A trap with a big, bad smiling wolf in it, waiting to devour her.

"Good," said Ms. Nelson. "I take it you two will come to terms with the visitation arrangements, so unless there is anything else that comes up I won't need to see either of you again till the DNA test results come back."

"That's fine," Trent said. "I feel sure me and Lana will be able to come to an agreement."

"I'm sure we will," Lana said. *An agreement?* She'd have to remind him that she would be the person in control of their meetings.

"Thank you for your time, Ms. Nelson," Trent said, blessing the social worker with another one of his smiles as they rose to leave.

Lana walked beside Trent as they left the office building. He'd been quiet as they had ridden down on an overcrowded elevator. It had been uncomfortable, being squeezed next to him. It seemed that no matter how much she tried, she couldn't get away from the man.

They could play nice together in front of the social worker, but that was as far as she could go with it. Just standing next to him was enough to fire up her defenses. This man was a threat to her and she knew she had to stay alert.

Of course there was that saying about keeping your enemies closer than your friends. Was that what Trent was doing by coming to work where he knew he'd be able to observe her? Not that there was any dirt he could dig up on her. She had never lived much of an exciting life. She had even started to think lately that she was getting to be just plain old boring.

Maybe after Maggie's adoption had taken place she'd take up a hobby, or get back in the dating pool. *Maybe*.

Thoughts of Joe and the way their relationship had ended left her shaking her head. Even though the man had professed that he loved her, it hadn't been enough. Not enough to make him want a future with a woman who couldn't give him children.

Her dream of a forever marriage—a marriage filled with love and support like her parents'—had been destroyed the day they'd broken up and she'd had to accept that she would probably never be able to find a man who would accept her as she was, damaged and broken.

No, she wasn't going anywhere near heartache any

time soon. She had created her own little family with Maggie and that was enough. Now she just had to find a way to keep her family intact and get this cowboy back to Texas. And, as much as it was going to kill her, it was going to mean spending some time with him.

"Look, we need to talk about this visitation. There will have to be some rules. Are you hungry?" Lana asked.

"Yeah, I skipped lunch so that I could get off on time," Trent said.

"There's a little Cuban deli I usually stop by when I'm down here," Lana said. "The food's good and the people are friendly."

Lana watched as Trent's lips twitched, as if he was unable to decide how to take her invitation, and then they parted. Something about his bright smile caused her warning bells to go off. *Danger, danger*, they said, but it was too late. For the second time that day she felt as if she was the fly that was getting caught up in Trent's web.

Maybe from now on they should discuss these visitations over the phone.

"Sounds good," Trent said. "Do we walk or drive?"

"Walk," Lana said.

She found herself about to smile back at him before she caught herself. She couldn't let herself be influenced by this man's charms. They would discuss the necessary arrangements and maybe she'd also try to pry a little information out of him. This was about Maggie—not the stupid way his smile made her legs wobble as she started walking up the street.

She had found Café MaRita on one of her visits to the Children and Families Department office, and she was glad to see the two sisters who owned the deli were working when she arrived at the walk-up window.

"Hey, Rita," Lana said, then waved to Mary in the back, where she was putting together the spicy sandwiches they were known for. "Can I get two Cubanos, an iced tea and…?" Lana turned to Trent questioning.

"A coffee, please," Trent said. "A *cafecito*?"

The small Cuban woman smiled at his pronunciation of the word for a coffee topped with sugary foam.

"I like this one," Rita said, and she winked at Trent. "He's dark and hot. Like my coffee. If you decide to get rid of him let me know."

"Oh, no," Lana said as she felt heat spread up her face, "it's not like that—"

"I'll make it a point to look you up when she's finished with me," Trent said, interrupting Lana.

Did the man have to flirt with every woman he met? Taking the sandwiches, she found an empty picnic table set out in the front of the deli and started dividing the food while she waited for Trent.

Watching him as he talked to the older Cuban woman while she prepared their drinks, Lana was impressed at how at ease he seemed with people. He had the ability to charm everyone he met—well, everyone except for her. The only thing *she* would find charming about him would be his backside headed out of town.

Trent watched Lana as she bit into her sandwich. He could see she was concentrating on something, and he didn't think it was just the sandwich she was eating— though she did seem to be enjoying it. It was nice to see a woman eat her food without any posturing about diets and calories.

He watched as the pink tip of her tongue slipped out and caught some of the juice running down the side of her mouth. From nowhere a burst of desire filled him, and he felt a jolt of arousal as it spread down his groin. Another swipe of her tongue along the crease of her mouth had his pants becoming uncomfortably tight.

He shifted in his seat, causing Lana to suddenly look up from her meal, and he knew the second their eyes connected that he wasn't hiding the hunger that had hit him. The surprise came when her eyes changed and she lifted her eyebrows, silently questioning him. If this was any other woman he might have thought she was purposely playing with him, but that just didn't seem like Lana's style.

"Sorry, I haven't found a way to eat these without making a mess," Lana said.

"That's okay. I'm actually enjoying watching you." Trent said, then watched spots of color flush her cheeks.

"Tell me why you decided to go into medicine instead of staying in the family business," Lana said, changing the subject.

His gut tightened as he thought of the decision he had made to follow his dreams. Would his brother still be here if he hadn't left him behind with his father? He had let Michael down when he'd walked away from his father's expectations for him. In saving himself from becoming the heir apparent to the Montgomery empire he had left his brother to deal with their father's unreasonable demands and bouts of temper.

No one had ever been good enough for their father. No one had been able to stand up to the old man's expectations. Not him, not their mother, and certainly not his brother. He had urged his brother to follow after him and get away from his father's influence, but Michael hadn't been strong enough. He'd even tried to talk his brother into the two of them joining together and using their share of the company stocks to oust their father from his position as head of the company, but Michael had refused.

Instead, Michael had continually tried to earn their father's approval, and when that hadn't happened he had turned to the same thing their mother had used to escape their father: alcohol. And when that hadn't been enough he had turned to drugs, until finally the two had killed him.

"You could say I did follow in one of my family's footsteps. My Uncle Jim was a surgeon. He had a lot of influence on my decision," Trent answered. She didn't need to know the turmoil his decision had caused to his family.

"Any regrets?" Lana asked.

"What?" Trent asked, startled by the question.

Did she know about the division in his family? Had she somehow learned about the threats and bribes his father constantly sent him, trying to get him to come back to the family-run business?

"I don't know much about the oil business, but I do know about all the demands and sacrifices a medical career requires. It just seems you could have had a pretty good thing going for you, working in your own company," Lana said.

"I find being a pediatrician very satisfying and challenging. And I can make far more of a difference as a pediatrician than as a businessman, don't you think?" Trent said.

He stood and started gathering up items from the

table to throw out. For now, the less this woman knew about his business, the better.

"You said you wanted to discuss the visitations?" Trent said.

"Yes, I do. I hope you understand that just because I'm letting you spend time with Maggie it doesn't mean I've changed my mind about keeping her?"

"I think you've made that plain," Trent said.

The only way she could have made her intentions any plainer would have been for her to tattoo them on her body. He had no doubt this woman was going to fight him all the way.

"Okay, then. I'm willing to allow visitations as long as it's understood that I'm in charge of everything that concerns her. I'll always be present and I'll have the final word on when and where."

After the short walk back, Trent watched as Lana's car pulled out of the parking garage. Nothing he had learned so far, today or at the hospital, indicated that she was anything other than a young woman working as a midwife and raising a child she loved as her own. He couldn't help but like her, and he hated that she was being pulled into this mess with his father, but he didn't see any way out of it. And it was better that she had to deal with him instead of the old man. At least he fought fair. He couldn't say that about his father.

They had arranged a time for him to visit Maggie during their walk back to their cars and Lana had been more than fair with him. Everything he had heard around the hospital about Lana had been positive. He even felt a little guilty that he had taken a job here to see what he could dig up on her. From what he had seen so far there wasn't anything in her character that made him think he needed to be worried about his niece not being cared for, or that there was anything he could use against her in the court case.

But he knew how appearances could be deceptive. Hadn't his mom had everyone fooled until it was too late? No one had ever known about the fights between his parents. or the times when his mother had never even got out of the bed in the mornings, leaving two little boys to care for themselves.

He knew first-hand that no one ever really knew what went on behind the closed doors of a home. No matter how much Lana Sanders looked like the perfect mother, he would be sticking to the woman like glue until he had custody of his niece and knew without a doubt that she was safe.

# CHAPTER THREE

TRENT STOOD ON the sidewalk outside Lana's home. He had seen a lot of these small block houses since he had arrived in Miami and though they were older buildings, he liked them.

The neat bungalows reminded him of the difference between his life in Houston and Maggie and Lana's here. While his condo in the busy metropolis area was modern, with all the amenities available, Lana's front yard was full of pink and yellow blooms and looked friendly and inviting. And whereas a doorman met visitors on arrival in his building, a colorful gnome sat on Lana's small porch, holding a "Welcome" sign which made even Trent feel as if he would be greeted warmly.

Of course neither of the two places compared to his father's ranch, where he had grown up. Even with the chaos that had made up his parents' relationship he had always felt at home there, with its sprawling acres of pastures. He had been able to escape for long rides on one of his horses and he'd come back feeling better every time. He had to admit he missed that feeling of being at home, of belonging somewhere.

Lana answered the door looking every bit the suburban mom in her tee shirt and jeans. While he might have thought the "mom look" would put him off, he was surprised to find that he liked it on her. She looked comfortable in the mommy role.

"Hey," Lana said as she held the door open.

There was a nervousness about her today that had him thinking she was having second thoughts about letting him into her home.

"Is everything okay?" Trent asked. "If you've changed you mind and want to…?"

"No," Lana said. "I'm sorry. Come in. Maggie's in her room, playing."

Lana directed Trent down the hall, where he found a room decorated in light pinks and purples. Sitting in the middle of the floor was a little girl, pouring what had to be pretend tea into a group of small cups. The table where she sat was surrounded by tiny chairs, upon one of which a rabbit was waiting to be served.

"Maggie?" Lana called the toddler's attention to her. "This is the man I told you was coming to see you. His name is Trent."

The raven-haired child looked up at Trent and a long-forgotten memory hit him as if it were a physical blow. While Maggie's eyes were blue, like both his and his brother's, the shade was slightly different. He had only seen that shade of clear cerulean blue once and, though his memories of his mother after all these years were few, he could still remember her eyes. The same eyes that now stared back at him from the face of the small girl who was studying him with a seriousness he was surprised to see in one so young.

"Maggie, will you let Trent play with you while I get your snack?" Lana asked.

"Cookie?" the child said as she looked back at her.

Trent watched as the toddler turned her smile on Lana. It was easy to see that Maggie had already begun developing the Montgomery negotiation skills.

"You can have two," Lana said as she held up two fingers, "with your juice."

Maggie smiled back at Lana, then got up and walked over to him. "Play?" she asked as she looked up at him.

"Ah…okay…" Trent said, surprised by the nervousness that suddenly hit him.

He was a pediatrician, for heaven's sake. He cared for kids of all ages in his practice. There was no reason for this one little girl to scare him, but inside his heart he knew there *was* a difference between this child and his patients. This was his brother's little girl. She was *family.*

Before the panic had time to overwhelm him, the child said something in an unknown language, then pulled on his hand. He shot a look back at Lana, who just smiled at them, then turned and left the room.

Lana stood and looked out the kitchen window. She couldn't help the smile she saw reflected in the window pane. The look on Trent's face had been priceless. How could a man who took care of sick children every day at work be scared of one little girl?

Just knowing that he was as uneasy about this meeting as she was made her feel a little better. She had been nervous about having Trent in her home. She knew her home was old and small, but she had made a comfortable place there for herself and Maggie. Would a man like Trent be able to appreciate the small house for what it was? A home where she and Maggie had become a family?

She watched as the smile that had been reflected just moments earlier disappeared.

A family—everything a little girl dreamed of. But when you were fifteen years old, and adults were telling you that you had cancer, the last thing you thought of was your infertility. She had just wanted to know if she would live long enough to make it to junior prom. But while she had worried about the chemo and the radiation causing her hair to fall out, she should have been worried about what the treatments were doing to the inside of her body instead.

Being told that you would not be able to have children at any age was a horrible thing. Being a teenager and learning that you would never be able to give birth to a child had been devastating.

She had given up on her dream of having a family and instead had thrown herself into high school and later her college education. Once she had gotten her degree in nursing she had found her calling in labor and delivery. If she could not have a child herself, at least she could help bring children into the world.

Then during her last year at midwifery school her Prince Charming had come and she had thought her life would be perfect from then on out. When a year later she had discovered that her prince, Joe, was really a frog, warts and all, it had been too late.

When the man she'd loved had told her that he just couldn't settle for a woman who wasn't able to give him children she had hit the lowest point in her life. But then Maggie had come along and everything had felt right. She *knew* she was meant to have Maggie, but how could she convince the man in the next room?

She finished fixing the drinks—two iced teas for

them and one sippy cup of juice for Maggie—and then stacked some of the cookies she had made earlier that morning on a tray. She stopped at the door, then covered her mouth to hold a laugh inside as she watched her daughter initiate Trent the manly cowboy into the world of playing pretend with a little girl.

He sat on the floor cross-legged, in front of the small table, with a pink polka dot hat on top of his head, and pretended to drink from a small plastic cup.

"Would you like some real tea?" Lana asked. "Sorry, I don't have any coffee."

"Tea's fine," Trent said. "But it will have to be some brew to compete with Maggie's. Isn't that right, Maggie?"

Maggie gave Trent a beaming smile. Somehow in the few minutes Lana had been gone Trent had managed to charm her little girl—not that she could blame her. There wasn't a female around who could withstand this man when he was smiling like he was right then.

She had heard all the rumors about the hospital nurses making fools of themselves around him, and if she was honest with herself she had to admit that being around him made her feel just as enchanted as the rest of womankind.

That was just what the man *wanted* her to feel, but she wasn't stupid enough to let a little bit of physical attraction muddle her brain. If he thought that he could charm her into letting her guard down around him, he was wrong.

Getting Maggie to settle down for a nap after finishing her snack had been a chore, but finally the toddler had tearfully waved goodbye to Trent and Lana had carried the worn-out baby to her room and put her in her crib.

She shut the door quietly and found Trent standing behind her.

"She's beautiful," Trent said, with a reverence that touched something deep down inside her.

Lana felt the same way every day she spent with Maggie. She was surprised at how sharing this feeling of caring for a child made her suddenly feel so close to him. Was this another ploy on his part?

"Thanks for letting me see her," Trent said softly.

Lana pushed her hair out of her face and looked up at him. It was easy to see that he had been moved by the time he had spent with Maggie. It had to be hard for him after the loss of his brother—to see this reminder of him.

"Are you okay?" she asked.

"It shouldn't be me standing here," he said. "It should be my brother."

"What happened to him, Trent?"

"Michael had the same problems as Chloe. His addiction of choice was alcohol, though recently he had begun combining it with drugs. One night he just took too many…"

Michael's voice cracked for a second, and then he cleared his throat.

"And now he's not here to enjoy that beautiful little girl," he said.

Suddenly she was aware of the closeness caused by the small hallway, and for a moment she felt the need to reach out and touch him, to smooth away the pain she saw in his face. And then she remembered the reason he was standing here in her house. He had come to establish a relationship with her daughter—a relationship that he intended to continue by taking Maggie away from her.

"I won't let you take her without a fight," Lana said.

Her body was relaxed, more comfortable with the anger inside her than with the attraction that had wound so tightly inside her body just seconds earlier.

"I know," Trent said.

His whisper seemed to bounce off the walls of the hallway. He reached up and pushed a stray hair behind her ear, his touch leaving a soft tingle behind. Then he turned and walked out of her house, leaving her alone with her young daughter, and for the first time since she had moved in it felt empty.

She'd worked hard to make her home a safe place, her retreat from the world after a hard day. She had accepted that she might never meet a man who could give her the forever love that she longed for—the type of love she'd witnessed between her parents—but she had made a home here for her little family and she would not let anyone take that away from her.

"You are doing *great*, Jaden," Lana said as she watched her patient breathe through another contraction.

The fetal heart tones were reassuring, but the labor process had slowed down. If there wasn't a change soon, the OB on call would start questioning if Jaden was going to be able to have a vaginal birth. The baby's posterior position was just not allowing it to come farther down into the birth canal.

"We can try moving you back onto your knees and see if we can get the baby to turn, if you'd like," Lana said.

"It didn't help last time," Jaden said as she took a deep breath and prepared for the next contraction.

"I know you wanted to do this without any type of pain control—" Lana started.

"She went through all the classes," Jaden's sister said.

"I know, and she's doing great. But the labor has gotten long now, and I really think we need to consider all our options. That includes an epidural," Lana said as she took the cool washcloth a nurse handed her and wiped Jaden's face.

"They said it would slow down labor," Jaden said.

"Sometimes it can, but right now your labor is not progressing at all," Lana said.

"I'll think about it," Jaden said.

The phone clipped to Lana's green scrubs pocket vibrated. She knew it had to be the office again.

"I'm going to step out for a moment," Lana said. "Why don't you think about whether getting an epidural is something you want to do while I take this call?"

Lana nodded to the nurse and walked out of the room. A call to her office told her that the department was packed with patients waiting to see her. The crowd was getting restless and her staff needed to know what to tell the women who were waiting.

Some days Lana needed to be cloned. Today was one of those days.

After talking with her office nurse, and catching up on Jaden's progress notes, she returned to the labor room. The sight of the anesthesiologist standing at the bottom of the bed and talking to her patient told her Jaden had decided to opt for the epidural.

"They decided on the epidural," the nurse, Shelley, whispered as she leaned toward Lana.

The door opened and Trent walked in, carrying a clipboard. He nodded to her, then moved over to Jaden as the anesthesiologist started setting up his tray.

"Trent is so good with the patients," the nurse said. "He makes a point to come and see them before they deliver, and they love him."

"His name is Dr. Montgomery," Lana said, and then regretted it as soon as she saw the questioning look on Shelley's face.

It wasn't any of her business if Trent got friendly with the nurses. She couldn't even blame them for wanting to get his attention. The man appeared to be a sexual magnet for women. Didn't she know it herself? She couldn't keep her own traitorous body from responding to the sexual pull of him, but that didn't mean she had to like it.

She moved over to the bed and helped the nurse position Jaden for her epidural. Trent stood to one side while she answered some of Jaden's sister's questions.

She thought about that moment in her hallway, when for a second she had felt a connection with him, When he'd touched her she had been sure he had felt it too. Had that moment been real or had she just imagined it? And why was she standing in the middle of a labor room thinking about Trent instead of her patient?

Forcing her attention back to where it should have stayed, Lana took her place to help her patient concentrate on her breathing and remain in the proper position. Just as they were ready, her phone rang.

"If you need to get that I can help," Trent said. "Unless you want to?" He addressed the patient's sister.

"Oh, no, I hate needles," the sister said, and she moved across the room as far away as she could.

As her phone went to voicemail Lana relaxed. Then

it immediately rang again. Someone was certainly being persistent.

"Have you ever helped with an epidural before?" she asked.

"I can't say I have, but I'm willing to learn," Trent said.

"Okay, come over here and help support her," Lana said as her phone continued to ring.

She traded places with Trent, then left the room to take the call.

When she stepped back into the room she was hit with a picture of Trent bent over Jaden, talking quietly as he assured her that they were almost finished. Anyone else walking in might easily have thought he was just another father helping his wife get through her labor.

The thought caused a small pain in her heart.

Fifteen minutes later Jaden was lying down and tilted onto her left side. While it would take several minutes for the medication to reach its full effect, Lana could tell by the way Jaden was starting to relax into the bed that she was already starting to feel some relief.

Lana checked the fetal monitor, then suggested a nap for both Jaden and her sister.

"Since you seem to always be feeding me, I thought I'd buy you lunch this time," Trent said as they stepped out of the labor room.

Lana glanced down the hallway and saw that two of the labor nurses had stopped and were looking their way. While she and Trent were standing outside one of the hospital rooms it would look as if they were discussing a patient's care, and no one would make any comments. But if they were sitting together at a table in the hospital café…?

That would definitely stir up the rumor mill.

"It might not be a good idea," Lana said.

"I promise I won't discuss the court case," Trent said, and then leaned against the wall looking at her expectantly. "I heard they're serving fried potato casserole today. You wouldn't want to miss *that*, would you?"

"So I treat you to the city's best *cubano* and my famous chocolate chip cookies and the best you can do is that? Besides, I need to get back to my office."

"I'd be happy to do better," Trent said. "How about dinner Saturday night?"

Lana felt her senses go on alert. The teasing tone in his voice was gone now. Was this another one of his tricks to get to her?

"I thought we had agreed to a visitation with Maggie on Saturday at the beach?" Lana asked.

"I'm talking about after our day at the beach," Trent said.

Lana watched as Trent pushed off the wall and took a step closer. That flirty smile he had flashed earlier was gone, leaving her in no doubt that he was serious in his invitation.

"What do you want from me?" she asked, unable to keep the stress from her voice.

Was this another ploy to get her to cave in to the Montgomery demands for custody of Maggie?

"Look, Lana, whether we like it or not, until the court makes its decision we're going to have to get along. It just seems like it would be easier if we got to know each other better."

And then his smile was back with all its magical appeal.

"I'm really not a bad guy, you know."

Maybe he wasn't a bad guy, but he was still the enemy.

"Okay," Lana said.

If he wanted to get to know her better—fine. It wasn't as if that was going to change her mind about keeping Maggie. Besides, maybe if he got to know her better he'd see that Maggie was where she needed to be. It would definitely be harder for him to take her daughter away from someone he'd come to know instead of a stranger.

It was a long shot, but she would take any chances she could get to keep her daughter.

"But don't say I didn't warn you about the fried potato casserole. You'll need to get your cholesterol checked as soon as lunch is over."

She arrived back on the labor and delivery unit to find Jaden almost ready for delivery. After less than an hour of pushing she delivered a healthy eight-pound baby boy. As Trent handed the new mom her baby her patient thanked him for all his help, and as Lana left the unit she thought about how Trent had been so good with her.

The quick lunch they had shared had been relaxing. They had discussed some of the differences between his job on the pediatric floor at his Houston hospital and the neonatal unit he was working in here. She'd been able to tell he had a true love for his job in Houston, and she couldn't help but wonder again at his choice to leave it to pursue his court case.

Neither one of them had brought up the custody case, and for the first time there hadn't been any conflict between them. Was it possible that they could work together without letting their outside problems get in the way? It looked as if they might be able to, but she knew she was walking on thin ice when it came to any type of relationship between the two of them.

It would be a very easy man to let her guard down around a man like Trent, and no matter how at ease she might feel around him she needed to remember they were on opposite sides when it came to Maggie. That was truly all that counted.

# CHAPTER FOUR

As SHE DRAGGED HERSELF through the front door, the quiet house told Lana that Amanda had already put Maggie to bed. She hated to miss that time of day, when Maggie, with damp curls and smelling of baby wash, would climb up into her lap and snuggle while they read a book together, but as hard as she'd tried she hadn't been able to catch up at the office without staying late.

As soon as she shut the door Amanda stepped out of the kitchen carrying two glasses of some kind of pink fruity-looking drink.

"Energy smoothie," she said as she handed one of the drinks to Lana. "You sounded like you could use a pick-me-up when you called."

"Thanks," Lana said.

The refreshing liquid slid down easily, bringing a soothing feeling through her body. She took a quick peek into Maggie's room and found her sleeping like an angel, then headed back into the living room. She let herself slump down on her couch and found herself relaxing for the first time all day.

She toed her shoes off and wiggled her tired feet. Dorothy in *The Wizard of Oz* was so right. There was no place like home.

"I left some pasta on the stove. You want me to fix you a plate?" Amanda asked.

"No, thanks. I'll get it later."

"Bad day, huh?" the young woman asked.

Amanda had been Maggie's live-in babysitter since Maggie was two months old. She had been there on those days when Lana had come home thrilled with the experience of having been a part of bringing a new baby into the world, and she had been there when Lana had come home emotionally torn up after giving an expectant mom news that had destroyed their hopes and dreams.

Today had been neither of those. It had just been very long.

She played over the events of the day, remembering the delivery she had done and the part Trent had played in it.

She hadn't been able to get his invitation to dinner off her mind. She would have to decide what she wanted to do about it. It should be an easy decision. She had told herself not to let their relationship become any more personal, but after their lunch together she was finding it hard to ignore her desire to see him some more.

"Lana...?"

"Oh, sorry. I zoned out for a minute," she answered. "Not really bad. I just ran late all day after a long delivery."

She sipped her drink and considered her options. She could try to ignore Trent, with the hope that he would soon go away, or she could let him get to know her better, with the hope that she would make him see that she was the perfect mother for Maggie.

The question of why he was pushing to spend more time with her kept circling in her mind, reminding her to beware of good-looking men with possible hidden agendas…reminding her of the need to stay on alert. What was he up to?

"What do you think about Trent Montgomery?" she asked.

Amanda studied her over the rim of her glass, then finally asked, "As an uncle to Maggie?"

"No. Not in relationship to Maggie."

Lana sat up straight and adjusted the pillows on the couch. Grabbing one, she hugged it close to her body, then combed her fingers through the satin cord tassels.

"So you mean as a man?" Amanda asked.

Lana nodded at Amanda. While she knew the baby-sitter was very protective of both her and Maggie, she also knew that she'd be honest and fair in her opinion.

"Well…" A big smile spread across Amanda's face. "If it wasn't for his involvement in stopping the adoption, I'd probably be thinking about jumping his bones— just like you."

"Amanda!" she said, feigning shock and throwing the pillow she'd been holding at her friend's laughing face. "I haven't—"

"Well, maybe you should." Amanda laughed again as Lana grabbed another pillow and shot it toward her.

She could feel the heat of embarrassment spreading up her face. Okay, maybe since they'd had that moment in her hallway she *had* been having dreams which included getting Trent out of his scrubs. Or his suit. Or whatever he had been wearing the last time she saw him. But she wasn't going to admit it.

"He asked me out."

"Like on a date?"

"More of a let's-get-to-know-each-other-better kind of thing, I think," Lana said.

"Wow," Amanda said. "Are you going?"

"I'm thinking about it," she answered.

The look of surprise on Amanda's face mirrored her own. Was she seriously thinking about spending time alone with Trent? Was she crazy?

"I don't know if I should be more shocked by the fact that you're even considering going out or by who you're considering going out *with*," Amanda said.

"Trent wants Maggie, Amanda—nothing else."

"What about you? What do *you* want?" Amanda asked.

And that was the problem. One moment the man was irritating her, with his *I'm Maggie's uncle and I know what's best for her* attitude, and the next he was charming her with that Texas drawl and that sexy smile of his. And then there was that irritating tingling she felt whenever he was near—a physical awareness of him that made her want to run far away but at the same time want to seek him out.

None of it made sense, and spending more time with him would be like playing with fire. No matter how safe you thought you were, there was still a possibility that you'd get burnt.

Of course the good thing was that he'd be leaving as soon as the court came up with a ruling on Maggie's custody. A ruling that could result in her losing Maggie.

That thought sobered her out of her daydream. Making sure that didn't happen was what she needed to concentrate on. As soon as the adoption was finalized she would think about getting back out in the dating jungle. The attraction she was feeling for Trent was just another sign that she'd been too long without a man in her life. She'd thought after what she'd gone through with Joe that she had accepted she had no need for a man in her life. Apparently she had been wrong.

"I just want life to go back to the way it was before he showed up," Lana said. "But I need to keep an eye on him. Hopefully he'll be leaving soon."

"And without Maggie," Amanda said, with a confidence that Lana wished she felt.

"Without Maggie," Lana seconded, and the two of them clinked their glasses together.

As the bikini clad blond roller-skated around them Lana considered her choice of beach once again. While she was usually comfortable with her body, now, seeing all the perfectly tanned beauties who flocked to the South Beach location. she felt self-conscious, knowing her body was not like the thin, willowy specimens out on display today.

She had what her mother had always referred to as "a curvy figure." She had never been lacking in the breast department, and her hips and thighs were definitely wider than those belonging to the women on all the magazine covers that tried to tell you what you should look like.

Her body was basically just like the rest of her— nothing above average—and up until now she had always been okay with that. She knew the only reason she felt inadequate now was because she had seen the women Trent was normally photographed with. But she wasn't one of those women. She was just herself and she needed to accept it.

"Here?" Trent motioned toward the crosswalk over to the beach.

He had insisted on carrying Maggie through the crowd, instead of using the stroller she kept in the car to help with carrying both baby and all the items that were needed when traveling with a toddler.

"Let's wait till the next one," Lana said, not wanting to mention that she was trying to avoid the topless section of the beach.

"You know, we have beaches in Texas, but they're not nearly as entertaining as this," Trent said as a second barely clad woman skated past.

A sleek cherry-red muscle car drove by, blaring music out the windows, making it impossible to talk. It was still quite early for the weekend crowd, but it appeared they were all ready to party even at this hour.

Lana had chosen to go early so that she could get Maggie back home in time for a nap, but she was also hoping to escape before the afternoon crowd showed up, making it impossible to get through on the small streets crowded with shops and restaurants.

"We can take the next crossover."

Lana moved in close, trying to avoid a group of tourists standing outside the old-fashioned soda shop. She felt the warm heat of Trent's hand when he reached around her waist and guided her through the crowd. They crossed the street to the entrance for the beach. When they reached the thick sand he moved his hand to grip her elbow, helping her as she plodded down to the shore.

They found a space with room to stretch out a blanket and Trent let the toddler down, but kept hold of her hand as she pulled him closer to the waves.

Grabbing some sunscreen, Lana joined them and began to slather lotion over Maggie as she giggled and stomped her feet in the water.

"Be still, you little wiggle-worm!" Lana laughed as she fought to make sure there weren't any areas not covered.

Maggie, deciding it was a game, squirmed around Trent's leg, causing Lana to miss the intended cheek and smear lotion across Trent's leg. At the feel of the coarse hair on this intimate part of Trent's thigh Lana's face flushed with redness. This had been such a bad idea.

"I'm so sorry…" Lana said, and she scooted back fast, almost tripping over Maggie.

"No problem—thanks for helping me with the sunscreen," Trent said.

She watched a smile curve across his lips that let her know he found her embarrassment amusing.

He picked up Maggie and held her out at arm's length. "I'll hold her for you."

Lana quickly finished with the lotion and then grabbed the little hand Maggie held out to her after Trent put her back down on the sand.

"Me play. *Now*," Maggie demanded, and she pulled down on both the adult hands holding her back from the waves.

They walked out a couple feet until Maggie could feel the cool water lap against her legs. Again she pulled down on Lana and Trent's arms, and she started swinging back and forth while dragging her feet through the water and giggling.

All around them people were wading out into the water or stretching out on the coarse sand. It was a great place for Maggie to play, and in minutes all three of them were laughing. with water soaking through their clothes.

They walked back to their blanket, where Trent set Maggie up with her pail and shovel. Lana started to peel her wet shirt off, then turned just in time to see Trent lift his own shirt over his head. For a second she had a full view of a firm, toned chest with a small strip of hair. She followed the dark line down to where it disappeared into a water-soaked bathing suit that molded around his groin, leaving very little to her imagination.

Realizing she had been guilty of staring, she looked up to find Trent's eyes glued to her face. She had definitely been caught. Where was a Florida sink hole when you needed one?

She jerked her tee shirt up over her face and then peeked through the armhole to see him still staring at her. The stupidity of hiding there, with her shirt over her head, just increased her embarrassment. Acting like a sex-starved female was bad enough—not having the courage to own up to it was worse.

She finished pulling off her shirt, moving slowly to disguise her nervousness. One look at Trent had her wishing her shirt was back in place. A smile still filled his face, but the heat now in his eyes out-burned the Florida sun.

A warm stream of desire began in her chest and then flowed down to pool deep into her core. How did he *do* that? It was as if he was touching her with those beautiful eyes, melting her with the heat she saw in them. As if reading her mind, he swept her body with one more appreciative look, causing her body to respond with a need she had long forgotten and didn't want to remember.

"Me, me!" Maggie cried as she pulled down on

Trent's bathing suit, not happy that she had lost her new friend's attention.

"What a beautiful child—you must be very proud."

The voice cut through her thoughts and Lana looked over to where an older couple had stopped to admire Maggie. She was used to being stopped by strangers, commenting on her little girl.

"Thank you," Lana said.

"It's so nice to see a young family spending time together," the elderly woman continued.

"Oh, we're not—" Lana started to correct her.

"You're a lucky man," the white-headed man complimented Trent.

"Yes, I am," Trent said as he placed his arm around Lana's shoulders and pulled her close to his side. "Thank you."

The couple waved goodbye to Maggie, then continued their walk down the beach hand in hand.

"Okay. Let's make us a big castle," Trent said as he let go of Lana and knelt down to help fill the pail full of wet sand.

"Why did you do that?" Lana sputtered.

"Did you *really* want to try to explain our unique relationship to them?"

Unique? Yeah, that would be a good description for them.

No one seeing the two of them together with Maggie would think there was a battle going on between the two of them. For a minute while they had played together in the water she had forgotten herself. It had just seemed so natural and right for the two of them to be enjoying time with this beautiful child.

She knew she needed to take a step back from Trent

and see what was really happening here. She had no doubt that there were ulterior motives behind all the attention he had been giving her lately.

Playing "Mommy and Daddy" with Trent would only get her hurt. It was too close to the happily-ever-after dream she'd carried with her for years—the dream that had died when Joe had walked out on her.

She and Maggie made a great family. They didn't need anyone else in their life.

"I think I'll stretch out and catch some sun, if you don't mind watching her," Lana said as she stepped away.

"Sure. Relax. I've got Maggie," he said as he looked across at her.

Knowing he hadn't meant that in any way except to say that he was watching over her little girl, Lana tried to make herself think of nothing except enjoying the salty breeze and Maggie's laughter as her little girl played with Trent.

Sometimes you just had to pull a Scarlett O'Hara and save your worrying for tomorrow, so you didn't waste the day you'd been given. That was a lesson that cancer had taught her very early in life.

Trent hung up the phone after listening to his father's message right before he turned into Lana's drive. He had known his father would be curious about his missing the latest board meeting of Montgomery and Lord, and that it was just a matter of time before his father started to make inquiries into his absence.

He had to make a decision about whether to continue with his plans or to trust Lana with the information that as of now was only known by him and his lawyer.

It had seemed so simple when he had first decided

to come to Florida and get custody of his niece. First he would hire a nanny and make sure the child was taken care of. Then he'd approach his father with his brother's will and make sure the old man knew that he no longer had any power to manipulate others the way he had his wife and younger son.

Trent got out of the car and smoothed his dark dress pants as he tried to clear his mind of all the pain and anger that immediately consumed him when he thought of his father. The old man had a lot to answer for, and for the first time in his life Trent might have the means of making him pay for his sins.

But first he had to decide what to do about Lana. Could he trust her to understand the danger his father was to Maggie? More importantly, would she trust *him* if she learned about the stipulations in Michael's will?

He had no explanation for the intimate tug he felt drawing them closer together, but it was easy to see that the physical attraction between them made Lana uncomfortable. With the little he had learned about her he knew she was as much out of her comfort zone with him as he was with her.

He had felt her pull away from him as soon as they had left the beach and he hadn't liked it. After Maggie had fallen asleep in her car seat Lana had been quiet until they had arrived back at her place, where she had very curtly thanked him for the trip to the beach. Then she had stated that she didn't think it was a good idea for them to go out to dinner together.

He'd somehow managed to turn the conversation around, though, so that she had agreed to go out with him tonight to "discuss their options" in relation to Maggie. He couldn't help but smile when he thought of that clipped tone her voice took on when she turned all Momma Bear on him.

He ran his hands through his hair and let out a heartfelt groan. Why was he rethinking all his carefully laid plans *now*? It had been a lot easier to think of taking his niece away from some stranger than it was to execute that plan now. The more time he spent with Lana the harder it was going to be to take Maggie away from her.

It seemed as if his plan to stick close to Lana and Maggie was starting to backfire on him and he only had himself to blame.

Maggie checked the mirror one last time, turning to get a view of the way the black dress followed the curve of her hips, stopping a few inches before reaching the back of her knees. Turning back around, she admired the way the jeweled neckline that circled her neck sparkled. It had been a long time since she had dressed up for a date. Okay, so maybe it wasn't really a date, but she still deserved a little mirror-time.

"You look hot," Amanda said from where she sat on the edge of the bed. "Doesn't Mommy look hot, Maggie?"

"Hot?" Maggie asked, giving Lana a questioning look.

"No, Mommy's not hot," Lana said as she picked up the sweet-smelling toddler and snuggled her close. Nothing could be as angelic as a freshly bathed toddler all ready for bed.

"See?" Lana told Maggie as she tickled her belly. "Not hot."

"I'll have to ask Trent his opinion when he arrives," Amanda said, reaching over to take the toddler.

"You do and I'll tell that resident on the oncology floor that you were ogling his backside the other day when I stopped by."

"I was not… Okay, maybe I was." Amanda giggled. "But have you seen how cute he is in those scrubs?"

"Yeah," Lana said "it was all the nurses could talk about until…"

"Until the cowboy doctor showed up?" Amanda teased. "Too bad for them that the only person he seems to be looking back at is you."

"He just wants to get to know his niece," Lana said. "That's all it is," she insisted as she saw Amanda's expression in the mirror. "The only reason I agreed to go tonight was to see if I could find out more about him," she said. "I need all the ammunition I can get in this fight."

"Are you trying to convince me or yourself?" Amanda said as she hurried off to answer the door.

"Behave!" Lana called after her friend.

The last thing she needed was for Amanda to insinuate that there was something romantic going on between them. There was too much tension between them as it was. She didn't need Trent thinking that she was like all the other nurses in the hospital, who had joined the Team Trent fan club.

She would go out tonight and listen to what he had to say, and then she would get her turn to explain to the man why her daughter needed to stay with *her*.

# CHAPTER FIVE

TRENT HAD KNOWN he was in trouble the minute Lana had stepped into the tiny living room wearing that sexy as hell black dress. His hands had clenched with the need to explore the body wrapped up in all that slinky black material and the woman dressed in the package hadn't had a clue what she was doing to him.

She had stood there in her living room, with that same sweet smile of hers that screamed innocence, while every delicious curve of her had sent him into sexual overdrive. Then there were those ridiculously high gold heels that had her almost coming up to stand eye to eye to him. Did she have *any* idea what having her lips that much closer to his was doing to him?

If it had been one of his usual dating partners he'd have had no doubt that this was a calculated move to reel him in—but this woman? No, one of the things he found so surprising about her was her honesty. She said what she thought and expected the same of others. She didn't play crazy games that ended up causing hurt feelings and resentment.

As a young man he'd learned quickly that there were women in the world who would use their bodies to manipulate you if you gave them a chance. It was something he did not put up with. He'd seen enough drama in his life as a child with his parents; he didn't need any in his adult life.

It was going to be a long night, he decided as he joined Lana in the car and headed for the restaurant.

As they drove he kept the conversation to common small talk as he tried to get his body under control—something he found almost impossible with her sitting close beside him. Keeping his eyes on the road, he reminded his overheated body of all the complications getting involved with her would cause.

He was relieved to find that by the time they drove up to the entrance and he handed his keys over to the valet the self-control he depended on had taken over once more. He couldn't afford to show any sign of weakness to Lana.

Lana took her seat at the linen-draped table. Except for discussing his choice of the newest Brazilian steak house in town, they'd kept their conversation to discussions of work and weather. She waited until the waiter had taken their orders and moved away before trying to turn the conversation to a more personal topic.

"So, are you missing Houston yet?" she asked.

Maybe if she could get him talking about his home he'd open up more about his brother. She had to figure out if there was more to his seeking out Maggie and moving to Miami. She could understand he would have an interest in seeing that his niece was being taken care of, but most unmarried men would have made a fast check on the child then flown out of town as soon as possible.

But not Trent. No, he had dug in with both feet in

this custody battle. Somehow she just knew there was more going on than she was aware of. Just the mention of his brother and he turned to stone. Was he grieving? Yes, she was sure there was pain in his eyes when the subject came up, but there was much more that he was keeping to himself. It was the key to his being here in Miami and she wanted to know just what he was holding back from her.

"I miss my colleagues, and of course I miss Tanglefoot," Trent answered.

"Tanglefoot?" Lana asked. "Is that the name of some sort of animal or do you have a very clumsy friend?"

"She's a very stubborn horse," Trent said, "but I love her."

Lana watched the smile that lit his face as some unshared memory seemed to come to his mind. It was nice to see the man truly relax and lower those shields he kept up between himself and others. Or was it just *her* that he was trying to keep out?

They each chose a selection of meat from the platter one of the gauchos was serving from and then continued.

"So, where does Tanglefoot stay?" Lana asked. Maybe if she kept him on what seemed like a safe subject he would finally open up to her.

"She's at my family's ranch," Trent said.

"But you live in the city, right?" Lana asked between bites of thinly sliced beef.

"I have a place in the city, but I try to get away at least once a week," Trent answered. "I spend as much of my off-time helping around the ranch as possible"

"Like what? Riding fences and looking for stray cattle?" Lana asked.

"Yeah, some…" Trent answered.

"Really?" Lana asked.

Trent gave one of his killer smiles that had her imagining him in his jeans and boots. She had no problem envisioning him on his horse, waving his hat as he rode off into the sunset.

"There's only a few hundred head of cattle left now. My father is more interested in the oil industry. But the ranch has been in my mother's family for a long time, so I try to keep an eye on the place. I like to spend time with the horses and do some of the necessary maintenance around the place."

"I can't really see you as a handyman," Lana said. No, she definitely saw him more as a cowboy.

"I might surprise you," Trent said, and flashed her another one of his potent smiles. "I'm pretty good with my hands."

Lana looked down at her plate, trying to ignore his intended innuendo. She wasn't stupid, and she had noticed that any time she started making headway into his personal life he turned on that flirty charm of his. It might work with some women, but she wasn't about to fall for it.

Not that she was unaffected by the thought of his hands. She had no doubt that those hands were very talented, and she'd seen how gentle they could be when he held tiny newborn babies…

"What?" she asked when she allowed herself to look up from her plate and caught his amused look.

"I like that flustered look you get whenever you're embarrassed," Trent said. "And then there's the blush…"

She had felt warmth spread through her cheeks barely a second before his comment. How did he *do* that? It was if he had been studying her and knew her responses even before she did. Was she that transparent?

"Sorry," Trent said. "I really didn't mean to embarrass you."

"I was asking you about the ranch," Lana said.

"Yes, you were."

"You mentioned your dad…what about your mom?"

Lana noted the change in Trent immediately. All joking was gone now and sadness touched his eyes.

"She passed away when me and Michael were still kids," Trent answered.

"I'm sorry," Lana said.

Reaching over, she covered his hand with hers. Though it had been a long time since his mother's death, she could tell he was still grieving. Some deaths were like that. They touched you forever. She had seen it in patients who had lost a child many years earlier.

For a second the thought of losing Maggie crossed her mind. She closed the door on those thoughts quickly. She wouldn't go there tonight.

"Thanks, but it was a long time ago."

"It had to have been hard on the two of you," she said.

"Especially Michael—he was so young that I don't think he even had many memories of her," Trent said.

"But you do. I'd think it would have been harder on you, really knowing what was missing from your life," she said as she removed her hand and went back to her meal. Even with his mother's death, Trent was determined to put his brother before himself.

"Maybe, but then again I have memories. He didn't."

"So who took care of you when the two of you were growing up?"

"My great-aunt Flo came to live with us. My mother's aunt. She still lives there."

Trent watched as Lana pushed back her plate so that the restaurant staff would stop the continuous flow of food to their table. He ordered a coffee for himself when she turned down dessert, then leaned back in his chair. The tension that had been with him when they had started the evening had drained to only a tinge of discomfort now centered in his upper shoulders.

He rolled his head to ease the pulling on his muscles. He had been worried when Lana had started with the questions about his brother, but though he usually didn't discuss much of his personal life with others, talking with Lana hadn't been the uncomfortable conversation he might have thought it would be. Not that he hadn't recognized all this interest in his life for what it was: Lana was fishing for anything she could use against him.

"You look tired," Lana commented. "Are we working you too hard?"

Was that concern in her voice? How could she possibly care about how he was doing when he had brought all kinds of trouble into her life?

"I'm fine," Trent said.

He was about to leave it at that when he saw a flicker of distress flash through her eyes. Taking a slow, deep breath, to prepare himself to be hit with all her accusations, he continued.

"I'm sorry, Lana. I know my coming into your life like this has to be a nightmare," Trent said. "I bet you wish I'd get on the first plane out of town."

"I was thinking more like you would ride off into the sunset, Cowboy."

He watched as a small twitch played at the corner of her mouth, then she looked down at her hands, which were tangled in the napkin in her lap.

"I can't say what I would do if I found out my brother had a kid out there I hadn't been told about, but that doesn't make the position you've put me in any easier. Haven't you wondered why Chloe picked me to give Maggie to?" Lana asked. "She could have gone with any one of a dozen private adoption lawyers in town, but she came to *me*."

"I know you were her midwife," Trent answered.

"I was." Lana said. "And you must know how sometimes you just develop a bond with your patient? When they just seem to touch something inside of you? That part of you that you feel you have to protect, because you know if you let it the heartbreak you see every day will cause you to burn out, and then you wouldn't be able to help anyone anymore?"

Trent nodded his head toward her. He'd learned at an early age that you had to keep those feelings that left you vulnerable to the outside world locked up inside, where they couldn't be used against you, and during his clinical rotations he had been able to put up the walls that protected him. Until he had started his pediatric rotation. It had been the young ones, the innocent ones so filled with hope and trust, that he hadn't been able to help but feel his heart soften toward.

And wasn't that what was happening with the woman sitting across from him? Somehow, no matter how he built up those walls he knew he needed to keep erected between them, she could find a way over, around or through them. And that made her a weakness he couldn't afford.

"I knew Chloe was all alone in town—she told me when I first saw her in the office. And she had been very open about her addiction problem with prescription drugs, and about her rehab and methadone treatment. But it really wasn't until after Maggie was born that I got to know her."

"Ms. Nelson at Children and Families told me about Maggie's withdrawal," Trent said.

"You know how that is. It's like going through hell when someone goes through withdrawal. Watching an adult patient go through it is hard enough, but watching a baby... Maggie..." Lana stopped and reached for her glass.

The tremble in her hand as she raised her glass to her mouth told him that Maggie had to have been really sick. He'd seen infants go through withdrawal many times, and it was a horror for the staff as well as the parents. He could only imagine how hard it had been for Lana to watch Maggie experiencing the pain and agitation her withdrawal would have caused. The thought of it had him clenching his fists.

Why were children always the ones who had to pay for the mistakes of their parents? It was a question that had haunted him for years as he had watched his brother's drinking spiral out of control.

"I'd find Chloe sitting beside Maggie's crib in the neonatal unit, just staring at her baby. She looked so lost and alone that I found myself sitting with her there, talking to her for longer and longer each day."

Lana looked up at Trent, capturing his eyes with hers until he felt himself drawn into her sorrow.

"I'm not trying to make excuses for her. But after Maggie got out of withdrawal, when Chloe decided she couldn't take the stress of caring for her, she did the most unselfish thing she could do. She put the care and well-being of her baby first. I can't imagine what it took for her to come to my house the night she brought Maggie to me," Lana continued. "And I'll admit I'm not nearly as brave. I can't give Maggie up. I *won't* give her up," Lana said as she rose from her chair.

Trent could see the pleading in her eyes, the innocent hope that shone out of them, asking for his help. She could have asked him for anything right then. Anything except for what she needed—his assurance that everything would be all right. Of course it wouldn't. They both knew that. Only one of them could win custody of Maggie, and right now he wasn't sure who he was hoping that would be.

It was only knowing the harm that his father could do to both Maggie *and* Lana that assured him he was doing the right thing.

"I saw them myself!"

"Saw who?" Lana asked as she walked into the nurses' break room.

She watched as two of the nurses who had been in there excused themselves. The other four nurses were either looking down at the floor or at Kat, the department's queen of gossip.

"We were just talking about what we did on our time off," said Laurie, the charge nurse.

"Did *you* do anything exciting this weekend?" Kat asked, and leaned toward Lana.

The room suddenly became quiet and everyone in

turned toward her expectantly. It was becoming very obvious that there was some piece of information they were all waiting for her to share. And by the way they all seemed to be anticipating her answer she knew this wasn't a casual question.

And then it hit her. Someone had seen her out with Trent. And that someone was apparently Kat, who she could see had been only too happy to run back and share the news with her colleagues.

She couldn't blame them for their interest. While the hospital was quite large, they were still a tight-knit group who seemed to share everything with each other—even things that were really none of their business. But that didn't mean she was prepared to go into details about her and Trent's relationship.

She had enough problems keeping Trent and her court case from interfering with their work relationship. So far her explanation that a last-minute complication had temporarily postponed Maggie's adoption had been all the reason she had needed. No one knew that the "complication" was Trent—or at least if they did she hadn't heard any talk about it. If it got out there that they were seeing each other socially, the gossip fire would be raging out of control. There was no way she was going to give it any more fuel.

"Nothing special. I just took Maggie to the beach Saturday. She loved it, of course. Besides that it was just a normal weekend."

Lana almost laughed at the look of disappointment on the group's faces. There would be more talk when she left the room, she was sure. And if Kat ws being her imaginative self by the end of the day she was also sure the hospital would be full of gossip about her and

Trent's torrid affair. She'd have to warn him, but besides that she decided just to ignore it.

"Laurie—Hannah Bowers has texted me that she is on her way," Lana told the charge nurse. "Hopefully she's just having Braxton Hicks contractions."

"How many weeks is she now?" Laurie asked as she got up and began to clear the space where she had been eating.

"She was thirty-six last Friday, when I saw her," Lana answered. "I checked her cervix and she was thinning out, but not dilated yet."

"Thirty-six is pretty good for twins," Kat commented.

"We won't stop her if she's in labor," Lana said. "Just call me when she comes in and I'll come over and do an exam."

Hoping that the excitement of possibly having a twin delivery would give the staff something to talk about besides her love-life, Lana headed back to her office to catch up on her daily appointments.

The prospect of a twin delivery thrilled her too, but she'd have to use some good time management or things would back up fast in the office.

Lana had only managed to see a couple of patients before Laurie called to say that Hannah had arrived with her mother and was having contractions.

After signing out with the office she made the quick walk over to the labor unit. Looking at the contraction pattern of two minutes apart, Lana wasn't surprised to find Hannah's cervical exam showing that she was definitely in labor.

"Ready to meet these two?" Lana asked as she motioned toward Hannah's stretched belly.

"Really?" Hannah asked. "I've got to call Jimmy. Momma—you call him. I've had so many false alarms that he'll never believe me."

"Probably would be a good idea to go ahead and make that call," Lana said. "You're progressing pretty well. When did the contractions start?"

"Just before Jimmy left for work. I didn't want to tell him. He'd have insisted on staying home and I didn't want him to miss work. Are they okay?" Hannah asked as she indicated the monitor screen, where four different lines graphed out, each in a different color.

"Their heart-rates look great," Lana answered. "They're early, but it's not unusual for twins to come early."

"Probably because they've run out of room in there," Hannah said as she rubbed her large belly.

"I'm going to order an ultrasound. I can tell that Baby Anna is presenting with her head down, but I need to check on James Junior," Lana said. "I know we discussed you trying for a vaginal delivery…"

"If I can," Hannah said.

"Is that safe?" asked Hannah's mother. "When my sister had her twins they just cut her and took them out."

The middle-aged woman came to stand near her daughter and Lana could see the concern in the woman's eyes.

"Things have changed since then, Momma," Hannah said as she reached over and took her mother's hand. "Remember one of the girls at your church delivered her twins vaginally?"

"I'll wait for the ultrasound results and then I'll talk with the obstetrician on call. If both twins are positioned correctly it will be okay to let the labor continue to progress," Lana said. "But don't forget—if the second baby decides to change position after we deliver the first, you probably will end up with a Cesarean section."

"You mean she could have *both*?" Hannah's mother asked as she got up from her chair and walked over to the monitors to study the readings.

"Momma worries," Hannah explained.

"And I don't blame her one bit," Lana said as she headed for the door. "I'm going to go get that ultrasound ordered now. You just get Jimmy on his way here, and after the ultrasound we'll all get together to decide how we're going to go from here. I also think you should consider going ahead and getting an epidural."

"This soon?" Hannah asked as she shifted in the bed.

Lana watched as the contraction that was tracing on the monitor peaked, then slowly went down. She had noticed Hannah instinctively take deeper breaths as the contractions had come and gone.

"You're going to need one soon. We can get some IV fluids going too, so that you'll be ready when Anesthesia gets here."

"Thanks, Lana," Hannah said.

"And just remember," Lana said when she reached the door. "The most important thing today isn't *how* you deliver—it's that we end up with two healthy babies and a healthy momma."

As she shut the door she heard Hannah's nervous mother say, "Amen." She couldn't blame her for having concerns about her daughter. Even knowing everything she knew about childbirth, Lana still knew that if it were her Maggie in there she would be a nervous wreck.

But what if she wasn't around when Maggie grew up and had children of her own?

That thought had her stopping to lean against the

nearest wall. She took a deep breath that would have made any labor doula proud, and let it out slowly as she tried to calm herself. She was starting to have more and more periods of anxiety over the custody case, and was afraid that one day she was going to find herself in a full-blown panic attack.

And how would *that* look to the court? And to Trent? He was always so in control of his emotions. He would never understand what she was going through. There had to be something she could do to help ease the anxiety she was feeling.

Of course the only thing that would really help would be Trent dropping his petition with the court and returning to Texas, so that she and Maggie could get back to their life together.

Yes, Trent leaving would be the answer to all her troubles—but what could she do to make that happen? She'd shown him that Maggie was happy and safe with her. He had to be able to see how much she loved her little girl. What more did he want?

And to top everything off she *didn't* need the complication of her hormones going crazy every time she was around the man. There had never been a man she was so sexually aware of in her life, and it made her feel self-conscious and unsure of herself at a time when she needed to be portraying someone who was totally confident in her life.

She took another deep breath to help cleanse her thoughts, then continued down the hall. She'd call her mother tonight. Between sharing her heartache with her momma and a pint of chocolate ice cream she would surely come up with some strategy to get her through the next couple of weeks.

* * *

Trent entered the labor and delivery unit and went in search of Lana. He was telling himself he needed to get an update on her patient's condition so he'd know how soon he and the nursery team would be needed, but he knew it was just an excuse to go and see the midwife. He hadn't seen her since their night out, and he had already planned to hunt her down later that day to make more arrangements to see Maggie.

Of course he could have just called to set that up, but that wasn't what he wanted.

What was it about her that had caught his interest and refused to let it go? She was certainly a beautiful woman, with her seductive curves and that thick blond mane of hers, and those green eyes that filled with love when she talked about Maggie. But he had dated plenty of beautiful women who hadn't affected him like she did. Even Maria hadn't captivated him the way Lana did, and Maria had been the perfect woman.

Maria had been everything he had wanted in a woman—beautiful, smart, and most importantly independent. He'd never had to worry about her throwing a fit if he got called into work, or complaining about him not spending enough time with her. If he'd been late for a social function due to a case going long she'd never been angry with him.

It had been the perfect relationship and he had been surprised when, after dating him for several months, she had called him one day to tell him she wouldn't be seeing him anymore—that she wanted to see other people and didn't feel that he could give her what she needed out of a relationship.

While he couldn't say that she had broken his heart, he *had* been hurt. No, he'd never felt that all-consuming love everyone talked about, but he had cared about her.

He'd seen her a few weeks later in a corner of the hospital cafeteria, holding the hand of one of the residents. Stopping to study them for a moment, he'd noted the flush of Maria's face and the way those deep brown eyes of hers had never left the young man. He had waited for jealousy to fill him, but he'd felt nothing.

It was then he'd realized that, no matter how intimate they had been, what they'd had was just a close friendship and nothing more. Maria had realized that too and wanted more. He hadn't.

And that brought him back to Lana. The two of them had managed to create a good working relationship and, even with everything between them, if not a friendship at least they'd managed a truce. He didn't want to endanger that because of some misplaced attraction between the two of them. Maybe if she was another woman they'd be able to scratch the itch and move on, but everything he'd learned about Lana told him that wasn't her way.

Lana was the kind of woman who would want roses and candles before she became in any way involved with someone, and then she'd be wanting the house with the white picket fence. She had quickly shown him that she was all about family, which put her at the top of his list of women to stay away from.

He'd learned a long time ago that he didn't have anything to give a woman other than his friendship and sex, and that was enough for him. He had no desire to be responsible for someone else's happiness. He'd heard his mother's claims of love for his father and it had destroyed not only her but the rest of their family. He never wanted to get caught in that trap, where everything depended on someone's feeling for you or your feelings for them.

He owed Lana a lot for taking care of his niece, and he wouldn't repay her by letting her think there could be more between them than there was. He was already trying to take the baby she loved away from her, and he knew that already made him just as much of a cold bastard as his father.

He'd found himself wrestling with that fact each night when he lay in his bed. On one hand he wanted to leave Maggie with Lana, knowing that she would always be loved and taken care of. But on the other hand Michael had asked him in his will to take care of the little girl. Couldn't Lana understand that he had to honor his brother's request?

And then there was Maggie's inheritance… So far Michael's lawyer had been able to stall his father concerning the contents of his brother's will, but he knew his father would have his own lawyers looking into it soon.

No one except for him and his brother's lawyers knew that upon gaining custody of Maggie he, Trent, would have control of the majority of the shares to Montgomery and Lord, but if his father found out that little tidbit before the custody case was settled he knew Maggie would be in danger of being used like everyone else Calvin Montgomery touched, and he couldn't let that happen to another person he cared about.

It was up to him to protect his niece and he was going to have to find a way to make Lana understand—even if it meant airing some of his family's dirty laundry. And there was plenty of that.

Trent was about to give up on finding Lana when he saw her in the nurses' break room. For a moment he just watched as she laughed with the two labor nurses she was sharing her lunch with. It was nice to see her laughing with her friends. With all the stress he had added to her life, it was amazing that she could still relax for a moment. And no matter how much he told himself the woman was dangerous, he had to admit he enjoyed looking at her.

"Excuse me," Trent said as he interrupted the three of them in their meal. "I was wondering if I could see you for just a minute, Lana?"

He stepped out through the door to let her pass, and was surprised when she grabbed his arm and pulled him down the hall to one of the empty exam rooms.

"What are you *doing*?" she asked him in a voice not much over a whisper.

"I'm not sure," he whispered back as he looked down to where Lana was still gripping his arm. "And why are we whispering?"

Lana dropped his arm. "Do you know who that was I was eating with?"

"Well, I know Kat…" Trent said.

"Of *course* you do," Lana said, then walked across the room away from him.

"What does that mean?" he said as he followed her.

"Nothing," she said.

Trent watched her as she stood there with her arms crossed, glaring at him while she chewed at her bottom lip. Then, as if coming to some conclusion—although on what he had no clue—she marched up to him.

"Kat is the biggest gossiper in the unit—probably in the whole hospital, for that matter," Lana said.

"And I should be concerned about that…why?" Trent asked.

\* \* \*

Was the man dense? Lana had been tiptoeing around questions about her weekend all day, and then he'd walked right into the break room and asked to speak to her. By now everybody on the floor would be speculating about what was going on between the two of them.

"Because somebody saw us out together the other night, and now everyone has got it into their head that there's something going on between us."

Lana watched as that information hit him. And then the stupid man smiled.

"It's not funny!" she said as she punched him in the arm.

"Ouch," he said, rubbing his arm.

"Will you just be serious for a moment?" Lana asked. "The last thing I want is for everyone to find out that there's something going on between us."

Lana watched as Trent sobered. He leaned back and then sat on the tightly made hospital bed.

"And what exactly *is* going on between us?" Trent asked.

"They don't know about your brother, or the reason my adoption of Maggie has been put on hold," she said. "I don't want to have to walk around this hospital with everybody talking about it."

She'd had enough of those pity-filled stares when she was a bald-headed teenager after her chemo and radiation treatments. She didn't want to live through that again.

"Sorry," he said. "I just wanted to ask you about this weekend—about me seeing Maggie."

Lana stopped and looked at him. He hadn't meant

to cause trouble. It wasn't his fault that tongues were wagging.

"No, *I'm* sorry," she said. "I shouldn't be so sensitive."

Walking across the room she took a seat beside him, and for a few seconds they sat there together in silence. She was starting to realize that in some ways Trent was just as much a victim in this nightmare of a court case as she was. *He* hadn't left Maggie's mother when she was pregnant. He hadn't come to Miami to stop her adopting Maggie for himself. Everything he was doing was for his brother.

While it was easy for her to see that taking Maggie away from the only home she had ever known was not the right thing for the child, she knew he was just trying to do what he thought was best for his niece—even though she knew he was wrong.

"Let me check my call schedule for the weekend…"

"Oh, *there* you two are," Kat said as she stuck her head in the door. "Dr. Miller called for an update on Hannah's progress. I told him I couldn't find you, but that I'd be glad to have you call him back."

Lana looked at Trent before jumping down off the bed. By the silly smile he gave her as she left the room she knew he was aware of just what the next set of rumors would be. She'd have some explaining to do to the people she worked with if they got wind of the fact that the two of them had been caught together on one of the hospital beds.

Because one look at Trent and no one would believe they were innocent. At least no female would.

# CHAPTER SIX

WITH HANNAH'S TWINS in the right position, they decided to go through with a vaginal delivery. As soon as Hannah was fully dilated and ready to push, they moved her to an operating room to deliver in case there were any complications.

Lana saw Trent dressed in his scrubs helping the nursery team set up when she entered after scrubbing up.

"Twins, huh?" Trent said.

"You don't do vaginal delivery of twins in Texas?" she asked.

"We do. Just most of ours are delivered by doctors," he said.

"I've done several, and Dr. Miller is on standby in the unit in case the second baby decides to misbehave. Trust me—I've got this," she said with a smile, then winked at him.

She knew the adrenaline rush was making her cocky and hoped she didn't regret the words later.

Trent watched as Lana moved over to her patient and couldn't help but smile back. If the look on her face was any indication, Lana had certainly found her calling in midwifery. While she was definitely full of confidence, he saw that she checked through the instruments arranged for the double vaginal delivery, as well as checking that she had everything they'd need if things changed and they had to do a C-section.

After having one of the nurses confirm that Dr. Miller, the obstetrician, was on the unit and available, she had Hannah start to push.

Several minutes later the first twin started to crown and Trent gowned and prepared for the delivery. when Lana handed the crying little girl to him, he carried her over to the warmer and checked her out from head to toe. She was a bit small for her gestation, but nothing that wouldn't be expected in a twin.

One of the nurses name-banded and bundled the baby, then carried it over to the waiting father.

Lana was busy doing an ultrasound on her patient. "Okay, Hannah and Jimmy—you ready to meet James Junior?"

Hannah nodded her head excitedly, then started to push again. Trent had to give it to the woman—and to women in general. He didn't know a man alive who would be able to go through what these mothers did.

With the top of a second little head crowning after a few pushes, he watched as Lana carefully delivered the head, then the shoulders.

"James Junior's been stealing the food from his sister," she said as she held the much larger baby boy up for them to see.

She cut the cord, then handed the newest member of the family to Trent. Within seconds of stimulating him with a firm rub on his back he had the baby boy as pink and as loud as his sister.

* * *

"Congratulations!" Trent said later, as Lana took a seat on one of the benches across from him in the locker room.

"Thanks. How are the babies?" Lana asked.

"They're doing good. They're both with their parents. We're watching their sugars, but besides the extreme difference in size they're perfect," he said. "The nurses are all talking about how good you did. And I didn't hear a word about us being caught in bed together."

Lana made a face at him and then broke down in giggles. She knew she was still on an adrenaline high from the delivery, but it felt good to just relax and enjoy it for a minute. Today was a day to celebrate the two new lives that had come into the world. Nothing could be better for renewing a person's hope in life than seeing a baby starting out it's life.

Trent watched her as she talked about what a privilege it was to be a part of the twins delivery. Joy seemed to flow out of her as she described the two babies who had just come into the world.

It was as if the beauty that he had learned was inside her was blooming out into her sparkling green eyes. Her cheeks glowed bright with color from her excitement and he had never been so turned on by just watching a woman talk.

He felt something in him thaw as the beautiful sound of her laughter touched him in a place he had closed up inside himself years ago. Her laughter warmed him and her smile teased him into wanting more. Would it be so bad just to enjoy this moment without worrying about all the complications that could follow?

* * *

Realizing she was on the point of blabbering, Lana stopped and looked up to see Trent had come to stand in front of her. Gone was the man who had earlier in the day joked with her about her concerns over gossiping nurses. The playful teasing she had become accustomed to had been replaced by a dangerous intensity that seemed to fill him, leaving his body taut with tension and reminding her of a wild cat preparing to pounce.

Everything about him had become hard now—everything except for his eyes.

Lana stood and moved closer, as if drawn into them. They seemed a deeper blue today. A blue she knew she would drown in if she wasn't careful. Then Trent took a step forward and his eyes went from calm sea to hungry storm—a storm that had the power either to pull her in or toss her away.

Fear about which he would choose, and what she herself wanted, had her taking a step back and moving around the wooden bench that penned her into the tight space.

"Trent?" she heard herself say, the sound barely audible as if it came from far away.

When he ignored her plea and took a second and then another step toward her, instinct had her continuing her retreat until she felt the door against her back.

She held herself still as he reached around her and locked the door. The warmth of his breath fanned her face, and when she glanced up at his lips she was surprised to find them so close to hers. So close that she could feel the warmth of them.

No longer willing to wait for his advance, she pushed up on her toes and met his mouth with hers. A white heat scorched her as it rushed through her body, then puddled in her core. The excitement of the twin delivery was scattered away as a new, more dangerous thrill filled her. Soon hard lips were meeting soft tongues as they battled, both of them advancing and retreating.

She felt Trent's hands as they skimmed over her back, then came to rest on her hips. He pulled her body closer until she felt the length of his erection as it rested between her legs. When he pushed himself against her, pinning her against the door, she was left with no doubt as to what he wanted. What they both wanted.

As their mouths continued to war she felt herself surrender to him. He was hard for her and she was aching to let him take her. Right then. Right there. Against the locker room door.

The memory of where they were suddenly broke through her clouded mind. She was about to have sex in a locker room. In the middle of the day. With the man who was trying to take her daughter away from her.

For a second Trent ignored her when she tried to pull away.

"Trent," she said when she managed to free her mouth, "we've got to stop."

She felt his fingers relax on her hips, but still he didn't move.

"I guess we were about to give the staff something to *really* talk about," Trent said as he rested his chin on the top of her head, so that her face was cradled against his chest.

Lana took a deep breath in, enjoying the tangy scent of hot and bothered male. She would take that smell with her. But it was *all* she could take of him. She had never been a woman who could handle a sex-only relationship.

She needed more from a man. But with her body still aching for his she knew she had to get away from him.

"I've got to go," Lana said as she shifted against him.

"You never answered my question," Trent said.

She pulled back and looked up at him.

"What *is* going on between the two of us?" he asked.

"Nothing," she answered, then looked away, afraid that her eyes would show a longing for something more that she knew she couldn't have.

"If that was nothing, I don't know if I could live through your something," he said, with a touch of humor that surprised her.

He held her to him for just a second longer before he released her and moved away.

"I got a call earlier from Ms. Nelson," he said.

With the mention of the social worker's name the warmth that had been between them faded. *This* was why she knew the right thing to do was to step back from Trent. Anything that they could possibly have would never survive the battle they would soon find themselves in.

"What did she say?" Lana said as she tried to stomp down on the panic that wanted to rise up and take control.

"Nothing that we weren't expecting. The DNA testing came back. I'm Maggie's uncle, Lana," Trent said. "Maggie's a Montgomery."

She watched him reach down and lift his duffle bag onto his shoulder. She walked across the room and kicked off her shoes. Feeling a bit shaky, she sat on the bench in front of her locker. She took her time changing into her street shoes and storing her work pair, and by the time she looked up the door was shutting, leaving her alone with even more questions than she'd had before.

Lana walked into the social worker's office knowing she was a coward. She had spent the week avoiding Trent as much as possible. The few times they had ended up on the labor unit at the same time she had made a fast retreat to her office.

If only it was that easy to run away from the dreams that haunted her nights, leaving her in tangled sheets with an unsatisfied need that filled her days.

She could deny that there was anything between them to Trent, but she wasn't able to lie to herself. She was letting herself get too close to him and that was dangerous. She couldn't allow herself to put anything before her family right now. She had to be totally professional from now on, and that meant no nights out with Trent and no moments alone together.

Then he walked into the room, and all her determination to keep things strictly business between them fled. How was she supposed to ignore this man who could turn her libido into a hormonal teenager's just by entering the room?

Dressed in soft gray dress pants and a black polo shirt, he had the look of a wealthy oil tycoon, with his charcoal cowboy boots and the black Stetson hat he held in his hands. She remembered the night at the restaurant, when he had told her about working on the family ranch and joked about how good he was with his hands.

The room suddenly heated up with her memories of those hands holding her in place while he pressed himself tight against her, his lips hot against hers. His hands were not the only things he was good with...

"Ms. Nelson… Lana," he said as he took the seat next to her.

"Thanks for coming down," the social worker said. "I think the two of you have gotten the information on the DNA testing from your lawyers?"

She continued when they each nodded their heads.

"I just wanted to get the two of you together to discuss how the visitations are going and to let you know what our plans are from here forward. I've talked with Nathan, Lana, and he has told me you're planning on continuing with the adoption."

"Yes, I plan on continuing with my plans for custody of Maggie," Lana said, hoping she had managed to keep the tremble she felt out of her voice.

"And I will need to continue with my petition also," Trent said.

"And your visitations with Maggie?" asked Ms. Nelson.

"We've done very well together," Trent commented, then looked over at Lana. "At least I think so."

"Trent is very good with Maggie," Lana answered. "He had no problem winning Maggie over. I think he's a natural in the uncle department."

"Well, thank you, ma'am," Trent said in his deepest Texan drawl.

Lana tried to stop the smile that always came when he was in this cute flirty mood.

"I think he just can't help charming every female he meets," she said.

"What?" Trent said. "I want you to know I take my wooing of a woman very seriously."

"*Wooing?* Who uses a word like 'wooing?'" she

said as she turned back to Trent. "What does that even mean?"

"Well, I can tell you that any woman I woo will definitely know what it means."

Ms. Nelson cleared her throat and they both turned toward the social worker, who was looking at them as if they had lost their minds.

"The visitations are going well," Lana said, and she sat back in her seat, then looked down at her hands.

"So I see," the social worker said, and gave them a friendly smile.

Lana took a deep breath and decided to dive into the speech she had prepared on her way to the office. She made sure that when she looked up she avoided looking at Trent. She locked her eyes on the older woman and hoped to see some understanding in the gray eyes that met hers.

"Trent can come to visit Maggie as often as he wants—" Lana started.

"Thanks," Trent said.

"Let me finish," Lana said. "But while I plan on continuing Trent's visits with Maggie…"

From her seat beside him Lana felt the tension as it coiled through him and he visibly straightened in his chair. This wasn't going to be easy, but she had to have her say. Squaring her shoulders, she moved up to the edge of her seat and began again. She had practiced, she had memorized, and she *would* get through this.

"Trent will always be Maggie's uncle, and I will always allow him to see his niece," said Lana. She let the breath she had been holding out and took in another one, this one deeper, as she tried to get her thoughts together. "But with all the things Trent can provide for her, the one thing he can't provide is something every little girl needs. A mother."

"Are you saying a single father can't raise a child?" Trent asked. "Aren't fathers important too?"

"No. I mean, yes." Lana fumbled over the words as she tried to ignore the anger she could hear rising in Trent's voice. "Yes. Fathers are important. But Maggie's being raised with a mother figure. I'm all she's ever known. What happens when you take that away from her? What happens when she wakes up in the middle of the night crying and I'm not there, Trent?"

"It sounds to me like what she really needs is the both of you," Ms. Nelson interrupted, and then continued before either of them could comment. "Trent, I need to discuss a few matters with you, if you have a few more minutes? I appreciate you coming down to see me, Lana, and I understand your concerns. If you need anything, or have any questions, you know you can give me a call."

Lana stood and thanked the social worker before leaving the office. She had been dismissed.

Turning back, she saw the woman get up and shut her office door. She couldn't help feeling as if she was being shut out of something that might have a big impact on her little girl. She turned and headed for the elevators, trying to decide how she would get through the next few days while she waited to see what step the courts would take next.

"I think you can understand Lana's concerns," Ms. Nelson said.

Trent took a long look at the social worker. She wore a friendly concerned look that he knew must put her clients at ease, but she was shrewd too. She knew how to get information when she needed it to get her job done.

"I do understand where Lana is coming from," Trent said.

"What we need to remember here is that a little girl's future is about to be determined and it is our responsibility to make the best decision we can in her interests. Anything besides honesty between the three of us would be going against what is best for Maggie."

Trent nodded his head in agreement, then waited for the social worker to continue. He had agreed to be honest with her. He tried to push back the guilt he felt about keeping information about his brother's will from both the social worker and from Lana. It was something he would eventually have to deal with, but now was not the time.

"I like Lana, and I know that Maggie couldn't be any more loved or cared for then she is with her." The social worker removed her glasses and rubbed at her eyes. "But it's my job and the judge's job to make sure that everyone's interest in the child is explored and taken into consideration. Having said that, I'm going to admit that right now I feel the best place for Maggie is still with Lana."

Well, she couldn't be any more honest than that, thought Trent. And what kind of argument did he have to use against her?

"That doesn't mean you won't win custody," she continued. "As a family member, you have a strong case. Your biggest job is going to be to prepare yourself to take on everything raising your niece will require, and it's not going to be easy. I'm not sure you're ready for this change in your life. As a pediatrician, I'm sure you know there's more to raising a child than just providing for their needs."

Was she right? Was he fooling himself, thinking he could take on the job of raising a toddler? And this was adorable little Maggie, who had already been through so much in her short life. The last thing she needed was for him to do something that could screw her up.

Just look what had happened to Michael. He had been supposed to take care of him. He had been the oldest and he'd known his mother expected him to look out for his little brother. He had failed Michael and he didn't want to fail his niece too. But no matter what Lana and the social worker thought Maggie needed him. He was the only one who would be able to protect her from his father's control.

Trent quickly agreed to the home visit the state required before leaving the social worker's office. He had a lot to think about after this meeting.

Lana should have felt at least a little bit of guilt about what she was about to do to Trent, but she didn't. The idea had come to her in the middle of the night, when thoughts of losing Maggie had kept her awake.

While Trent talked a good game as far as wanting to be a responsible uncle and taking on the duty of caring for his niece went, in truth he had no idea of what taking care of Maggie would entail. Sure, he was qualified as a pediatrician to give proper medical care to a child, but she was pretty sure he wasn't really prepared for the day-to-day care a toddler needed.

An early call to Emily, the midwife covering deliveries this weekend, and everything had been set up. The fact that Maggie had woken up cranky from the teeth she was cutting was just the icing on the cake.

"I'm so sorry about this," she said to Trent now, trying to keep the evil laugh inside her from exploding, "but I didn't know I was going to have to cover the hospital today, and Amanda is out of town visiting with her parents."

"So, what exactly do I need to do?" Trent asked as he looked down at Maggie, who was still in her sleeper, with a good amount of oatmeal smeared on her face, her nose crusty with the mucus caused by her teething.

"You'll be fine," she said. "I've laid her clothes out in her room, and her lunch and her supper are in the fridge."

"Supper?" he asked.

"You know how deliveries are—some of them take hours, and there's no way for me to know when I'll get off. But don't worry—I'll be relieved early enough in the morning that you can make your shift tomorrow. You did say you were working Sunday, didn't you?"

"Uh, yeah... Sunday," Trent said.

Had the man's skin paled, or was that just wishful thinking?

"You'll be fine, Trent," she said.

Reaching down to hug her little girl, she took a second to make sure she didn't have a temperature. Maggie had never been one to run a fever while teething, but there was always a first time. She had no doubt that her daughter would be safe with Trent—she just wasn't sure if Trent would survive the day with the cranky toddler.

Trent looked down at the little girl holding on to his leg. Had she just wiped her nose on his jeans? This child, dressed in some kind of one-piece jumper, with food caked on her mouth, looked nothing like the Maggie he knew. Picking her up in his arms, he made another discovery: she smelled worse than she looked. The first order of business would have to be cleaning her up.

After fighting with her to get her face washed, taking off her dirty sleep outfit seemed a breeze. Putting new clothes on his niece was another matter. He tried all the tricks he knew from his practice. The tickle move he used before giving shots, his funny faces for after the shots, the calm voice he had learned to use with stressed-out kids.

Nothing in his box of tricks worked. It seemed the child was a nudist at heart and had no desire to wear any clothes. By the time he'd managed to get a clean diaper and a shirt on her, he gave up the battle. If running around half dressed made the child happy, so be it.

"I surrender to Princess Maggie," he said, then bowed his head to the toddler.

Maggie giggled at him, then ran to get a little plastic and crystal crown that was sitting on a small bookcase. She stopped and looked through the books stacked in piles, then pulled one out, sending the rest of them tumbling to the ground. Walking over to where he sat on the floor, she sat down on his lap and handed him a book.

He looked at the title. "A princess book for a princess?" he said. "I can do this."

Opening the pink sparkly book, he wasn't surprised to see a young girl dressed all in pink wearing a crown. He started to read.

Four books later he noticed Maggie's eyes drooping. Closing the book, he carefully got off the floor, trying not to disturb the sleepy baby. Laying her down in her crib, he tiptoed out of the room and smiled. What had he been so afraid of? Taking care of Maggie was nothing he couldn't handle.

He had just shut the door when the crying began.

Lana opened the door and stared at the chaos of her living room. Every toy Maggie owned had to be in that room—plus what looked like half the clothes from her dresser. She leaned down to pick up a large stuffed elephant that was in her way, then froze.

Stretched out on her couch was Trent—a sound asleep Trent. He held her sleeping daughter on top of him, with one of his arms laid protectively around her.

While wide-awake Trent, with his powerful frame and those mesmerizing blue eyes of his, was a seductive temptation even to her, this version of the man took her breath away. Thick, dark lashes lay resting on copper-toned skin, while lips usually turned up in a smile were relaxed in soft invitation.

She'd felt those lips against hers. She bent down closer. Had they really been that warm? That firm?

Bright blue eyes stared up at her and she jerked away from him. Heaven help her—had she really been about to kiss him? No, of course not. She'd never do anything like that.

"I need to put Maggie down in her crib," she said, trying to keep her voice even while her heart tried to come out of her chest.

Lifting Maggie up into her arms, she held her tight against her racing heart as she carried her into her room and laid her in her crib. She took a minute to catch her breath, then walked back into the living room where she found Trent sitting up and rubbing the back of his neck.

"I can't believe you did that," he said.

"What?" she said. Her heart sped up. Had he caught her?

"You got her to stay in her crib," he said.

She watched him walk toward the door, shoulders slumped and feet all but dragging, and said a silent thank-you to the sleeping Maggie.

"Just one of those tricks you learn when you're a mother," she said.

"You're a good mother, Lana," he said. "I just want you to know that. This isn't about me not thinking you can take care of Maggie."

"Then *what*, Trent? What *is* it about if not what's best for Maggie?"

She stilled as Trent's hand came up to her face. He ran the back of his hand down one cheek, then cupped her chin. He pulled her to him and laid on her lips a kiss so soft that she wondered if she'd imagined it.

He pulled away, a half-smile on his lips, and walked out the door.

As the door shut behind him she took a deep breath and let her body relax. From what she had seen she'd have to say that operation Teach Trent a Lesson about Parenthood had been a success—but would it be enough?

She still had so many unanswered questions. She knew that Trent's guilt concerning his brother's death was part of what was driving him to seek custody of Maggie, but she couldn't help but think there was something he was keeping from her—something important that would explain everything.

Trent sat in his car and watched as other employees came and went from the staff entrance to the hospital. So it all was about to hit the fan. The text he'd received from his lawyer that morning had been short, but to the point.

He looked down to read it one more time.

Time running out. Getting pressure. Must address other parts of your brother's will which includes your father. Will is set to go into probate this week.

His plan had been so simple. Go to Florida. Get child. Protect child from his father. Show the old man that he didn't have the power to control everyone's life anymore. So simple—and yet it had turned so complicated. And that complication was named Lana. Watching her interact with his niece had changed everything.

He never should have come here. He should have stayed far away from both Maggie and Lana and had his lawyer handle everything. But it was too late. He had got involved and now he had to take control of the situation.

He knew his next move should be to have his lawyer start applying pressure to the courts to get this thing done, but he had been dragging his feet. He was normally a very decisive man, but suddenly he couldn't determine a plan of action that he felt comfortable with.

His knew his father would be on this before he even left the probate hearing. He needed to come up with a new plan. One that was sure to protect his niece. And although he had ignored the social worker's earlier comment, about Maggie needing both him *and* Lana, after Ms. Nelson had shared her concerns with him he had caught himself considering her observation.

After taking care of Maggie all by himself, he had to admit that caring for a toddler was going to be harder than he had first considered. Oh, he could hire a nanny to take care of Maggie, but that didn't sit right with him. That wasn't what he wanted for his niece.

Possibilities entered his thoughts and he mentally made notes. Maybe instead of fighting Lana he could find a way for them to work together. With all the force of his father's lawyers about to descend on them, he had to come up with a plan soon. He didn't have just Maggie to consider—he had to protect Lana too.

Getting out of the car and heading in to work, he willed himself to put everything behind him as he walked into the cool air of the hospital. He prided himself in being able to give his patients his complete attention and he wouldn't let anything get in the way of their care and safety. He'd deal with everything else after his shift.

# CHAPTER SEVEN

"I WASN'T EXPECTING YOU," Lana said as she entered her office to find her lawyer, Nathan, sitting in one of the three chairs that circled her desk.

It had only been a few days since she and Trent had met with the social worker and she really hadn't expected to hear any news for at least another week.

"Thought I'd stop and see if you wanted to go out to lunch," Nathan said, and then he saw the sandwich she had laid out on her desk. "But I guess you have that covered."

She had planned a quick lunch and then to use an afternoon free of appointments to catch up on her charting. She had been leaving the office as early as possible the last few days, in order to spend every minute possible with Maggie. The number of file entries she needed to make were beginning to pile up and she had to get caught up. Being behind at work was just one more thing to stress over and she had all the stress she needed right now.

"I have a feeling that I'm not going to feel like eating after all," she said, after taking a seat behind her desk.

Nathan's wife had been one of her first patients when she'd begun her midwifery career. But that didn't explain why he'd shown up here instead of calling. Warning bells started going off in her head, making it almost impossible for her to remain in her seat.

"There's no way you came down here just on the off-chance that you might catch me for lunch," she said. "Especially with having to fight through the noon traffic."

Lana forced her hands to relax on her chair and tried to practice the deep breathing from the labor classes she taught. She had found in the last few days that it helped her get through those times when thoughts of losing Maggie started to overwhelm her.

"So, either you have some really good news that you couldn't wait to share with me or you have some really bad news you didn't want to give me over the phone."

"I got a call from Karen Nelson today that I wanted to talk to you about," Nathan said.

"And here comes the really bad news, I take it?" She sat up straight and braced herself for the blow. "Go ahead. I can take it."

"She's received a call from a lawyer in Houston about Maggie," Nathan said.

She had been wrong. She hadn't been ready for that bombshell at all.

"Trent has hired a new lawyer?" Lana asked.

"No, this one represents Trent's father," Nathan said.

Lana felt the pain of prickling needles shoot through her body as the shock of Nathan's statement hit her. *Maggie's grandfather.* Why hadn't she considered this? Of course the power of two Montgomerys would be stronger than just one. It was taking all she had to fight against one of them—what chance did she have against two of them? How could Trent do this to her?

"Karen Nelson just wanted to give us a heads-up,"

Nathan said. Leaning over her, he gave Lana a look that would have had her running if she hadn't known he was on her side. "We are going to *fight* this, Lana. I know I told you that we would have a hard time because of Trent's biological relationship, but we still have your history with Maggie. And the fact that the biological mother wanted you to adopt Maggie will play heavily on our side."

"But you know that when one of the biological family requests custody the court usually sides with them. Now there will be two. Two to one, Nathan."

Lana looked down to where her hands now gripped the armrests of her chair. So much for learning to deal with her stress. There was no way she was going to be able to ignore this hit. But Trent should have told her he was going to do this. They had agreed to be honest with each other, hadn't they? Even if there hadn't been any way to talk him out of it, he could have warned her. The fact that he hadn't told her caused an ache deep down inside her chest.

Suddenly, the butterflies that had been in her stomach for the last couple of weeks stopped doing jumping jacks. Now they seemed to have picked up pitchforks and were trying to fight their way out. A wave of nausea rolled over her and she made herself take a deep breath to calm her stomach.

Then a new emotion hit her. A burning anger boiled up from a stomach that only minutes ago had been ready to spew. How *dared* the man worm his way into her life and then blindside her this way?

The more she thought about it, the madder she got. Maybe it was time for her to show Trent that she was ready for a fight too.

* * *

When Nathan had finally quit trying to talk her out of rushing over to Trent's, he called his office and got the address for her. She wouldn't approach him at work, but if she had to hunt him down at his place she would do it.

After promising that she wasn't going to commit murder, she talked her lawyer into leaving the office. She hated it that the poor man would be worrying about needing to have bail posted for her for the rest of the day, but she knew that this was something she had to do.

Even if confronting Trent didn't get her anywhere, at least she'd feel better. She was tired of just sitting back and letting everybody else have a part in deciding her daughter's future. Maggie was *hers* and she wasn't going to just lie down and let somebody come down from Texas and take her child away from her.

She called the hospital and asked for Trent's schedule. Marty, the prenatal technician on duty, seemed suspicious about her needing the information, but with some sweet talk she managed to find out that Trent had gotten called in during the night and had been given the day off in exchange.

Marty was one of the quieter techs in the department, who normally just went about his business, but she would still be surprised if he didn't leak details of her call to the other techs in the department. She could expect a resurgence of gossip by the next time she was on the labor unit, but that was the least of her problems.

She had trusted Trent and he had let her down by pulling this last strategy on her. He needed to know that she wasn't going to be scared off by him and his father. If the Montgomerys wanted a fight she would give them one. What did she have to lose?

Just the most important person in her life—her daughter.

The ride over through bumper-to-bumper traffic just got her more ready for a fight. By the time she pulled up into the driveway of a two-story townhouse she was prepared to confront Trent.

She couldn't believe she had fallen for that sweet Texas drawl of his and let down her guard. Okay, it hadn't been just that sexy accent he had. No, Trent had been blessed with the whole package. From his hard body to his sweet smile. She hadn't had a chance. Had that been the plan all the time? Was he just the front man for his father?

Yeah, the gloves were coming off now and she wasn't going to leave till she got some answers.

When ringing the doorbell didn't get a response she began pounding the decorative knocker on the front door. It didn't get any better results, but it sure did make her feel better. She had become a fountain of adrenaline, and she was about to spill over if she didn't get to burn it off soon.

Finally, she heard the door being unlocked and saw the knob turn. She was ready to blast Trent with everything she had when the door opened.

One look at the man standing in the foyer had her swallowing her words and forgetting her name. His inky dark hair was bed-tousled and his eyes, heavy with sleep, were seductive and inviting. His chest was bare and she followed the fine line of dark hair down his taut abs until it disappeared under a pair of silk sleeper pants that rode low on his hips and made no secret of the fact that he wore nothing under them.

He could have been born of any of the thousand fantasies that had filled her nights since meeting him. For a second she just stopped and drank him in as she thanked the fates that had seen fit to give her at least this moment of pleasure. How was she supposed to fight with this man when her whole body had suddenly melted into a puddle of need that had to be steaming up his front porch with its heat?

And then she remembered Maggie—sweet little Maggie who needed her so much.

She watched Trent scrub at his jaw as he tried to shake off the remnants of sleep that seemed to be holding him captive. She could almost feel the rough sensation of the bristly stubble as it nuzzled her neck and tickled her chin.

Dreams, she reminded herself, those had just been dreams.

"Lana?" Trent said as he rubbed at his eyes, as if he was trying to get everything awake and operable. "Did I oversleep and miss something?"

"What…?" she said.

"Come in. Let me go change. I'll be right back." Trent said, and then turned to walk into his house.

Lana felt cool air hit her as she walked into the foyer. And after a couple steps into the room she felt herself surface from her lust-induced fog. This would never do. She couldn't keep letting him do this to her.

"Wait," she said as she caught up to him in a large room that opened into a modern stainless steel kitchen and a formal dining and living room. "Nathan told me about your father."

Trent stopped and turned back toward her. Was that remorse she saw in the pained expression on his face? For her? Or was it for himself? Did he regret that she had found out his plan? She wouldn't have known anything about his father's lawyer if the social worker hadn't informed Nathan. Maybe he had planned to throw her off by waiting till the court date to hit her with this news.

"Let me get some clothes on," Trent said, then turned to walk away.

*Yeah, clothes.* Clothes would be good. Maybe if the man covered up some of that inviting skin of his she would be able to think.

A glance around at the cool white-upholstered couches and off-white carpeting and walls had her imagining the damage one little toddler could do to a room like this. Images of Trent playing tea party with Maggie came to mind, and for a second she imagined a future with the three of them together, sharing lazy Sundays and evenings curled up together on the couch.

She shook her head, forcing the fantasies from her mind. She was happy with her daughter and their little block bungalow with its toy-strewn rooms. They had become a family. *Her* family. She wasn't going to let anyone destroy that. Not Trent and not his father.

But would the court see it the same way? She couldn't compete with all the things Trent and his family could give Maggie. She did okay in her midwife practice, and could certainly provide for Maggie, but looking around the expensively furnished room reminded her of the difference between her life and the Montgomerys'. It was just another thing where the judge could find her lacking.

"Ready to talk?" Trent asked as he walked into the room.

He had changed into a pair of worn jeans and a pale blue tee shirt but he'd left his feet bare, which gave him a casual look that did nothing to squash the desire she had felt for him earlier. She stared down at the long toes peeking out from the hem of his jeans. Who knew bare feet could be so sexy?

Lana shook her head. She was lusting after his toes? *Toes?* Someone really needed to come up with a vaccine she could take to keep her safe from this man. She had to snap out of it. She had to get back in control of herself. She had to get some answers.

"So what was the plan, Trent? Come to Florida and play nice with the little midwife while your father was back home putting together a legal team to fight me?" Lana asked.

The anger that had spurred her into hunting down Trent had died somewhere between his opening the door and her walking into the house. She was so tired of playing games with him. Why couldn't he just be up-front with her? Didn't she deserve that?

He dropped his eyes for a minute, and then looked up as he rubbed the back of his neck. He looked more like a sheepish kid who had gotten caught with his hand in the cookie jar then a man who was trying to tear her world apart. How did he break her heart one minute and then rev it up the next? She felt as if she was being pulled in two when she was around him and she just couldn't keep going like this. Something had to give—and soon.

"I was going to call you and explain to you today…" Trent started. He ran his hands through his hair, then held them out to her. "Look… It's not what you think. I've tried to keep my father out of this. If anything, I've been trying to keep him out of Maggie's life—and yours."

"I don't understand," Lana said.

"Come sit down," Trent said as he reached for her hand.

She looked at the hand he held out to her. Another ploy? But one look at him had her doubting her earlier suspicions. He was pulling off the performance of his life ifthe pain she saw in his eyes was just an act. She knew better than to trust him, but still…

Trent sat, then pulled Lana down next to him. The warmth of her body eased the coldness that seeped into him whenever he had to deal with his old man. Her rigid posture told him she still didn't trust him. And could he blame her?

How much to tell her? He had to gain back her trust if there was any way for them to move on and do the right thing for his niece. She would need to be prepared for the force of his father's influence.

He had no doubt his father would be pulling out all the stops now that he knew the conditions of Michael's will. Would she even understand what his father was like when it came to the family company? Of course it was more of an empire now. He had to give that to his father. The man had taken the small-time oil company his mother had inherited and made a multi-billion-dollar business out of it.

But how did he explain the dysfunction his father's

obsession with the company had caused? He would have to start at the beginning. Digging into his past would be painful, but he had to make her understand what she was up against. What the two of them were up against.

"My parents came from totally different backgrounds. My mother was an only child and, while my grandparents weren't nearly as successful as my father has been with the oil company my Grandfather Lord started, she was well provided for. She went to all the right schools and had everything she wanted."

He felt Lana relax against him and some of the tension in his own body eased. Maybe he would be able to win her trust back. Maybe she would realize he hadn't had any choice other than to try to protect his niece.

"But my dad was a different story. Grandpa Montgomery worked for Grandfather Lord out on the ranch. He worked hard, and he had a wife and four kids. From what I've been told, my dad grew up helping his dad out with ranch chores," he said.

"So your parents grew up together?" Lana asked.

She was so close now that he could feel the vibration when she spoke. It was nice. He wasn't a man usually comfortable with someone in his personal space, but this felt good. Safe.

"Yeah, they did. Eventually they grew up, and I guess they fell in love and married."

"You *guess*?" she asked.

"I don't know. I think they loved each other at first. I do remember some times when I was young when they seemed happy together, but in the end all I remember is their fighting."

And his mother crying. He remembered his mother crying and his dad storming out of the house.

"My uncle has told me that my father buried himself in the business because he needed to prove to himself and the company that he could handle it."

"It couldn't have been easy for him to come into the company that way," said Lana.

"No—knowing where my father came from, I'm sure there were often people making comments about him marrying into the company."

His uncle had said as much on the many times he had taken sides with his brother when Trent had complained about his father ignoring Michael's problems.

"I'm sure it was hard at first, but by the time my mother died he had doubled the company's size and he should have been able to spare some time for Michael."

"You say Michael—what about you? You were just a boy yourself when your mother passed. Didn't you need a father too?"

"Michael was the youngest. He needed him more."

Trent looked away when Lana responded with a snort.

"You've got to understand... Michael was the baby of the family."

"What you're saying is that he was left to do whatever he wanted and there was no adult there to hold him accountable," she said.

"Unfortunately, yes," Trent agreed. "And it just got worse as he got older. I tried to help him, but he wouldn't listen to me. By the time my father decided to take an interest in him he was already in trouble. That's when things got really bad at home."

"Why?" she asked.

Trent felt his body tense. Talking about his brother was difficult, but it had to be done.

"Michael got into some trouble with the law and suddenly my father decided he needed to take control of the situation." He hated the bitterness he could hear in his voice. "By that time I had gone off to college and made it plain that I wasn't going to follow in the old man's footsteps. I guess my father knew that his only chance to pass on the company was through Michael."

"And Michael wasn't interested?"

"No, actually, just the opposite. For a while it looked like he was going to straighten out his life. But it seemed the harder he tried the more my father wanted from him. I think eventually he just gave up."

"What happened to Michael, Trent?"

"It was just too much for him. He started playing around with drugs. Street drugs, prescription drugs… I think he tried them all. Before I knew it he was hooked. We sent him to the best rehabs in the country, but in the end the drugs won. One night he just took too many and that was the end."

"Was it an accident or…?" Lana reached over and wrapped her arms around him.

"I don't know." But, God, how he hoped it had been an accident. Losing his brother to drugs had torn him up inside. Thinking that his brother had ended his own life was more than he could bear.

"I'm so sorry that you lost Michael, but what does this have to do with me and Maggie?"

"My father likes to take control of situations. It's what he did with my brother—what he tried to do with my mother. He'll want to take over Maggie's life too. He's powerful, Lana. He has the means to take Maggie away from you and I'm afraid he won't be satisfied until he does."

Trent felt tears on his shoulder where she had laid her

head. He knew the tears were as much for him as they were for her. That was his Lana. She had a big heart. One that she had opened up to a young mother and a little baby. And now he was tearing her heart out when he should be thanking her for taking that little baby in and giving her a home.

Turning, he hugged her close to him, then slipped his hand under her chin. He began wiping his thumb across the smoothness of her wet cheek and then replaced her tears with soft kisses that led down to her mouth. Taking small sips of her lips, he worked to draw her out of her sorrow. It tore him apart to see her hurting.

"I'm sorry too," he whispered into her mouth. "I'm so sorry."

"Then show me," she whispered as she began kissing him back. "Take away the pain…make it all go away."

Lana let go of the hurt and the worry and gave in to her body's demands. Somehow it had separated her desire for Trent from her fear. She needed to forget all the pain, all the fear that haunted her every second of every day. She needed him to satisfy this ache, this itch, this all-consuming desire he made her feel that left her waking each night tangled in her sheets, frustrated and hurting.

She always did the right thing, the safe thing. Just for once she wanted to be able to do what she wanted without worrying about the consequences. To let go of all the reasons this was wrong and allow herself the freedom to just enjoy the moment.

She plunged into him.

Pleasure coursed through her at the feel of his hot, wet mouth. He tasted of spicy mint, and as his tongue circled hers she let the last remnants of anger leave her body.

There was nothing to hold her back now. She combed her hands through his thick curls, then tightened her grip to anchor his lips against hers.

His hands stroked up and down her back in a rhythm that matched the mating of their tongues. He deepened his kiss, then ran his hands lower until they cupped her butt and lifted her up over him. She felt him long and hard against her belly and her body answered his with a wet need that pooled between her legs.

"Ah, Lana…" he groaned as he pulled back.

She reached for the bottom of his shirt, then ran her hands up inside till she found his nipples. She let her thumbs caress the twin nubs till they puckered for her. She felt his hands undo the clasp of her bra, then circle back around to her freed breasts. Her breath caught inside her when she felt him cup their weight. The feel of his coarse hands against her nipples had her arching into him. She'd wanted this—no, *needed* this since that first kiss in the locker room.

She let her hands trail lower as they followed the soft line of hair down his chest. The feel of his abs tightening at her touch urged her on to her target. She felt him tense, heard him moan as she teased the skin along his waistband. For the first time in her life she felt power in lovemaking and it was exhilarating. Trent made her feel like a real, whole woman—not broken like Joe had made her feel.

Yes, Trent had been with more experienced women then her—women who would have known how to attract and satisfy him—but there wasn't any way that a woman had ever wanted him more than she did at that moment. Maybe she had never learned the art of seduction, but she wasn't going to let her old insecurities stop her. She was too far gone now. No way was she going to let her feelings of inadequacy spoil this. No more waiting for what she wanted. She would take it this time.

Surprising herself, she let her hand wander down to his fly, where she let her nails run up and down over the teeth of the zipper. Feeling the hard ridge beneath the clothing, she teased herself as much as him—until she could no longer stand the thought of being this close yet still not touching him. She undid the button of his jeans and eased the zipper down.

Feeling the pressure ease as Lana lowered the zipper of his jeans, Trent fought for control. Backing away, he grabbed her hand, stilling its motion while at the same time pressing it against the length of him. Resting his head against her forehead, he took a deep breath…and then another. He needed to gain control or he would end up taking her on the floor where they stood.

What was it about her that heated his blood so hot that he couldn't think when she was around? As she closed her hand around him his whole body tensed with a need he had never known before. This woman, with her pure heart and sweet curvaceous body, undid him. If he didn't get her hands off him right then it would all be over. His body was going to go up in flames any minute.

He removed her hand and held it tightly in his own. They had to slow down. He needed to think.

Looking down into her wild green eyes, he was amazed by the trust he saw there. She was amazing in her capacity to love and nurture. It was unlike anything he had ever seen or known. The thought of being the one who was able to gift her with what she needed right then humbled him. He felt his own need as it pounded into his heart. He knew he wasn't worthy of the honor, but he felt no shame in his desire for her. Maybe in this one thing they could come together and give each other the comfort they both needed right now.

Keeping his eyes connected with hers, he threaded his fingers through hers and drew her up from the couch. He led her down the hall into his bedroom, where there would be no one but him and her, choosing to grab this precious time for themselves. He had to do this right. Things were so complicated between them now and he couldn't mess this up.

He shut the door behind them and turned to her.

"We leave everything, everybody, on the other side of that door. Can you do that, Lana?" he asked as he closed the space between them.

Lana forced herself to concentrate on his words. There would be no going back from here.

Sex had never been something she took lightly, but she had spent the last two years feeling like only half a woman, and she didn't want to feel like that anymore. She knew the intimacy of this moment would change her, touch her deep down in places she had kept guarded since Joe, but she knew it would be worth it.

Sometimes you just had to trust blindly. There could be no love without trust.

Love? Was she that far gone?

Fear suddenly flamed inside her at the thought of loving Trent, but then she remembered his words. He had told her to leave everything outside the door for just these few moments they had together. Could she? Should she?

"Yes," she heard herself say.

No matter how much her brain questioned the insanity of this, there was no other option for her. Both her body and her heart needed him. Right then, right there.

He led her over to his rumpled bed and she watched his face as she released his hand and backed up toward the bed, removing her shirt and letting it fall to the floor, following it with her bra and skirt.

As the afternoon sunlight filtered through the closed blinds she stood there in only a white cotton thong. She should have felt cold and exposed, but as Trent walked towards her she felt the warmth of his eyes as they covered her body. She reached for his hand and led him with her to the bed.

When his arms circled her she let all her misgivings go. She pulled him down and then his hands were everywhere as they stroked and kissed. She let herself explore his arms and chest as she returned his burning kisses, reaching lower until she was circling him with her hands. She thrilled at the hard length that proved his desire for her.

His hands came between them and he began stroking her. She spread her legs to welcome him. Sensations flooded through her as her hips rocked against the thick hard length of him. And then he was there, thrusting inside her with a rhythm she fought to match until she was drenched with sweat.

He arched and stiffened inside her as his body rushed to its climax. Then he reached between them once again and with one shattering stroke she joined him.

Everything around them flew away as they held on to each other. For a brief second she felt them suspended in time, where nothing existed except for the two of them. And then they were crashing back down—together.

* * *

Lana glanced at the alarm clock sitting on the nightstand. She would have to leave soon. Amanda had a night class so she would have to pick up Maggie at daycare. She looked across the room, taking in the same simple white color scheme that had been present in what she had seen of the rest of the house.

There was nothing in the room that hinted of Trent's personal taste. White walls, off-white carpet, even shabby-chic white furniture throughout the room. The only thing with any color was the natural oak window trim and the door. The door that kept the world away… the door that allowed them to escape from all the reasons why they shouldn't be here, together, right now.

Wasn't that what everyone had to do sometimes? Just shut everything out and escape into a world where they felt secure and safe, away from all their troubles and free of all their responsibilities, even if it was just for a short time? Was it so bad that they had grabbed this little bit of time for themselves?

She thought of her agreement with Trent. *Leave everything, everybody, on the other side of that door.* But what happened when the door opened? When once again they found themselves in the heated fight that was turning them both inside out? What happened when they both had to face the fact that they were on opposite sides in a battle that had the highest stakes possible and that only one of them could win?

"Shh…" Trent said, and he shifted and drew her closer, trailing his hands through her hair, soothing her with his touch.

Letting go of a breath she hadn't known she was holding, she snuggled down into him. Resting her head on his chest and listening to the steady beat of his heart, she let her body recede into that calm place where Trent had taken her.

She just needed a few more minutes to enjoy the feel of him. Enough time for her to capture this memory. She would wrap it up and take it with her. And when things got bad she would take it out and it would remind her that at least she'd had this moment. This little bit of time when life had been right between the two of them.

Trent combed his hands through the thick blond mass of hair that lay across his chest, then bent his head and took a deep breath. The soft scent of honeysuckle filled him, making him smile. It was a scent that he had come to recognize as Lana. It was fresh and feminine, with a touch of sweetness that was guileless in its simplicity and so like Lana, who had no desire to be anything but herself.

He had always enjoyed the smell of the little yellow flowers that grew wild on the rickety old fence that lined the entrance to the ranch. Though he could remember many an argument between his dad and mom about the trailing plants, with his dad calling them weeds and fussing about having to clear them every year after they'd died out. But his mom would always just ignore his dad and go right on picking the vines and sticking them into the old Mason jar that she'd kept sitting on the kitchen window sill.

Things were different around the ranch now, but the same old fence still stood, and every year the honeysuckle would grow back. He'd caught his dad staring out the window and looking at the fragrant yellow flowers once, and wondered if possibly the old man was thinking about the wife he had lost.

"I was eight and Michael only four when my mother left and never came back."

He felt Lana turn to him, but he knew he couldn't look down at her. He had promised her that they would keep everything out of the bedroom, but he could fill the world creeping in and knew they would soon have to return to their separate lives.

"She just walked out on you?"

"No. Well, not exactly," he said.

Once more he pulled her up close to him and turned her so that he could rest his chin on the top of her head. He let the scent of her soothe the raw hurt he felt every time he thought of that night twenty-four years ago.

"Mom and Dad had had a bad fight that day. He'd found where she'd hidden her whiskey bottle and had thrown it out the back door. She'd screamed at him about going through her things and he'd hollered back that she had promised to quit drinking. That she had promised there wouldn't be any more alcohol around the house. Then she started crying and telling him that he didn't understand. It was the same argument that they had almost daily. They argued about him always being at work and her always being left alone, but this time it was worse.

"Dad told Mom he'd have her put in a rehab clinic if she didn't stop drinking, and that's when my mom threatened to take the company away from him. My dad finally walked out and I thought things would be okay. That he'd come back in a little while and Momma would tell him that she was sorry and beg him to forgive her. Say that she'd try harder. It was how all their fights ended. They'd hug and kiss and everything would go on just fine."

Trent stopped. He had forgotten about those times when they had made up—the times when they had disappeared for an hour or two alone. Had they been happy together then?

"Your mother was an alcoholic," Lana stated.

"Yes. Looking back now, I can see all the signs. All the times she slept through the day, never getting up to check on either me or Michael. Then there were the times when I would find her hugging the toilet, too sick to hold her head up."

"But you couldn't have known what was wrong with her then. You were just a child," Lana said.

Trent clasped the hand she'd entangled with his. He hadn't really ever talked about that night with anyone. Not even Michael, who had been way too young to understand what was happening at the time.

"No, I didn't know what was wrong—but I did know something wasn't right," he said. "And that day when Momma left us home alone I knew she shouldn't have gone. I knew that moms didn't go off and leave their kids all alone like that. And when it got to be dark and she still hadn't come home, and Michael started crying that he was scared and wanted his momma, I got real mad. I got mad at the both of them."

He'd been scared too. Scared that his parents had both gone off and forgotten about them. But he hadn't told Michael he was scared. He'd had to be strong and take care of Michael.

"Momma said she'd be right back. She was going to run to the store and then she'd be right back. She said that I needed to take care of my little brother because I was the oldest, but that she wouldn't be long. Just a few minutes…that's all it would take her."

Trent remembered how relieved he'd been when he'd seen the lights from his dad's rusted old pick-up pull into the drive. But then his dad had found out that their mom wasn't home and that she'd left them all alone. He'd never seen his dad so mad. He'd been scared all over again. He'd tried to tell his dad that Momma had just gone to the store and that she'd be right back.

Then Harry from the sheriff's office had driven up. He'd seen his daddy shake his head as tears ran down his weathered face.

That was the last time he'd seen his dad show any type of emotion for anything except his damn oil company. His father hadn't even cried at Michael's funeral— but then neither had he. Just how much like his father *was* he?

"Something happened to her, didn't it?" Lana asked in a voice that could barely be called a whisper.

"They found her car where she hit a tree, but I found out later—when I was older—that she had been thrown out of it," Trent said. "The accident report said that they found an open bottle of Jack Daniels on the seat."

For a few minutes they just lay there in silence as they held each other. Lana couldn't imagine what it had been like for the two little boys, all alone and scared one minute, while they waited for their momma to come home, and then the next to be told she was never coming back.

They'd both been so young, and there was no doubt that they'd been affected by the events of that night. Even Michael, at four, had to have known that their mom was supposed to *be* there. That she was supposed to take care of them. And her asking Trent to watch his brother so that she could go out and buy alcohol had been so irresponsible that it made her wonder if there had been other times when she had put the bottle before her two little boys.

"After my mom died and my great-aunt came to live with us my father devoted all his time to the oil company. Before long it had grown to one of the largest in the state," he said. "That's when he really changed."

Lana felt his hand under her chin, strong but tender as he raised her head up to his.

"The company was the center of his life. It became impossible to please him. No matter what Michael or I did, it was never good enough. By the time I started applying to colleges I knew that I didn't want to be involved with the family business, so I decided to go into medicine. My father has never forgiven me for that decision. He doesn't like it when things don't go his way."

He was *warning* her about his father. "You're not involved with him against me in the custody battle, are you?" she asked.

"No, I'm not," he said. "And now you know all my family's dirty secrets."

A chill washed over her. "We all have secrets," she said, pulling the sheet up higher.

"And you, Lana? Do you have secrets?" he asked.

The outside world was starting to seep into the room and none of it was pretty. He had shared so much with her. Was it not right that she did the same with him? Where things would go between them after this she didn't know, but she knew she needed to be honest about everything with him.

"I need to tell you something," she said, then swallowed.

She felt the slightest tightening of his muscles against her skin.

"Okay," he said.

He settled back in the bed, curling himself around her and pulling her against him, as if protecting her. If only he could… But there were some hurts that even Prince Charming, or in this case a sexy cowboy doctor, couldn't fix.

"When I was sixteen I went to my pediatrician for a school physical and he found a cancerous mass in my abdomen. I was lucky they found it early, but the chemo and radiation…" She took a deep breath, reaching for the strength she needed. "They damaged my ovaries. I can never have children, Trent."

They lay there with nothing but silence between them for a minute, Trent still wrapped around her.

"I'm so sorry, Lana," Trent said. "Cancer is such a harsh disease, and you were so young."

She shrugged her shoulders and pushed herself up, pulling herself away from him. The last thing she wanted Trent to feel for her was pity.

"It was a long time ago. I just thought you should know."

She needed to leave.

She wiped the tears away from her face and reached for the alarm clock to bring it closer to her. Propped up against a crystal lamp was a small picture of her and Maggie as they played in the sand on their trip to the beach. She hadn't known he was taking it—which was a good thing. With her hair soaking wet from their dip in the cold salt water and her face bare of everything except the red hint of sun on the tip of her nose, it was not a good picture of her.

Of course he had been taking pictures of Maggie that day—she had probably just happened to be in this one. But the fact that he had it there, where he would see it every night before he went to sleep, helped ease the pain of knowing that she would never be in this bedroom, behind this door, again.

"I've got to go pick up Maggie," she said as she climbed out of the bed.

Her body immediately felt cold, and she knew it had nothing to do with the air-conditioning in the house. All the warmth that had comforted her earlier was now gone.

She picked up her clothes from where they had been dropped earlier and told herself that everything would be okay between them. They were adults. They had both agreed to keep this time separate from everything else in their life and they would do it. Knowing what she did now about Trent and his father's relationship, there was no doubt that the two of them weren't working together against her, but that still didn't make him an ally. They were still on opposite sides of what was best for Maggie.

"Lana, I'm sorry. About everything. I'm *so* sorry."

Looking back at him, she saw pain in his eyes. And as she left to go back into the world outside she knew that somehow nothing and yet everything had changed since she had walked inside that bedroom.

Trent watched as Lana left the room. His heart went out to the sixteen-year-old girl who had been through so much and then had so much taken away from her after surviving cancer. He had seen the pain that still haunted her eyes when she'd talked about not being able to have children.

Looking over at the picture he had placed on the

nightstand, he was hit with how unfair it was that the beautiful woman in the photo, who had so much love to give, and who had helped so many women as they labored to bring their children into the world, would never know what it was like to bring her own child into the world.

And as he turned over in his bed he was hit with the realization that his bed felt cold and empty without her.

# CHAPTER EIGHT

IT HAD BEEN two days and thirteen hours since she had walked out of Trent's home. She had been waiting for him to contact her. She'd believed him when he'd said he wasn't involved with his father's plans, but she knew there was something going on between him and his father that he was holding back from her. There was a bitterness in Trent's voice whenever he spoke of his father that was inconsistent with everything else she thought she knew about him.

She decided to stop by Labor and Delivery after rounding on her patients on the recovery floor, hoping not only to see him, but also to talk to the charge nurse about the gossip Amanda had heard earlier that week, concerning her and Trent. She needed to address some of the tongue-wagging that was going around the hospital. She could have approached the people she thought were spreading the stories around, but she felt it would be better to have the charge nurse remind them to watch what they were saying.

Arriving on the unit, she found the nurses' station empty, which was never a good sign. Recognizing the flashing emergency light that was going off over Labor Room Five, she sprinted down the hall.

"Lana, we need some help," said Laurie, who was the day charge, as soon as she saw Lana enter the room.

Lana recognized the two nurses who were trying to strip the clothes off a pale woman whose rounded belly indicated that she was due at any time.

"What do you need me to do?" Lana offered as she approached the bed.

The metallic smell hit her before she saw the blood that pooled between the patient's legs. The young woman looked to be of Asian descent and she seemed to be pleading in a language that Lana couldn't understand.

"What's she saying?" she asked as she grabbed the heart monitor and applied it to the swollen belly.

"Save my baby," said the man standing at the other side of the bed, holding her hand. "She doesn't want to lose our baby."

Lana touched the woman's abdomen and felt the hard tone of the uterus. Looking further down, she saw the outline of a faded scar. "Did she have surgery when she had another baby?" she asked the man.

"Yes—with our three sons. She was supposed to have another C-section."

"Ruptured uterus?" Laurie asked as she passed her a small hand-held ultrasound.

"No, I think her placenta is abrupting," Lana said as she looked at the black and white screen.

The labor monitors started to beep and the fetal heart-beat began tracing across the screen. It was lower than normal, but if they got the baby out fast it would have a chance.

The blood pressure machine went off too, and the cuff on one of the patient's arms began to tighten.

"Who's the doctor on call?" Lana asked as they worked to turn the patient and remove the rest of her clothes.

"Dr. Bradley and he's on his way," Laurie said. "We've already called the nursery and Dr. Montgomery is on his way over too."

The charge nurse finished inserting an intravenous needle and hung a large bag of fluids to help replace some of the volume of blood the patient was losing.

"We need to get her to the operating room *now*," Lana said as she looked at the low blood pressure reading that flashed up on the monitor. "I'll assist. Where's anesthesia?"

"Right here," said Debra, the nurse anesthetist, as she walked into the room. She grabbed a pair of gloves on her way to the bed when she saw the blood that was quickly filling the clean pads they'd just applied.

"Okay, let's roll," the charge nurse ordered her staff.

While Debra rushed to get her equipment ready, Lana stopped to put her arm around the father of the baby. She walked him out to the small waiting room outside the operating theater. The man had begun to tremble the minute he had left his wife's side and she knew he needed to sit down.

Lana was very familiar with the feeling of helplessness that the man had to be feeling, with both his wife and his child's life in danger. Bending down so that they were on eye level, she took his hand and gave it a squeeze. "What's her name?" Lana asked.

"Joy. Her name is Joy," he said.

"Is she allergic to anything that you know of?" she asked.

"No," he answered, then looked up at her with dark troubled eyes. "Will she be okay?"

"We're going to take good care of her," Lana said, then rose to her feet and headed for the door. "I'll let you know any news as soon as I can."

"And the baby? Will the baby be okay?" she heard him ask as she was leaving the room.

She wanted to ignore the question, knowing that her answer wouldn't bring the relief that this father wanted, but that was the cowardly way out and what he needed was honesty. He needed to be prepared in case the worst happened.

"I don't know," she answered quietly, then turned and headed for the scrub sink.

The operating room would have appeared to be in chaos to anyone who didn't know that every one of the staff members there was competently doing their job. As she dried her hands on the sterile towel one of the techs handed her, Lana turned in a circle so that one of the nurses could tie her up in a sterile gown.

Checking the fetal monitors, she saw that the fetal heart tones, which had been dipping down with the contractions earlier, were remaining low. They needed to hurry and get the baby out—but they had no choice but to wait for the surgeon.

She looked over as the swinging doors opened and Trent walked in with the neonatal team. They went straight over to the warmer unit and began setting up the resuscitation equipment. They had already opened the crash cart so that they would be ready as soon as the baby was handed to them. This was a situation where a few wasted seconds could be a matter of life or death.

"What do we have?" Trent asked as he moved over to her.

She had thought she would be uncomfortable the next time she saw Trent after their afternoon together, but right now all she felt was relief at the sight of him. If there was anything that could be done for this baby when they delivered it she knew Trent would do it.

"Patient's name is Joy. Past C-section times three… placenta abruption on arrival. She doesn't speak much English," she said.

She watched as he moved over to the neonatal team and started giving orders. And the whole time, as people turned the woman from side to side, stuck monitor pads on her arms and chest and applied all the necessary monitors, she kept pleading with that sad voice for her child's life.

"Is everyone ready?" asked Dr. Bradley as he entered the OR and reached for a sterile towel to dry his hands.

Lana's breath came a little easier at the sight of the OB doctor entering the room. As the circulating nurse reviewed the patient's history and her presentation at the hospital he gowned and gloved. He called for the patient's name and then did a time-out, to assure everyone was aware of the procedure and the patient.

While everyone in the room listened to Laurie's report the staff positioned the instruments where they could easily be handed to the doctor. Debra from Anesthesia was injected some medicine into Joy's IV and then inserted the endotracheal tube, so that she would be able to control her breathing while she was under anesthesia.

Seconds after the team was in position Dr. Bradley made an incision into the abdomen. Lana operated the suction, trying to clear all the blood and fluid so that the doctor could see as he made his way through to the uterus. He cut into the uterus and removed a pale, still baby girl.

Lana remembered that Joy's husband had said they had three boys at home. This mother must be so excited about having a little girl. Lana felt the mask that covered her nose and mouth become damp as she watched Trent and the neonatal team begin to work on the quiet baby.

"We're not finished here, people," Dr. Bradley said, getting back the attention of his team. "Let them work on the baby. Our job is to fix this momma."

Lana quickly returned her attention to assisting while the doctor delivered the placenta and then repaired the uterus and closed the incision. Meanwhile Trent had quickly intubated the small baby and was working on getting intravenous access.

Finally the doctor closed the last layer of the earlier incision and the staff could relax.

"I have to go check on the staff," Laurie said as she pulled off her mask. "Melody, you take over here."

"I've got her," the nurse responded.

Lana moved over next to Trent as he finished putting a line through the umbilical cord. One of the respiratory team continued to bag the baby, but her color was still a dusky blue.

"Will she make it?" she asked him.

"I don't know," he answered. "Her heartbeat is still a little slow, but we've ordered blood to transfuse. The sooner we can get that in her the better."

A shrill alarm sounded and Trent quickly turned back as the monitor showed the baby's oxygen saturation falling rapidly.

"Rate?" he asked the nurse who was listening to the baby's heart with a stethoscope.

"Fifty-six," she answered.

"Start compressions," he ordered. "Where's that blood?"

"It's on its way up from the lab," another nurse said. "I'm drawing up the epinephrine now."

"Go ahead and give it," he said.

Lana watched as yet another nurse walked in with a small packet of blood and began setting up the tubing. She waited as all the nurses coordinated their compressions and ventilations, feeling helpless but knowing there was nothing she could do but pray for a miracle.

"Pulse-check," Trent ordered.

"One hundred and twenty," said the nurse checking the pulse.

"Let's go," he said to the team, and they rushed out with the new baby.

Lana looked down at the blood on her scrubs. Unless she wanted to give her staff and her patients a scare, she would need a new pair before she went back to her office.

She pulled out her beeper and was surprised to find that it had only been thirty minutes since she had walked onto the unit. It always felt so much longer when you knew there was a life depending on your speedy response.

Lana was just stepping out of the locker room when Trent walked in. He couldn't get his thoughts off the woman who had been on the operating table. He knew that she would be physically okay once she got into Recovery. It was the woman's emotional reaction to hearing that her baby was in critical condition that would affect the young mother the most.

Would she be able to cope if her baby didn't make

it? What about Lana? Would *she* be able to cope if she lost Maggie?

It was thoughts of Lana that had sent him here, looking for her.

"The baby?" she asked when she saw him.

"Now that we've got a transfusion going her color is better, but it's too soon to know how she'll do. I just wanted to grab some new scrubs," he said.

"'Save my baby. Don't let me lose my baby,'" Lana quoted as she leaned against the locker room wall. "She kept telling us that. And I can't lose *my* baby, Trent. I can't lose Maggie."

He felt his heart break when Lana looked up at him, her eyes brimming with tears.

"Don't, Lana…" he said as he came over and put his arms around her. Pulling her down to the closest bench, he rubbed his hands up and down her arms, where goosebumps peppered her skin.

"I don't know if I'm crying for her or for me," Lana said as she wiped away her tears with the back of her hands. "Selfish, huh? To be thinking about myself when that poor woman doesn't know if her baby is going to live or die?"

Trent moved her hands out of the way, then used the pads of his own thumbs to wipe at her tears. How could she ask that? She was the most unselfish person he had ever met.

He had watched her with her patients. She could be falling-down tired, but she remained at their side no matter how long they needed her. She thought of everybody's needs—even his—before herself. She only asked for one thing for herself. To be able to raise the little girl she had taken into her heart.

"No, I don't think you're selfish. I'm surprised you haven't broken down before now," Trent said as he held her face between his hands. "Look at me," he said when she tried to look away. "I came here without any thought of how it would affect anyone except me. But I think I have a way to make things right—to fix this. But I need a few more days to work things out."

"I stopped by to see her husband. He says the baby's name is Hope."

Trent looked down into those pure green eyes that swam with tears. There was hope there now. He couldn't let her down. A hint of doubt sparked through him. He had let Michael down, hadn't he? How could he know that he wouldn't fail Lana too?

"I've got to get back," Trent said, then pulled away from her.

As he opened the door he looked to where she sat on the old wooden bench. She was bent over, with her elbows resting on her knees and her beautiful blond hair falling around her face, staring down at the dull gray carpet on the floor. He was doing the right thing—the only thing he *could* do right now. But that didn't mean it was over. He would find a way to work this out. He just had to.

He had no doubt that she would agree to anything to keep his niece, but his plan would come at a cost for both of them. He felt the weight of guilt hit him at his thoughts of sacrifice. He should tell her about the stipulations of the will. But would she understand how important it was for him to be able to protect Maggie from his father's influence? Or would he lose the trust he'd just seen in her eyes?

He walked back into the nursery with new determination as he remembered Lana's face as she had looked up at him, with all her faith in him in her eyes. She trusted him, and the weight of that trust lay heavy on him.

He wouldn't let her down. This time he would protect those who were depending on him. He couldn't fail Lana and Maggie.

"Of course I understand that you want to know your granddaughter, Father."

Trent tried to relax his grip on the phone. He was getting nowhere fast in this conversation. But he had enough experience in dealing with his father that he knew not to push at this point. He'd let the man try to convince him that this was all about family. As if Calvin Montgomery knew *anything* about family...

Trent had been thinking a lot about his childhood since his talk with Lana. There had been times when he was young when his father had spent time with him and his brother. It had been his father who had taught him to ride his first horse. And there had been a few fishing and camping trips with the whole family together. He would have sworn that his parents had been happy then—would have sworn that his father had truly cared about his sons.

But things had changed when his mom had passed away. It had been as if his father had just given up on his family after that. They'd all been damaged, with his father devoting more and more of his time to the business and Michael getting into more and more trouble. And Trent had found himself hiding behind his school work and spending as much time at his uncle's house as possible.

Hitting the "end call" button on his phone as soon as his father had ended their conversation, he gave himself some credit for not throwing it against the wall. His father reaching out to him like this was just a sign of things to come. He could expect more pressure now that the lawyers would be getting involved. There were too many people fighting over one little innocent girl.

He'd realized the night before, while he was lying in bed, looking at his picture of little Maggie and Lana, that really none of them had taken into account the fact that not only did Lana love Maggie as if she was her own, but Maggie loved Lana too.

That was what Lana had been trying to tell him in the social worker's office, but he hadn't listened. He hadn't wanted to hear what she was saying. But it was there in the picture, where Maggie was smiling up at Lana with all the love in her little heart. What would Maggie think if they took her away from Lana? That her mother had just gone off and left her?

He'd remembered the feeling he'd had when he had realized his mother wasn't coming back. He had been so scared. The thought of Maggie being scared like that had tied his stomach into knots, and he had known he couldn't let anything happen that would leave the child feeling like that.

So he'd woken up this morning and decided to take action to protect both woman and child.

Now, after glancing at his watch, he poured the coffee he'd let get cold while he was talking with his father into the sink. He had half an hour to get to Lana's for his visitation with Maggie and he didn't want to be late. There were plans to be made and action to be taken.

Lana stopped and looked outside her window for the second time in as many minutes. At this rate she would never get anything done. She was in a bad mood today, and it was the irritating man who was supposed to be here at any minute who had her that way. One minute he was all over her—the next he was walking away. A woman could get permanent whiplash, trying to keep up with his coming and going. And what had he meant when he had said he could fix things?

"Maggie, I found your purple puppy!" she called out as she bent down to pick it up off the floor. The toddler was busy pulling out all of her toys, looking for the prized stuffed animal.

She remembered when she had bought the silly-colored toy dog. Maggie had just started to crawl then. She'd been so cute, trying to hold onto her puppy and crawl at the same time. The poor puppy was missing an eye now, and it needed one of its ears to be sewn back on.

She heard a car door slam and felt her body relax. He was here. She hadn't been sure if he would show or not after his cryptic vow to make things right yesterday. She had been afraid that he intended to walk out of her and Maggie's life, and the thought of something that a couple of weeks ago would have thrilled her now left her feeling empty and alone.

She tried to tell herself that the only reason she didn't want Trent to leave was because of Maggie. Her daughter had become very attached to her uncle, and now that she had gotten to know him Lana knew she'd never keep him from seeing his niece.

Taking the stuffed animal into Maggie's room, she glanced at the mirror in the hall. It was a good thing that Amanda had decided to go out shopping with some of her friends today. Her babysitter would have seen right through her if she had seen her primping in front of the mirror.

So maybe she *had* spent a little more time on her make-up than necessary this morning? It certainly wasn't a crime to want to look good when you were doing housework and laundry, was it?

Who was she fooling? It had been years since she had been this concerned about how she looked. Trent had brought out the woman in her—the one that had been dead for the last couple of years. All those feelings of insecurity were almost gone now, and the excitement that filled her at the anticipation of seeing him was new.

She couldn't remember feeling like this even when she had been dating in college. It had to be the absence of a man in her life that was doing this to her. She had been wrong in thinking that since she had given up on marriage she didn't need a man at all. When Trent left she would have to find someone to take his place. She could do that. Couldn't she…?

"Who are you trying to fool? You've got it bad, girl." she said to her reflection, then looked down to see her daughter looking up at her. "Your momma's got to get herself together, Maggie-girl."

She picked the little girl up and gave her a big hug as the doorbell went.

"Now, let's go answer that door and see if we can talk some sense into your Uncle Trent."

She let Maggie greet him first. She couldn't help but smile when he picked her up and she gave him hugs and kisses. Maggie had always been a happy baby, but she had never been so comfortable around a man before. Lana had always blamed it on the fact that she had never been around a man except for Lana's dad, whom Maggie had loved immediately.

"Daddy!" the little girl said as she patted Trent's face with her small hands.

Lana felt the blood leave her face. Maggie had seen other children at daycare being picked up by their dads, so she must have decided that was what all men were called.

Lana reached out and took Maggie from Trent's arms. "I'm so sorry," she said. "I guess she thinks that's what men are called."

"It's no big deal," Trent said as he followed Lana into the house and shut the door behind him. "I've been called a lot of things, but I have to admit that is a first."

Lana looked up at Trent and noticed a tinge of color under his golden tan. Had he been embarrassed by Maggie calling him Daddy? But why? As he'd said, it wasn't a big deal.

"This is your Uncle Trent, Maggie," she told the little girl as she squirmed her way out of her arms.

Maggie immediately went back to Trent and pulled on his jeans leg, asking to be picked up. "Daddy?" she said in her sweet little voice.

"I'm sorry. She must be going through a phase," Lana said.

"It's not a problem, Lana," Trent said as he leaned down to pick the little girl up.

"So, what's the plan for today?" she asked. "Do you just want to hang out here with her or is there something you want to do?"

"I saw a park down the road," he said. "I thought we could go there. The weather is beautiful today, and we can talk while Maggie is playing."

"Let me grab a bag for her," Lana said, and headed down the hall.

So they were back to talking again. She didn't know why they bothered. She wasn't going to change her stand on Maggie's adoption. And he was too tied up with his feelings of being responsible for his brother's actions. They'd just end up chasing the same rabbit down a hole and they'd never come out in the same place together.

Trent watched the two little girls as they played in the sandbox. Even with a fairly small vocabulary the toddlers managed to communicate and play together. Kids were amazing. It was too bad that people seemed to lose that ability when they got older...

He and Lana had been sitting there watching the toddlers for several minutes and he still didn't know how to approach this. Would she go along with his unorthodox plan?

"I thought you wanted to talk?" Lana asked, then turned toward him.

He noticed the way she had pulled back her shoulders, as if she was getting ready for a fight. Well, either that or she was trying to show off the cleavage that was peeking out of the fitted pink tee shirt she was wearing today. He knew if he had to choose between a fight and looking at her breasts, the breasts would win every time.

He tried to smother the laugh he felt coming, but then decided he could use a good chuckle after the week he'd had, so he let go of all the happiness he felt in just this moment and enjoyed it.

"What's so funny?" Lana asked, then looked down to where his eyes were still trained. "Trent Montgomery, are you staring at my breasts? This is not the time!"

Lana had leaned in to whisper, which just gave him a better view.

When she saw his eyes, still peeking down her shirt she laughed herself. "Behave! There are little kids all around us."

He watched Lana tug at the top of her shirt as she pretended to be scandalized by his behavior, but he wasn't fooled. Memories of her in his bed had his body responding in ways that definitely weren't appropriate, considering their location.

He shifted in his seat and crossed his legs so that he wouldn't embarrass her any further.

She peeked over at him from under her thick lashes while she pretended to take in all the people walking and playing in the tree-lined park—though he noticed she didn't let her eyes stray from Maggie for more than a few seconds.

She was such fun to tease, and it was such a beautiful day. He was a lucky man, to be sitting out in the sun with two of the prettiest girls around. Too bad he was going to have to ruin it.

"I talked to my father today," he said.

"Did he mention Maggie?"

"Yes, he did." He stretched out his legs as he turned toward her. "He fed me some bull about always wanting grandchildren. He even had the nerve to give me a hard time about not having any kids."

"Why haven't you?" she asked.

"What?"

"Why haven't you gotten married? Had children?" she asked. "You know—all the things people normally do by our age?"

Because the thought of living like his father and

mother scared the life out of him. He would never be able to live like that. It was better to live alone than to spend his life on a rollercoaster of ups and downs such as his parents had called a marriage.

But maybe, for a little while, he wouldn't have to be alone. Surely if anyone could manage to make a temporary arrangement work for the security of little Maggie, he and Lana could.

"Why haven't *you*?" he asked.

"You know why," she said. "I can't have children."

Trent looked over to where Maggie played. "Would it make any difference to how you feel about Maggie if you had given birth to her?" he asked.

He watched her lips curve up in a smile as she watched Maggie playing.

"No, of course not. But it's not that simple," she said, then changed the subject. "What did you mean when you said you could 'fix things,' Trent?"

# CHAPTER NINE

LANA WATCHED AS he cleared his throat. She sensed in him the same nervousness that she had felt while discussing her infertility. Was it something so bad that he was scared to tell her?

"I think Ms. Nelson is right. Maggie does need both of us. We need to get married."

The shock of his statement hit her instantly. For a second she thought she would pass out, and then she remembered to breathe. She tried to open her mouth and ask one of the hundreds of questions spinning in her mind, but her voice wouldn't come.

He couldn't be serious. Could he?

"Trent…"

She let him take her hands in his and waited. She had to have misunderstood him.

"Just hear me out, Lana," he said. "Right now we're fighting against each other, when we should be fighting together for what's best for Maggie."

"You know I only want the best for her," she said.

"And with both of us working together we can make sure of that," he said.

"But that doesn't mean we have to get *married*,"

she said. "This has something to do with your father, doesn't it?"

She couldn't understand what his father could want with her little girl when from what Trent had said he hadn't cared for his own children, but it was plain to see that Trent thought his father was a real threat. Why else would he come up with such a hair-brained idea?

*Marriage?* To *Trent*?

She fought down a flutter of excitement that wanted to float to the surface. She couldn't let herself get pulled into that happily-ever-after dream again. Marriage was not meant for her. She had gotten her hopes up once, and when Joe had rejected her after he'd learned about her infertility it had nearly destroyed her.

She wouldn't go through that again. Better to accept that her future didn't hold any hope of the traditional family she had always planned on.

"What could be better than the two of us together?" he asked. "We've shown that we can work together and we get along well."

Yes, they did work well together—both in and out of bed—but that wasn't enough to build a marriage on. Was it…?

"And, yes, this has a lot to do with my father," he said. "There's something I should have told you—something you need to know that concerns my brother's will and is the reason I'm so worried about my father. I should have told you sooner—when we first met—but I didn't know you then. And later it always seemed the wrong time… No, that's not right. The truth is I was afraid you'd think I was just here trying to take advantage of you and Maggie and I didn't want that."

He pulled himself away from her, stretching his legs out in front of him as he looked out over the park.

"I'd never think that. I know you care about Maggie. Just *tell* me. What is it that I need to know?" she asked, knowing that whatever it was it had something to do with his desire for them to marry.

"When Michael died he didn't have much. He'd gone through most of the money we had inherited from our grandparents. But he still had the shares in the family business he inherited when our mother died. When he learned about Maggie he had his will updated, leaving everything to her. Those shares are worth a lot of money, Lana, but more importantly having control of them is worth a lot to my father."

"I don't care about any shares in your father's company, Trent. As far as I'm concerned he can have them. I just want to protect my daughter."

"The will specifies that Maggie is to keep them until she turns twenty-one. Then she can do whatever she wants with them. For now Michael's lawyers are in charge of them—till custody is decided by the courts. And that's where we are right now. The court can decide on only one of us. When my father decides to get involved in the custody battle—and he will, I promise you—we could both lose. This way we can both be there to protect Maggie."

"Of course after the case is settled we can both go back to our old lives, but until then we'd have to play the part of a loving couple for the court's sake."

Of course he would go back to his life in Houston. Had she really thought a man like Trent would be interested in actually setting up a home with her? It was only his sense of responsibility that had him willing to do something as drastic as marrying her.

She knew she shouldn't be hurt that he had come up with what might be the solution to all their problems. She should be happy that he was willing to go this far for his niece. But playing a part for the court? Living together day in and day out? How could she do that without falling for the man completely?

"I need to think about it," she said. "You should have told me everything before, Trent. For me to even consider this we need to be honest with each other."

"I'll do anything I can for you and Maggie," he said. "You know that."

*Anything, but love us.* How could she go into an agreement like this without her feelings for him getting stronger? But how could she not when this might ensure that Maggie would always be hers?

"I need some time," she said.

As she stood to leave she watched Trent as he walked over to the sandbox to get Maggie. He would be such a good father—a great father—but would that be enough?

She had so much to consider before she could make a decision of this magnitude. She would have to talk to Nathan so that she would know the legal requirements, and she would have to come up with some guidelines for their relationship. She knew she needed to protect her daughter, but if she was to survive this fake marriage she would have to find a way to protect herself too.

She had already let herself get too close to Trent. If she took this step it would just make her more vulnerable. Could she take that chance? Could she survive another heartbreak? She wasn't sure she would.

A scream cut through her thoughts and she turned to

see Trent, still holding Maggie, running toward a young woman holding a limp child.

Lana caught up with him and reached for Maggie, freeing his arms to take the child. As he knelt beside him Lana looked up at the woman whose face was filled with horror. She knew her. Sally—or was it Sandy?—and her little boy came to the park often when she was there with Maggie. They'd talked a few times, sharing something cute or horrible that their kids had recently done.

Shoving Maggie into the mom's arms, she leaned down to see if she could help.

"What happened?" Trent asked the mother.

Lana watched him check the child's breathing, then his pulse.

"Call 911," he said.

"He was playing, just running around like normal. Then he coughed…he kind of coughed… I don't know… he sounded funny… And then he fell… I thought he was playing…just playing." The woman sobbed as she clutched Maggie to her.

Lana watched as Trent assessed the child even as she gave their address to the operator on the line. "Pulse?" she asked.

"Too slow," Trent said.

"An ambulance is on its way," she told him, and she continued to hold the phone, giving the operator a play-by-play on the situation.

"Any history of asthma?" he asked the mother.

"No. He just fell down…" the mother said.

Trent was about to give the child a breath, then he paused. Lana watched as he glanced around the sidewalk. Following his gaze, she saw the apple core at the same time he did.

"Was he eating an apple?" she asked the mom.

"An apple?" the mom said.

Lana could tell the mother was going into shock, panic overwhelming her.

"Could he have choked on an apple?" Trent asked as he opened the child's mouth and looked inside. "Nothing," he said to Lana.

"Yes!" the mother said. "I gave him an apple for a snack. Oh, God, is that it?" The mother was now sobbing.

Maggie whimpered in the woman's arms and the woman held her tighter, unconsciously soothing her with her hands.

Trent positioned his hands on the child's body, then thrust up several times before returning to the child's mouth.

"I've got it," he said as he pulled out a piece of apple and threw it on the ground. Then he gave the child a couple of breaths and they both watched as the small chest rose with each one.

The child suddenly started to cough—a sound as sweet as the most beautiful music Lana had ever heard.

Trent checked the little boy's pulse then looked up to Lana and smiled. "His pulse is stronger," he said.

The child opened his eyes and then took in all the people surrounding him and started crying for his mother.

Lana took Maggie from the woman so that she could hold her son, then reached over and hugged Trent to her.

"I'm so glad you were here," she said, and reached over and gave him what had to be the biggest kiss she'd ever given him, ending it with an audible smack.

"Me too," Maggie said, and she planted soft baby kisses on Lana's laughing face and then Trent's, before he moved away to talk to the ambulance team who had arrived.

Lana held Maggie close as other people in the park approached her, asking what had happened, and watched Trent help the crew load the little boy on a stretcher. The mother gave Trent a hug and thanked him.

Trent was a good man. He had saved this woman's child. He was prepared to marry her so they could protect her little girl. The truth was that a fake marriage was more than she had ever expected. Yet the thought of faking something as important as marriage didn't sit right with her.

If she couldn't have the real thing, could she settle for an imitation?

Trent walked out of the nursery and felt like a jerk even before the door had closed behind him. He had been short with the nurses for days now. Baby Hope had not made the progress he would have liked to see, and that along with the pressure of waiting for his father to make his next move was getting to him.

Of course his bad mood didn't have *anything* to do with the fact that Lana hadn't jumped at the chance to be Mrs. Montgomery. Sure it didn't.

He decided that he would walk up to Labor and Delivery and check on the laboring patients there. And if he just happened to run into Lana up on the unit that would be okay. It was time for her to make a decision… time for both of them to move on to the next step that would secure the future for her and for Maggie.

"Kat told me you were on the unit," Lana said as she walked into the break room.

"How does that woman always know where I am?"

Trent asked as he poured himself a cup of coffee. He started to offer Lana a cup, then remembered she preferred tea.

"I wouldn't be surprised if she knew where every good-looking warm male body in this hospital is right now. It's just a talent she has," Lana said.

"You doing okay?" he asked her as she moved from the table to open the fridge and then shut it. She was as nervous as the mares at the ranch when they were about to be mounted by one of the studs.

Suddenly memories of their lovemaking flooded his mind. Okay, he really *didn't* need that in his thoughts right now.

"Lana, come here," he ordered her.

She was a nervous wreck, and he needed to find out what he could do to settle her down. Was this what the thought of marrying him did to her? So much for all his charm and good looks.

Pulling her close to him, he moved his hand down her soft cheek, then tilted her chin up till her troubled green eyes were forced to meet his. The feel of her body against him had his body responding instantly, while at the same time the emotional strain that had plagued him for the past few days eased away.

"Someone could come in," Lana said, and pulled away. "I got a call from Ms. Nelson," she told him.

"And…?" Trent asked as he moved closer.

"He's done it," Lana said.

She looked at him with eyes shadowed with the dark circles that told him he wasn't the only one not sleeping these days.

"Your father's lawyers contacted her today to see where the custody process stood," she said.

"She hasn't contacted me yet," he said as he pulled his phone out of the back pocket of his scrubs and checked to see if he had any missed calls. "Or she called my lawyer and he hasn't had time to pass on the information yet. I don't want to pressure you," he went on, "but if we're going to have any chance of pulling off this marriage for the benefit of the court you're going to have to make a decision soon."

Marriage to Trent. It was the only thing she had thought of since that day at the park. It wasn't a terrible idea. And she did see the advantages it would give them. With her history with Maggie, and Trent's biological relationship, together and presenting a happy home for her daughter, they would have a good chance against anything his father might throw against them.

But would she be able to pull it off? She wasn't a good actor. Her drama grades in high school would attest to that. But surely they should be able to play the role without much effort? She would have to be comfortable with Trent touching her in public, and with showing the normal affection a couple in love would share, playing the happy newlyweds. It would hurt, but she could do it.

Yet still she couldn't bring herself to say yes.

There would be real problems after the marriage was over and Trent went back to his old life, but that wasn't what was stopping her. The problem was that even after all the warnings she had given herself she was falling in love with Trent a little bit more every time she saw him. How was she going to be able to hide the way she felt from him if they were living together?

Part of her wanted to believe that he cared for her too. She had to believe that he cared for her in some way, or he wouldn't be willing to go to such extreme measures. And there was no doubt that they got along well together in bed. He had never mentioned that it would be a marriage in name only, and just the thought of being back in his bed made her want to agree, but she knew that the intimacy between them would just make it harder to walk away later, when the need for their marriage was over.

She was willing to sacrifice everything for Maggie, but surely there had to be another way.

"I know," she said as she pulled away from him. "I just need a little longer."

Trent threw his jacket across the back of the first chair he came to when he got home. An emergency Caesarean section had come in right when he had been about to get off, and he had volunteered to stay and help out.

He saw the blinking light flashing on his answering machine, but decided to get himself a cold bottle of water from the fridge before he checked to see who had left a message. He had given the number here to only a few people since he was only in town temporarily.

He took a refreshingly clean swallow of water, then picked up the phone to check the message. His stomach twisted itself into tight knots as he listened.

He ran his hands through his hair, then began to undress. His father was coming to town and there was nothing he could do about it. Lana would have to give him an answer—and soon. There was no telling what his father was planning and he would have to be prepared for anything—including telling Lana about what he intended for Maggie's inheritance.

But how did he bring that up with her? *Oh, by the way, I forgot to tell you that I plan to use Maggie's share*

*of my family's oil company to get revenge on her grand-*
*father for ruining her father's life.*

Would Lana really believe that a man she had known
only for a few weeks was more concerned about his
niece's welfare than an inheritance worth millions?
Would *he* if he was in her shoes? Had he really come
with Maggie's welfare as his priority he could have returned to Houston as soon as he had gotten to know Lana
and seen how much she loved the little girl, but instead
he'd let his own personal experiences with his parents
cloud his judgment.

One look at Michael's little girl and he had been reminded of how his brother had been treated by their father, so he had continued with his plan to grab custody
of Maggie before his father could get involved.

What had he been thinking?

Lana caught sight of Trent as he entered the cafeteria.
He smiled at her as he headed over to her table, but she
noticed his high-voltage smile had been turned down
to just a low-wattage gleam today, and his eyes had the
same look she was becoming accustomed to seeing in
her own mirror.

Stress was beginning to take its toll on both of them.

"May I sit down?" he asked as he approached.

She wasn't sure what had him doubting his welcome.
She was thinking about *marrying* the man, for heaven's
sake, and yet now he was back to acting as if they were
strangers?

"Sure. Is everything all right?" she asked as she
watched him lay his tray on the plastic table and then
arrange his food.

"Yeah—why?" he asked as he looked up at her.

"You just don't seem like yourself today," Lana said, and she reached out and covered one of his hands with her own. "What is it, Trent?"

Trent looked around at the other staff and visitors sitting at the tables and then back at her. Whatever was bothering him clearly wasn't something he wanted to discuss in public. Was it the fake marriage? Or was it something his father had done?

She placed her fork back down on the table, the thought of having to deal with more complications in her fight to keep Maggie dulling her appetite.

She started to remove her hand from where it lay over his, then stopped when he turned his hand over and gave hers a slight squeeze. She'd have to wait till they were alone to find out what had caused this change in him.

"Eat your lunch," Lana said as she removed her hand from his. "Though I'm warning you: the tuna surprise is a step down from the fried potato casserole."

"So I've been told," Trent said as he picked up his own fork and stared down into the pale-looking noodles and sauce.

They ate in silence, with Lana just moving her food around on her plate while she watched him somehow manage to finish the cafeteria's special of the day. As they went to drop off their dirty trays she tried to think of somewhere they could go and not be interrupted.

She needed to know what had happened to cause this change in him. And there was one place where no one in the hospital would see or hear them and they could have the privacy they needed.

It was risky, going down there, but it would be worth it if she could find out what was bothering him. They would talk, she promised herself as the idea formed. *Just talk.*

"You got a few minutes?" Lana asked as they walked side by side down the hall that led to the bank of elevators that went up to the patient care floors.

"I'm checked out on the roster for the rest of this hour," Trent said as he studied his watch. "Why?"

She could tell that he was shocked when she grabbed his hand and pulled him away from the main elevators and down the hall to where one old, dented metal elevator door stood.

Okay, maybe they'd do a little more than talk. Maybe she would kiss his sad mood away…just a few kisses to bring the warmth back into that spectacular smile of his…and then they'd talk.

They'd had such little time alone together lately, and she couldn't help but feel that he was pulling away from her. And if she decided that she couldn't go through with a fake marriage, where would that leave them? She'd had a taste of Trent and she wanted more. Whether or not she agreed to marry him everything between them would soon change. She needed just one more time alone with him before that happened.

"You want to show me the freight elevator?" Trent asked.

The doors opened and Lana pulled on his hand until he reluctantly got into the elevator. She pushed the button that took the elevator to the basement, and then froze when the reality of what she was doing hit her.

What she was doing was crazy and dangerous, but she wouldn't let that stop her. She'd have to give him an answer soon and then everything between them would change. She needed to be held in his arms one more time. Because she knew in her heart that it would have to be the last time, no matter what she decided about marrying him.

When the doors opened Lana poked her head outside to make sure there wasn't anyone around to see where they were headed. Looking both ways, she was relieved to see that they were alone. She pulled Trent out of the elevator with her.

"Okay, now I'm getting a little freaked out," Trent said as he pointed to the arrow indicating the hospital morgue.

"It's not that way," Lana said, and began walking down the opposite hall.

It had to be close to here. She had heard one of the nurses talking about it not long after she had come to work there, and then one of the labor and delivery nurses had dragged her along on a dare —to see if the room really existed or if it was just an urban legend.

"If you tell me what you're looking for maybe I can help you."

"It's right here," Lana said as she made one more turn and then saw the door she was looking for.

"What *is* this?" he asked.

Lana tried the doorknob and was relieved when it turned easily. She had gotten her nerve up and she didn't want to lose it now. She pulled Trent in by the hand she was still holding, then shut the door quickly before she flipped the light switch and locked the door behind them.

"It's the hospital make-out room," she said, and smiled when she saw the shock hit his face.

Trent glanced around at the mix of broken furniture filling the room. Looking back at sweet, honest-to-the-core little Lana, he watched as she seemed to turn into a siren right before his eyes.

"We need to *talk*, Lana," Trent said as he pulled away.

"You see this door?" she said as she leaned back against it.

Surely she couldn't mean what she was about to say? With everything that was going on with them right now?

Guilt slammed through him as warning bells began to toll inside his overstimulated body. This wasn't right. He had planned to tell her everything—come clean about his plan to use Michael's will against his father, and tell her everything that he should have told her long before they had gotten to this point. He wanted everything out in the open so that there was nothing hidden between the two of them and the decision she had to make.

"We leave everything and everybody on the other side of this door," she continued. "Can you do that?"

"Lana, we need to talk." Trent said again.

He was going to tell her all the reasons this wasn't a good idea. He would swear in a court of law that he was. But then she walked over to him and laid one small finger against his lips.

"We'll talk later," Lana said. "I promise."

Trent tried once more to stop things from going any farther, and then she stood on her tiptoes and whispered in his ear.

"I *need* you, Trent. Do you need me?"

Urgent desire struck him as her warm, sweet breath blew into his ear. If he'd been a better man then maybe, just maybe, he could have withstood the want that flashed through him as her lips worked their way down the side of his neck.

But he had a weakness where Lana was concerned.

One moment alone with that sweet body of hers and he was done for. Somehow he had let his desire for her seep deep down inside him—until he could no longer control the need that flared up and consumed him.

"Yes," he answered as he lifted her up so that he could meet her lips.

The taste of her filled him as his tongue circled with hers. He had missed this—her—so much. He tilted his head to let his tongue delve deeper into her mouth, then crushed her body to his and took the weight of it.

The feel of her returning his kisses with the same feverish need that he felt had him losing control too fast, so he pulled back. Her moan of protest was almost too much for him, and for a moment he thought of just taking her right there, against the wall.

Barely managing to clamp down on his body's demand that he take her *now*, he pulled away from her. Looking around the small room, he saw a dilapidated plastic chair within reach. He used one of his feet to hook one of the chair legs and pull it close.

As he sat down with Lana in his arms he arranged her body so that she faced him, with her legs straddling his body. When her hand reached down between them and pulled the cord that held his scrub pants closed he lifted her and hiked up her skirt. He let his hand run down the thin line of her thong then pushed it aside so that his fingers could slide deep inside her.

A hot bolt of desire ran the length of him as her hand circled him and his groan filled the room. He ran his hand once more between her legs, then pushed her hand aside as he lifted her until he could feel his tip at her entrance. Thrusting up, he brought her down on the full, hard length of him in one swift move.

He stopped and took a moment to look at the flushed face and bruised lips of this woman who had clearly caused him to lose his mind.

And then she started to move.

This was so much more then she had planned but, oh, it felt so good to be with him like this again.

Lana eased herself down around him as she stared into his eyes. Never had she felt such an intimate connection as she did at this moment. In this stark room, totally absent of any romance, it was as if they were the only two people in the world.

She let him increase speed as he tightened his hands against her hips, and her breath caught with each stroke as she fought to keep her suddenly heavy eyes open. She loved the feel of him sliding in and out of her, loved the sweet, almost painful stretch of her body deep down inside her.

She could feel her body tightening around him, but she fought against it. She forced her eyes to stay open, letting herself drown in his deep blue eyes as his body stroked her into unbearable pleasure. His hands came up and cupped her breasts, then he bent his head and took her lips with such hunger that it destroyed her.

It was too much for her to take—too much for her to withstand. Her hands gripped his hair and she tried to pull his mouth closer. The demand of his lips, the hard length of him as he drove deep inside her, filled her completely. Her breath caught, then held. This was too much. He was taking her too far.

She felt herself losing her hold as she soared higher and higher, her core tightening, her body reaching for its climax. She tightened her arms around him, holding on to him as if her life was dependent on that connection between them, the joining of their bodies anchoring her to him. He thrust into her once more and her body shattered into a million pieces.

# CHAPTER TEN

LANA, WHO HAD NEVER had the privilege of experiencing the walk of shame before, snuck into the back entrance of her unit. Trent had reassured her that she looked great, but she knew there was no way she could look the same coming out as she had going into that storage room.

Had she lost her mind? Thank goodness none of the other midwives she worked with, were in the office. They would have seen right through her casual act. All she would have had to do was look one of them in the eye and she knew she'd spill everything.

It wasn't every day that she managed to have mind-blowing sex in the most scandalous of places. Was it just a few weeks ago that she had been calling her life boring?

She knew that making love with Trent again had added more complications, but she would never regret it. She didn't even want to *think* about what the consequences of their getting caught together would have been. But at the same time it seemed she had spent too much of her time worrying about what the staff were saying about her and Trent. Why not give them something to really talk about?

Not that she would actually *tell* anyone about what

had happened between the two of them, but she might as well be guilty of some of the rumors going around about them.

But what had been wrong with him today before the mind-blowing sex? He had become known around the hospital for having a big smile and a quick sense of humor. Even in the fight they'd had in the court he had still been friendly to her.

Not that she had always been the same with him. And she wouldn't apologize for that. She'd had every right to be angry with him when he had first come to town. But she hadn't been able to stay mad at him for long. Watching the gentle man he was while caring for the smallest of babies, and the way he eased the concern of anxious mothers, and then seeing him interact with Maggie, it had just become too hard for her to hold a grudge against him.

He had looked much more relaxed when they'd parted—or at least until he had stopped her before she got on the elevator and reminded her that she couldn't avoid making a decision about their marriage much longer.

She'd seen the stress return then. Had he sensed the conflict inside her?

The consequences of *not* going through with the marriage were so high that she knew she shouldn't even be considering turning him down. She should agree to Trent's plan and just hope she would be able to find the strength to survive when everything was over between them.

But how would that be possible when her heart already hurt at the thought of him leaving?

If she'd felt that Trent had even the slightest desire

to marry her for any other reason than to protect his niece, she would jump at the chance. But that wasn't the case, and she needed to get over any daydreams she was having of them being together as a family and accept the inevitable.

Trent was only interested in marriage because of his need to protect his niece—which was as honorable a sacrifice as anyone could make. But she had vowed after her break-up with Joe that she would never let someone make her feel that marrying her would be a sacrifice. She had always wanted to have someone love her just the way she was, but maybe it was time to accept that wasn't ever going to happen.

She grabbed the lab coat she kept hanging on the back of her office door and put it on to help hide the wrinkles that she had in her skirt and then headed down to the reception area to call for her first afternoon appointment. Everything in her personal life was coming to a head, but life kept going. Women continued to get pregnant, and that meant there were still babies who needed her to be there to deliver them.

As Trent rounded the corner of the Labor and Delivery nurses' station he saw Lana as she was coming out of one of the labor rooms, and he watched her as she spoke with the family members who had been waiting outside the patient's door. She was wearing scrubs today, so he knew she was planning on spending most of her time on the unit.

"Hey, Trent," one of the nurses called as they walked up beside him. "We're almost ready to go back if you want to meet us in the operating room."

"I'll be right there," he said, and turned to walk toward Lana.

She gave him a little wave, then walked back into the labor room. He'd have to catch her after they'd finished the next delivery.

The surgery went off without any problems, and in less than an hour another mother was holding a perfect little baby in her arms as her husband took pictures to show the rest of the family in the waiting room. He checked at the nurses' station and found that Lana had just gone into another delivery.

"You have a great team here," Trent told Dr. Miller as he joined him at the nurses' station to finish his paperwork.

"They're a great group of nurses," Dr. Miller said as he looked up from the chart he was checking for his notes. "I've heard you're here just for one a short time," the doctor said as he stretched back in his chair. "You ought to consider staying."

"I'm here for an eight-week assignment right now," Trent said. "I have a permanent position in Houston."

He turned as Lana came into the nurses' station. She walked over to some of the nurses who were talking.

"We'd be happy to have you stay," Dr. Miller said. "Good pediatricians are hard to find."

The doctor rose out of his chair, then turned to see where Trent's attention had gone.

"Just think about it," he said. Smiling, the man gave Trent a hearty slap on the back and left the unit.

Trent was glad to see Lana heading over to where he stood leaning against the station's countertop. He nodded his head toward the exit door and then accompanied her out of the unit. He only had a few minutes before he needed to get back and take the next case in the operating room.

"Lana, I—"

"Look, I've got to get back to the office right now, but why don't you come over tonight? You can see Maggie and I'll fix dinner."

They came to the elevator doors just as one opened its doors with the button's light showing it was headed up. A group of visitors bearing flowers and pastel-pink-wrapped presents walked out, pushing the two of them together. Her body brushed against his, sending a quick burst of desire through him.

Desire he couldn't act on. Not here, not now.

He reached out to tuck a loose piece of hair behind her ear and let his hand linger on the soft lobe, then slide down the side of her neck.

"Trent…?"

The hoarse whisper of his name was too much. Before he could do something that would surely shock the staff he pulled away from her.

"Tonight," he said.

Turning away, he headed for the stairs. Maybe a little physical activity would get him cooled down before he made it to the OR.

Lana was in a better mood when she got home. She'd made peace with her decision concerning Trent's marriage proposal and, while she was nervous, she knew she was doing the right thing.

She'd taken Maggie with her to the grocery store, where she'd bought all the ingredients for one of her daughter's favorite pasta dishes.

"Hey, you're home!" Lana said as Amanda walked out of the house.

"Class was canceled tonight," Amanda said as she reached over and took the toddler out of Lana's arms.

"Thanks. I bought a few more groceries then I had planned." Lana juggled the bags in her arms, then reached back into the car for the last two.

"Yeah, it looks like you're going to feed an army," Amanda said. "Did Momma invite a football team over for supper?"

Maggie laughed up at her babysitter, then struggled to get down as soon as they made it inside the house. The toddler ran down the hall to her room as soon as she was let down, then was back in seconds, pushing her plastic play shopping cart around the kitchen, where the bags of food had been taken.

"No, but I did invite Trent," Lana said.

"Are you sure that's a good idea?" Amanda asked.

"Have you gotten a *look* at the man?" she teased her friend, and then stopped as she saw the look of confusion on her face.

"Okay, I know this is hard to understand," Lana said as she walked around the room, putting everything in its proper place.

"It just seems like you're getting more and more involved with him," said Amanda.

"Does it?" Lana asked.

She began sorting through the vegetables she would need to get ready for the evening's meal.

"Lana, are you okay?" Amanda had walked over to the sink and was staring at her as if she had grown a second head. "Oh, my God—you're in love with the guy."

"I didn't say that," Lana insisted.

She began slicing a tomato on the wooden butcher block, making sure that she had a good excuse not to look up at her friend.

"You didn't have to. I can see it," Amanda said.

Lana felt the heat of the blush that she knew stained her cheeks.

"Have you had sex with him?"

Looking up, she watched Amanda's eyes go wide before a big grin spread across her face.

"I can't *believe* it. You've had sex with the hunky Dr. Montgomery!"

"Hey, no S-word in front of Maggie," Lana said, hoping to change the subject—as if that was going to happen now.

"So the rumors about you two hooking up were true?" Amanda asked as she went over to the table to sit down. "I want details."

"I'm not telling you about—" Lana stopped as Amanda doubled over with laughter. Crap—the brat had tricked her. She knew there was no way she would share what was going on between her and Trent.

She didn't even know for sure herself what it was that was happening between them. It was as if they had two separate relationships. In one they were talking about marriage as if it were a business arrangement between the two of them. In the other they weren't only friendly… they couldn't keep their hands off each other.

No—they both had to leave their personal issues out this. Maggie had to be their priority.

Lana ignored her friend's teasing for the rest of the day. Amanda was just having a good time, picking on her, but deep down Lana knew her friend was right.

Even after all the warnings she had given herself, she had fallen head over heels in love with a cowboy doctor who had come to town to break her heart.

# CHAPTER ELEVEN

LANA WAS SURPRISED at how smoothly the meal had gone. If only their next conversation would go as smoothly.

Dinnertime with a tired toddler could quickly turn into a messy, crying affair, but instead of running from the house screaming Trent had pitched in and helped.

Deciding to give him a realistic view of parenting, she had assigned him the task of bathing Maggie while she cleaned up the kitchen. He'd survived his one day alone with the toddler, but that was different from the day-in and day-out demands of parenting. The sight of him drenched to the waist and grinning madly as he held a sparkling clean Maggie had sent her into uncontrollable fits of laughter.

"She's really asleep this time," he said now, as he joined her back in the kitchen.

"You sure she's not playing possum again?" she asked.

"Hey, I happen to be an expert on child behavior," he said.

She looked up from the sink and raised an eyebrow.

"Okay, she fooled me once," he said, "but I'm on to her tricks now. She's definitely destined for the big screen when she grows up."

"I'm thinking more of her as a teenage drama queen," she said.

One look at his horrified face had her laughing again. "You do realize she's going to grow up some day?" she said.

"I don't want to even *think* about it," he said.

She didn't either. It seemed like only days ago that Maggie had learned to crawl. Now she was walking everywhere, and learning a new word daily. Next there would be school, then boys... *Boys?* She definitely wasn't ready to think about *that*.

"You were great with her tonight—well, except for the half-hour it took you to actually get her into her crib," she said, "But that's not really your fault. She knew you'd be an easy mark so she played you."

"But those were *real* tears," he protested.

"That she quickly turned off as soon as I walked into the room. Like I said—she played you."

Trent took the glass of tea Lana offered and sat at the small table, waiting for Lana to sit down too. Finally they would have a chance to discuss their plans to keep his father out of Maggie's life.

He knew Lana had reservations about the idea of marrying him, but he knew they would be able to make things work out together. They were both level-headed adults. There would be none of the dysfunction of his parents' marriage.

Still, it would be for the best if they ironed out some of the details. If they set up the terms of their marriage now it would be easier for both of them, but for some reason the more they tried to make this feel like a business deal the more uncomfortable he felt.

He put his hands in his pocket and felt for the ring he

meant to surprise her with. He tightened his hand around it, then let go and pulled his hand out.

This was what he wanted. No drama, no chaos, no fights that ended with one of them crying or, worse, one of them dead. They needed to keep this separate from any feelings they might have for each other. They were putting a good plan in motion and sticking to it so there would be no misunderstandings.

"So, have you come to a decision?" he asked. He felt his pulse quicken as he waited for her to answer.

From the hesitancy before Lana's response he knew she was uncertain, but that was to be expected. Most people didn't go into marriage like the two of them were doing. Of course most people weren't in the situation they were in either.

Trent watched her as she seemed to gather herself together. This wasn't going to be easy for either of them, but it would be harder if they didn't start off on the right foot.

"Trent," she said, "I want you to know how much I appreciate your offer. I know you'd do anything for Maggie."

Trent watched her as she took a sip of tea, a sinking feeling invading his chest.

"That's why I think we can work things out between us so that we don't have to do anything as drastic as getting married," she went on.

"I don't understand. If we married everything would be taken care of," he said.

"Stop and think about it, Trent. What about after the adoption? After you go back to Houston? We'd be right back at the same place we are now, trying to work out custody of Maggie. We can't do that again. It's not fair to either of us and it certainly isn't fair to Maggie."

"I promise this is not some type of trick. I'm not trying to take Maggie away from you, Lana. You're her mother. The only one she will ever know. I lived most of my childhood without a mother—I don't want that for Maggie. But I still want to be part of her life. This way I can be."

"And what are we going to tell Maggie when suddenly you're not there every day? How will that make her feel, Trent? She'll just be more confused. It's not right to do that to her. But if we work together and show the court that you support my adopting her we can both do what's right for her. Maggie can live with me and still have an awesome uncle who she goes to visit and who spoils her as any uncle would. Instead of being confused about your part in her life, she'll have the security of being loved by the two of us. And with you handling her inheritance I know she'll be taken care of just as your brother wanted."

He got up from the table, unable to sit still any longer. He didn't want to confuse Maggie—he just wanted to protect her. And Lana. Why couldn't she see that this was the answer to keeping Maggie safe from his father?

"We wouldn't have to end the marriage immediately," he said as he began to pace.

"Listen to yourself," Lana said as she stood up and joined him. "You're already changing things. Can't you see how complicated marriage would make things between us?"

"It wouldn't have to be that way. We can set out the terms of the marriage. Have a lawyer draw it up, if you like, to make it all legal if you don't trust me."

He heard the bitterness in his voice, but couldn't control it.

"It's not that I don't trust you—it's that I don't trust myself," she said as she shook her head.

"What does *that* mean?" he asked, even more confused now. If she truly trusted him why wouldn't she marry him?

Lana had expected Trent to try and get her to change her mind, to see the reasons he thought this was the best thing to do for Maggie, but she had never thought he would be this upset.

The man standing in front of her was not the Trent she knew, who always remained calm and controlled no matter what was going on around him. This man was anything but calm, with his body coiled tight, his face a beautiful mix of confusion and frustration, his hands running through his thick dark hair.

Hair she'd once run her hands through. Hair she'd never have the right to touch again after tonight.

Her body heated with memories of tangling her hands in Trent's hair as she pulled him closer, as she anchored her lips to his, felt his tongue deep inside her mouth, his hands roaming her body. Those were the other times she'd glimpsed this man in front of her now.

She watched as he took a deep breath, then walked over to her and took her hands in his. How could she continue this relationship without him utterly destroying her heart? How could she make him see that faking a marriage with him was impossible for her without telling him what she felt for him?

"What *is* it? What do you mean you don't trust yourself?" he asked, his voice now calm and caring. "I would trust you with anything."

"Anything?" she asked, her heart stuttering as she took the biggest risk she'd ever taken. "Would you trust me with your heart?"

"What?" he asked as he pulled his hands from hers.

"I don't want to settle for a fake marriage, Trent. I want a real marriage. A marriage like my parents', where you plan to grow old together, a marriage filled with love and respect."

"And what would *I* know about those types of marriages, Lana?"

She could hear the bitterness in his voice. She couldn't blame him for being bitter. He'd been given a raw deal as a child. But he wasn't a child any longer. He needed to see that things could be different for him.

"I know your parents' marriage wasn't perfect..."

"That's an understatement. It was a war zone, with me and my brother as prisoners. I'll never live like that again."

"But that's not what marriage has to be. When two people love each other they can make it work. Yeah, they might argue and disagree sometimes, but they also learn how to compromise and support each other. That's what I want, Trent. Not a marriage filled with lies. I want someone to be there when things are good, but also to be by my side when things go wrong. I want someone to love me no matter what. In sickness and in health."

"Till death do us part?" Trent asked, and the sarcasm in his voice was almost palpable.

"Yes, that," she said.

"And you think you could have that with *me*?" Trent

asked, his eyes wide as he backed further away from her. "This was supposed to be about Maggie—not about us."

"And it was—until I fell in love with you," she said, her hands covering her heart, as if to protect it from the pain she knew would come.

It hurt to see the panic in his eyes, but she'd known before she'd admitted her feelings for him that he wasn't ready for this—not for any type of real commitment, let alone one that included messy emotions such as love.

How long had it been since someone had told him that they loved him? Months? Years? Had anyone really, truly, *ever* loved this man the way he deserved? She knew he could love—she'd seen it in his eyes every time he looked at Maggie—but did he know how to *accept* love?

"I love you, Trent," she said, and her voice was stronger as she poured everything she felt for him into it. "I love the way you comfort your patients' parents when they're scared and worried, the way your eyes light up with laughter when you're playing with Maggie, and the way you want to protect her so much that you're willing to marry me—even if it is for all the wrong reasons. I love the way you make me laugh, the way you have of calming my worries, the way you make me feel like a whole woman when I'm in your arms."

"It's not you…" he said.

"I know it's not. It's about you being afraid to take a chance on us. Life's all about chances, Trent. Do you know how hard it is for me to stand here and wait for you to reject me like Joe did?"

"Joe was stupid," he mumbled.

"Yes, he was—but I didn't see that until I met you. You made me see that I could have it all if I was willing to take a chance. I just need to know if you can take that same chance with me."

She waited as Trent looked at her, sadness in his eyes.

"I don't think I can give you what you need," he said.

She watched him reached his hand into his pocket, then slide it back out again, empty.

"I don't know how to be what you want...what you deserve."

"Yes, you do," she whispered as he walked away from her. "You just don't know it."

Lana tried to keep her mind on the patient's chart that she was updating. She'd been having a hard time concentrating since the night Trent had walked out of her house. It had been two days now and she hadn't heard from him.

She'd spent hours second-guessing her decision to refuse Trent. Would it have been so bad to take what he had offered? To have what time with him she could have, even though she knew it would have ended with a broken heart?

A knock at her office door sent her thoughts back to the present, where they needed to be.

"Come in," she called as a second knock sounded.

"Hey, Lana, there's a Mr. Montgomery is here to see you," the young receptionist said as she stepped into the room.

"Send him in, Lily." Lana stood and removed her lab coat, then straightened her skirt, her hands unsteady. Trent had never been to her office before and she couldn't imagine why he was there now. Could he have realized that she was right?

The man who walked into her office wasn't Trent, but

she had no doubt that he was a Montgomery. His face was so like his son's, in all its lines and angles, but it was aged and hardened. His brown eyes were cold, so unlike the warm blue of Trent's, and the straight line of his lips showed no hint of humor.

He wore an expensive suit that screamed power, and his large six-foot frame overwhelmed her small office. Now she understood why Trent had been so worried about his father's interest in Maggie. If this man wanted something, he'd take it. But he wouldn't be taking her daughter anywhere.

"Mr. Montgomery—come in." Surprised when her voice came out with no trace of a tremor, she indicated the chair in front of her desk with a wave of her shaky hand.

"Please have a seat," she said, then waited till he sat before sitting down in her own chair.

"Thank you," he said as he folded his body into the small chair.

She watched as he looked around the room, taking in the setting as if preparing for battle. His eyes stopped on the bulletin board behind her, where she displayed pictures of the babies that she had delivered. She knew the second his eyes found the picture she had added just that morning.

It had been taken on one of their trips to the park and it showed Maggie giggling with joy on one of the toddler swings. But it had been the look on Trent's face that had caused her to pull her phone out of her purse and snap the picture. He looked so relaxed and free. And *happy*— as if spending the day pushing a swing in the park was just what he wanted to be doing.

"What can I do for you, Mr. Montgomery?" she asked.

"I'm sure you know I'm here about my granddaughter," he said.

"Maggie's fine. She's a beautiful, healthy little girl," she said. "If you'd like to meet her I'm sure me and Trent can arrange it."

"I was under the impression that you had sole custody of the child at this time."

"I do, but Trent has become a very important part of our lives," she said. "We discuss everything concerning Maggie together."

His cold eyes melted with the heat of the temper that flared there now. *Why?* Why couldn't the man just be happy that his granddaughter was going to be taken care of?

Being studied like a bug under a microscope was uncomfortable and she was tired of it. "Mr. Montgomery, if you didn't come here to arrange to see Maggie then why *did* you come?"

The smile on his lips didn't touch his eyes. How could a man so cold and calculating have raised a son like Trent? Of course the obvious answer to that was that he hadn't raise him.

"I came to make you an offer."

An offer?" she said. What was he going to do? Offer to *buy* her daughter?

"My youngest son…"

"Michael… Maggie's father," she said, with a hint of annoyance evident in her voice.

"I do know my son's name, Ms. Sanders. No matter what *Trent* has told you…" he emphasized the name "…I do care for my sons. Both of them."

"I'm sorry," she said. "And I'm sorry for your loss."

He accepted her apology with a nod of his head.

"As I was saying, Michael made certain stipulations in his will concerning his daughter—Maggie."

His lips parted in a small smile at this acknowledgement of the little girl's name.

"My son apparently wanted to make sure his child was taken care of financially on a long-term basis. Simply put, he left her all his shares in my oil business—shares that could be used to gain control of the company. I'm willing to make an arrangement that would allow you to keep Maggie and still have the financial stability her father wanted for her. I just want the *control* of the shares—not the ownership."

Disbelief filled her. No, this man didn't want to *buy* his granddaughter—instead he was willing to sell her for the right to control some of the shares in his company. No wonder Trent was scared to trust anyone with a father like this man.

"I'm sorry." She stood up abruptly, surprising both of them. She grabbed the top of the, desk using it to steady her. "I'm going to have to ask you to leave. If you want to discuss Maggie's inheritance you'll need to talk to Trent."

He stood and reached into his pocket, then pulled a card from a case and laid it on her desk.

"Here's my contact information. Hopefully we will be able to come to an agreement. I'm sure neither one of us would like to have to take this to court."

# CHAPTER TWELVE

TRENT PULLED THROUGH the gated entrance. He was tired and he needed to grab a shower. He'd barely slept since he'd left Lana's house two days ago, and his mind was swirling with thoughts of life without her and Maggie. The only thing that had gone right that day had been with baby Hope's progress. The baby girl was showing herself to be a fighter and if she kept up the progress she had shown in the last couple of days he had no doubt he'd be able to take her off the ventilator by the end of the week. He couldn't help but be inspired by the fight in one so small. He laughed to himself. Baby Hope gave him hope.

The long black car sitting in his driveway had him taking his foot off the gas pedal. There was only one person who would be waiting for him in that limo. His father was in town. That was *just* what he needed to have to deal with today.

He left the front door open for his father to follow him. It was rude, but it was the mood he was in. Why couldn't his father have called and at least informed him of his visit? Instead now he'd have to deal with everything between the two of them when he was already as tightly wound as a rattlesnake about to strike.

"And hello to you too," his father said as he followed him into the living room.

Trent turned around to face him. He tried to corral the anger that sprang up within him, but it was too strong. He'd held it under such tight control for so long that he was afraid of its power. But he couldn't afford to let his anger at his father take him back to that black hole he had been in when he'd left Texas—before he had met Lana.

Lana and Maggie. They were what was important now.

"Father, I wasn't expecting you." With his thoughts on Lana and little Maggie he felt the anger subside to a manageable irritation.

"Weren't you?" his father asked.

His father took a seat on the sole chair in the room, leaving him to the couch. It was a move he had seen him carry out before. His father was holding court and he was just another one of his subjects, expected to bow down to him.

Trent remained standing.

"I knew you'd be coming eventually, but I expected to hear from your team of lawyers first."

"I find out I have a granddaughter and you expect me to send my *lawyers*? This is something of a personal nature, wouldn't you say?"

Things of a personal nature? Was that what his father was calling family matters now?

"If you'd like to meet Maggie I can see that it is arranged," Trent said.

"The child's foster mother has offered to let me see her and, yes, I would like to meet her. But first I'd like to know what your intentions are concerning the girl and the shares she is to inherit."

"So you've met Lana?"

"Yes, she seems a lovely young woman who has no idea of the worth of my grandchild's inheritance."

"Lana doesn't care about Maggie's portfolio. She loves Maggie for herself."

Just like she loved *him* for himself, he thought.

He bit down on his anger as it returned. "She's one of the most caring women I've ever met and we both owe her our thanks for the way she has taken care of Maggie. She's a genuinely good person. And, unlike most of the people you're used to dealing with, she's honest and sincere."

He could go on and on about what a good person Lana was, but his father would never understand. In his father's world Lana would be considered weak and easy prey. But in the new life Trent had found Lana was all the good things he'd never had in his life. She and Maggie had shown him a whole new world that he could have if he was willing to take a chance.

"And what are your feelings for this woman?" his father asked. "Apart from gratitude."

"I…" He stopped with the word *love* sitting on his tongue. *Love*… Not a word he was comfortable with, or one that he really understood, but it had come to him so easily, so naturally. Was it possible that these crazy feelings he had for Lana were more than just friendship? More than just desire? *Could* it be love? *Was* he in love with her? How would he even know?

But he did. Somehow he knew—had known for a while, if he was honest with himself, that what he felt for her was more than he had felt for anyone else in his life.

"No, Father, it's not gratitude, and it has nothing to do with Maggie or with Michael's will."

He heard his voice rise as he felt joy such as he had never known fill him. *Hell, yeah, it was love.* How had he not known it? If just thinking about her made him feel this good, how could it *not* be? He *loved* Lana Sanders. Not only did he love her, but he was going to marry her if she'd have him. They were going to be a family—him and Lana and Maggie. *His* family.

He looked at the man sitting in the chair inn front of him. He had never understood his father—probably never would—but he couldn't help but feel sorry for him. With all his wealth and power, he was living his life all alone.

They'd both isolated themselves emotionally from others, never letting anyone get close. But then Lana had come into his life and now he was a different man. His life was nothing like his father's and it never would be again.

He needed to tell her. Let her know what she meant to him, how she'd saved him. That he was willing to take a chance on marriage even though it still scared him.

"Look, I don't have time to explain it right now. If the only thing you came for was to see what my intentions are as far as Maggie's shares in the company are concerned, you can relax. I no longer have any plan to use her shares to make a move against you. As long as you agree to let me and Lana adopt her, Maggie's shares will be under the control of the lawyers I'll be setting up for her trust fund. Neither one of us will be able to use them. I won't use your granddaughter against you unless you decide to fight us for custody."

He watched his father's shoulders relax and for the

first time noticed how tired his father looked. The man was working himself into an early grave. And for what? More money? More power? Would this have been him thirty years down the road if he hadn't found Lana?

"And now that's settled, I really need to get a shower," said Trent.

He headed off down the hall, then turned around and caught up with his father, who was heading out the door. As his father turned toward him he felt a surge of guilt. He'd dug up a lot of memories lately, and he had to admit that not all of them had been bad. There had been a time before their family had been torn apart when his father had been close to both him and Michael. There was no going back to those times, but he owed it to his brother to give Maggie a chance at a relationship with her grandfather.

"Let me know when you want to meet Maggie. She's a special little girl. I think you'll like her."

"I'm sure I will," his father responded, then started back out the door.

"She has Momma's eyes," Trent said.

His father stopped, then turned back. The glimmer of dampness that filled his father's eyes told him what he needed to know. His father had loved his mother.

He watched his father get into the car, its door being held open by a uniformed driver. No, there was no going back. But maybe with the help of a little girl they could go forward on a different path than the one they had been following all these years.

Lana had folded the same washcloth three times, but she just hadn't got the energy to stop her toddler from playing in the clean laundry. The visit from Calvin Montgomery had sent her into autopilot. She couldn't even remember the trip home. And, while she'd tried to act normal while she fed and bathed Maggie, she just couldn't keep up the act.

She finally put the child to bed after a quick game of peekaboo with one of the clean towels.

Her whole conversation with the senior Montgomery had been surreal, the man's attention blinded by his greed. How could anyone be so calculating as to offer their granddaughter to a stranger for strictly financial reasons? And how dared he threaten to cause trouble for her with the courts?

She had no intention of letting him intimidate her. She just hoped that she could still depend on Trent to back her up after she'd scared him with her confession of love for him.

A knock on the door startled her out of her dark thoughts.

Opening it, she found a different Trent from the one who had left her house two nights ago. His eyes were bright, his body full of nervous energy, and his smile was dangerous and sexy.

"Can I come in?" he asked as he stood there, one hand in his pocket.

"Of course," she said, and she stepped back from the door, turning her back toward him, unable to meet his eyes.

Having a man run from your house after a declaration of love had a tendency to make things a little awkward.

"Lana, I heard that my father came to see you. I'm sorry if he upset you."

"Upset me?" she said as she walked over to the couch and sat down. "The man was ready to bulldoze me, and when he couldn't do that he threatened to make trouble with my adoption case. I take it he came to see you?"

Trent took a seat on the other end of the couch. She noticed he didn't try to move closer. She'd known there would be no going back after she bared her heart to him. Their relationship was bound to change.

"You won't have to worry about my father anymore. We discussed his concerns and I settled things in a way that he understood. He won't get involved with our adoption of Maggie."

"*Our* adoption?" she asked. Did he still think she was going to go through with his fake marriage plan? "I thought you understood that I can't marry you, Trent?"

If she sent him away now he'd be lost forever.

"Lana, I will do whatever it takes to protect you and Maggie—that will always be a priority in my life. But I know I messed up, asking you to fake a marriage to me. You were right. A marriage built on lies wouldn't have been fair to either of us. I know that now. And that's not what I want."

Trent rose from the couch and looked down at Lana. What a lucky man he was to have a woman like her love him. He didn't know how to talk about his feelings. It was something they'd have to work on together. But for now hopefully the three little words that had scared him into running away from her just two days ago would be enough.

He knelt down in front of her and pulled the ring he'd been carrying with him for days from his pocket. "Lana, I love you. I want to marry you. And it has nothing to do with my father, the will, or even the adoption. I want to marry you simply because I'm in love you."

"Will you marry me, Lana? Marry me for real?"

Trent had reached out and taken her hand. He *loved* her? He was the prince she had always dreamed of and he *loved* her. The life she had always wanted was just within her reach. But she had to know for sure that he understood what he would be getting.

"We'll never be able to have biological children of our own," she said, feeling her wounded heart stutter as he raised her hand to his lips, then placed it over his heart.

"I'm sorry you had to go through so much when you were young, but I'm thankful that the treatments saved you," he said. "You and Maggie are more family than I ever thought I would have. More than I deserve. The two of you are all I need."

"Are you sure? What if you decide you want to have more children later?"

"We can always adopt—just like we're doing with Maggie," he said. "Lana, we can't build our family on a past that neither of us can change, but we can build it on our future together…on our love for each other."

Could life really be that simple?

"I love you, Trent," she said as she wiped tears from her eyes. "And there's nothing more I want than to marry you."

She watched as he took her hand in his and slid a sparkling ring on her finger. Standing up, he reached down and scooped her up in his arms, silencing her surprised scream with his mouth as he carried her down the hall.

She'd gotten her fairy tale prince and her cowboy all roped together in this man she would soon call her husband. And whether they rode off into the sunset or she was carried away in her prince's arms, she knew they would find their happily-ever-after together.

# EPILOGUE

LANA RUSHED UP the courthouse steps. She was going to be late again.

"Don't even say it," she said to Amanda, who was standing at the front door waiting for her.

"Say what? That I told you running off to a delivery wasn't a good idea?" Amanda said.

"You know I had no choice. I've been there for every one of Lacey's deliveries. The fact that this one was going to be a Caesarean section was freaking her out," Lana said as she rushed down the hall toward the courtroom.

Stopping outside the door, she straightened the hemline of the tea dress, then checked her hair in the mirror that Amanda had pulled out of her pocket. The nurses on the unit had all helped her get dressed. Even Kat had helped with her hair and make-up.

"You look beautiful," Amanda said.

Lana smiled at the woman looking back at her from the mirror. It wasn't the perfectly applied make-up, or the hair combed into a flawless knot. No, what she saw was the beauty that only real happiness could bring.

"Ready?" Amanda asked.

"Definitely," Lana said as she opened the heavy wooden door—and stopped.

He wore the same dark suit he'd worn that first day they'd met, with a thin string of a tie he called a *bolo*, and she knew that if she looked down at his feet she'd see a pair of black pointed cowboy boots. In his arms he held a beautiful little girl, dressed in soft pink ruffles.

The sight of the two of them together filled her heart with love. He turned as she entered and the force of his smile almost knocked her over. It was more than she could take. This was her life. How had she got so lucky?

As she walked toward the front of the room she saw her parents, and Trent's great-aunt and uncle, along with Ms. Nelson sitting to one side. They'd decided to make it a quiet ceremony, with a larger reception at the beach to follow.

"Well, here she is," said Judge Hamilton as she approached the bench.

"I'm sorry I'm late, Your Honor," she said.

"Well, I could hold you in contempt of court, I guess, but I think that would make this young man of yours very unhappy."

"Your Honor," Trent said as he shifted Maggie in his arms and took her hand. "I'd be beholden to you if you could show some leniency in this case."

"I promise it won't happen again," said Lana.

"In that case, let's get started," said the stately judge.

"Yes," Lana said as she looked up at Trent and her daughter, "let's get started."

They repeated their vows with hands joined and Maggie at their side, and her sweet giggles filled the courtroom as they shared their first kiss as husband and wife.

Then the judge called the court to order again.

"There's one more piece of business we need to handle," the judge said, "and that's the finalization of this little girl's adoption. Miss Maggie," he said, as Trent lifted her up in his arms so that she could see the judge up close, "do you take your mommy, Lana Montgomery, to be your forever mommy?"

Lana thought her heart would burst from her chest as she watched her little girl's curls bounce around her head as she nodded yes to the judge.

"And, Miss Maggie, do you take your uncle, Trent Montgomery, to be your forever daddy?"

Astonishment filled the little girl's face, then her mouth lit with a smile and she grabbed Trent's face between her hands. "Daddy!" she squealed, patting his face, and the whole courtroom broke out in laughter.

"You have to answer the judge," her new daddy reminded her.

Turning her head back to the judge, she nodded while Trent reached over and wrapped Lana in his other arm.

"Well, then, by the power invested in me by the State of Florida, I now pronounce you husband and wife, father and mother and daughter, and the cutest darn family I've ever had the privilege to unite."

Trent smiled down at Lana, his arms full of their daughter, his eyes full of love.

"Thank you, Mrs. Montgomery," he said.

"For what?" she asked.

"For loving me," he said, "for teaching me how to love."

"Oh, cowboy," she said as she grabbed his tie and pulled his lips down to hers, "you haven't seen anything yet."

\* \* \* \* \*

# COMING SOON!

# MILLS & BOON

## Coming next month

### THE ARMY DOC'S BABY SECRET
Charlotte Hawkes

Tia had no idea how she got home. One moment she was leaving the lifeboat station, shifting her car into gear and hurtling out of the car park. The next, she was pulling into her father's driveway, blinking away the tears that threatened to spill out over her cheeks the entire eight-minute drive. And as she hurried up to the house her heart lifted at the sight of Seth's face peering out of the window, and his elated grin as he blew her frantic kisses.

She couldn't get her key in the door fast enough as she heard him racing down the hallway, already babbling to her about his day with Grampy. What was it about the prospect of a squeezing hug from her son that promised to settle her churning stomach and the turmoil of the past few hours better than any antacid ever would?

The door was barely open before Seth was dragging her inside, a finger painting in one hand and a sticky piece of toast in the other.

Reaching out, she began to close the front door when a foot wedged itself in the way.

A big, biker-booted foot.

She almost tipped backwards in her haste to stand up. Instinct making her send her curious son to his grandfather and closing the living room door behind them.

She hadn't even noticed him following her, let alone heard his bike. Yet there it was, parked right on the driveway as though he had every right to be there.

And Zeke, looming and furious, in the doorway. His eyes locked onto the closed door as she gripped the handle as though that could somehow delay the inevitable.

'What the hell, Tia?'

'Zeke…'

She should have told him. Back there in the lifeboat station. It was why she'd come back to Delburn Bay the moment she'd discovered Zeke was in Westlake.

Waiting for the right moment had been a mistake, because there was never going to be the perfect opportunity for giving a person that kind of news. And in delaying, she'd only made things ten times worse. A hundred times.

'I have a son?'

*Continue reading*
**THE ARMY DOC'S BABY SECRET**
Charlotte Hawkes

*Available next month*
www.millsandboon.co.uk